THE TUPPENNY CHILD

Sadie Linthorpe is the talk of Ryhope when she arrives there, age seventeen, alone, seeking work and a home in the pit village. But Sadie is keeping a secret — she is searching for her baby girl, who was taken from her at birth a year ago and cruelly sold by the child's grandmother. All that Sadie knows about the family who took her daughter is that they live in Ryhope. And the only thing she knows about her daughter is that when the baby was born, she had a birthmark on one shoulder that resembled a tiny ladybird. But as Sadie's quest begins, a visitor from her past appears — one who could jeopardise the life she's beginning to build and ruin her chances of finding her beloved child forever . . .

GLENDA YOUNG

THE TUPPENNY CHILD

Complete and Unabridged

MAGNA
Leicester

First published in Great Britain in 2019 by
Headline Publishing Group
London

First Ulverscroft Edition
published 2020
by arrangement with
Headline Publishing Group
An Hachette UK Company
London

A catalogue record for this book is available
from the British Library.

ISBN 978–0–7505–4832–8

Published by
Ulverscroft Limited
Anstey, Leicestershire
Set by Words & Graphics Ltd.
Anstey, Leicestershire
Printed and bound in Great Britain by
T. J. International Ltd., Padstow, Cornwall

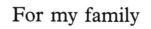

For my family

For my family

My thanks go to: Sunderland Museum & Winter Gardens, Sunderland Antiquarian Society — especially Norman Kirtlan and Ron Lawson, Sunderland Local Studies Centre, Sunderland Central Library, Ryhope Heritage Group — especially Rob Shepherd and Peter Hedley, Anth Croft of the Railway Inn at Ryhope, Durham Mining Museum at Spennymoor, Durham County Records Office, my friend Emma Hynes for making me aware of the wonderful Irish custom of the Women's Little Christmas, my brother-in-law Robin Smith for his knowledge of trains, Sharon Vincent for her knowledge of women's social history in Sunderland and my sister-in-law Marie Young for inspiration at the Railway Inn in Ryhope. To my agent Caroline Sheldon and my editor Kate Byrne. And to Barry, as always, for the love and support and endless cups of tea when I lock myself away to write.

1

Escape

May 1919

'Where to, miss?'

Sadie glanced behind her to ensure she hadn't been followed. Her heart hammered in her chest.

'Miss?'

'Ryhope, please,' she said, snatching another look behind her, just in case. 'Third class.'

'Single or return?' the ticket clerk asked.

'Single,' she replied. She had no intention of ever coming back.

'That'll be one and six, please.'

She lifted her small blue bag to the wooden counter. Her hands were shaking as she spilled the coins from it to the counter top. As the clerk expertly flicked each coin towards him, totting them up one by one, Sadie looked around the ticket office. It was a neat and tidy little place, with timetables and schedules pinned to the walls, a clock ticking above an oak desk, and a small coal fire burning in the hearth. There was a quiet hush about it, a sense of order that helped calm her racing mind.

'You'll be needing the Sunderland train for Ryhope. It's due at half past the hour,' the clerk said as he handed over her ticket. 'You can wait in the ladies' room if you wish.'

'Me, sir?'

'Yes, miss. West Hartlepool railway station is proud to open its waiting room to all ladies, whatever their ticket class.'

Sadie walked out of the ticket office, relieved to see that the platform was clear apart from a porter gathering a pile of wooden crates, laying one on top of the other. He whistled as he worked, a tune that she didn't recognise. She turned and saw the sign for the ladies' waiting room and quickly walked towards it. She'd never been inside one before, but she knew it was the safest place, somewhere she could hide. Her heart continued to thump as she glanced behind her one final time to be certain she hadn't been followed. Then she took a deep breath and reached out her hand. The doorknob was cold to her touch but turned easily, and the green wooden door swung open.

It was the fire she noticed first. The roaring blaze in the huge blackened fireplace dominated the small room with its noise and heat and its musty, smoky smell. In front of the hearth was a black iron guard, wrapped around the fireplace to protect skirts and bairns. Sadie felt drawn to the fire; she wanted to walk towards it, to lift her coat and warm her backside. But a quick glance around the room at the three ladies already seated suggested that this was not the thing to do.

All eyes turned towards her as she hesitated by the door. In the centre of the room was a large table, scattered with worn magazines and a copy

2

of *The Hartlepool Northern Daily*. On the wall high above the fireplace, the waiting room clock loudly ticked the minutes until the next train arrived.

'Shut the door, pet,' the woman closest to the fireplace barked. 'You're letting in the wind.'

Sadie moved quickly at the demand, and swung round to close the door. She gave a brief nod by way of apology, but all she got in return was a blank stare from a pair of dark and deadened eyes. She fell into the seat closest to her, landing heavily, the bench as hard on her legs and as uncomfortable underneath her as it looked. But it was warm in the room, and she was grateful for that, for although it was early May, it was cold and windy out.

She pressed her back against the wall and allowed her gaze to settle on the stone floor before she slowly lifted her eyes to fully take in her surroundings. On the wall to her right was a blue and white tiled map of the north-east coast, next to it a colourful poster advertising the twin resorts of Roker and Seaburn, with their sweeping bays and golden sands. On the opposite wall were two large windows, frosted to stop prying eyes looking in from the platform, providing the women inside with privacy. Underneath each window, on deep sills set in the stone walls, stood white enamel jugs holding golden daffodils.

Sadie glanced at the older woman by the fire who had spoken so abruptly when she'd entered. She guessed that the woman was travelling in third class too. Her boots were worn, and her flat brown hat sat askew on her head as she slouched against the wall. To Sadie's right was a young woman who looked about twenty, slightly older than her own seventeen years. But from the look of her, she would definitely not be travelling in third. The girl's clean, pretty bonnet partly shielded her unlined features, and her concentration went into reading a book with a light brown cover that she held in her small, soft hands.

To Sadie's left was another well-dressed young woman. Whether she was a mother or a maid, Sadie couldn't tell, but she had a large black perambulator in front of her with a sleeping baby inside. The pram was turned towards Sadie and she could see a baby's tiny pink face peeking out. She had grown used to seeing women with bairns over the last ten months, though it hadn't been easy at first. In those ten months her life had been turned upside down. As she gazed into the dancing flames of the fire, she cast her mind back to the Hartlepool lodging house she'd left only that morning, where she'd been living with Freda McIntyre and her son, Mick.

★　★　★

Sadie had been left with little choice but to move into Freda's house after the Spanish flu ravaged Hartlepool and took her parents in its deadly wake. With no relatives to take her in, she was handed over by the authorities into Freda McIntyre's care, to live as a lodger in her spare room. But there was nothing caring about Freda, as Sadie soon found out.

4

Freda was a woman who looked older than her years, her face made heavy from the drinking of ale. But she must have been pretty as a girl, for there was a touch of something to her features and her long dark hair that made her popular with gentleman callers. Sadie would scuttle away and hide from the men who came into the house, afraid in case any of them climbed the stairs to her room. Freda enjoyed the company of her men friends more than she cared about Sadie's welfare. Sadie hadn't been sure, when she first moved into the house, what Freda's business was, but she soon found out when she became friendly with Mick, Freda's son. He was the one who explained to her that the men who came to the house paid to spend time with his mam, and in her bedroom too.

When she first arrived at Freda's, Mick walked Sadie to Hartlepool market each morning. He was friendly enough at the start and Sadie was glad of his companionship. She was just one of the many girls who lined up at the market, waiting for the women from the fancy houses to appraise them and pick them off one by one to work in service. If they were found suitable, a shilling would be placed in their hand to contract them for however long they were needed. Sometimes Sadie was hired for a day, sometimes just an hour. If she was lucky, she was given a job that would last all week.

She was obliged to hand over her earnings to Freda, every single penny. In return, Freda provided her with a roof over her head, a bed to lie in and breakfast and supper to eat. But it was

5

a breakfast that Sadie had to prepare before she went out to work, and a supper that she had to cook no matter how tired she was at the end of her working day. And she was forced to cook not just for herself but for Mick and Freda too before she climbed the stairs to her cold, damp room.

She proved herself a hard worker, and word spread amongst those who hired at Hartlepool market that she was good in the kitchen. It was said she had perfect hands, cold hands, for making pastry for pies. When she was given a job with a cook or a chef in one of the big houses, she tied back her long fair hair into a plait and happily got down to work. The warmth of the coal oven and the sweet aroma of baking reminded her of helping her mam.

She was always eager in the kitchen, always keen to know more and to learn, but when she was chosen at the market to work with a house-keeper, she dreaded her days. The endless cleaning and scrubbing were not to her liking. It was back-breaking work. Worse still were the times when a housekeeper contracted her services on a Friday, for all the girls knew that Fridays were the worst days of all, when the heaviest cleaning was done ready for entertaining at the weekends, and there were always stairs to be scrubbed.

Sadie would be given a stiff brush and a tin bucket filled with scalding water and washing soda and left to get on with it. With the houses so big and so grand, there were always plenty of stairs, wide too, with as many as four flights — and woe betide any girl if she didn't do a good job, for the work would be checked. The housekeeper would peer at each stair with a candle in her hand, and if she found dirt in any corner, she would put down the candle long enough to give the girl a tongue-lashing. After that, she'd give her another bucket of steaming hot water and make her do the stairs again, every single one of them. Only once had Sadie, unknowingly, left a scrap of dirt on the stairs. After having to clean the whole four flights again, she never made that mistake again.

At first, at the end of her working day, Sadie looked forward to talking to Mick, telling him about where she'd been, in whose house she'd worked and what she'd seen inside. But as time went on, Mick became increasingly absent from the house, at his mam's beck and call, and Sadie saw him less often after she finished work. In the mornings, when he walked her to the market, his mood increasingly turned dark, and where once he'd been chatty and friendly, now he answered her questions with a simple yes or no.

Freda sent her son nightly to the Red Lion to buy a jug of ale to bring back to the house, and Mick took a liking to it. Sadie often found him drunk, slumped on the stairs, when she came in from work. No more would he want to sit and talk to her about her day's domestic work. He'd try to kiss her and hold her, telling her he wanted to lie with her in her room.

Life with Freda and Mick couldn't have been more different to the life Sadie had lived while her parents were alive. She was happy then, close to her mam and dad in the warmth of a loving family home. Now she had no friends, or even a kindly neighbour to talk to; only the girls she worked with while in service, who changed almost daily. She battled her loneliness, but it was a solitary existence for her, and one she struggled to resign herself to. She knew that there had to be more to life than this, for hadn't she experienced the warmth and love of a family once? And she wanted to believe she could find it again, if only she knew where to look.

It was this that kept her hoping for a renewal of her friendship with Mick, but his moods and behaviour were changing daily as the ale took hold. Desperate to keep him — her only friend — close, one winter evening she allowed him into her bed while Freda was sleeping. One night was all it took, and in the weeks following, she discovered she was pregnant with his child.

At first she didn't understand what was happening to her body. But when one of the cooks she worked with at Hartlepool joked about her getting fat, the joking soon turned serious as the woman asked her if she might be pregnant. They had a hushed conversation as they worked together, with the cook filling Sadie in on as many details as she could.

'A baby?' Sadie whispered. 'Me?'

The cook eyed Sadie's apron, which had grown tight across her chest and stomach. 'I know a woman who can get rid of it for you,' she said. 'She'll charge you for it, but I can ask her if you like?'

A cold shiver ran down Sadie's spine. There was nothing she wanted less than to lose the baby growing inside her. She thought of her mam and the miscarriages she had suffered, losing child after child.

'No,' she said firmly. 'I want to keep it.' She put her hands to her stomach. 'This baby is mine.'

★　★　★

At first, Sadie was hopeful that the news of the child might somehow soften Mick again. She carefully picked her moment to tell him, one evening at Freda's house after a miserable day spent cleaning. Mick followed her to her room as she requested. He was keen, thinking he was to take the same pleasure he had taken from her the last time. Sadie sat on the edge of her bed.

'Please, Mick, sit with me,' she said.

Mick sat heavily next to her and immediately tried to kiss her, forcing her down to the bed.

'No, Mick! No!' she cried, fighting him off with her fists. 'That's not what I want.'

'You wanted it last time,' he breathed in her face.

She struggled to turn her head from his as his lips pressed down, and pummelled her fists against his back. Reluctantly Mick eased away.

'Then why have you brought me here?' he asked dully.

Sadie's disappointment at Mick's actions mixed with anger now as she shifted from under the bulk of him. The two of them moved uncomfortably into sitting positions on her bed.

'There's something I need to tell you,' she said firmly.

'Oh aye?'

She put her hands to her stomach, then raised her gaze to meet Mick's. 'I'm going to have a baby,' she said. 'Your baby. I didn't know it at first, but I spoke to a woman I worked with and she told me it was true. She knows about these things; she's got three bairns of her own.'

They both sat in silence, letting the weight of her words sink in.

'Say something, Mick,' Sadie pleaded, but he simply sat staring at the worn floorboards in front of him. Then, without a word, without warning, he pulled her sharply from the bed by her arm, yanked her across the bedroom floor and out to the landing at the top of the stairs.

'Mick? What the . . . ?'

Sadie struggled, but she was no match for him. He was taller and stronger and she never stood a chance against the shove that he gave her. It came out of nowhere, completely unexpected, and she lost her footing just as he had planned, tumbling down the stairs and landing in a heap at the bottom. Mick followed her down, but when he reached her, he simply stepped over her and carried on walking.

It was a miracle the baby survived and Sadie didn't break any bones. But from that day on, she kept out of Mick's way and they never spoke again.

★ ★ ★

10

Throughout her pregnancy, Sadie continued to line up each day at the market, but the work came less frequently to her once the swell of her stomach started to show. She was often the last to be chosen, and on the days she wasn't picked at all she would return to the lodging house to be put to work by Freda, scrubbing the house clean and cooking meals. Of course she guessed that Mick had told Freda about the baby, but she kept the swell of her belly covered as best she could, and for weeks it went unmentioned in the house.

Freda's mind was elsewhere, too busy sleeping off her hangover each morning when Sadie got up for work and too busy drinking each evening when she returned. But when the pregnancy could be hidden no longer, she began to eye Sadie like her own prize cow. Sadie began to hear her whispering with Mick on the landing outside her bedroom door. And when she entered the kitchen to make meals, their hushed conversation would break off, leaving her feeling uneasy and more unwelcome in the house than ever. Snippets of conversation that she did hear unsettled her. There was talk of money to be made and a sale to be agreed. But when she questioned them, demanding to know what they were talking about, Freda hissed at her: 'We're talking about you, not *to* you — now scram!'

★   ★   ★

Sadie's baby was born in the cold of her room to Freda's bloodied hands. Sadie immediately

11

reached out for her daughter, and Freda gave her that much, at least: a few days of holding her child to her and feeding her from her breast. There'd been a little birthmark on the baby's shoulder, a mark Sadie would never forget. It was the colour of the red wine she served in the houses she worked in, and she remembered touching it, running her finger across the raised patch. It reminded her of the shape of a ladybird, like a ruby, a living, breathing gem.

'I'm going to call you Birdie,' she whispered to the child. 'And I'll do whatever it takes to look after you and love you. Do you hear me, little one? You don't know it yet, but I'm going to do everything I can to get us out of here, away from these people. We'll have a life of our own, Birdie, just you and me. We'll never be apart, it'll be the two of us against the world, and you won't work in service, I'll tell you that now. No daughter of mine will have to clean and scrub. You'll have the best of it all, the finest things I can buy.

'Oh Birdie, we'll look out for each other, won't we? I'll protect you and keep you from harm. I'll tell you all about my mam and dad, and how much they would have loved you. And if there really is a heaven, like folk say there is, then that's where they'll be. They'll be looking down on you now and I know they'll be smiling and waving and blowing you a kiss. Mam will be saying to Dad, 'Look, there's your grandchild,' and Dad will be proud, Birdie, I know that he will.'

★   ★   ★

In the days following the birth, Sadie heard Freda and Mick talking outside her bedroom door.

'Shame it's just a girl,' Freda was saying.

'How much will we get?' Mick asked.

'We'll be lucky if we get more than a few shillings. It's got the mark of the devil on it, a red patch of skin touched by evil. All these months we've waited, and when it comes out, it's not right.'

'We'll make something, though, won't we?'

Freda gave a harsh laugh. 'She's not worth more than tuppence, that child! Don't worry, though, I'll find someone to buy it. There's always someone wanting a bairn, no matter if their skin is diseased.'

★　★　★

Freda never once touched the child after the blood from the delivery had been washed from her hands, and Mick never came to see his daughter while Sadie was nursing her. Sadie heard him about the house, though, laughing with his mother, the two of them deep in drink. Freda came to Sadie's bedroom once a day to check on the baby, to ensure Sadie was feeding her correctly and to bring a tray of food. But any hopes that Sadie might have had that the woman was softening towards her after the birth of her grandchild ended as quickly as they had entered her head. Far from being kind, Freda was simply looking after her investment.

At the end of the first week, when Sadie had

bonded with her newborn baby, Freda came into the room with a man following behind. Sadie sat up straight in the bed, assuming he was a doctor, come to check on the baby's patch of red skin. But as he approached the bed, she was puzzled to see no doctor's bag about him. She was further confused because this man was better dressed than any doctor she'd seen, in his black suit with matching waistcoat and tie. His shoes were shined, she noticed, and he was dressed as neat as a pin. He was thin, too, with a pinched face and dark eyes and short black hair smartly combed to one side. But it was his moustache she would remember, the tidy, clipped black moustache of a man whose appearance was as important to himself as it was to others.

He walked into the room with an air of efficiency about him, and if he was shocked at the state of the place, with its walls peeling from damp, and torn curtains at the window, his face gave nothing away. Sadie hugged her baby to her breast, for if this smartly dressed man was not the doctor, then who was he and what did he want?

'Show him the mark,' Freda commanded.

Sadie hugged the child tighter.

'Show him, or I'll come over there and rip that blanket off it myself.'

Sadie looked up into the man's face, hoping for a smile, but she was sadly disappointed. 'Are you the doctor?' she asked.

The man dropped his gaze to the floor. Then he straightened and gave a little cough. 'I'm here to see the baby. I hear it has a little mark on its skin.'

'No,' Sadie said, swinging the child in her arms away and across to the other side of the bed. 'No. I won't let you see her. Not if you don't tell me who you are.'

'Sadie!' Freda cried. 'For God's sake, let the fella see the mark.'

But even as Freda's angry words were leaving her, she was already striding across the room towards the bed. She barged straight past the man standing at the bedside, grabbed the baby from Sadie's arms and pulled the blanket from its shoulders. The man remained silent and unmoving when he saw the scarlet patch of skin.

'Well?' Freda demanded.

'Is it healthy otherwise?' he asked.

Freda nodded and held out her hand expectantly. 'Do we have a sale?' she demanded. 'If you don't want it, I've got plenty of others who'll take it.'

Sadie sat and watched, her stomach turning, her breath coming out of her fast and shallow with the shock.

'Yes,' the man said. He held out his own hand and Freda took it in a tight handshake. 'I'll take it now. I've got my man waiting outside with the car.'

'Wait!' Sadie cried. 'What's happening?'

The man shot her a look, just the briefest of glances exchanged between them. Then he turned and strode out of the room, ignoring her cries. He'd been in the room for just a few minutes, but that was all it took for Sadie's life to be changed in every way.

Sadie moved quickly and swung her legs from

the bed, but Freda saw her trying to stand and pushed her back with her free hand. Then, without another word, she walked from the room with the baby and slammed the door shut behind her.

Sadie struggled up again, using the bedpost as support. She stood still for a moment, gathering her strength and calling out over and over for Freda, for the baby. In her desperation, she even called for Mick. From out on the landing, she heard the sound of a key in the lock. She moved to the door and banged on it with her fists, all her anger and hurt and fear coming from her. But she knew they wouldn't answer.

She turned and walked towards the big sash window. Using all the strength she could find, she heaved at it until it gave way and started to move. It opened an inch, and then another, but she could get it to budge no further. On the road in front of the house she saw a fancy black car that she'd never seen before. In the front seat a man sat at the steering wheel. The car window was lowered and he was smoking a cigarette, his elbow resting on the window ledge. In the back seat she could make out another figure. It was a woman, her face shielded by a wide-brimmed black hat.

Suddenly he appeared, the man who minutes ago had been at Sadie's bedside, and in his arms he held what looked like a bundle of rags. But with a sickening lurch to her stomach, she knew immediately what it was. She watched as the back door of the car swung open and the man leaned inside, handing the precious parcel to the woman in the hat. Sadie bent low to the open window.

'No!' she cried. 'You can't do this! You can't take my baby!'

The man at the steering wheel glanced up in the direction of her cries and caught her looking down. She watched as the thin man with the moustache walked from the back of the car towards the driver.

'Back to Ryhope?' the driver asked as he threw his cigarette to the pavement.

Just three little words, but Sadie heard them clearly through the gap in the window.

The man with the black moustache nodded, then walked to the passenger side of the car and disappeared inside. Sadie's cries were lost as the throaty hum of the engine started and the car began to move away. As it edged forward, she caught sight of the number 3 on its licence plate.

★ ★ ★

Hours later, Freda came to her room with a tray of food — and harsh words too.

'I want you back working tomorrow,' she commanded. 'You've lazed around here long enough now. First thing in the morning you'll be at Hartlepool market. Get yourself some work and start earning again or I'll throw you out on the streets.'

Sadie glared at her but didn't reply.

'Got nothing to say for yourself?' Freda snarled. 'No, you'll still be crying about the bairn, I'll bet. Well, pull yourself together. It wasn't anything more than a tuppenny child. I almost had to give it away. A child like that with the mark of the devil on it is best out of my house.'

'You sold my child?' Sadie gasped at Freda's callous words. The confirmation of what she had seen from the window hit her like a bullet to the heart. 'You took her!' she cried, louder now. 'And you sold her? For tuppence?'

Freda pointed a bony finger towards Sadie and poked her hard in the chest.

'Don't you forget that I am the child's grandmother and I have the right to do what I choose! And never you mind how much we got. It's none of your business. You need to remember this, lass — you knew the rules when you took this room: no babies allowed. You should think yourself lucky I got rid of it for you. A young lass with a bairn brings shame on my house, and you bring shame on yourself. Besides, it's bad for business having a bairn about the place, and I've got a living to make.'

Sadie stayed silent. She would cry later, when Freda was downstairs with Mick, mother and son lost in their nightly drunken haze. She wondered if that night's beer would be bought with the proceeds from the sale of her child.

Left alone in her room, she made a decision. She had no friends or relatives or anyone else she could turn to for help, but she was determined to get out. She didn't know when and she didn't know how, but she knew that she couldn't continue living under the same roof that housed the evil of Freda, not after what she had done.

One morning while she was waiting at the market to be chosen for domestic work, Sadie noticed a new stallholder. It was an older lady wrapped in a blue and yellow wool shawl, with swept-back white hair and a weathered face, and Sadie felt sure that she'd never seen her before. She watched intently as the woman set up her stall in the spot close to where she stood, carefully laying out a cloth of black velvet over a shabby wooden bench. Onto the velvet she placed tiny silver-coloured items in long, neat rows. Sadie was close enough to see they were tiny charms in the shape of animals: birds flying with their wings wide, cats, dogs, even an elephant and a horse. There was a butterfly charm, and Sadie noticed the intricate detail on its wings that had been lovingly worked and crafted. And then she saw it, the ladybird charm that the old woman placed carefully on the black cloth.

'How much are your silver trinkets?' she whispered.

'Oh, they're not silver, lass,' the woman laughed, revealing blackened teeth. 'Just tin. I work them myself and I could never afford to use silver.'

'They're beautiful,' Sadie said.

The old lady looked at her, taking in the length of her all the way from her black boots up to the sadness in Sadie's face.

'You waiting for service?' she asked.

Sadie nodded. 'I'm here every day. I never

19

know where I'll end up working.'

The woman gathered her shawl about her shoulders and stared long and hard at her. 'Which one do you want?' she said at last.

'Sorry?'

She pointed to the trinkets on the cloth. 'Pick one. Before I change my mind and think better of it.'

Sadie's mouth opened in shock. Before she could even think of what to say in reply, another woman appeared right in front of her.

'Do you have nits, girl?' she demanded. She was smartly dressed in a long brown coat, and she was wearing stockings and shoes, not boots. She even carried a handbag too.

Sadie looked from the stallholder to the woman in front of her and straightened her shoulders. 'No,' she replied.

'Hold out your hands,' the woman instructed.

Sadie did as she was told, holding them out for inspection, palms up.

'You'll do,' the woman said. 'It's one day's work with our pastry cook. Clean hands are needed. Follow me.' She strode ahead towards the road from the market. Sadie began to follow, then quickly turned back to the stallholder.

'Can I really pick one?' she asked.

The old lady nodded. Sadie's hand went straight to the tiny ladybird charm that was no bigger than her thumbnail. She held it tight inside her clenched fist, then dropped it into her boot for safe keeping.

'Thank you,' she said. The old lady smiled in reply, and with that, Sadie ran to catch up with the woman, following her to wherever she was to spend her day's work.

★ ★ ★

Being contracted into domestic service this way had been Sadie's life for the two years since Freda had taken her in. But now things would change. They would have to. Oh, she would go to work each morning as she'd done in the past. She'd keep on working, keep earning. But it would be a harder, tougher Sadie from now on. After what Freda had done, after she'd stolen her child and sold her, Sadie knew she would never find it in her heart to forgive.

The last two years living at Freda's had been a struggle the like of which Sadie had never known as she lived with the grief of losing both parents. But now she'd lost her child too, the child she had carried for nine months inside her. She wondered if her heartache would ever end. Would life always be painful? She knew that the only way to ease the emptiness inside her was to find her baby girl. But how? Could she do it? Could she make her escape, and if she did, what then? Thoughts and doubts spiralled around her mind for days, forcing her to lie awake in bed at night. She thought about her past, the warm and loving past with her family, and of the cruel conditions she now found herself in. And she thought about her precious child who had been cruelly taken away.

When she woke after another fitful sleep, Sadie's decision was finally made. She'd need

21

money to flee, she'd need resolve and spirit, and by God, she'd need nerves of steel in case Freda and Mick came after her. But she would do it. One day, somehow and some way, she would break free from Freda's house and leave. And then she would head to Ryhope to find Birdie, her child.

In her room at night, she became expert at stitching a double hem in her clothes in which she hid a farthing or a ha'penny every time she found work. She hoarded the coins in a hole in the wooden floor, which she covered with a blanket, and Freda, not once taking it upon herself to come into the room to clean or air it, never discovered her secret. Also in this gap in the floorboards, Sadie hid her ladybird charm. She threaded it with string, and in the dark of her room, she would take it from its hiding place and loosely tie it around her slim neck. Wearing the charm this way brought the mark of the ladybird to her skin, just as it had been on her child.

It wasn't easy to save the coins. As soon as Sadie walked in through the front door at the end of the day, Freda stood with her grabbing hand held out, ready to take her wages from her. But such were the vagaries of the work that Sadie was given, each job at a different rate of pay, that Freda never truly knew the difference between what she was actually earning and what she was bringing home. Besides which, Freda's liking for the ale meant that she was often drunk by the time Sadie returned home, and increasingly careless in counting the coins.

It didn't take Sadie long to realise that she could play this to her advantage, not just in handing over fewer coins to Freda. She knew where Freda kept her money to pay for ale and food, in a red pottery jug high on a kitchen shelf. Sadie wouldn't have dared touch it, not in a million years, but if she just kept on saving ha'pennies, it would take forever and a day to earn enough to pay for her train ticket to escape. She eyed the red jug each time she was in the kitchen, wondering how much money — her money — it contained.

One night when she knew that Freda and Mick were sleeping, she took the jug down from the shelf. But there was more in it than coins. There were pound notes, three of them, all with the King's head on. Sadie gasped when she saw them. She hesitated, holding her breath in case Freda or Mick came creeping down the stairs. She felt her heart thumping in her chest. They'd skin her alive if they found her stealing from the jug. But it wasn't stealing, not really; it was her own money she was taking back, that was all. She stuffed all three notes into her pocket, then crept back upstairs to her room, where she put the money in the hole in the floor. The next morning, she made her escape.

* * *

The clock on the wall in the ladies' waiting room showed twenty-five past the hour. The Sunderland train was almost due; Sadie would not dare leave the safety of the room until she heard it arrive. What if Freda had learned that Sadie hadn't been seen at the market that morning? What if Mick was waiting outside, ready to drag her back to the loneliness of her cold room?

Outside, there was an almighty roar and hiss as the train pulled into the station. A shouting started up on the platform announcing the stations it would call at: Horden, Seaham Harbour, Ryhope East, Sunderland. The women around Sadie stood to leave, and she followed the girl with the pram. Her eyes scanned the platform; she was nervous in case there was any sight of Freda or Mick, but they were nowhere to be seen. Sadie heaved herself up into a third-class carriage.

Only when the train began moving, huffing from the platform, leaving Hartlepool behind, did she breathe a sigh of relief. Her hands were still shaking. So many times she'd dreamed about this moment as she lay in bed at Freda's house. For months she had planned her escape. Not a day had gone by since her child had been cruelly snatched from her arms that she hadn't thought about her. Not one single day. And now here she was, on the train, on her own, with money in her blue bag and a ticket in her hand.

A lot could change in almost a year. She knew that her daughter might have been moved on, away from Ryhope. The man with the moustache might be impossible to find. Her child may have died. The black car with the number 3 on its plate might no longer exist. But there was a chance, wasn't there? There was a chance that her bairn was alive and living in Ryhope, thriving even. And while there was a chance, she had to take it, no matter how slim it was. She would hunt for her child, she would do all she could to find her, and she would make the most of her life away from the loveless Mick and his evil mam. After months of planning and secrets and hardening herself, she had done it, she had finally escaped.

Sadie touched the ladybird charm at her neck. She'd waited long enough. For almost a year she had bided her time. Now it was time to get her baby back.

2

Arrival

The train snaked its way north from Hartlepool, hugging the coastline. It ran along sea cliffs standing guard over bays of coal-blackened sand. Sadie looked from the window, staring out at the expanse of the grey North Sea and wondered what Ryhope would be like.

The fear she had felt at Hartlepool station hadn't yet left her, and her hands were still shaking. With every turn of the train wheels, doubts filled her mind as the madness of what she was undertaking became real. She had no job to go to, nowhere to live and knew no one in Ryhope. All she had in her bag was a tiny remainder of the money from her train ticket savings, while hidden in her boot were the three pound notes she'd taken from Freda's red jug. She had nothing else but her wits about her and knew she would have to turn her hand to whatever she needed in order to find work. There could be no going back now.

Sadie's reverie was broken when the ticket collector came into the carriage, calling for all tickets from Hartlepool station. She delved into her bag and brought out her ticket, ready to hand it to the tall, hefty man in his railway uniform who was making his way towards her.

As he handed it back to her, his gaze lingered on her for a little longer than Sadie felt comfortable with. She felt as if it were she being inspected, rather than her ticket. She turned her head from him to look out of the window again.

The ticket collector walked on, racking his brains, wondering where he'd seen the girl before. It was a few moments before it came to him, and when he remembered, he made a mental note to let his friend Mick know that he'd seen the bonny lass with the long fair hair from Freda's lodging house riding north on the Sunderland train.

★ ★ ★

A droplet of rain splashed against the train window, then another. Soon, fat drops were running into each other and tearing down the glass. At the end of the hour-long journey, when the train finally pulled into Ryhope East station, the heavens opened and rain poured down. Sadie was the only passenger to alight, and she stepped out onto a short platform puddled with rain. With one hand she gathered her hair and brought it down inside her jacket. She hugged her blue bag to her, afraid of it soaking through, and ran along the platform towards the exit gate.

Outside the station, the road ahead of her stood empty, with not a soul around. To her left was a row of terraced houses, fine-looking houses too, almost as big as Freda's, and straight ahead of her was a lime-washed building: a pub, the Railway Inn. It looked a clean building, decent, despite the mud on the roads around it. The impressive sign that bore its name faced the railway station, designed to entice rail travellers inside. Sadie had never been inside a pub before, but if it was an inn, as the sign suggested, she might be able to afford a room for the night, using one of her pound notes if she must. She lifted her skirt with one hand and ran as fast as she could through the rain.

The pub was empty apart from a woman behind the bar, who turned with a start when Sadie burst in through the door.

'Hey! What's your hurry, lass?'

Sadie let the door swing closed behind her. Rain dripped from the end of her nose, and she felt the arms of her jacket damp against her skin. In front of her was a long, narrow bar with bottles of all colours and shapes lined up in front of a mirrored wall. On the right-hand side were small round tables with chairs at each one. The woman behind the bar was staring at Sadie, waiting for her to explain herself. She was older than Freda, and her dark brown hair was pinned back from her face. Sadie noticed a hardness around her mouth and chin, but there was a warmth in her eyes that made her feel brave enough to speak up.

'It's raining out and I thought I might take shelter here until it eases, if I may?'

The woman cocked her head. 'Oh aye. Shelter is it? It's a pub I'm running here, not a charity mission hall.'

'I'll buy a drink while I wait, then,' Sadie said, taking a step towards the bar.

'You'll do no such thing!' the woman replied sharply. She put her hands on her hips. 'Young lass like you, coming into my pub like this on your own! How old are you anyway?'

Sadie pushed her feet forward in her boots and straightened her spine. 'Seventeen.' She shivered as a raindrop made its way down into the collar of her coat.

The woman didn't move. She looked across the bar at the newcomer. 'I haven't seen you in here before. You're not from Ryhope, are you?'

Sadie shook her head. 'No, I . . . I've just got off the train.' Her mind raced as she desperately tried to think of a place, any place that wasn't the truth. 'From Seaham,' she said at last, remembering the name of one of the railway stations the train had stopped at before Ryhope.

A dark look crossed the woman's face and she hesitated before she spoke again. 'You've never travelled all the way from Seaham on your own, have you?'

Before Sadie could reply, a small white dog made its way towards her feet and started sniffing at her boots.

'Pip!' the woman cried. 'Back here! Now!'

The dog did as it was told.

'Don't mind him,' the woman told Sadie. 'He always likes to greet new customers. He's harmless enough.'

'Is that what I am, then?' Sadie asked, with a note of hope in her voice. 'A new customer?'

The woman sighed. 'You can sit in the corner with a lemonade, and as soon as the rain stops, you can go, you hear me?'

She turned back to the bar and pulled a glass and a bottle towards her. She filled the glass with lemonade and slid it across the bar towards Sadie.

'What brings you here anyway, all the way from Seaham?'

Sadie took a sip of the drink, grateful for it. It was the first thing that had passed her lips since the meal of eggs and bread she'd cooked the night before at Freda's. That world already seemed like another lifetime away, and yet it had been just a few hours since her escape. She took a deep breath. There was something about the warmth in the woman's eyes, the way she asked her direct questions, that made Sadie want to tell her the truth.

'I've come looking,' she began. 'I've come looking for something.'

She was going to continue; it was on the tip of her tongue to tell the woman the truth. But she remembered Freda's words about an unwed lass with a baby bringing shame on a place. And if a woman with loose morals like Freda thought it shameful, then Sadie realised it might be best to keep quiet. She bit back her words and took another sip of lemonade.

'Looking for something in Ryhope?' The woman laughed. 'The only things you'll find here are pit-black miners, or if you're lucky, one of the farmers might be looking for a wife.'

'No, not a man,' Sadie said quickly, embarrassed that she'd given such a poor account of herself. 'What I mean is, I've come looking for something that was taken from me. Stolen. All I know is that it's here in Ryhope, or at least it was. And if it's still here, I hope to find it.'

The woman behind the bar softened her tone when she spoke again. 'I've already told you I'm not a charity mission, and I'm not a lost property office either.' She reached her hand across the bar. 'My name's Molly Teasdale, and the Railway Inn is my pub.'

Sadie took her hand and shook it firmly. 'I'm Sadie . . . ' She paused, making a split-second decision not to give her own surname, just in case word spread about her escaping from Freda's. It was unlikely, she knew, but she wanted to cover her tracks as best she could. As she stood there in the calm of the pub, she was certain that all hell would be let loose in Hartlepool just as soon as the red jug was found empty in Freda's kitchen. 'Sadie Barnes,' she added. 'And I've come looking for . . . '

Say it, she thought. Just tell her you're looking for your bairn. But there was something within her that wouldn't allow her to share her secret with a stranger, not yet.

'I've come looking for a job.' The words were out of her mouth before she could stop them.

'I knew it,' Molly said. 'The minute I saw you storm in through my door, I thought to myself, that girl looks like she's got a hunger for something, and I knew it wouldn't be the ale. Not a bonny lass like you.'

'Could I take off my jacket, Mrs Teasdale?' Sadie asked. 'It's awful wet from the rain.'

'Course you can, pet,' Molly replied. 'If you give me half an hour, I'll get the coal fire burning and you can warm up and get dry before you head out again. I don't open for another half-hour, see? You caught me getting the bar ready for the day ahead. Not that there'll be many who'll brave the rain today.'

Sadie removed her jacket and laid it over the back of a wooden chair at one of the tables. She kept her blue bag in her hand.

'What sort of work are you looking for?' Molly asked her.

Sadie shrugged. 'I'll do anything. I'll clean, bake, cook, polish and scrub. Is there a market square I can go to where domestics are hired?'

Molly put her hand to her ample chest and gave a long, throaty laugh. 'You're kidding, aren't you? A market square in Ryhope? You're a long way from home, lass. We've not got a market in Ryhope, not like the big fancy ones down yonder. There's a market in Hendon, in the East End of Sunderland, but it's not somewhere a young lass like you would go looking for work. Well, not the sort of work I think you're after, that is.'

'Where would I go to find work then?' Sadie asked.

'Can you really clean and scrub?' Molly asked. Sadie nodded. Molly thought for a moment.

'And you say you can cook and bake, too?'

'I've worked in domestic service for almost three years,' Sadie replied proudly. 'Never in one place for very long, though; we got picked from the market each day to work somewhere different.'

'Who's *we*?' Molly demanded.

32

'The girls in Seaham,' Sadie replied quickly, knowing she was going to have to tell another lie to cover herself. 'I'm looking for a new start. I had to leave my lodging house when I turned seventeen; those were the rules.'

Molly appraised Sadie slowly from her spot behind the bar.

'Well, you've already met my dog, Pip, and now you've met me. If you give me a hand getting the bar ready, Sadie Barnes, how would you fancy a job here, working at the Railway Inn?'

Sadie's eyes opened wide. 'Really?' she cried.

'Really,' Molly said gently. 'I can't promise much, but I do need a hand around the place. I've been running the pub almost single-handedly during the war. My son Eddie helps out when he can, but he works hard at the pit, poor lad.' She glanced at Sadie again. 'Eddie's not much older than you, just nineteen. And now the soldiers are starting to come home from the battlefields, they need their thirst quenching and I'm finding I need more help. I reckon you might be the sight for sore eyes they'll want to see when they return. That's if you want to give it a try?'

Sadie's heart thumped in her chest. 'I need to tell you something, Mrs Teasdale.'

'Go on, lass.'

'It's not that I'm not grateful for the offer of a job. I'd love to take it, I really would.'

'Sounds to me like there's a 'but' coming,' Molly said. 'What is it, lass?'

Sadie lowered her gaze to the pub's wooden floor. 'I've got nowhere to live,' she said.

'Oh,' said Molly, taken aback. 'I see.'

'But you're an inn,' Sadie said quickly. 'I thought I might be able to afford a room for a night.'

'No, love, this place hasn't been an inn for a while. There used to be lodging rooms upstairs, but that was long before I took the place on. Eddie lives up above, and my other son Tom,' here Molly's face lit up with a wide smile, 'he's due back any day now. Been serving with the Durham Light Infantry.'

'A soldier?' Sadie asked.

'He's been fighting out in Belgium,' Molly said. 'He's kept in touch all the years he's been away, sent me telegrams from the front, and I've kept every single one.'

'You must be very proud of him,' Sadie said.

Molly beamed. 'Oh, I am, lass. I am.'

'Well, if there are no rooms here, do you know where in Ryhope I might find somewhere to lodge?'

Molly tapped her index finger against her chin, lost in thought for a moment. 'Come with me,' she said, beckoning Sadie behind the bar.

Sadie followed Molly as she entered an archway at one end of the bar. It led into a tall, narrow passageway with walls covered in red paint. At the end of the corridor was a door, which Molly pushed open into the pub yard. The rain was coming down more heavily now, and splashes landed on Sadie's face. She wiped them away with her hand. Molly pointed across the yard, to where a short flight of stone steps led up to a wooden door.

'Go and have a look,' she told Sadie. 'It's the old storehouse. It's not much to look at, and it'll need tidying up and the coal fire lighting. There's hardly room to swing a cat, but if you can put up with it for now, you'd be welcome to stay. We can come to some arrangement for payment out of your wages. That's if you decide to stay on once you've seen the state of it, of course.'

Sadie knew without seeing it that she'd accept it. She'd accept Molly's kind offer of a job, and of a home too, whatever state it was in. To Molly it might just be the Railway Inn's old storehouse, but for Sadie it was her new home and the beginning of her new life.

★ ★ ★

In the days after Sadie's arrival, she busied herself with learning everything she could about working the bar at the Railway Inn. Under Molly's watchful eye, she quickly became adept at pulling a pint of Vaux ale with the perfect, creamy head to it that the customers liked. She got to know the regulars who came into the pub and learned their names off by heart. She enjoyed her chats at the bar with them, and soon saw that each had their favourite seat. She remembered the names of their wives, their children, and even their pigeons and dogs. She learned which men had recently returned from the front and which ones had remained in Ryhope working at the pit. She listened to their ailments and their politics, their grumbles and their moans. And after a few too many ales, especially on the first Friday and Saturday night she worked there, she heard their hopes and dreams and their favourite songs as they sang out around the pub.

Molly was pleased with Sadie's work. Ever since Sadie had burst in through the doors of her pub, she'd suspected that the lass had a capable head on her shoulders. Nothing was too much bother. Sadie could lift the heaviest boxes, and she helped in the cellar when the barrels were delivered by the brewery boys. She wasn't one for sitting around waiting to be asked to do a job, and she always put her hands to good use. If the pub was empty or quiet, Molly was pleased to see the girl taking it upon herself to push the sweeping brush around the outside of the building, shifting the muck from the pavement to the road. There was no doubt about it, Molly Teasdale had fallen on her feet the day she'd taken on Sadie Barnes in her pub. The lass had turned out to be one of the best workers she'd had.

Sadie also worked hard to turn the old storehouse into her bedroom. She cleaned the place from top to bottom, not even flinching when she found a dead mouse. She'd seen a lot worse than that when she'd been working in the big houses in Hartlepool. The floorboards were scrubbed with scalding water and the tiny window scraped free of its dirt. She cleaned the hearth and set a coal fire ready every morning to be lit at night when she finished work. By the fire was a pan that she cooked her food in, food that Molly bought for her when she went to the village shops.

Inside her room at night, with the fire's embers glowing, she felt secure in a way that she had never felt at Freda's. There was silence around her. No shouting or jeers from the men who visited Freda. No raging from Mick as he drank himself daft. Just a hush about the pub after everyone had gone home and Molly had locked the doors. Some nights, lying in her bed in the storeroom, Sadie could hear the sea as the tide surged against the cliffs on the other side of the train tracks that ran past the pub. She wondered if her child could hear it too.

She longed to visit the beach and walk around Ryhope, to explore the village that was now her home. All she'd seen was the edge of the village green when she swept the pavement outside the pub. Every time she was out there, she kept her eyes peeled, hoping to catch sight of the black car she'd seen outside Freda's house all those months ago. But she saw nothing as fancy as that car in Ryhope.

Although Molly couldn't have been more welcoming and kind, Sadie's heart hung heavy at first. She knew she needed to settle into her new life, and she determined to give herself time to feel comfortable there before she started asking questions. She needed to know who in Ryhope she could trust. It had been over ten months since Birdie had been born, ten months in which anything could have happened. But at least she had made her escape from Freda and Mick. Whatever the future brought her, she knew she had within her the courage to make a change and the strength to take control of her own life.

She felt certain her mam and dad would be proud.

Behind the bar of the pub, Molly and Sadie worked amicably together, with Sadie respectful and ready to learn. She would find Molly watching her sometimes, as if she had a question on her lips that she wanted to ask but then thought better of it and kept her thoughts to herself. Molly talked often of her boys; of Eddie, who worked at Ryhope pit, but of whom Sadie had not seen hide nor hair yet. According to Molly, he was either working the night shift or asleep in his bed, leaving his mam to run the pub herself most days.

'It's what I'm used to doing, love,' she told Sadie. 'This place is my little palace. I've run it on my own since Henry passed on, and I'll continue to run it on my own until I pass too.'

But when she spoke of her other son Tom, her eyes shone and she chatted happily about the excitement she felt at the thought of his return from the war. All she was waiting for, she told Sadie, was the telegram with the date he was due to come home.

'And oh! what a day that will be, Sadie! What a day!' she enthused.

Beside Sadie and Molly as they worked behind the bar was Pip, Molly's little dog. He had the look of a Jack Russell terrier about him, but Sadie wasn't sure what breed he really was. He was small, though, and white all over except for a patch of brown on his ear. He often fell asleep behind the bar, and Sadie would find herself having to step over him rather than risk a telling-off from Molly for disturbing her dog. But when he was awake, he was a friendly little thing, always with his tail wagging to greet customers as they walked into the pub. Rarely did Sadie hear him bark and never did she hear him growl.

Each time the pub door opened, Sadie glanced up quickly to see who was stepping inside. On the one hand, she was terrified in case it was Freda or Mick. However unlikely it might be that they'd found out where she'd gone, she lived in terror of being hunted down and dragged back to Hartlepool. But on the other hand, there was one familiar face she wanted very much to see: the pinched face of a man with a black moustache, steel-grey eyes and black hair parted to one side.

She wore the tin ladybird charm around her neck, hidden under her blouse, rarely removing it. At night, she brought it to her lips and kissed it gently before falling asleep in front of the fire in the storeroom. Doubts flooded her mind daily — was she crazy to think about finding her child again? Surely the chances were so slim it was laughable. And even if her daughter was presented right in front of her eyes, how would she recognise her now? She would no longer be a baby. She would be grown, ten months old and changed in every way from the babe in arms that Sadie had nursed and loved for just a short week. But being in Ryhope, in the place she knew her child had been headed for when she had been taken from her arms, was enough for Sadie for now.

★　★　★

At the end of Sadie's first week, Molly gave her a small brown envelope, heavy with coins.

'Your wages. You've more than earned this, lass,' she said. 'I've just taken out a little for the rent of the storeroom. And I'm over the moon with the way you've cleaned it up in there. I've not seen it that tidy in years.'

Sadie slipped the envelope into the pocket at the front of her blue apron.

'Anyone serving here?' a voice behind them barked.

Molly swung round, and the sight of the man at the bar wiped the smile right off her face. He was as skinny as a rake, with short dark hair and rings under his eyes.

'How long have you been standing there, Bill Scurfield?'

'Long enough,' he replied, eyeing Sadie. His gaze fell to the pocket of her apron, where the brown envelope was nestled. 'Bonny new lass you've got working here. If I'd known, I would've been in sooner.'

'Never mind her,' Molly said quickly. 'Pint of the usual, is it?' Without waiting for his reply, she started pulling a pint of stout.

Bill propped an elbow on the counter top and rested his foot against the rail that ran around the bottom of the bar. It was a position he didn't move from over the course of the afternoon. After each pint he downed, he pushed his glass forward to be refilled and insisted that it was Sadie who served him.

40

'Go and have a breather,' Molly told her after the afternoon rush had died down. 'Get some fresh air out the back, go on.'

Sadie glanced over towards Bill Scurfield at the end of the bar and didn't need to be told twice. She wanted to get away from the man who'd been watching her since he arrived, eyeing her up and down. She knew that if she had any trouble with any of the men, if they went too far with her, if their chat and their jokes turned sinister or lewd, all she had to do was tell Molly and she'd soon set them straight. But there was something about Bill Scurfield that she noticed had unsettled Molly. And Pip hadn't come out from under his favourite seat by the fire to greet the man when he'd arrived.

Sadie stood at the back door and looked out into the yard. She breathed in the fresh air, glad to be away from the smoky interior of the pub. With the coal fire burning in the hearth and the smoke from cigarettes and pipes, she was glad of Molly's offer to take a short break. Around the yard ran a high stone wall, and by the back door was a water trough fed by the luxury of an outside tap. She'd heard that some of the pit rows in Ryhope didn't even have water at all, and that people who lived in the colliery houses had to share taps in the back lanes. They even shared netties, too. Sadie didn't think she would like that at all, having to share a netty that everyone in the street had used. A shiver ran down her spine at the thought.

'What are you shivering for? Cold enough out there for you?'

41

She turned to see Bill Scurfield behind her. She stepped forward from the doorway into the yard so that he could pass by. She assumed he'd come out to use the netty. But Bill didn't move, just reached out his arm to block the doorway so that Sadie couldn't move either. She forced a smile to her face.

'Just getting a breath of fresh air, like Mrs Teasdale suggested,' she said politely.

Bill stepped forward, and before Sadie could move away from him, he reached out both hands and pulled at her apron pocket. Instinctively, she threw her fists at his chest.

'Molly!' she screamed, hoping her cries would be heard all the way through to the bar. 'Molly!'

Bill snatched the envelope from her pocket and the pennies scattered to the stone yard. As Sadie struggled to fight him off, the tin ladybird around her neck shifted so that it was no longer inside her blouse, but glinting in full view of Bill's gaze. He grabbed at it with both hands and yanked the string from her neck.

'Get off her!' Sadie heard a man's voice behind them. 'Get off her now, or by God I'll knock your bloody block off, Bill Scurfield.'

Bill fell to his knees on the stone floor, scrabbling to pick up the coins. Sadie saw a heavy black boot land on top of one of his hands. She turned to see a man with a face as black as night. Only the whites of his eyes and his teeth could be seen. On his head he wore a cloth cap, and a black woollen scarf was wound tight around his neck.

'Get off,' Bill hissed. 'Take your flamin' foot off my fingers.'

'I'll let go when you apologise to the lass.'

Bill muttered something under his breath. It wasn't loud enough for Sadie to hear, but the boot was removed.

'Now get out,' the man scowled. 'Get out and don't let me see you in here again.'

'You can't bar me,' Bill spat. 'It's not your pub!'

'No, but it's my mother's. She's barred you once before and she'll bar you again. Or at least she will as soon as I tell her what you've just done.' He turned towards Sadie. 'Are you all right, miss? Did he steal any of your money?'

'He's got my necklace,' Sadie gasped. 'It's in his hand.'

Bill Scurfield opened his clenched fist to reveal the ladybird charm on its string. 'Call this piece of old tat a necklace?'

Sadie lunged towards him to get the charm back, but Bill opened his hand and let it drop to the ground.

'It's just a worthless piece of rubbish,' he spat.

Eddie marched Bill through the pub and as both men disappeared Sadie slumped to the ground, intent on picking up her necklace and the coins. She ran her free hand through her hair, pushing back strands that had come loose in the struggle. The man with the coal-black face reappeared and crouched low beside her, helping her collect the coins. He picked up the ladybird charm and handed it to her.

'Unusual little thing, that,' he said.

Sadie took it from his hand. 'It's just a necklace,' she said hurriedly.

When the coins had been collected, both of them stood.

'See you've met Mam's least favourite customer.' The man smiled. His face looked as if it would split itself in two, and his white teeth shone out from the blackness.

'Mam?' Sadie said. 'Are you Eddie?'

'I am. And you must be Sadie. Mam's told me a lot about you. She's quite taken by you, says you're a hard worker.'

Eddie studied Sadie, seeing for the first time the girl that his mam had been talking about for days. She was a lot more bonny than Mam had given her credit for, with her long fair hair and a smile he found appealing.

'I've heard a lot about you too,' Sadie said. 'Only I was starting to think you mightn't exist, seeing as I'd never seen you since I started here.'

'Night shifts,' Eddie sighed. 'They're a killer. But they pay well. Listen, I would shake hands with you and introduce myself properly, but you can see how I'm fixed, covered in coal dust. I've just finished at the pit, but if you give me half an hour to have my bath in the kitchen, I'll come into the bar and we can meet properly.'

'That'd be nice,' Sadie replied.

Eddie glanced at the coins in her hands. 'Bill didn't steal any, did he?'

She opened her hand. 'It's all here,' she said. 'See you later, Eddie,' she added as he turned to walk back inside the pub. 'And thank you. For Bill, I mean.'

Eddie nodded in reply and then disappeared inside along the dark red hallway.

★ ★ ★

A little while later, when Sadie and Molly were busy working, Eddie came to sit on a stool at the bar. Sadie didn't recognise him at first, as he was scrubbed clean from his bath, and the pit black that had covered his skin when she'd first met him had gone.

'I hear you've met my son,' Molly smiled, nodding towards him.

Sadie glanced along the bar. Eddie's head was bent over a copy of *The Sunderland Echo*, and she saw a mop of short brown hair atop a long, pale face. His strong chin was like Molly's, and he had the same warmth in his eyes too.

'Here, give him this,' Molly said, pulling a pint of ale.

Eddie smiled broadly when Sadie appeared in front of him.

'Your necklace isn't damaged, I hope?' he asked, pointing at the ladybird charm around her neck. In her hurry to fasten it after the fight with Bill Scurfield, Sadie had forgotten to hide it away under her blouse. Her fingers flew to the charm and she tucked it away out of sight.

Eddie reached his hand across the bar top. 'I think a proper introduction is called for this time, don't you?' He smiled. 'Eddie Teasdale.'

Sadie took his hand. 'Sadie Barnes,' she replied, still not comfortable using the fake surname she had given herself.

'Mam says you're from Seaham,' Eddie said. 'And you've come looking for something in Ryhope. Is that right?'

'Sort of,' Sadie replied. She didn't feel ready to tell anyone the truth about her business in Ryhope, not yet. And certainly not Eddie, whom she had only just met.

'Well, if you need any help, let me know. I know Ryhope like the back of my hand. It's a small place, where gossip spreads fast. If something's gone missing, it's likely it'll turn up once word is out.' Eddie took a drink from his pint. 'Are you staying long?'

Long enough, thought Sadie. Long enough to find my child.

'I might do,' she replied with a smile. 'It seems a friendly place, although I haven't seen much of it yet. I hear the beach is nice to see, and the church.'

'Well, I'm not one for churchgoing,' said Eddie, taking another sip of his pint. 'But I'd be more than willing to show you around. I'll ask Mam to give you an hour or so off and take you on a tour. We can walk the streets up to the colliery and down to the beach. It's a pretty little place. You've got to get out and see more than the four walls of this pub.'

Sadie could see the advantages of taking a walk around the streets of Ryhope with someone like Eddie, who knew the village well. She could ask questions without seeming to pry, without revealing the real reason she needed to know who lived where and what they were like.

'I'd like that, Eddie,' she replied. 'I'd like it a lot.'

'We'll do it tomorrow, if you're free? I've got a day off and the weather looks set to be fair.'

'That would be lovely, thank you.' Sadie's attention was drawn from Eddie to a customer waiting to be served.

'Has Mam had a word with you about the Select yet?' Eddie asked as she pulled two pints of Castle Eden ale.

'The what?' Sadie replied, glancing from Eddie to Molly.

Molly caught the drift of the conversation from her end of the bar, and when she'd finished serving, she wiped her hands on her apron and walked towards her son. Sadie joined them after she'd taken payment for the beer.

'Me and Eddie have been talking,' Molly began. 'And I was thinking, now that war's over and the lads are coming back, well, if you were willing, Sadie, I was thinking we could reopen the Select at the back of the pub.'

'What's the Select?' Sadie asked.

'Back in the days when the pub was a proper inn, we used to get a more mixed class of customer in here, different,' Molly explained.

'A better class,' Eddie added.

'More moneyed, certainly,' Molly agreed. 'The Select is just a small room, but we used to offer waitress service there. There are bells, you see, little bells you can press on the wall when you're ready to be served or have your glass refilled. And the bell tinkles in the main bar so we know they need serving without them having to come in here. Course, we charged a little bit extra for those who preferred to sit in there as it's more

47

private. We used to get more women, rather than them having to come into the bar. The Select offered them a bit of privacy; it was nicer than the main bar. I used to waitress it myself when Henry was alive and the two of us were running the place together.'

'And you're thinking of reopening it?' Sadie asked.

'I'd love to,' Molly sighed. 'I've long wanted to, but it's not been worth my while during the war. Folk haven't had the money to come out and drink like they used to, and with all the Ryhope lads away fighting for our country — '

Eddie straightened on his stool and lifted his pint glass. 'Not all of us, Mam. Some of us have been doing our bit here, keeping the place going. There'll always be a need for coal, now more than ever.'

'But Tom's been away fighting for four long years. He's put himself in every danger imaginable and some I daren't even think of.'

'And I suppose working underground all the hours God sends isn't dangerous enough for you, is it?'

'Now, Eddie, don't be like that!' Molly scolded.

Eddie took a long drink from his pint and brought his glass down to the bar. Sadie dropped her gaze, embarrassed to be caught in the crossfire of harsh words between mother and son.

'Anyway,' Molly said, addressing Sadie. 'What I've been thinking is that now you're working here, we can open the Select again and offer the waitress service like we used to. Mind you, the place will need a thorough clean; it's been locked up for years.'

'I'd be pleased to help,' Sadie replied. She felt

48

a slight flutter in her chest at Molly's words. For if she was being asked to stay on at the Railway Inn, it meant she had more of a chance to get to know folk in Ryhope. And the more she knew, the more questions she could ask, questions that might lead her to Birdie.

'Oh, here he comes,' Eddie cried, turning towards the pub door.

Sadie saw a man enter the pub, someone she hadn't seen before. He was short, stocky, with a round pink face. He wore a small black hat unlike any she had seen, and his jacket was smart with brass buttons. Across his body he wore a large bag with a wide strap and in his hand he held an envelope. Molly flew from her spot behind the bar to greet him.

'Is this it?' she cried.

The man in the black hat handed her the envelope. 'It's a Post Office telegram, Molly. You know that's all I can tell you,' he replied.

Molly ripped the seal open and all eyes in the pub turned towards her as she read the words within. Sadie watched as Eddie walked to his mam's side and she handed the telegram to him. It was hard to tell from their expressions just what news it contained. Finally, Molly took it from Eddie's hands and held it to her chest.

'He's coming home!' she cried, thrusting an arm into the air and waving the telegram wildly. 'Day after tomorrow! Tom's coming home!'

Sadie saw the joy on her face, the way it lit up. But it was a joy that wasn't shared by her other son. Eddie was unsmiling, his mouth set in a thin, hard line.

'Sadie!' Molly cried. 'Drinks for everyone! On the house!'

A cheer went up around the pub. Molly sank heavily into a chair, overcome with the news, and her customers came to pay their respects. Some wanted to read the telegram themselves, and she was only too willing to share it around. Sadie busied herself pulling pints for each customer and was surprised to see Eddie come behind the bar to join her.

'I'll help you,' he said.

'Looks like it's going to be all hands to the pump now that Tom's coming home,' Sadie said, glancing at him.

'Free beers today, fatted calf tomorrow,' Eddie muttered under his breath.

A toast was raised — 'To Tom!' — and everyone in the pub raised their glass. Everyone, Sadie noticed, except Eddie Teasdale.

3

Tom

'Did I hear you say you could bake, Sadie?'

Sadie paused in cleaning the bar top and looked over to where Molly was sitting in the corner of the pub. On the table in front of her lay a sheet of lined paper and in her hand she held a red pencil.

'I can make good pastry, they say.'

Molly scribbled quickly on the paper. 'We'll do pies then, steak pies if the butcher at the Co-op's got beef at a good price. Tom always liked his pies.'

'I know how to make cakes too, if that's any good?' Sadie offered, but Molly shook her head.

'He never had much of a sweet tooth,' she replied. 'And anyway, cake will put folk off drinking. Savoury things, that's what we need, give them something to get their teeth into, and they'll need to keep buying beer to wash it all down.' She winked at Sadie. 'Got to keep an eye on my profits.'

'Is there anything else I can help with?' Sadie asked.

Molly checked her list. 'Just the cooking, pet,' she said. 'As soon as I come back from the Co-op, we'll make a start. We'll do as much as we can today, and then tomorrow all we'll have to do is make the sandwiches. I think that's just about it.'

She sank back into her chair and laid her pencil on the table, then reached down to stroke Pip, who was lying at her feet.

'Four years Tom's been gone. Four years. It's too long for any mother to be parted from her child.'

Sadie took to cleaning the bar top again, polishing it with a little extra vigour as Molly's words sank in. She raised a hand to her ladybird charm.

'No mother should be parted from her child,' she said, too quietly for Molly to hear.

Molly stood up and tucked her list into her apron pocket. 'But he's coming home tomorrow and that's all that matters. He's alive, and I've got my lucky stars to thank. I know how fortunate I am. There's a fair few in Ryhope who won't see their sons again. Have you met Hetty, the woman who runs the Albion pub across the village green?'

Sadie shook her head.

'Her son was killed out there. Philip, he was called. Terrible shock it was to her and her husband Jack.' Molly sighed. 'They say Jack's a shadow of the man he once was since the telegram arrived from the front. Seems a bit wrong to be giving Tom a welcome party when so many of his friends didn't make it home, but we have to count our blessings in this life.'

Molly walked towards the bar, where Sadie was now arranging glasses into neat rows. Pip followed her. 'And speaking of blessings, where's my other son this morning? I thought he was going to take you on a walk around Ryhope?'

'Just as soon as I finish cleaning the bar,' Sadie said. 'I wanted to get this done before I went out. I'll be back in time for afternoon opening, Mrs Teasdale.'

Molly smiled. 'Can you not call me that, pet? Only the doctor and the vicar call me by my Sunday name.'

'But you're my employer,' Sadie said. 'It's what I was taught. We always had to refer to those we worked for in,' she paused and remembered to correct herself in front of Molly, 'in Seaham. We weren't allowed to call anyone by their first name.'

'Well, I might be your employer, Sadie love, but you're living in my house, and while you're under my roof, you're part of the family. So please, no more of the Mrs Teasdale. It makes me sound like a schoolteacher. If you and me are going to get on, you've got to call me Molly. All right?'

'All right, Molly,' Sadie smiled.

Molly joined her behind the bar, taking bottles of ale from wooden crates and positioning them in front of the mirrored wall.

'Are we opening the Select for Tom's welcome home party?' Sadie asked as they worked. 'I could set to on cleaning it instead of going out this morning.'

'You'll do no such thing!'

Both Sadie and Molly turned to see Eddie coming towards them along the corridor that ran behind the bar.

'I've been looking forward to showing off

Ryhope to you,' he laughed.

'Go on, the pair of you, get yourselves out for a wander and some fresh air,' Molly said.

'Fresh air? Up the colliery? We'll not find much of that.'

Molly shook her head. 'Oh Eddie, you're never taking her up to see the pit, are you?'

'It's all part of Ryhope, Mam. I promised Sadie the grand tour of Ryhope, and the grand tour of Ryhope is what she's going to get: village, beach, pit, colliery bank and all.'

Molly tutted. 'Go on then, get going. I'll see you both later. Sadie, we'll set to with the baking as soon as you return.'

'Yes, Mrs . . . Molly,' she replied.

'And Eddie? Don't forget I need your help sorting out Tom's room before tomorrow.'

Eddie nodded in reply. 'Come on then, Sadie Barnes,' he said playfully. 'Get your coat on and I'll show you the delights of this place we call home. Where do you want to go first — beach or colliery?'

'Colliery,' she replied. 'Let's leave the beach for the way back.'

'Up to the colliery it is then.'

The two of them walked from the Railway Inn towards the village green. It felt comfortable to be walking out with Eddie, Sadie thought, comfortable and safe. After her experiences with Mick back at Freda's house in Hartlepool, she'd never imagined that she might feel happy in herself again. But there was something about Eddie, about the gentle way he moved and spoke, that she warmed to. And she'd met his

54

mam first and hadn't Molly treated her with kindness, offering her a job and a room? So there was no need to fear Eddie, Sadie felt, no need at all.

'You've worked for Mam for over a week and you've not seen the village green yet?' Eddie asked her. 'I can't believe it. You must be sick of the sight of the inside of the pub.'

'I wanted to feel comfortable first,' Sadie replied quickly. What she really wanted to say was that she needed to feel safe, to be sure that neither Freda nor Mick nor anyone she recognised from Hartlepool had come looking for her before she ventured further.

'Mam likes you, I can tell,' Eddie smiled. 'It's not everyone she lets call her by her first name.'

'She's a good woman,' Sadie said.

'She has her moments,' Eddie replied, turning his face away.

Sadie pointed to a large, imposing pub at the corner of the village green. It was at least three times the size of the Railway Inn, with tall brick chimneys. To one side was land where horses stood grazing.

'That must be the Albion Inn,' she said.

'It's a good pub,' replied Eddie. 'Gets a lot of business from folk who pass it on their way to Sunderland. Mam's pub gets the railway passengers and the Albion gets those who travel by road. Since the trams started running, more people are seeing it from the road than ever before.'

'The village green's nice,' Sadie said. 'Pretty with the trees around it.'

'Suppose it is,' Eddie replied. 'Never think

much of it myself; it's just something that's always been there. Guess we take things for granted when we see them all the time.'

Eddie noticed Sadie taking in the large stone houses that stood proudly around the edges of the green.

'That one's Ryhope Grange,' he explained, pointing to a house surrounded by a black wrought-iron fence. Beyond the fence were trees, their branches heavy with pink cherry blossom. Sadie saw two men working in the garden, one digging with a spade, turning over soil, the other staking a climbing plant around the front door.

'Morning, John!' Eddie shouted as they walked nearer.

'Morning, Eddie!' came back the reply. The gardener looked older than Eddie, Sadie noticed. He was wearing dark trousers with a matching waistcoat and tie, and a brown flat cap. He paused at his digging when he caught sight of Sadie. 'Got yourself a lady friend at last?' he laughed, nodding towards her.

'She's our new barmaid,' Eddie replied. 'Just showing her the sights of Ryhope.'

'Why, that'll take all of five minutes! What's your name, flower?'

'Sadie. Sadie Barnes,' she replied. She was growing more confident in using the fake surname, although she still disliked having to lie.

The gardener doffed his cap. 'Pleased to meet you, Sadie Barnes. You're not a Ryhope lass, are you? Haven't seen you around here before. I'd be sure to have remembered a bonny lass like you.'

'I'm from Seaham,' Sadie said.

'Seaham, eh? Which bit?'

Sadie faltered for a moment. 'Close to the railway station,' she said at last, hoping it would be enough to stop John's questions.

'Nice place.' He nodded. 'Hope we see you again, Sadie.' And with that, he returned to his work turning over the soil.

Eddie and Sadie walked on.

'Is everyone so friendly in Ryhope?' she asked.

Eddie laughed. 'They're nosy, if that's what you mean. It's a small place. Everyone knows everyone else's business, whether you want them to or not. And if they don't know your business, they'll do their best to find out. But yes, apart from that, it's a friendly enough place.'

'Who lives in these big houses, then?' Sadie asked.

Eddie nodded back towards Ryhope Grange. 'Pit manager lives in that one. Mr Marshall. Nice enough bloke, a bit quiet. We don't see much of him, truth be told. Managers tend not to mix with the likes of us miners at the pit, not if they can help it. From what I hear, his wife's had a bit of trouble. Bad with her nerves after a bout of Spanish flu. But you can never know for sure in Ryhope if gossip is true or not.'

'And what's that over there?' Sadie said, pointing to a squat stone building ahead.

'Village school,' Eddie replied. 'Me and Tom both went there as nippers. And just around the corner here is our church.'

'It's beautiful,' Sadie said, taking in the impressive sweep of the path through the grounds up to the huge door of St Paul's.

'And the vicar's a decent man,' Eddie said as they walked past the stone wall that separated the church grounds from the pavement. 'Reverend Daye, he's called. He gets a lot of respect from folk in Ryhope for the way he brings those from the village and the colliery together.'

Sadie made a mental note of the vicar's name as someone she might be able to talk to, maybe someone she could trust with her secret. Eddie pointed to the left, where the road opened up.

'See that big building there? That's Ryhope Electric Grand cinema. Do you like the films, Sadie?'

Sadie couldn't believe the size of the cinema; it was almost as big as the church they'd just walked past.

'I've never been,' she replied, still keeping her gaze on the large red-brick building with its rounded roof.

'Maybe I could take you one night, if you'd like to?' Eddie asked, not daring to look at Sadie for fear she might think him too forward. But there was something about the lass that he liked. He admired the way she wasn't afraid to work hard, to get her hands dirty at the pub. He liked the fact that his mam had warmed to her, and the way she had about her that made her easy to talk to and comfortable to be with. And he liked the way she looked, too.

'Maybe you could,' Sadie said, turning slightly towards him, and the two of them locked eyes before Sadie turned her gaze away.

'What's that building there?'

Eddie started walking on and Sadie followed.

'The Guide Post Inn,' he replied.

'Blimey, there's a lot of pubs in Ryhope,' Sadie said.

Eddie laughed. 'This is just the half of it. Wait till you see them all up the colliery. It's thirsty work, is mining, and the pubs are happy to quench that thirst in exchange for a bit of hard-earned cash.'

They walked on in silence and the road began to rise ahead of them to a gently sloping hill. Sadie noticed that in the short time it had taken them to walk from the village, past the church and up to the colliery, the air had begun to change and was soon thick with coal smoke. Gone were the sturdy houses of the village green with their large gardens and fences, their trees and flowers. In their place stood rows of lime-washed cottages, squashed together in rows as if that was the only way to keep them from falling. Row after row of these small houses were laid out, and between each row were the back lanes, where shared netties and water taps stood.

Behind the houses was the pit itself. Eddie pointed out the workings to Sadie. She saw tall, narrow buildings with black iron wheels connected with pulleys, which Eddie explained were the winding gears. Black smoke belched from the chimneys, high enough to reach the darkened clouds. She wondered if her child was living in one of the long rows of houses, asleep in a room warmed by a coal fire. Or was she lying in a soft feather bed in a large house with a black car parked outside? Was she even still alive?

'Penny for them?' Eddie said, cutting into her thoughts.

Sadie shook herself and looked ahead at the pit. 'I can't believe this is all part of Ryhope,' she said at last. 'I mean, the village is so pretty and peaceful, and then there's this. I've never seen anything like it.'

'The pit's what keeps Ryhope as busy as it is. But it's a village of two halves and that's a fact,' replied Eddie. 'And you haven't even seen the beach yet. It's different again down there.'

They carried on walking, up past a muddy field where the flat leaves of rhubarb were spreading, pushing up from the soil. The large plate-glass windows of the Ryhope and Silksworth Co-operative Society store came into view.

'There are stables at the back of the store, see? The Co-op keep their delivery horses there.' Eddie pointed to a fenced area of land. 'And beyond the stables, in the store field, is where some of the fellas keep pigeon crees.'

'What are pigeon crees?' asked Sadie, confused.

'Some of the lads would say it's their second home,' Eddie laughed. 'They spend so much time there when they're not working at the pit. A cree is . . . well, it's like a shed for birds to live in. A big one. Big enough for a dozen or so pigeons. They're homing pigeons, see, and the miners race them, for money. They can win a lot in some of the races.'

'Can we go and see them?' Sadie asked, but Eddie shook his head.

'They don't much like strangers going in

there,' he said. 'They reckon it brings bad luck to their birds. They're a superstitious lot, truth be told, although if you ask me they're just wanting a bit of quiet time alone with the pigeons after working their shifts at the pit. It's not an easy life underground, and the lads make the most of the open air when they're not at work. Some of them go fishing at the beach, some of them take to their gardens and grow leeks and potatoes and some of them, like these lads, keep pigeons.'

Sadie glanced at Eddie and saw his face had taken on a sadness she'd not seen before.

'And what do you do, Eddie?' she asked. 'I haven't known your mam mention that you go fishing, there's no garden at the pub, and I know you don't keep pigeons in the yard at the Railway Inn. Where do you find your relaxation in the fresh air when you're not at work in the dark?'

Eddie smiled. 'I walk pretty lasses around Ryhope and give them a tour of the place.'

He saw Sadie looking at him, a shocked expression on her face.

'Sorry,' he said quickly, aware that his joke had been lost on her. 'I'm only kidding. What I really mean is that in my free time I'm expected to give Mam a hand in the pub. And when I'm not doing that, well, we live close enough to the beach, so I walk there a lot. I like to skim flat stones out across the waves, see how many times I can get them to bounce on the water. I can usually skim them three or four times, but I managed a sixer once. And I love the sound of the waves. You can hear them from the pub some

61

nights, when the sea's rough and the weather's bad. There's something special about it, living on the coast, right at the edge of the country. I don't think I could ever live anywhere that's not by the sea. You must feel the same, surely, coming from Seaham?'

Sadie simply nodded in reply. The lie she'd created about where she was from wasn't sitting easy with her. She'd never told such lies before; she'd never needed to. The more she was getting to know Eddie and the more she was starting to like him, the more she was finding it difficult keeping the truth from him.

'Come on,' Eddie said. 'We'll cross over and head back to the village on the other side of the road.'

They walked back down the colliery bank, past the mucky rows of pitmen's houses, past the miners' hall and the Co-op.

'Tell me more about the pitmen,' Sadie said as they walked. 'You said earlier they were a superstitious lot.'

'Oh aye, they are,' Eddie laughed. 'It's working underground that does it, dangerous work, you see. So anything the lads can do to get themselves in the right frame of mind, they'll try it.'

'What sort of things?'

'Well,' Eddie began. 'Take the pit ponies, for instance. If you get to work and the pony you're working with is fit and in good spirits, then you're going to have a good day underground. But if the pony's acting up, or in a bit of distress, it sends a bad signal, see.'

'Like an omen?' Sadie asked.

'Exactly! If the pony's being difficult, some of the lads refuse to work with it and they have to bring along another. Oh, and it's unlucky to meet a woman on the way to work, and if you see a crow, that's not a good sign either.'

Sadie laughed.

'I bet you think I'm making all of this up?' Eddie smiled when he saw the look on her face.

She shook her head. 'No, not at all. What happens if you see a pigeon on the way to work? Is that unlucky too?'

'Oh, that's the worst kind of luck,' Eddie joked. 'Because it means the cree has been burgled and the pigeons have got loose. Mind you, some of the miners won't have pictures of crows in the house, or any kind of bird — apart from pigeons, of course. Pigeons are special round here. The top flyers, those that win the races, they have their portraits painted, and those pictures hang proud in miners' homes.'

'But not next to a picture of a crow,' Sadie smiled.

'Never next to a picture of a crow,' said Eddie. 'Or any ornament of a crow either. Oh, and cats, they're unlucky too, so they say.'

St Paul's church came into view ahead of them as they walked further down the bank.

'Is there anything the miners consider lucky?' Sadie asked.

Eddie thought for a moment. 'Just their pigeons, I guess,' he said at last. 'The lads send them out to race and they all come home to roost, every single one of them. It's an instinct in them, something to do with an internal compass;

they always know which way they're going. Think I could do with one of them myself.'

'A pigeon?' Sadie asked.

'No!' Eddie laughed loudly. 'An internal compass to keep me on the right track. Mind you, maybe I don't need one. I've got the homing instinct already. I don't know if I'll ever spread my wings and leave the pub.'

'Is that what you want to do?' Sadie asked. 'Move out, away from the Railway Inn?'

Eddie shrugged. 'Sometimes I want things to change. And other times I like things just the way they are. I've got a decent job, a good home.'

'Do you wish you'd gone to war?' she said quietly.

He took his time before he gave his answer. 'Sometimes,' he said. 'I see the way Mam is with Tom coming home and I wonder, you know, about what it's like to be a hero like him. I get taken for granted working down the pit.'

'At least Tom's safe, he's alive,' Sadie said. 'And tomorrow he's coming home. There's a lot to look forward to.'

Eddie didn't reply, just stared straight ahead. Sadie thought it odd, but then she had little experience of the way other families worked.

They walked on, past the church and the village school, skirting the village green. Along one side of the track that led down to the beach was a broken-down wooden fence, covered in trailing stems of green that Sadie recognised. She walked close to the tangled shrub.

'They're sweet peas, growing wild.' She smiled at Eddie. 'Or at least they will be sweet peas when they flower this summer. I recognise the stems and the leaves; my dad used to grow them.'

'I don't know much about flowers.' Eddie shrugged.

'They've a gorgeous smell on them when they bloom,' Sadie said, but Eddie was already walking on. She ran to keep up with him and they continued along the track under a bridge carrying the railway above.

'This is my favourite bit of Ryhope,' Eddie explained.

As they drew closer to the ocean, they could hear the waves crashing to the shore, dragging the shingle back. The track ran between high cliffs to either side of them and it wasn't until they reached the very end of the pathway that the full expanse of the beach could be seen. Sadie gasped when she saw it.

'It's not as black with the sea coal as you'll be used to seeing on Seaham beach,' Eddie said. 'Some days we even see pure yellow sand between the rocks, depending on the way the tide takes it.'

'It's beautiful,' Sadie said. She took in the tall stack rocks and the caves in the cliffs on either side. Ahead of her were rock pools of black in the frothy white ocean spray.

'Beautiful's not a word I'd use to describe it,' smiled Eddie. 'But it's got a rugged charm, I'll give it that.' He pointed towards the base of the cliffs, where honey-coloured stones as big as a man's head were washed up in piles. 'See those stones there? The village school was built of them. Before the pit came, Ryhope used to be all farms. Mind you, this was over a hundred years ago. The farmers gave a day each in turn to carry the stones from the beach, pulling them up the track all the way to the village to help build the school. It makes the beach as important a part of Ryhope as the village and the pit.'

'Do people come here in the summer, to swim and enjoy the sands?' Sadie asked.

'You'd be surprised how many of them do,' Eddie replied. 'They bring picnics and spend all day here. The Earl of Scarborough even comes to spend his summer break. You remember the big house we passed next to the village school, the one that was almost as grand as Ryhope Grange? He stays there. We never see him, though. It's not as if he pops into the Railway Inn for a pint while he's here. He's got folk running around after him when he comes to Ryhope. I expect he brings his own ale with him too.'

As Eddie was speaking, Sadie felt a splash of water against her cheek, then another and another as the rain began to fall.

'Come on, we'd best get back to the pub,' Eddie said. He took off his weathered brown flat cap and handed it to Sadie. 'Wear this, it'll help keep your hair dry.'

Sadie took the cap and placed it carefully on her head. There was a warmth to it from where it had been sitting on Eddie's own. Then the two of them ran back along the track that led through the cliffs. Under the railway bridge, sheltered from the rain, they paused for a second to catch their breath.

66

'Thank you, Eddie, for showing me around your village,' Sadie said.

'It was my pleasure,' he smiled. 'I've really enjoyed it. Are you ready for the last part of the tour?'

'There's more to see? I thought we were going straight back to the pub.'

'We are,' Eddie laughed. 'Your tour of Ryhope concludes at a traditional railway tavern, once used as an inn. We even had stables at the back.' He glanced out beyond the shelter of the bridge. 'It's still pouring down. We're going to have to run for it. Come on.'

He held out his hand to Sadie. She wavered, but only for a second, before she grabbed it. Eddie squeezed her hand and smiled at her, and she felt warm inside, warm and safe and happy in a way that she hadn't felt in years.

★   ★   ★

Back at the pub, they were just about to cross the road when a car came into view to their left. Sadie let Eddie's hand drop and pulled his cap down over her eyes as they waited for it to pass by. Eddie's focus was on the pub door opposite, but Sadie was looking at the car. There was something familiar about the shape of it, its size, colour and make. With a gasp, she realised where she'd seen it before. But it couldn't be, could it? Not the very same car? She stared hard as it drove past, but its windows were steamed up and it was impossible to see inside. She quickly glanced at the registration at the back of the car, and there it was, the number 3 in exactly the same spot that she'd seen it from her window at Freda's.

Eddie grabbed her hand again and pulled her across the road.

'Come on, Sadie daydream,' he laughed. 'You'll get soaked through standing there gawping.'

Sadie looked at him. 'That car! Did you see it? The car?'

Eddie pushed open the door of the Railway Inn and the warmth of the coal fire rushed at them from the hearth.

'It was just a car, what of it?' He shrugged.

'Do you know who it belongs to? Have you seen it before?'

She never received her reply. Eddie had stopped in his tracks. At the bar stood a soldier in uniform with a pint of ale in his hand. Five brass buttons ran up the front of his serge jacket. His trousers were tucked into long thick socks and on his feet were heavy boots. He turned and locked eyes with Eddie but neither of them said a word.

There was something about his face that Sadie recognised immediately. He had the same strong chin and jawline as Eddie, the same dark brown hair. But there was no warmth in this man's eyes the way there was with Eddie and his mam. He was a little shorter than Eddie, thinner, and he looked older and entirely overwhelmed.

Eddie nodded towards him. 'Mam know you're back? She wasn't expecting you till tomorrow.'

The soldier took a long swig from his pint.

'She knows,' was all he said.

Eddie walked towards the bar and thrust out his hand. 'Good to have you home, Tom,' he said as evenly as he could.

Tom looked at his brother's hand just for a second, then he picked up his pint again and turned his gaze back to the bar. Eddie let his hand drop to his side. The clatter of Molly's footsteps as she walked along the corridor into the bar broke the tension between the two men.

'What do you think about this, then?' she beamed. 'Tom's home a day early when we're not ready for him, and do you know what, I couldn't be any happier if you paid me to be. I've just been making up his room.' She reached across the bar top and patted Tom's free hand. 'It's good to have you home, Tom. Isn't it, Eddie? Good to have him back?'

So wrapped up was she in joy at the return of her son that Molly didn't notice Eddie had chosen not to reply.

'And who's this?' Tom asked sharply, nodding towards Sadie.

Sadie whipped off Eddie's cap, which was wet through from the rain.

'Sadie Barnes,' replied Eddie firmly. 'She's working in the pub now, helping Mam.' He turned towards Sadie. 'Sadie, this is my brother Tom.'

'Nice to meet you, Tom,' Sadie said politely.

Tom gave a weak smile in reply but offered no further comment or conversation.

'You look tired, love,' Molly told him. 'Get yourself up to your room, get some rest.'

'Might just do that,' he said, draining his pint.

He picked up his kitbag from the floor and disappeared behind the bar with his mam.

By the time Molly returned, Sadie was already working, preparing the glasses and the till.

'Oh, leave that, girl,' she said kindly. 'I'm relying on you to get the food ready for Tom's welcome home party tomorrow. We might as well go ahead with it even though it won't be a surprise for him any more. Folk have been invited and they'll be expecting a decent spread. I've got the coal fire burning in the kitchen and the oven should be good and hot. The butcher had a nice bit of beef when I went out this morning, not too pricey, so you can make plenty of pies.'

Sadie took off her damp jacket, handed Eddie his cap back and walked from the bar to the corridor behind. At the end of the corridor was the narrow stairway up to the bedrooms. Opposite that was a short passage that led to the pub's kitchen. This was a large square room where meals had been prepared for the Railway Inn guests when the place had been run as a lodging house. Now it was where Molly cooked the family meals. It was also where she rested in her wooden rocking chair in front of the fire at the end of the night when the last of her customers had left. The coal fire provided the warmth for the room but also the means for cooking too. And in front of the fire was where Eddie took his bath when he came in from the pit. When it wasn't called into use, the tin bath hung on a metal hook on the brick wall of the yard.

70

Sadie enjoyed spending time in the kitchen. She loved the space of it, the light and airy feel, and the warmth of it too. Even with just a small window, there was a brightness in the room from the whitewashed walls and stone floor. Against the wall under the window stood a long wooden table where food was prepared, and on either side of the window were wooden shelves. The fireplace took up the whole chimney breast, being as wide as it was tall, with sturdy black iron bars affixed above from which all shapes and sizes of pans hung on hooks. In front of the fire was also where the laundry was dried on the days when the weather didn't allow it to be blown on clothes lines zigzagged across the yard. The oven at the side of the fireplace had three shelves for baking, and in front of the fire were round blackened iron plates. The largest one was used to boil up water in the kettle and the others were for cooking pans. Also in front of the fire lay the pub dog Pip, curled up and asleep, snoring gently.

Sadie felt happy in the kitchen, in control of her own little world. She'd worked so often in domestic service in Hartlepool in kitchens of all sizes, and now she had one of her own. Well, almost. It was Molly's, of course, and Sadie knew she must never forget her place. She set about her work, draping a pinny over her head and tying it in a bow at her back. As she sought out the paper bag of flour and the earthenware bowl of salt, her thoughts returned to the car that had passed in front of her earlier. Could it really have been the same car, the same man who had taken her child?

She picked up a knife and sliced through the fat, being careful to take just enough to make the pastry that Molly had asked for. Then she chopped the fat into small chunks and dropped the lot into a large brown bowl with the flour and the salt. Using the very tips of her fingers she began to rub the fat into the flour, slowly at first, and again her mind turned to the car. Had she imagined it? Was she wanting so much for it to be the same car, for it to be the same person who had taken her baby, that she was willing to believe it was? She sighed. She'd ask Eddie about it again, she decided, but not yet. She'd speak to him later, when he was more relaxed. She'd seen the way he'd reacted at the sight of his brother; it had put an abrupt end to their time together that day, time that she'd really enjoyed. She liked Eddie, but there was more to it, something she couldn't yet name. But she knew she was looking forward to seeing him again.

Her fingers worked quickly, turning the flour and fat into what looked like breadcrumbs. And what of Tom himself, Sadie thought, back from the war with not even a handshake for the brother he hadn't seen in years? She didn't understand that at all, but didn't feel it was her place to get involved with the business of a family she didn't truly know. Still, it had upset her to see Eddie's offer of a handshake dismissed in that way.

She paused, her fingers still, and glanced out of the window into the yard. There was nothing to see out there, nothing but the whitewashed wall and a square of cloudy sky. She thought of

Eddie again, the comfortable way she'd felt with him today. She picked up the jug of water that Molly always left ready in the kitchen and tipped a little of the cool liquid into the bowl. Then she plunged both hands into the gooey mix, turning it quickly and effortlessly into a tight dough. When it was ready, she took a pinch of flour from the bag to sprinkle on the tabletop, then kneaded the dough briefly and rolled it flat with the long wooden pin. Sadie's pies went down a treat at Tom's welcome home party the following day. Molly was overjoyed and praised her highly, saying she'd never tasted anything so good. The pub customers echoed Molly's sentiments, and requests were made for her to offer the pies for sale at the pub.

Molly was in her element at the party, loving every single minute of having her son back home, a hero from the war. Eddie was there too, but in the throng of the packed pub, he managed to stay at the opposite end of the bar to his brother. He and Sadie chatted across the counter as she worked. And when there was a lull in service, when the pies came out of the kitchen and everyone tucked into the food, she pressed him about the car they'd seen the day before. But Eddie simply shrugged and said that he'd paid it no heed.

He was curious about her questions but didn't want to put the lass off by being nosy about her business. He was enjoying her company a lot more than he'd expected and didn't want to say or do anything that would cause any kind of friction between them.

'Don't you want to sit with your brother to celebrate his return?' Sadie asked.

Eddie shook his head. 'I'm happier just letting them get on with it, him and Mam,' he replied. 'Me and Tom . . . we don't really get along. We never have. I mean, as lads we were always fighting, over daft stuff mainly. And now he's back, acting the big hero, and everyone's pleased to see him, and what have I got to show for the four years he's been away? I've been working underground all of that time, hewing coal from the earth. Tom always said I was good for nothing, and now he's back, he's lording it over me again. It's bringing back all the old rivalry between us, just like when we were lads. Only this time we're not physically fighting. He just turns up in his uniform and he's won, hasn't he? How can I compete with that? Black my face with coal? It's like I've only been second best for Mam all the time he's been away. She's never once said to me how proud she is of me, did you know that, Sadie? And he's back here five minutes, and she can't do enough for him. Well, I'll leave them to get reacquainted and sit here on my own for a while. I'll be all right.'

His tone of voice warned Sadie against saying anything more on the subject. 'Will I get you another drink, Eddie?' she asked instead.

'Please. I'm just nipping out the back for a minute,' he said, and he pushed his empty glass towards her.

As she filled the glass from the pump, Tom appeared in front of her, in the very spot where Eddie had been sitting not a minute before.

'Where did you learn to bake pies like that?' he asked her. There was no smile on his face.

'At home,' she replied. 'I mean, I worked in service. In kitchens. I was taught.'

'Very nice they were,' Tom said, eyeing her closely. 'And what about you and Eddie? Is he your boyfriend?'

Sadie shook her head, shocked at the directness of Tom's question. 'No, we're just friends,' she said quickly.

'So if I asked you out to see a film at the Grand Cinema one night, you'd come?'

Sadie looked down at the pint she was pulling, taking care not to let too much froth gather at the top. Molly always told her that the customers didn't like it, for once the froth had settled, they felt cheated of a full pint.

'Leave her alone.'

Sadie glanced up to see Eddie walking towards them, his face full of thunder.

'Leave her alone, Tom. I'm warning you,' he repeated.

'Can't blame a fella for trying.' Tom smiled at his brother, but there was something hard in the expression, something cruel that Sadie didn't like. He turned from the bar, and in doing so, Sadie saw, he gave a deliberate push against Eddie's shoulder. Eddie chose not to react to the provocation and sat heavily back on his stool.

'Was he bothering you?' he asked.

'He asked me to go to the pictures with him,' Sadie replied.

Eddie glanced up into her brown eyes. 'And will you go?'

She shook her head. 'No.' She smiled. 'There's only one Teasdale brother I'm interested in spending time with.'

A smile spread wide across Eddie's face. 'Are you serious?'

'Yes. I mean, if you'd like that.'

'Oh, I'd like it,' he replied. 'I'd like it very much.'

4

Secrets

Summer 1919

Over the coming weeks, Sadie and Eddie's friendship grew. They fell into easy conversation after hours in the bar when Molly had gone to bed and left the two of them to close up the pub. Eddie listened intently to Sadie as she began to reveal a little of her past, about losing her parents to Spanish flu, and the domestic work she'd been forced into after their deaths.

'What were they like, your mam and dad?' he asked.

Sadie smiled at the memories. 'Mam worked in a shop, selling groceries and bread. And Dad worked on the ships.'

'In Seaham?'

Sadie's heart dropped. How she hated maintaining the lie she'd created. 'Close by,' she replied. 'And they loved gardening, both of them. Dad had an allotment about half a mile from our house and he grew flowers there. Mam helped him and I'd go and dig weeds out for them. I thought I was helping too, but I was probably in their way most of the time. Dad grew sweet peas; those were his favourite. Even now the smell of them brings it all back, you know, living as a family, the three of us.'

'No brothers or sisters?'

Sadie's gaze dropped to the floor. 'Mam lost a few babies over the years after I was born. And then she got pregnant again when they thought she couldn't any more.' She paused before she continued; talking about the loss of her parents was hard. 'She was pregnant when she caught the Spanish flu. But there was no saving her. I was taken to hospital with it too, but I was spared the worst of it. When I recovered, I was told my mam and dad had passed away. I was moved to an orphanage but wasn't there long. They told me I was lucky: a woman called Freda McIntyre wanted to take me in. She'd care for me, they said, but they were wrong. Freda cared for no one but herself.'

'Must have been awful for you,' Eddie said, trying to comprehend Sadie's experience and make sense of what she had been through.

'It was,' she replied softly. 'It still is. I miss them every day.'

Sadie went on to hint at her life in Freda's house, but she never drew Eddie the full picture, instead just giving a broad outline of how bad things had been. She kept the truth from him still about her home town really being Hartlepool, not Seaham, and about her real name and the reason she'd come to Ryhope. There was something in her that wouldn't allow herself to open up to him yet. The more time she spent with Eddie, the more she realised how much she liked and trusted him. She saw the warm way he treated his mam, and how the

78

Railway Inn customers respected and liked him. Perhaps if she could get him to tell her more about his problems with his brother, then she could trust him with the truth of her past too.

Spending time with Eddie made her content, calm in a way that she hadn't felt since she was a child at home with her mam and dad. They didn't need to talk; they were happy to spend time in each other's company, working around each other, collecting glasses and pulling pints.

Other times, Eddie offered to take her for a walk to the beach or around the village green. She always felt proud to be seen in his company, excited to be walking with her arm through his. While their blossoming relationship made her happy, never once did it take the focus away from finding Birdie, who was on her mind every second of every day.

Each time they went for a walk around Ryhope, Sadie kept looking for something, someone: a car, a man with a moustache, a child that might be hers. When a woman with a perambulator walked towards them, she would turn and look inside. Could it be Birdie? And if it was, how could she ever know? The sadness she felt some days was too much to bear. As they walked past the big houses on the village green, along the pit rows up the colliery, or around the farm buildings to the beach road, she always looked. She peered through windows into kitchens and parlours, shops and pubs, hoping to see something, desperate for a clue that would lead her to her child. But she saw nothing that would help. She didn't even see the black car again.

★ ★ ★

In the pub, Molly started to pass comment about Sadie and Eddie's friendship turning serious.

'You don't mind, do you?' Sadie asked, concerned that without Molly's approval their relationship was on a hiding to nothing.

'As long as my sons are happy, that's all that matters to me,' Molly replied. But she never seemed to notice that whenever Eddie spoke of his brother, his face clouded and his tone darkened.

Since Tom's return from the war, Sadie could count on the fingers of one hand the number of times she'd seen the brothers together in the same room. They never ate together in the kitchen or chatted at the bar. In fact, the more she thought about it, the more she realised that Tom had been spending most of his time elsewhere, anywhere other than in the pub. Where he went was a mystery, for not even Molly seemed to know what her elder son was up to. But from her bed in the storeroom at the back of the pub, Sadie often heard the gate slam shut in the small hours of the morning. The first time she'd heard it, she leapt out of bed, determined to tackle whatever intruder was intent on gaining access to the pub. Her first thought was to protect herself; her second was keeping safe the pound notes that she'd tucked into a hole in the mattress. But when she looked out from her door at the top of the steps, it was Tom she'd seen staggering across the yard to the pub's back door. There he'd stand a while, fumbling as he tried to turn his key in the lock. And then the next morning he slept off his hangover before going out in the evening and repeating the whole performance again.

'How's Tom?' customers would ask Molly when they came into the pub. And Molly would beam with pride as she always did at the mention of his name.

'He's upstairs, having a little rest,' she would reply.

But Sadie knew full well after seeing the state that Tom rolled home in each morning that far from just having a little rest, he was sleeping off a hangover every single day. She wondered if she should talk to Eddie about his brother's behaviour, but she still didn't understand the history of the problem that lay between the two of them, so she kept her thoughts to herself. However, a shudder ran down her back every time she saw Tom stagger home through the yard drunk, as her thoughts ran back to the cruel way Freda and Mick had behaved when they were taken the same way with the ale.

★　★　★

Eddie never pushed Sadie for more than the pleasure of spending time with her. He never pawed at her body the way Mick had done that night at Freda's house in Hartlepool. He kept a respectful distance from her when they were in the pub together. Even when they were alone, he'd sit at the opposite side of the table, his legs away from hers. The last thing he wanted to do was ruin their friendship by leaning in for a kiss that Sadie might not want. Despite her winning

81

way with people and her ready smile, Eddie picked up on a sadness about Sadie at times, a vulnerability that made him want to protect her.

Little did Eddie know that his kiss was exactly what Sadie wanted. But it would come in time, she hoped, when she found the courage to unburden herself and let Eddie and perhaps Molly know about her baby. Only when there were no secrets between them could she allow herself to be kissed by this man. This wonderful, calm, patient man who had come into her life and brightened it with his smile and warmth.

★ ★ ★

One morning when Sadie walked into the kitchen for breakfast, Molly was already seated at the wooden table. Pip was lying at her feet and in Molly's hands she held her favourite blue mug filled with tea.

'I've decided that today's the day to open the Select, Sadie,' she said. 'I'd like you to make a start on it this morning. The whole place will need going over from top to bottom. Now that Tom's back, it feels right to open up the whole pub again. His return has breathed a bit of life back into the place.'

Molly watched as Sadie opened the bread bin to search for the last of the baked stottie.

'Leave the bread, lass,' she said. 'There's hasty pudding in the pan by the fire. Made it fresh this morning when I came down earlier. Help yourself to that; it'll do you good with all the work you've got ahead of you today.'

Sadie took a bowl from the kitchen table and ladled warm oats from the pan.

'Here, add a bit of rhubarb for sweetness,' Molly offered, pushing a plate of stewed fruit across the table. 'I reckon we're a good team, Sadie, you and me,' she said. 'If you can look after the Select for me, I might be able to put a little more in your pay packet every week.'

For Sadie this was welcome news indeed. Although she still had the pound notes she had brought from Hartlepool, taken from Freda's red jug, she had vowed not to touch them until she was reunited with Birdie. That money was being kept for her child.

'And I was thinking,' Molly continued. 'Those pies you made, the ones for Tom's homecoming party, they went down a treat. Everyone said how good they were, and they all were eaten, every last crumb. I was wondering about offering them at dinner time for sale at the bar. It'd mean extra work for you, but what do you say?'

Sadie swallowed a spoonful of cooked oats and milk. 'I'd be honoured,' she said. 'I'm pleased everyone liked them.'

'Oh, they did more than that, pet,' Molly said. 'Folk were asking for the recipe, and when I told them I wouldn't give it to them for the world, they said they'd happily pay to buy it. I think we could be onto a little winner with your pies if we play our cards right.'

Sadie continued with her breakfast as Molly gazed into the flames of the fire. She looked relaxed and content, sitting with her hands cradling her mug of tea, but Sadie knew her well enough now to know that behind that calm facade, Molly's mind would be whirring twenty to the dozen. She'd be working out the profits that Sadie's pies would bring.

'What about bread?' Molly said at last. 'Can you make stotties, Sadie?'

'As flat and round as you'd like them.'

'Then we'll offer those too. We'll put on home-baked pies and stottie sandwiches at the bar. If we're quenching a thirst with the beer, we might as well feed our customers at the same time. But we'll leave that till tomorrow. Let's get the Select sorted today. I've not had it open since Henry passed; it didn't seem right somehow. Besides which, I've only got one pair of hands. But now that you're here, and Tom's back and — '

'And Eddie helps out when he can, doesn't he?' Sadie chipped in.

Molly took a long drink from her mug, then pulled it towards her chest.

'Eddie's . . . He and I . . . ' Sadie was about to say how much she enjoyed spending time with Eddie, but thought better of it. She didn't want to complicate her life and her work at the Railway Inn by letting Molly know just how much she was falling for her son. 'I'm enjoying the walks with him very much,' she said instead. 'Ryhope's a lovely little place.'

'Aye, it's not bad,' Molly agreed.

She stood and gathered the breakfast dishes from the tabletop.

Sadie took a deep breath. 'Molly?'

'What, pet?'

'Do you know anyone in Ryhope who drives a big car?' she began hesitantly, but once the words were out of her, she couldn't hold them back. 'It's black, fancy-looking, not a jalopy like some of them you see around here. And it's got the number three right in the middle of the plate at the back of it. Only I saw it a while back, it drove straight past the pub door, and I wondered if you knew who it belonged to.'

'Can't say I do.' Molly shrugged. 'What makes you ask?'

Sadie shifted uncomfortably in her seat. She lifted her hand to her ladybird charm and ran it through her fingers.

'Oh, nothing. Just thought it was a bit fancy for Ryhope, that's all.'

Molly turned her attention to the fire, stoking it with the poker so that the flames roared high. Then she filled the kettle with water.

Sadie smoothed down the front of her apron. 'I'll go and start on the Select then, shall I?' she said.

Molly nodded. 'It's open. I unlocked it this morning when I got up. It'll need a good airing while you're cleaning it, so put a chair in front of the door to the street to keep it open. You can fill your bucket with hot water as soon as the kettle's boiled, and there's soap here and a scrubbing brush too.'

★ ★ ★

Sadie tied her hair into a plait in preparation for the work. She rolled up the sleeves of her blouse and fastened her apron tight. Then, carrying the metal bucket of hot soapy water and the scrubbing brush, she set to cleaning.

It was a strange little room, the Select, being much smaller than the main bar of the Railway Inn and as square as could be. There were only four tables, and they came with the luxury of padded leather chairs. Sadie ran her hand along one of the seats, its comfort in sharp contrast to the wooden stools and chairs in the bar. The floor was more decorative than that in the bar too, with patterned tiles whose colours came up a treat once she started scrubbing them with hot water. The walls were lined with dark wood, which gave a cosy feel as there were no windows; the room would be lit by oil lamps. There were two doors, one that led directly to the street, and another that led into the bar. The outside door meant that those who wished to use the Select could do so in private, without having to enter through the main door that faced the train station. The outside door faced the road that led down to the beach.

Sadie scrubbed and cleaned it all. She washed the doors inside and out, wiping away muck blown against the paintwork by the wind. She clambered up on top of the tables, reaching high to the ceiling to clear the cobwebs away. She upended all the chairs and tables, wiping them clean. And when the water in her bucket was too mucky to be useful, she carried it around the side of the pub and chucked it out in the back lane. Then she refilled the bucket in the kitchen and started all over again.

Molly left Sadie to her work, confident that she'd be thorough. She often counted her blessings since the day Sadie walked through the door of her pub. For although Molly had always prided herself on her ability to keep the place going with just Eddie's help now and then, she wished that she'd met someone like Sadie months ago. The lass was a grafter all right, and Molly was more than pleased that she'd taken her on.

★ ★ ★

It was mid afternoon by the time Sadie's work was finished, and the first customers had begun to arrive in the main bar. It was the usual faces who came in early in the day: miners who'd finished their night shift at the pit, or farmers at the end of their day, having worked since the small hours. Molly attended to their requests for pints of Vaux beer or Castle Eden ale, and with every pint she served, she announced that Sadie's pies would be on sale before the end of the week. This was met by agreeable replies that Sadie was heartened to hear.

As Molly served her customers, she sent Sadie to the kitchen to make mugs of beef tea for them to drink as they worked. When Sadie returned with the two steaming mugs in her hands, she saw a woman enter from the main door. She was short, round and dumpy, with dark brown hair tied in a bun at the back of her head. On her feet were heavy black boots, and she wore a long, thick grey skirt and a black and grey striped jumper that had long lost its shape. She looked to be around the same age as Molly, but her face was heavier, without the warmth about the eyes and she wore a scowl as she entered the pub.

'Bessie Brogan! What brings you in here?' Molly cried.

Bessie walked straight to the bar, where she leaned across and gave Molly a peck on the cheek. Molly reached out to her friend and the two of them held tight to each other.

'How's Pat?' Molly asked.

'Pat's fine.' Bessie winked. 'Never better. His hip plays him up, but apart from that, he's fine, same old Pat.'

Sadie watched the scowl on Bessie's face disappear completely as she spoke to Molly. When she smiled, she looked like a different woman, her whole face lifted.

'What can I do for you?' Molly asked.

Bessie nodded towards Sadie. 'It's her I've come to see.'

'Sadie? Whatever for?'

'I heard about the pies. Folk have been talking about them all the way up the colliery.'

'Aye, news travels fast in Ryhope,' Molly smiled. 'If folk spent as much time working as they do gossiping, we'd be on the map as the hardest-working village in County Durham.' She turned towards Sadie. 'Sadie, this is my good friend Bessie Brogan. She runs the Forester's Arms up the colliery with her husband Pat.'

Sadie nodded towards Bessie. There was something unusual in the woman's accent, she realised. Oh, it had the warmth of Wearside tinged with that of Durham in the way of most Ryhope folk, calmer and softer than the accent of Hartlepool. But there was something else, something in the way Bessie spoke that appealed to Sadie. Her voice had a charm to it, a sing-song quality, as if she was reading out a rhyme with each sentence that left her thin lips.

'Thought it was about time I came to pay you a visit,' Bessie said, extending her hand to Sadie across the bar. 'I hear your baking's of a good standard and I wondered if you'd be interested if I put some work your way.'

'Hey! Now that's not on, Elizabeth!' Molly said sharply.

Bessie raised her eyebrows and smiled at Sadie. 'Oh, I know I'm in trouble when she calls me by my Sunday name.'

'I don't see you for weeks and you come in here trying to poach my staff! I'm not having that and you know it!'

Bessie tutted loudly. 'Can't blame me for trying, though, can you? You'd have done the same if she'd been working for me and you got to find out about it.'

'You old Irish goat!' Molly laughed. 'You're not pinching my staff and that's the end of it, got it?'

'Oh, all right,' Bessie smiled. 'But I'll have a small glass of stout while I'm here. If I can't steal your pies then I'd best check on how you're keeping your cellar.' She winked at Sadie. 'Got to keep an eye on the competition, you know.'

'It's nice to meet you, Bessie,' Sadie said as Molly prepared the drink.

'I've heard a lot about you, lass,' Bessie said, eyeing her. 'Heard you're from Seaham, is that right? Your family lives near the railway station?'

'Yes,' Sadie replied. 'Anyway, if you'll excuse me, I've got to check on the Select and make sure it's aired out properly.'

She turned to avoid any further questions and headed into the little room, where she lifted the chairs from the tables and put them down on the clean floor. She was pleased with the work she'd done that morning and took pride in the fact that the room was clean and welcoming. She peered through a crack in the doorway that led into the bar and saw Bessie deep in conversation with Molly. She didn't want to risk being asked any more awkward questions to which she would need to lie in reply. She decided to stay in the Select until Bessie was safely away.

As she watched, she saw Eddie walk into the bar. He was due at work much later that afternoon and she'd been hoping she would have a chance to see him before he left for the pit. She saw him pass the time of day with Bessie and his mam at the bar. And then she saw the three of them look up towards the pub door as it swung open and a young man with a mass of dark curly hair walked inside.

Sadie gasped.

Mick.

She slammed the door to the bar shut and stood behind it, her breath coming out of her short and fast as her chest heaved with the shock. Since she'd left Hartlepool, she'd begun to feel safe, thought she had found a refuge away from Mick and Freda, but now Mick had walked into the pub, her pub, the one place she thought she was free of her past. How had he found her? Of all the villages up the coast from Hartlepool, why was he here, in Ryhope? And of all the pubs in the place, how did he know which one she was in?

⋆ ⋆ ⋆

Mick had received word from his friend Ned who worked on the trains that he thought he'd seen the girl from the lodging house alight at Ryhope station. And when Mick told his mam, Freda forced him to go after Sadie and find her. But it wasn't Sadie they wanted back, for they cared nothing for her; it was their money they wanted returned.

Mick did as his mam told him and Ned promised a free journey on board the train to Ryhope. But in order for Ned to smuggle Mick onto the train, they had to wait some weeks until his rota brought him back on the Hartlepool to Sunderland line. But at last they managed it, and now here Mick was.

⋆ ⋆ ⋆

Sadie breathed deeply, trying to calm herself. She laid her ear against the door to try to hear what was being said in the bar. But the Select was built to keep secrets, and all she heard was the sound of her own heartbeat as the blood rushed within her. With shaking hands, she gently pulled the door open an inch, just enough for her to put an eye to the crack to see what was happening.

Mick — the same gangly, skinny Mick that he'd always been — was questioning Eddie at the bar while Molly and Bessie looked on. Even with the door open, they were too far away for Sadie to hear what was being said, but she saw Eddie shake his head. Mick raised one hand to indicate height, and then with both hands gestured around his face at the memory of her long hair. Again Eddie shook his head before taking Mick by the arm and marching him to the pub door. With his other hand, he pulled open the door, then pushed Mick outside.

Sadie let the Select door close quietly and fell into the nearest chair, gasping for breath as tears threatened to fall. A second later, the Select door opened and Eddie walked inside. Without a word, he sat in the seat opposite her.

'He was looking for me, wasn't he?' she asked.

Eddie nodded. 'I sent him away. I told him we'd never seen a lass fitting your description. I didn't like the look of him, Sadie. He was a shifty beggar, whoever he was. Look, it's your business and I won't pry, but I think you owe me and Mam something of an explanation.'

He gently took Sadie's hands in his and she allowed them to rest there as sobs racked her body.

'You're not from Seaham, are you?' Eddie asked, already knowing the answer in his heart. 'That fella that was just here, he said he'd come to take you back to Hartlepool. Said a friend of his saw you get off the train at Ryhope, and he's asking around the village to see if anyone's seen you since. Mam trusted you, Sadie; you can't keep secrets from her while you're living under her roof, it's not right. And you can't keep secrets from me, not if we're to continue being friends.'

'I know, but I needed to feel safe first, I needed to . . . '

'What is it, Sadie? What troubles you that you have to keep a secret this way? We're friends now, aren't we? Won't you tell me as your friend?'

Sadie pulled back from Eddie's warm hands and lifted her apron to wipe her eyes. 'As my friend?' she said at last.

He took her hands again. 'More than that, Sadie,' he said. 'I think you know you're more than that to me already. I feel like I've known you all my life. From the minute I set eyes on you it felt like I'd found the other half to my heart. You're the missing piece of my jigsaw puzzle that I didn't even know I'd lost.'

Sadie smiled at his words. 'I feel it too, Eddie,' she said. 'It's come on me without warning, I didn't come to Ryhope looking for a fella, you must believe me. It's taken me by surprise, meeting you, falling for you.'

'Then let me protect you. But if I'm to do that, I need to know what's going on.'

Sadie nodded and she and Eddie locked eyes for what seemed like a very long time. She knew that once she'd confided in him, there could be no going back. He was willing her to speak, to tell him the truth.

Holding his hands tight in her own, and through tears of guilt and shame, she finally revealed her secret. Eddie sat silent and listened, encouraging her to go on when she faltered, when she spoke of her baby being snatched from her arms, caressing her face as the tears fell. And he finally understood about the black car she'd seen on their walk and how important it was for her to find out who it belonged to.

When she had finished, Sadie felt drained, spent, with no more tears inside and no more words. She had given Eddie everything; he now knew it all, including her real surname of Linthorpe.

'I expect you'll be turning me out now,' she said, wiping her eyes on her apron. 'Now you know I'm just a lass with a bairn.'

'I'll do no such thing,' Eddie replied. He was hurt that Sadie would even think that of him. For whatever had happened to her in the past, he was determined to make her future part of his own.

★ ★ ★

Unbeknown to Eddie and Sadie, their conversation had been overheard through the Select's open door to the street. Sadie had left it ajar when she'd been airing the room, and now every word she'd told Eddie, every single word, had been listened to. Her secret wasn't as safe as she thought.

Tom flicked his cigarette butt to the road and took a deep breath. This was what he'd been waiting for. He'd always known something like this would happen, something to ensure he could force Eddie out of Mam's favour and even out of the pub. The pub that by rights should be his. Mam had promised him as much before he went to war. She'd always said the Railway Inn would come to him when the time was right. Eddie wasn't fit for anything more than working underground, hewing the coal from the earth. Whereas Tom felt himself above that. And he knew the Railway Inn was a little gold mine, if only Mam would run it right.

Well, now he knew what was really going on with that girl she'd hired to work behind the bar, and with Eddie colluding with her, he had news big enough to take to his mam that could ruin his brother if he wanted it to. And oh, he did want it. He wanted it very much. It was all he had ever wanted since they'd been boys in short trousers scrapping at the village school. Tom was the worst for it by far, the instigator of many of the brothers' arguments and fights through the years. For he knew that although he was their mam's favourite, it was always his dad's love and attention he'd craved.

Henry had made it clear that he had more respect for the hard work that Eddie put in at the pit than for any of the money-making schemes that Tom devised and failed at. He had even said when Tom went off to war that miners were just as important to the nation as soldiers fighting at the front. Tom had resented Eddie more than ever then. He never knew how much Eddie hated having to stay in Ryhope, tied to their mam's apron strings, while his brother was lauded as a hero for going overseas.

When Tom had been called up, he went without question. He was afraid of what was to come, of course, but was more than happy to leave Ryhope behind. And in all the years he was fighting in the trenches, in the horror of the war, only once did his thoughts truly turn back to home. It was the day the telegram arrived to say his dad had passed away. The Spanish flu had taken Henry and had tried its damnedest to take Molly too.

With the war over and peace declared, Tom had returned home to Ryhope expecting to take up his rightful place at the pub. But what did he find when he arrived? A young lass working there. A young lass of whom his mam spoke highly and often, of her hard work and dedication, her friendly approach to the customers, and now of her pie-baking skills, which would be sure to bring in more custom. The matter of the pub being passed on to Tom had not even been spoken of since his return. And to make matters worse, the lass that Mam respected so much had fallen for Eddie.

Anyone could see just by looking at the two of them how crazy they were about each other, always deep in conversation at the bar, always whispering, always laughing. Well, if they thought they were going to take the pub away from him, take what was rightfully his, then they had another think coming. Tom felt his face burn with rage and jealousy. The heat always started in his face before it spread uncontrolled to his neck, shoulders and arms. He wanted to lash out, to hit and destroy. He'd always been angry, always a fighter, but since he'd returned from the war, his rage had worsened. He had to control it; had to keep it down.

Drinking was helping, he thought, drinking and sleeping and keeping out of the way of Eddie. He hated seeing his brother so happy. Hated seeing anyone in Ryhope happy. Didn't they know what he'd been through? Couldn't they tell? He steered clear too of any of his old pals who might say the wrong thing to him and set the red mist descending.

And the stomach cramps he was having; he could only hope they'd settle soon. When he did sleep, the nightmares came, terrifying dreams of being back on the front line, unable to withdraw his bayonet from a man's body, a man just like him. Returning home to civilian life should have been easier than this, surely? But still the nightmares and the anxiety and the rage burned within him, and he focused it now towards Eddie and Sadie and the secret he'd just overheard.

Tom took a deep breath and filled his lungs with sea air. He patted his jacket pockets again and searched for a final time in his trousers, but still he couldn't find his door key. It must have fallen out of his pocket up at the Colliery Inn during the last game of cards. He winced at the memory of it. It was a game he'd felt sure he would win, laying more money on the table with each hand he was dealt. The other players had dropped out one by one during the course of the night. Some of them left to walk home to their wives, families and warm beds. Others pushed their chairs back to the wall of the pub, keeping a watchful eye on the game as it continued in front of them.

Eventually, just Tom and Stevie Clark had been left. After four years serving with the Durham Light Infantry, both lads knew how to keep a face that revealed no emotion. Both knew what was at stake in this game as their friends sat around them, taking bets on who would win. It was Stevie who took the winnings at the end of the game, leaving Tom out of pocket again. No matter, he thought, he'd just dip into the till at the pub when Molly's back was turned. He'd take enough to get him into the next game, one he felt sure he could win.

Drinking and gambling had become Tom's way of life since his return, his method of coping with the rage and the fear, the nightmares and the shock of the war. He took every opportunity to get away from the Railway Inn and away from Eddie and the lass. The sight of them together made him sick to the stomach, and to hear his mam talking about Sadie and how hard she worked made the bile rise in his throat. Well now, he thought, let's see what Mam thinks when she finds out the truth.

★ ★ ★

Exactly as Tom had hoped, Molly did not take the news well. She was waiting, hands on hips, her face full of thunder, when Sadie and Eddie finally emerged from the Select. Behind her at the bar stood Tom, waiting to enjoy what was about to unfold before him.

'You two,' Molly barked. 'In the kitchen, the pair of you. Now! I want a word with you both. Tom? You stay and mind the bar. What I've got to say won't take long.'

Sadie and Eddie exchanged a look and Eddie reached out to hold Sadie's hand.

'Whatever it is, let me do the talking,' he whispered as they followed Molly behind the bar and along the corridor. Tom smirked as they passed him.

Once inside the kitchen, Molly ensured that the door was closed tight. By the fireside lay Pip, curled up fast asleep. Molly straightened her shoulders.

'Is it true? About the bairn?' she asked sharply.

'Mam, listen — ' Eddie began.

'I'm talking to *her*!' Molly pointed firmly towards Sadie.

'Molly, I wanted to tell you. I tried to — ' Sadie started to say, but Eddie cut her off.

'Mam, leave her be. That fella that came looking for her earlier, he tried to kill her! Is it any wonder she's not told us the full story about where she's from and who she really is? She's been scared witless the last few weeks in case he turned up looking for her. The least you can do is show her a bit of compassion.'

'Compassion?' Molly exploded. 'Compassion? I've given that lass a home. I've given her a job, and this is how she repays me! She's been lying to me from the minute she walked through the flaming door!'

Sadie dropped her gaze to the stone floor of the kitchen. 'I'm sorry, Molly,' she said quietly. 'I am so sorry. I wanted to tell you so many times. I tried to tell you, but I couldn't. I needed to feel safe first, I needed to know I could trust you.'

'When were you going to tell me exactly? Anyway, there's no need. I've heard all about your bastard now.'

'How?' Sadie gasped.

'You two, sitting in the Select, thinking your conversation's private. Well you were overheard, every word of it, clear as a bell.'

Eddie felt a rush of anger when he recalled the smirk on Tom's face. 'I'll kill him,' he spat.

'You touch him and I'll throw you out as well,' Molly said. 'Because I want you gone, Sadie. I want you gone today. You're not spending another night here, you hear me? A slip of a lass like you with a bairn, courting my Eddie? No. I am not having this, not under my roof.'

'Mam!' Eddie pleaded. 'You can't do this.'

'Just watch me,' Molly said, shaking her head. 'I've never felt so let down in my life. I've taken you in, Sadie, fed you, treated you like one of my own, and you've been lying to me all this time. The shame of it! Do you know what this'll do to the pub? To my reputation? When folk find out I've been soft enough to take in a dirty whore like you?'

Sadie gasped.

'Mam! There's no need for words like that!' Eddie was furious. 'Sadie was just a lass, an orphan, and that fella that was here, he tried to kill her when he found out she was pregnant. Do you know what he did to her? He chucked her down the stairs when she told him she was carrying his bairn. That's the sort of people she lived with, awful people, Mam. Anyway, she's not the first lass to get herself pregnant, and by God, I bet she's not the last.'

'That's as may be. But she's the first one I've had working for me in the pub,' Molly said sadly. 'And I cannot condone what she's done. When folk find out — and they're bound to find out around here — I can't bear to think of the scandal it'll bring to my door. I've got a business to run here, a proper, decent business!'

Sadie took a step forward. 'Molly, please. Forgive me, won't you? Please don't put me out on the streets,' she pleaded. 'This place is my home now. I've nowhere else to go.'

'Get her out of my sight, Eddie,' Molly said softly. 'Take her stuff from the storeroom and get her out of my pub today.'

Sadie walked towards the kitchen door. She paused as she reached Molly and looked into the face of the woman she had come to know as a friend. But there was no longer any warmth in Molly's eyes as she returned Sadie's gaze.

'I'm going to help her pack her things, Mam,' Eddie said. 'But I won't give her up. We've feelings for each other, the pair of us, we . . . ' He glanced towards Sadie. 'I love her.'

Molly let out a sharp laugh. 'Love? No, son. Once she leaves this pub, I forbid you to see her again. No son of mine is going courting with a fallen woman.'

Eddie stayed firm and gathered himself to his full height. 'Oh, I'll see her again, Mam. And I'll tell you another thing. I'm going to help her find

101

her daughter. Whatever it takes, I'm going to help her, and if her bairn — '

'Her bastard, you mean!'

'If her bairn is in Ryhope, we'll find it.' He glanced at Sadie again. 'Together.'

5

Reveal

Sadie left the kitchen without a word, and Eddie followed, leaving Molly with Pip at her feet. She drummed her fingers on the table, sighed heavily and then walked through to the bar, where Tom was waiting.

'I'll be needing your help with the Select,' she told him. 'In fact, I'll be needing your help a lot more about the place now that things have changed.'

'You've sacked her, then?' Tom asked, certain already of the answer, for he knew how much his mam abhorred gossip about her beloved pub, and Sadie's secret child would have brought gossip of the very worst kind.

Molly didn't answer. She didn't need to; her silence told Tom all he needed to know. Being asked to help at the bar, and help run the Select too, the room that hadn't been opened in years, well, it was a taste of running his own pub at last. He might even set up card games in the Select after hours once a week, after his mam had gone to bed.

★ ★ ★

Up in the old storeroom at the back of the pub, Sadie quickly gathered her belongings into a small pile. She hadn't brought anything with her from Hartlepool. All she owned was the clothes she stood up in and an extra skirt and blouse that Molly had passed to her that no longer fitted her ample frame. Eddie remained in the doorway, taking care not to cross the threshold. He watched her assemble her meagre possessions and extract the pound notes from the mattress.

'That's the money you took from Hartlepool?' he asked her.

Sadie nodded, and stuffed the pound notes into her boot. She tidied the bedding and swept the fireplace with the stiff fireside brush. Only when she was satisfied that the storeroom was as clean and tidy as she could make it was she ready to leave the place that had become her home.

'Where will I go, Eddie?' she asked. Her voice was breaking as she turned to him, and she felt a coldness run through her. She stepped out of the storeroom into the fresh air of the yard. 'You won't send me back there, will you? Not to Hartlepool?' she pleaded.

Eddie looked at her, alarmed. 'I wouldn't dream of sending you anywhere,' he said. 'Now that I've found you, I never want to let you go.'

Despite everything, Sadie smiled at his words, for it was exactly how she felt too. She felt lucky to have found him; she never could have imagined when she escaped Hartlepool that she'd feel so content with someone like Eddie by her side.

He took the clothes from her arms. 'Here, let me carry them,' he said.

'Where to, Eddie?' Sadie asked. 'Where are we going?'

'I've got an idea. Trust me, it might just work. You do trust me, don't you?'

Sadie didn't hesitate before she gave her reply. 'Yes,' she said. 'And I'm thankful after everything I've put you through that you haven't judged me in the same way your mam did.'

'Aye, well, Mam doesn't know you like I know you. And I'm sorry for what she called you, Sadie, that was uncalled for.'

Sadie headed towards the gate in the yard, but Eddie nodded towards the pub.

'I won't allow you to sneak out the back, Sadie. You've done nothing wrong.'

'Please let me do it this way,' she replied. 'What I've done is lied to your mam after she's looked after me and taken me in. I should have been honest with her right from the start.'

'Are you sure you don't want to walk out through the pub? It'd teach our Tom a lesson that you're not to be cowed.'

Sadie shook her head. 'For your mam's sake, let me go quietly out the back.'

'If you insist,' Eddie said, and he pulled the back gate open for her.

'Will you tell me where we're going?' she asked as they walked along Station Road at the back of the pub.

'You remember that woman who was talking to Mam in the bar earlier? The woman who was there when the fella from Hartlepool came in looking for you?'

'Bessie? Was that her name?'

Eddie nodded. 'Bessie Brogan. She runs the Forester's Arms up the colliery. You know she came in to try to poach you away from the Railway Inn, don't you?'

'She wasn't being serious, though, was she?'

'Where pub business is concerned, Bessie Brogan is always serious,' Eddie replied. 'The Forester's is a little gold mine. It's just a small place, not much bigger than the Select at the Railway, but it's always full to bursting and she runs a tight ship there with her husband.'

'I can't go and work for Bessie. She's your mam's friend.'

'Never mind about Mam,' Eddie said firmly. 'I'll take care of her. She'll come around, in time. I know her. She knows what a good worker you are. I'll smooth those waters over, although it might take a while.'

'Bessie was asking about the pies when she came into the Railway earlier,' Sadie said.

'She'll be over the moon to take you on. And Pat's a good fella. You'll be happy with the pair of them, just you wait and see.'

Sadie took a deep breath as they walked along St Paul's Terrace and wished she had Eddie's confidence. They continued walking in silence, up Ryhope Street North to the colliery, past the coal pit, the Co-op and the rhubarb field. They walked past the Miners' Hall and the Forester's Arms came into view. Eddie was right, it was a small place, much smaller than the pubs she had seen so far in the village. It was packed tight in a terrace of shops with bow-fronted windows. Above its front door hung a sign with the pub's name displayed in large black letters, and on the frosted windows was etched the Vaux brewery sign.

As Eddie took a step towards the door, Sadie put her hand on his arm. He spun round.

'Don't worry,' he told her when he saw the look on her face. 'Everything will be all right, you'll see.'

He pushed the door open with his hip, reached for Sadie and they walked into the pub hand in hand. Once inside, they were hit with a wall of noise, of men's chatter and laughter. Unlike the Railway Inn, no one turned to stare at the newcomers; no one was interested in anyone's business but their own. The men in the crowded bar were lost in their conversations under air heavy with smoke from cigarettes and pipes.

'Come on,' Eddie said, pulling Sadie towards the bar. It wasn't easy to reach as the pub was crowded and they had to push their way through. Sadie's eyes scanned the place, searching for the one face she would recognise, but Bessie was nowhere to be seen. She gripped Eddie's hand as she glanced around. A shelf ran around the wall, out of reach of grabbing hands, on which stood big glass boxes displaying stuffed birds with smooth, glassy eyes. She recognised the birds as pigeons, and each had a wooden plaque at the front of its box with its name painted on it. She squinted to read them: Macker, Dicky, Gee Up Gracie, Swift. Another glass box held a small stuffed dog; Sadie didn't know its breed, but a wooden plaque revealed that its name had been Champion Sid.

Just then, a voice behind the bar cut into her thoughts.

'Hey, Eddie lad! How you doing now? It's good to see you, so it is! What'll you be having? And who's this lovely lady you've got on your arm with you?'

Sadie turned to see the barman with his hand outstretched to Eddie. He was short and dumpy in the same way that Bessie was. Even his clothing reminded her of Bessie's own. His waistcoat and shirt had seen much better days, and the shirt was frayed around the collar. Wisps of white hair at either side of his head refused to lie flat. There was a twinkle in his eyes, though, and a smile about his face that was pleasant and welcoming.

'Pat, this is Sadie Barnes . . . no, Linthorpe,' Eddie said, shaking the barman's hand.

'Barnes? Linthorpe? What's it to be now?' Pat laughed. His voice had the same mild Irish lilt as Bessie's, mixed in with the warmth of the Ryhope accent. Sadie extended her hand towards him.

'Sadie Linthorpe is my name,' she replied, glancing at Eddie.

'You'll be wanting a glass of small stout, or my name's not Pat Brogan,' Pat proclaimed, shaking her hand.

'I don't . . . I mean, I've never drunk beer before,' she said quickly.

'That's as may be. But you're in my pub now and the least I can do is offer you a drink.'

'She's in whose pub?' a voice boomed from behind Pat.

Sadie smiled when she saw Bessie walk to the front of the bar. She was carrying a wooden crate of bottled beers.

Pat rolled his eyes. 'Your pub, my dear. She's in your pub,' he laughed.

'And don't you forget it, Patrick Brogan! It's my name above the door,' Bessie replied.

'Yes, dear,' Pat said, pushing the glass of stout towards Sadie. He leaned across the counter and whispered conspiratorially, 'Want to know the secret of a happy marriage? Those two little words right there: 'yes, dear'!'

When Bessie came to stand by Pat's side, Sadie saw them exchange a smile that they thought had gone unseen by anyone else.

Pat picked up a pint glass from underneath the counter. 'What'll you have, Eddie? A pint of the usual?'

Eddie shook his head. 'I can't stop, Pat. I've got to get to work. But I was hoping to have a word with Bessie before I go.'

'With me?' Bessie asked, turning her attention towards Eddie. Her eyes flickered to the pile of clothes he was holding in his arms, and then to Sadie, standing beside him.

'Come on.' She nodded towards them. 'And bring your glass of stout, pet. It's on the house. We'll talk in the sitting room.'

★ ★ ★

Bessie settled herself into her favourite chair by the fire and looked from Eddie to Sadie, who were sitting opposite her on the settee. Her face took on the dark expression that Sadie had noticed when she'd met her for the first time earlier that day. But as soon as she started speaking, her features lit up and the scowl disappeared.

'Doesn't take much to guess what's gone on down at the Railway,' she said. She nodded towards Sadie. 'I was there when your man came in this morning. I heard everything.'

'Everything?' Sadie asked.

'I know about you coming from Hartlepool, that you're not a Seaham lass like you told everyone. So I know you've been lying to Molly. What I don't know is why you've turned up in my pub.'

'Mam's chucked her out. She needs a job, Bessie,' Eddie implored. 'And somewhere to live.'

Bessie sucked her teeth as she gave the idea some thought. She could do with the help, that was for sure, especially from someone like Sadie, whose pies had been much in demand.

'What have you got to say for yourself, lass?' she asked Sadie at last. 'If I take you on here, how can I be sure that no fellas from Hartlepool or God knows where else are going to come knocking at my door at all hours trying to drag you away?'

Sadie sat up straight. 'I wish I could promise you that he won't come back, Mrs Brogan, but I can't.'

'Is there anything more I need to know?'

Eddie reached for Sadie's hand and gave it a gentle squeeze. 'You need to tell her,' he said. 'There's no point in keeping secrets now.'

'My bairn's in Ryhope,' Sadie began. Bessie's face didn't flicker, so she carried on. 'But I don't

110

know where. All I know is that she's somewhere here with a couple who drive a black car.'

'And you're hoping to find her?'

Sadie nodded, and her glance fell to the worn carpet at her feet. She missed the quick look that passed between Bessie and Eddie. Eddie quickly stood.

'Look, I've got to go or else I'll be late for work,' he said. 'Bessie, can I leave Sadie here with you? What do you say?'

Bessie took a deep breath and let the air out noisily through her mouth. She stared long and hard at Sadie.

'You'll do the baking if I take you on?'

'Pies, cakes, bread, anything you like,' Sadie replied.

'Cleaning and serving at the bar?'

'She's a grafter, you know that,' Eddie said. 'I heard what Mam said to you about her this morning. I was right there beside you.'

Bessie shook her head slowly. 'I don't know. I just don't know.'

'Is it because I have a child?' Sadie asked. 'I know it was enough for Molly to throw me out. I'd understand if I wasn't welcome here.'

'No, love, it's not because of the child. But Molly's my friend. I'm not sure I can poach her staff like that.'

Eddie laughed. 'Isn't it what you were trying to do this morning when you called in to see her? All we're asking for is a job for Sadie and a roof over her head. I know you've still not rented out your room next door, above the hardware shop. It'd be perfect for her. Come on, Bessie,' he pleaded. 'I'll square things with Mam. You know how she is. Give her a couple of weeks and it'll all be forgotten.'

'And when it is, what then, lass?' Bessie said. 'Will you be running back to work for Molly?'

Sadie shook her head. The further she was from the railway station, the better, just in case Mick came looking for her again.

'I'll be loyal to you, Mrs Brogan,' she said. 'I promise.'

'Promises, eh? But it's true we need the help. Pat's hip plays up something rotten and he can't stand behind the bar for as long as he used to.'

'And the room next door?' Eddie asked.

Bessie smiled, her whole face lighting up. 'You're a one-off, Eddie Teasdale, I'll give you that.' She nodded towards Sadie. 'You've got a good one there.'

Sadie smiled up at Eddie. 'I know.'

'All right. You can have the room next door,' Bessie said at last. 'It's not been empty long and there's some sticks of furniture in it. It's not much, but it's warm. Netty's in the yard, water tap's there too. Entrance is round the back of the pub and Pat will give you the key.'

'Thank you, Bessie,' Eddie said. He reached out to touch Sadie's arm. 'I'll call up and see you in the week once you're settled in.'

★ ★ ★

Once Eddie had left, Bessie stood too.

'I'm glad you're here, pet,' she said, smiling. 'Your pies have been the talk of the colliery and I

112

count myself lucky you've come to work here in my pub. We'll make a good team, you and me. You're a good worker and I like what I've heard about you. You'll find me firm but fair, and Pat's as easy-going as they come. You'll have no problem there, working with the two of us. But before you settle in and I show you up to the room, you and me are going to have a little chat. I want no secrets between us, you hear me?'

Sadie nodded.

'Right then,' said Bessie. 'So, what about you and Eddie Teasdale? Are you courting?'

'I think so,' Sadie smiled. 'We're not . . . I mean, we haven't . . . It's early days,' she said, aware of a heat rising from her neck to her face.

'Well, let me tell you something. I've known Eddie since he was born,' Bessie said. 'And do you know what? I don't think I've ever seen him so happy. Sadie and Eddie, eh? It's got a ring to it, don't you think? Makes the two of you sound like a vaudeville act.'

* * *

As the two women chatted in the sitting room, Pat Brogan was sitting on a high stool at the bar, resting his hip. The pub crowd had thinned out since Sadie had entered, but a man sat at one of the tables, his head bent over a newspaper. He had short black hair smartly combed to one side, and a tidily clipped black moustache. He kept himself to himself, drinking just the one glass of Vaux ale while reading his newspaper. When he had finished, he folded the paper neatly and tucked it under his arm. It was always the national newspaper he read, Pat noticed, never the local *Sunderland Echo*, which was the miners' choice. Then he stood and returned his glass to the bar.

'See you now,' he said as he placed it on the counter.

'Good day to you, Mr Marshall,' Pat replied.

Pat Brogan noticed a lot more about his customers than they ever knew. He saw who they talked to, who they sat with and who they avoided. He noticed the women they went around with. Pat had worked at the Forester's Arms since he and Bessie had moved from Dublin many years ago. The little pub was where they'd raised their two daughters, Branna and Cara, and sent them out into the world. The girls were both married with their own families now, and Pat and Bessie's grandchildren came often to stay overnight in the pub.

In all his years at the Forester's Arms, Pat had come across some very peculiar customers, and Mr Marshall was definitely one of those. He didn't come into the pub very often and he barely spoke a word when he did. He kept himself to himself, sat in the same seat by the window, drank just one pint and then left. Pat knew who he was, knew of his status at the pit as one of the managers. But he wasn't keen on his custom, for the miners who made up his regular clientele felt uncomfortable drinking in the presence of their gaffer. Pat had even heard gossip about the man keeping a girlfriend when he had a wife and a new bairn at home. But it was gossip that he chose to ignore.

114

★　★　★

Sadie took a sip from the glass of stout that Pat had poured her earlier. Bessie saw the look on her face as she tasted the drink.

'Leave it if you don't like it, girl. It's not a taste for everyone.'

Sadie placed the glass back on the small table at the side of the sofa. She felt Bessie's eyes on her and knew she was being appraised. And so, before Bessie could ask any further questions, she started talking. She confided in Bessie all the things she had wanted to tell Molly. She told her about Freda and Mick, about the lodging house and Freda's men, about Mick throwing her down the stairs. She even told her about taking the money from Freda's red jug. Bessie's face remained still as Sadie's words sank in. Sadie told her more about the baby, about the ladybird birthmark on its shoulder, about having her child taken from her just days after the birth and about the man with the fancy black car. Finally, when there was no more to tell, she sank back against the sofa.

Bessie sat in silence a few minutes more. She joined her hands together in front of her ample chest as if in prayer. She lifted her index fingers to make a steeple of her joined hands and then raised them to her face, tapping them lightly against her chin, lost in thought.

'And your child will be how old now?' she asked.

'One year and two days,' Sadie replied.

Bessie shook her head slowly. 'But . . . how

can you even think of finding her? You don't know what she looks like. You don't know where she is. You don't — '

'I don't have a choice,' Sadie interrupted. 'Birdie, my baby, she's the only thing in the world that's mine. I have no family, Bessie. I have to find her. She belongs to me.'

'And what if she's not here?' Bessie said gently. 'What if she's not in Ryhope and you've risked everything escaping from this Freda woman in Hartlepool? What if you've done it all for nothing?'

Sadie thought of Eddie and of Molly, the dramatic cliffs at the beach and Ryhope's pretty village green.

'It's not been for nothing. Being here, meeting you and Pat and Eddie, none of it's been for nothing. I have to make my own way, make my own life, make my own mistakes. I know Molly thinks I've lied to her, but I haven't, not really, I just couldn't tell her the truth.'

'She'll come around in time,' Bessie said softly.

'But if there's a chance that my child is here in Ryhope, just the tiniest chance, then I have to stay here and look for her. I have to.'

Bessie thought for a moment. 'And you say she'd be just over a year old?'

Sadie nodded. 'The birthmark could have faded, I know that,' she said. She felt a lump rise in her throat and swallowed hard against it, determined not to cry in front of Bessie.

'And what would you do even if you did find her? You say that Freda sold her?'

'She called her a tuppenny child,' Sadie said.

Bessie shook her head. 'Tuppence? For a baby? Well, whatever the price — and I doubt very much tuppence was all she got — there was a sale involved. What I'm saying, lass, is that even if you did find your child, even if she is here in Ryhope, there's a deal been agreed. Someone has bought your bairn.' She pointed towards the sitting room window. 'There's someone out there, some woman, who's sitting with your daughter in her arms thinking and feeling that she's her own. You can't just turn up and snatch her back in the same way she was snatched from you.'

Sadie felt the hot sting of tears prick her eyes and her gaze fell to the carpet.

'You know, lass, you could do worse than go and speak to the vicar at St Paul's. You're a young girl and it takes an old bird like me to say this to you, for I dare say no one has said it to you yet. She could be anywhere in the world, anywhere, and there's little chance you'll find her. I think in your heart you know that. Go and see the vicar. If nothing else, he'll help soothe your troubled mind.'

★　★　★

Bessie's words gave Sadie much to think about, and she kept in mind her advice about seeing the vicar. But it was a meeting that would have to wait, for over the next few days, Sadie was put to work behind the bar at the Forester's Arms with Bessie and Pat. The bustle and noise of the small pub was at odds with the quiet order of the

Railway Inn, which ran to the railway's timetable with its comings and goings each day. Sadie thought of Molly often, and each time she did, her stomach knotted with anxiety, knowing how disappointed Molly was in her for not telling the truth. She thought of Tom, too, and wondered if he was still creeping home drunk in the early hours to avoid his mam's gaze. Most of all she thought of Eddie, who was never far from her mind.

★   ★   ★

The kitchen at the Forester's Arms was tiny. There was no room for a table here, not like there had been at the Railway Inn. It was dominated by a coal fire with its oven to one side. Underneath the small window that looked out to the pub yard was a wooden bench that ran the length of one wall. Next to the kitchen was a tiny pantry no bigger than an alcove, in which were stored tubs of butter and lard, home-made rhubarb and ginger compote in glass jars with hand-written labels attached, cinnamon and nutmeg, even rosemary dried in a bunch. On the fireside hearth stood a pile of chopped wood in a basket next to a tin bucket of coal.

Bessie used the kitchen to cook the evening meal for the three of them, which they took into the sitting room to eat before Sadie went up to her room. But it had been a long time since it had been given a good clean, and Sadie set to scrubbing the place thoroughly before she began baking her pies. Once they went up for sale, they sold as quickly as Bessie had hoped — indeed, better than she'd expected.

In July, when Ryhope held its Peace Parade to celebrate the end of the Great War and all those safely home, Bessie and Sadie baked together. Generous slices of beef pie, mutton pie and sweetened rhubarb pie were laid on a trestle table outside the pub. They were not for sale this time, but to give away to anyone who wanted a slice — just as long as they'd bought a drink from the pub first. Sadie saw another side to Ryhope on the day of the parade, when the community came together in a way it had never done before. She helped serve at the table as Pat and Bessie worked behind the bar, the pub flinging its doors open early to cater for the celebrations.

Up and down the colliery, shops and pubs were decorated with bunting and flags, and Ryhope had never looked prettier. Eddie even took the day off work, but he saw little of Sadie apart from a quick chat with her at the Forester's before the Railway Inn opened. He was stuck helping his mam and Tom, for they were having a busy day of it too, with the parade ending in the village. At Sadie's request, he left his flat cap with her when they said goodbye. He was bemused but delighted she wanted to keep it. She said she wanted it to remember him by when they were apart.

'I'll look after it,' she promised as he handed it over. 'I just want to keep it for a while.'

Bessie had been right: she and Sadie did indeed make a good team. In the pub, the two of them worked happily together, Sadie taking instruction and learning every day. The pain in Pat's hip increasingly meant that he had to sit out his shifts at the bar, conversing with the customers about their jobs and their pigeons, their wives and their bairns. But there was little else he could do now: no more lifting wooden crates or helping with the barrels when the draymen arrived from the brewery with the horses. That was Sadie's job now, and she took to her tasks heartily over the balmy summer days.

She and Eddie spent little time together, what with him working at the pit and helping out at the Railway Inn. On the rare times that she did see him, he brought her news that his mam wasn't yet ready to forgive.

'Give her time,' he told her when she asked how Molly was doing. 'I know Mam. I know what she's like. She'll come round, just you wait and see.'

Eddie sounded so sure, all Sadie could do was trust him. But there was a tiny piece of her heart that wondered whether Molly was deliberately working Eddie hard at the Railway Inn to keep the two of them apart.

Sadie and Eddie's time together was precious, stitched together in conversations across the bar at the Forester's Arms when Sadie wasn't too busy. Eddie never asked for his flat cap back — he had another at home — and Sadie was happy to keep it in her room, hanging on the door handle. Every time she caught sight of it, it made her happy to think of Eddie. Sometimes she even wore it when she was in her room

120

alone, turning it this way and that as she looked at her reflection in the mirror. She tried tucking her long hair under it, pulling it up to expose her slim neck. She liked the way she looked with just the wisps of her fringe poking from the front of the cap. She liked it so much that she began to turn over an idea forming in her mind.

'Bessie?' she asked the next morning. 'Would you cut my hair for me, please?'

Bessie turned and saw that Sadie held a pair of kitchen scissors in her hand. 'You can't be serious, pet? You've got lovely long hair. It always looks a treat.'

'I need to do it,' Sadie said. 'You remember when Mick, the fella from Hartlepool, came looking for me in the Railway Inn?'

'Aye, go on,' said Bessie.

'I was watching him through the crack in the door as I was hiding in the Select. And I saw him trying to describe me, my height and my hair. I'm that scared he'll come back looking for me, and if he walks around Ryhope asking folk if they've seen a new lass with long hair, they'll know it's me. But if I cut my hair, change the way I look . . . '

'Aw, Sadie love,' Bessie said. 'Couldn't you just pile it up in a bun, like I do with mine? It'd be such a shame to take it off; it doesn't half make you look pretty.'

But Sadie was determined and her mind was made up. 'I've got to do it, Bessie. I can't risk him coming back here, not now he knows I'm in Ryhope somewhere.'

'But even if he did come back, me and Pat

would protect you. You're our lodger now, our employee. We pay your wages and you pay us rent. What hold has Mick got over you?'

'Him and his mam, Bessie, they're not nice people. Vicious they are, the pair of them.'

Sadie thought about the pound notes she had taken from Freda's. There could be no doubt that the missing money had been noticed, and that was what had brought Mick to Ryhope to find her.

'If Mick comes and finds me when I'm on my own,' she continued, 'without Eddie or you and Pat, what chance have I got? He could drag me to the train station and back to Hartlepool. I'd have to go back into service and hand my money to Freda. And I'm not doing it, Bessie, I won't. I've got to give myself the best chance of finding Birdie. And even if I don't find her, if the worst should happen . . . ' She paused and took a deep breath. 'If that should happen, I'd stay on here, Bessie, I've come to like the place.'

'And the people,' Bessie smiled. 'Especially a big strapping fella called Eddie, eh?'

Sadie felt a warm heat spread from her neck to her face. She put her hands to her cheeks.

'Is that you blushing now?' Bessie laughed. 'Sorry, Sadie, I didn't mean to embarrass you. But Eddie's a lovely fella.'

'He is,' Sadie replied quickly, feeling the heat in her face begin to dissipate. 'I feel lucky to have found him.' She held out the scissors again. 'Would you help me? Please?'

Bessie sighed as she took the scissors. 'Turn around.'

122

Sadie did as she was told.

'How much should I cut?'

'Enough so my hair will fit under Eddie's cap.'

'No, lass,' Bessie cried. 'I can't take that much off. You'll end up looking like a miner yourself.'

Sadie stood firm. 'Please, Bessie. It'll grow again. And by the time it does, Mick will have given up on looking for me and I can wear it long again.'

Bessie shook her head gently and took a deep breath before she allowed the scissors to make their first cut. Sadie's hair floated to the ground, softly at first and then more steadily until it pooled round her boots.

'I'm not taking off any more,' Bessie said at last.

Sadie put her hands to her head but could no longer run her fingers through her hair. She patted down the sides, and around the back too.

'Let's have a look at you,' Bessie said.

Sadie turned. 'How do I look?'

Bessie was too stunned to speak. 'Eh, lass. I wouldn't have thought it possible. You're even more bonny with your short hair than you were with it long. You're a little beauty. Go and have a look in the mirror.'

Sadie ran out of the pub into the yard and back in through the door that led up to her room. She ran straight to the mirror, and when she saw her reflection, she gasped. She looked younger, wide-eyed and innocent. Without her long hair, the focus was on her face, her eyes and her delicate lips. She smiled, liking what she saw, then picked up Eddie's cap and put it on her head. It covered her hair perfectly. There was no way that Mick, or Freda, or anyone who came looking for her from Hartlepool would recognise her now. She arranged the wisps of her fringe and looked again at her reflection. She was still the same Sadie, but there was a spark of something special about the way she looked now. She didn't look boyish, not exactly, but younger certainly. More like the girl she used to be before life turned her over to Freda's cold and callous hands.

'Sadie!' It was Bessie, shouting up the stairs to Sadie's room. 'Eddie's here to see you!'

Sadie gasped. Eddie! She hadn't considered what he would think about her hair. All that had been on her mind was changing her appearance in case Mick came hunting again. She raced down the stairs and back into the pub. Eddie smiled when he saw her.

'You still wearing my old cap?' he said.

Sadie put her hands to her head and slowly, gently removed the flat cap. Behind them both, Bessie busied herself at the bar, pretending not to watch but secretly intrigued to see what Eddie's reaction would be.

'What . . . what have you done?' he stammered. 'Where has your hair gone?'

'Do you like it?' Sadie asked.

'Like it? There's nothing there to like,' Eddie laughed. 'Where's it all gone?' He swung round towards Bessie. 'What happened?'

'Now don't look at me,' she said, holding her hands up in mock surrender. 'She made me do it. And I think you know her well enough now,

Eddie, to know she's a determined little madam when she puts her mind to things.'

Eddie reached out his hand towards Sadie and gently stroked the side of her head.

'I don't look like a miner, do I? Bessie was worried I might.'

'No, you don't look like any miner I've ever met,' Eddie grinned.

'I had to do it, in case Mick came back looking for me,' Sadie explained. 'You understand, don't you, Eddie?'

He stroked her hair again. 'I've never seen a lass with short hair like this,' he said. 'It makes you look . . . I don't know. It makes you look beautiful, Sadie. I mean, even more beautiful.'

'You've got a bonny lass there all right,' Bessie said. 'Now are you two going to stand there all day making eyes at each other or is there something you wanted, Eddie?'

Eddie dropped his hand. 'Sorry, Bessie,' he said, not taking his eyes off Sadie. 'I thought I'd call up and see if I could entice Sadie out for a walk before she starts work today. But only if you don't need her yet. It's such a nice day out, seems a shame to waste it being stuck indoors.'

'Go on, get yourselves out for an hour before we open up,' Bessie said, waving her hand to dismiss them.

Sadie put Eddie's cap back on top of her head. It covered her hair completely.

'Leave it off,' said Eddie. 'I want everyone to see how beautiful you look. And if anyone does recognise you, although I doubt very much that they will, I'll see them off, Sadie. You'll be safe.'

She slipped her arm through his and the two of them walked from the pub. Eddie led her across the road directly in front of them, heading towards the pit.

'Where are we going?' she asked.

'I meant what I said before,' he said. 'About finding your bairn. We're going to do it together. I've not had much chance to get away from Mam at the pub. She's putting all her store in Tom running the place, but he spends his days sleeping and I'm having to help her, and what with my pit work and everything . . . '

'I understand,' Sadie said softly. 'There's no need to explain. I haven't had much time to think about looking myself. It's been so busy with Bessie and Pat, and oh Eddie, I can't thank you enough for all the help you've given me.'

'I just wish I could do more,' he said. 'The least I can do is walk you around Ryhope, show you some of the back lanes and colliery rows, somewhere your bairn might be. We could ask around, see if anyone knows anyone with a baby about the age yours would be.'

'What then, though?' Sadie said softly. Bessie's words had played on her mind since they'd chatted by the fire on Sadie's first night in the pub. 'What if I do find her? What if I find a child that I am certain is mine, with the ladybird birthmark? What then? I can't steal her back. I've dived head first into searching for her without thinking through what'll happen if I find her.'

Eddie laid his hand on her arm. 'Not if; when,' he said.

'I wish I had your certainty,' she replied.

126

'Then let me help you,' Eddie said firmly, as if he'd given the matter considerable thought. 'Now that Mam knows the truth and Bessie knows too, and everyone knows we're mad on each other, where's the shame in me helping?'

'You'd do that? For me?'

'Course I would. You'd want me to, wouldn't you?'

Sadie leaned into Eddie's side and pulled him gently towards her. 'Course I would,' she replied.

'Right then, let's go and have a walk up and down the pit rows and see who we can find to talk to. There's bound to be someone who knows what's going on; gossip travels fast in Ryhope. Someone might know something about who drives that black car.'

They set off along the rows of mucky lime-washed cottages. At the back of each cottage was a yard with a high wall over which neither Sadie nor Eddie could see. As they walked, Sadie lifted the hem of her skirt to avoid the mud from the cobbled lanes. Holes in the uneven ground held the previous night's rainwater, blackened from coal dust. Eddie held tight to her hand as they walked. At the sight of the outside netty blocks and water taps at the end of each row, she was more grateful than ever for his help in finding her somewhere decent to live. At least she didn't have to share her netty with a whole row of neighbours, just the customers at the Forester's Arms. And her tap was one she shared with just Bessie and Pat.

She peered into a back yard as they walked past a cottage that had its yard door flung open.

Inside she saw a tin bath hanging on a brick wall and a metal poss tub for washing clothes. A broken chair, one of its legs missing, was propped up against the back door. She glanced up at the bedroom window, hoping to see . . . what exactly? A woman with a bairn in her arms? And what then? What then? The hopelessness of her task was starting to sink in, the realisation that what she was hoping for might never come true. Her heart turned heavy.

'Come on, Eddie,' she said at last. 'I've got to get back to work or Bessie will have my guts for garters.'

'Are you sure you don't want to keep walking? Keep looking?'

She shook her head. 'If only I knew that I'd find her,' she said quietly, turning her face away. 'If only I knew for sure.'

'If she's here, we'll find her. And when we do, we'll decide what to do.' Eddie put his hand to Sadie's head and stroked her short hair with his rough miner's hand. 'You can't give up, Sadie. You've come all this way. You left your old life to search for your child. You can't let her go.'

'She'll always be in my heart,' Sadie said, leaning in towards him. He wrapped his arms around her and pulled her close.

'And one day she'll be in your arms,' he said, glancing over her shoulder down the length of the back lane. But his words belied how unsure he really felt about finding Sadie's child.

★ ★ ★

After a busy night at the bar, Sadie headed to the sitting room at the back of the pub. Bessie brought in three mugs of hot tea on a tray and asked to have a word with her.

'You might want to sit down, love,' she said.

Sadie's face clouded over.

'Don't worry,' Bessie said when she saw her distress. 'Pat's coming to join us too. There's something we both want to talk to you about.'

Sadie heard a noise at the door and turned to see Pat coming through. He was limping heavily; his hip was clearly causing more pain. He rested with his hand against the back of the sofa.

'I'll not sit,' he said. 'Takes too long to get down and back up again.'

'Will you tell her, or shall I?' Bessie asked him.

'Think it'd be better coming from you,' Pat said with a quick nod.

'What is it? Is there something wrong? Is it something to do with Eddie?' asked Sadie.

'No, love,' Bessie replied. 'It's about your bairn.'

Sadie looked from Bessie to Pat. 'What is it? What?'

'It might be nothing, love. And we don't want you to get your hopes up, for it all might come to naught.'

'What is it, Bessie? Tell me, please,' Sadie urged.

'Well, it's what you said that first night you moved in here,' she said. 'When we had our chat and I said I wanted no secrets between us. You made a promise to me that you'd be honest from now on.'

'And I have been honest, truly,' Sadie said with tears in her eyes.

Bessie and Pat exchanged a look.

'It works both ways, pet,' Bessie said. 'We need to be honest with you now. No secrets, right, Pat?'

'No point,' Pat chipped in. 'No good ever comes from telling lies.'

'We've been talking, Pat and I. Ever since you came to live with us, Sadie, there's been something we've wondered about. Something we talked about a lot after you told us about your bairn. And I think we know something that might help you,' Bessie said.

Sadie's eyes widened.

'We know someone, love. Someone in the village who's got a bairn. Just over a year old you said yours would be by now. Well, about that time, this bairn came to Ryhope. Brand new it was, squealing like a pig by all accounts, but it wasn't delivered by any midwife here. It was given to the couple from an orphanage, or that's what we heard, isn't that right, Pat?'

Pat stayed silent and nodded in reply.

'Now it might not be yours, Sadie, and I don't want you rushing out looking for it. But we wanted you to know what we'd heard, because we thought it odd at the time when the bairn turned up like that out of the blue.'

'And did it have the birthmark on its shoulder? Was it a baby girl?'

'It was a girl, yes,' Bessie replied. 'But as for a birthmark, we can't say.'

Sadie's heart thumped. 'Where is she?' she asked. 'Who are the couple you mentioned?'

Bessie leaned back in her chair. 'Oh love, I'm not sure this is a good idea, really I'm not.'

'Bessie,' Pat tutted. 'You've come this far, you can't leave the girl hanging like this. You've got to tell her everything we know.'

Bessie took a deep breath. 'Over at the pit there are three bosses who run the place. Mr Wright, Mr Pascoe and . . . ' she glanced towards Pat, 'Mr Marshall.'

'Marshall?' Sadie breathed.

'It's his wife who has the bairn, love,' Bessie said softly. 'They live in the village, at Ryhope Grange.'

'He's a pit boss?' Sadie cried. She struggled to take in the news. She remembered Ryhope Grange from her first walk around the village with Eddie, with its gardeners working at the front of the house. 'Does this mean my child has a good life?'

'If it *is* your child. And remember, we have no proof.'

Sadie thought for a moment. 'Does he have a car, Mr Marshall? A big black fancy kind of car?'

Bessie shrugged and turned towards Pat. 'I'm not sure if it's his, but there's a black car the gaffers use for pit business. I know I've seen Mr Wright sitting in the back of it before, being driven down Ryhope Street South.'

'Then I need to see her,' Sadie said. 'I need to find out, to know for sure if it's Birdie.'

'All in good time,' Bessie replied firmly. 'If you go running down to Ryhope Grange demanding to see the bairn, even if it is your own, they'll have you carted away to the funny farm.'

'You don't want to mess with the likes of them, not the pit managers,' Pat added. 'They've got power in the village. You can't go storming in without thinking properly first.'

Sadie lifted her eyes to Bessie and Bessie saw the tears there. She reached out and took Sadie's hands.

'You need a few days for the shock of the news to settle in before you do anything, you hear?' she said. 'Then we'll decide what to do.'

She turned towards Pat. 'And we'll both help you, love. Won't we, Pat?'

Pat nodded. 'Yes, dear.'

6

The Grange

Late summer 1919

Over the coming days, Sadie's thoughts began to trouble her sleep. She needed to speak to Eddie, to let him know what she had learned, but she saw nothing of him, as his night shifts at the pit meant that he slept during the day, putting a stop to them meeting. Working behind the bar at the Forester's, her mind was elsewhere, constantly turning over Bessie's words, wondering if the child was hers, hoping in her heart that it was. Was she really close to finding Birdie? Could she allow herself to think, to hope, that her daughter was in Ryhope and living in the house of the pit manager, no less? And if she *was* living at the Grange, was she loved by the people there? There'd be money there, Sadie knew, money that could be giving her baby luxuries that she knew she could never afford. Her heart sank at the thought. What if Birdie was being given the kind of life at the Grange that meant she would be better off staying there?

She wanted to run out of the pub, down the colliery bank to the village, and bang on the front door of Ryhope Grange until it flew open. She dreamed about throwing herself inside, demanding to see her child. But she knew how futile such an action would be. As Bessie had told her, she needed to get her thoughts straight before she did anything. But how would she know when the time was right? And how would she go about approaching the Marshalls? She needed Eddie so much. He'd promised to help her and she knew she wanted him by her side, whatever happened now.

★ ★ ★

Late in the week, after the last of the customers had left, Sadie, Pat and Bessie locked up the pub, tidied the bar and washed the glasses ready for the next day. Bessie was pleased to see that all the pies had been sold, yet again. She allowed herself a satisfied smile. She was really on to a winner with Sadie and her pies; the lass could certainly bake, and profits had soared since they'd taken her on.

'Come on through to the sitting room and have a cup of tea before you go up to your room,' she said.

Sadie was glad to sit with Bessie and Pat in the quiet of the back room. It felt safe and warm there with the two of them.

'Your pies are selling well,' Bessie said as she handed mugs of tea to Pat and Sadie.

'Are you wanting me to make more? I could bake more stotties too, if they're selling for sandwiches?'

'Too many coffins,' Pat said without looking up from his tea.

134

'Sorry?' Sadie said.

'Coffins. In your bread.'

'He means holes, love,' Bessie explained. 'The miners call them coffins; they reckon it's bad luck for bread to have holes in it. Too much air, you see. They won't take it the way it is.'

Sadie thought for a moment. 'I'll change the recipe,' she said at last. 'I'll try a different shelf in the oven, see if that makes a difference.'

'Good idea, lass,' Pat said drily.

'Anyway, word's spread about the pies,' Bessie continued. 'Speaking of which, I've got some news for you about the Marshalls. It's news you might like to hear, too.'

Sadie sat up straight in the armchair by Bessie's coal fire.

'We haven't told you this before, love, but Mr Marshall drinks in here now and then.'

'Not often,' Pat chipped in.

'Here? In the Forester's?' Sadie gasped. 'But I haven't seen him. And I'd know him, I would. I'd recognise him. I remember his face, his moustache.'

'As Pat says, he doesn't come in very often. This is a pub for the miners, not the gaffers. We've never been sure why he comes in here at all; the lads don't like the pit bosses drinking in the same pub as them.'

'But what's this got to do with the pies?' Sadie asked, impatient to find out what Bessie had to reveal.

'He's become a fan of your baking, has Mr Marshall. So much so that he's asked if the pub will cater for a picnic his wife's throwing for

135

some of the pit managers' wives. Course, he'll likely have heard that we've got a girl working for us doing the baking, but he's not set eyes on you yet. You say you'd recognise him, but would he recognise you, Sadie?'

Sadie raised a hand and stroked the side of her head. 'With my hair cut short? I don't know. He looked at me for a long time on the day he took Birdie from my arms, though that was over a year ago. I can't say for sure, but he might remember the look of me, yes.'

'Then you're to visit Mrs Marshall when he's at work,' Bessie said firmly. 'Call in on her tomorrow morning and find out what she wants for this picnic. I'll help you with the baking. And we can split the profits between us. Sound fair?'

It took Sadie a moment before she could speak. 'I'm to visit Ryhope Grange?'

Bessie nodded. 'I know, love. And the bairn will likely be there. You've got to steel yourself, you hear me? Give it some thought and decide what you'll say to Mrs Marshall. Ruth, she's called, bit of an odd fish by all accounts. Standoffish, and very high church.'

'Pious, more like,' Pat said.

'Aye, well, that's as may be,' Bessie agreed. 'Do you want me to come with you when you go and see her?'

Sadie bit her lip and her gaze dropped to her hands in her lap. She was afraid of going alone, of what she might find there. What if she saw Birdie? She needed someone with her, someone who'd keep her calm with a voice of reason.

'Please,' she whispered.

'Then that's what I'll do. Pat can manage the pub on his own tomorrow, and we can have one day without any pies being sold at the bar, I'm sure, although we'll get complaints.' She gave a wry smile. 'Mind you, we'll sell twice as many the day after.'

★ ★ ★

That night, Sadie slept badly again, her thoughts and dreams running wild with images of stepping through the door of Ryhope Grange, the big oak door that she'd seen when she'd walked past with Eddie. She still hadn't seen Eddie since Bessie had told her about the child. She could have called into the Railway Inn to tell him the news that Birdie might have been found, but she was still keeping her distance from Molly, just to be on the safe side. Eddie had said he'd let her know when his mam was ready to be approached, but as yet his silence told her everything she needed to know. She'd make amends with Molly, she was determined to do so, but not until the time was right.

★ ★ ★

The next morning, Sadie and Bessie set off together from the Forester's Arms, down the colliery bank. Sadie slipped her arm through the older woman's as they made their way along Ryhope Street South, past the Co-operative Society store.

'Morning, Bessie!' folk shouted when they saw

137

her. It seemed to Sadie as if everyone in Ryhope not only knew who Bessie was but was delighted to see her outside the pub she spent so many hours working in. Bessie introduced Sadie to everyone who stopped to greet her, telling them that this was the lass who baked the pies. Word had spread, as Bessie said it had, and everyone seemed to know about Sadie's baking prowess. They carried on walking, past the tiny front window of an Italian ice-cream shop, down towards St Paul's church. The vicar, Reverend Daye, stood at the low iron gates that separated the church path from the pavement.

'Morning, Father,' Bessie said as they walked past.

'Morning, Mrs Brogan,' he replied. 'I haven't seen you in my place of worship for a while.' He smiled widely and his eyes twinkled with mischief, as if he already knew the reply he was going to receive.

'And likely you won't, Father,' Bessie replied with a smile. 'Until the day I see you in my place of worship.'

The vicar gave a sharp laugh, unable to contain himself. 'The Forester's, you mean, of course!'

'Aye,' Bessie replied. 'The day I see you there, you'll see me here.'

'You can't blame me for trying to get you to come along to Sunday service, now can you?' he laughed, then he turned towards Sadie. 'And who's this young lady you've got with you today?'

Sadie extended her hand. 'Sadie Linthorpe.'

'Nice to meet you,' Reverend Daye said.

138

She held on to the vicar's warm hand a few seconds longer than she needed, taking comfort from it. He didn't seem to mind. If he sensed her anxiety, he made no mention of it. She looked up into his open, friendly face. It was a face she felt she could trust, a man she could open up to if she needed to about Birdie and all that had happened. But right now, there was somewhere else she needed to be.

'We'd best be going, Vicar,' Bessie said kindly.

'Nice to see you both,' he replied. 'I think I'll wait here a while longer, see who else might be passing by.'

'You mean, see who you can round up and add to your flock.'

Reverend Daye gave Bessie a smile, and she and Sadie went on their way. As they rounded the corner of the village green by the school, a horse and cart came towards them on the road. Sadie looked in astonishment at the ragged state of the old horse, tired and worn. Her eyes widened further when she saw it was a young girl, seated on the cart, driving the horse forward.

'Morning, Meg,' Bessie shouted, and the girl waved in reply as the horse trotted on. Ryhope was turning out to be full of surprises, thought Sadie.

★ ★ ★

As Sadie and Bessie crossed the village green, Ryhope Grange stood ahead of them, as large and imposing as Sadie remembered from the

139

first time she had seen it. She felt her heart quicken with every step she took. Once again, two gardeners were working at the front of the house, sleeves rolled up and flat caps on their head. The taller of the pair turned when he heard the gate open, and Sadie recognised him as John, the gardener Eddie had introduced her to. He recognised her too, and doffed his cap before going back to his digging.

'Are you ready?' Bessie asked as the two women stood at the front door.

Sadie squared her shoulders and nodded. 'I'm ready.'

Bessie raised her right hand and knocked hard on the door. After a few moments, it was opened by a woman who was covered from the waist down by a pristine white apron. Above it she wore a green blouse with a cotton frill at the neck. Her hair was a pile of soft brown curls that had been tied on top of her head and were now escaping around her face. She looked flustered, Sadie thought, as if Bessie's knock had been an unwelcome distraction from whatever she was doing inside.

'Hello, Em!' Bessie beamed. 'I didn't know you were still working here!'

'Not for much longer, if I have my way,' the woman whispered. She leaned towards Bessie and the two women hugged. 'I hear you've got an appointment to see her ladyship?'

'Ooh! Still like that, is she?' Bessie whispered in reply.

'She's never changed. Never will, I expect.'

'I heard she was still unwell,' Bessie said.

But before Em could reply, a loud clattering noise reached them from deep within the house.

'Oh Christ! Not again!' she cried.

She left Bessie and Sadie on the doorstep and ran along the dark passageway behind her. The two women looked at each other, and Bessie motioned for Sadie to step inside. She closed the front door behind them and they waited in the hallway. They could hear Em's voice from the back of the house telling someone not to worry, that everything would be all right, that nothing was broken this time.

As they waited, Sadie looked around the entrance hall of Ryhope Grange. It looked no different to the fancy houses in Hartlepool that she'd worked in. There seemed to be too much of everything: too much pattern on the wallpaper, too many pictures in heavy frames on the walls, too many ornaments on the shelves. And for the maid who worked here and had to keep the house straight, Sadie knew from experience that there was too much to clean. Two deep brown stone pots stood at the bottom of a wide wooden staircase. Each contained a plant with long, shiny dark leaves that attracted the little bit of light that came into the hallway from the small window by the front door. Sadie remembered only too well having to polish leaves like those in the Hartlepool houses.

Still, there was something homely about the entrance to Ryhope Grange, something welcoming. Perhaps it was the smell, she thought, the sweet aroma of baking that wafted towards her from the back of the house. She glanced around the polished wood of the hallway, her heart quickening, knowing that this might be the place where Birdie was being brought up. Was she upstairs asleep? she wondered. Or maybe there was a nurse to take care of her, and she was in the back garden, lying in a pram with soft cotton sheets trimmed with lace.

Em came bustling into view, smoothing down the front of her apron and pushing wisps of hair behind her ears.

'Honestly, she's a danger to herself,' she whispered as she drew near. 'Come on through to the parlour; she'll meet you in there and I'll bring you some tea.'

'Don't go to any trouble, Em,' Bessie said, knowing how much time it would take from the woman's day to produce a tray of tea for them all.

'If I don't bring tea, my life won't be worth living,' Em replied as she led them into the parlour. 'Take a seat, she'll be through in her own time.'

Once Em had headed back to the kitchen, Sadie sat in one of the chairs by the enormous hearth, which was blackened to perfection. The fireplace around it was white marble, decorative, with more ornaments, vases and pictures in frames displayed on the mantel above. Sadie gasped when she caught sight of one of the framed pictures. It was of a child, a baby with a mass of dark hair, its eyes tight shut, caught sleeping by the photographer. Bessie looked too when she realised what had caught Sadie's attention.

'Now, love, you're going to have to steady

142

yourself, you hear me?' she said softly. 'Don't give Mrs Marshall any reason to be alarmed by your behaviour.'

'I'm pleased you came, Bessie,' Sadie said. 'I'm not sure I could have managed to do this on my own.'

'You'll be all right,' Bessie said, but Sadie knew it was more of a command than a reassurance. 'Just let me do the talking. And try not to stare at that picture; we don't want to give her any reason to doubt our integrity, do we?'

Sadie ran her hand along the armrest of her chair. She'd often wondered what it would be like to sit in the overstuffed furniture of the fancy houses in Hartlepool. She'd cleaned enough of them in her time. She'd wiped them down and changed dirty seat covers, but this was the first time she'd actually sat in one of them. It felt too big for her; there was room on the chair for her and Bessie to have sat side by side. She put her hands in her lap and straightened her back, then took a deep breath and readied herself to meet Mrs Marshall.

It was Em who bustled into the room first, with the tea tray in her hands. Sadie almost jumped out of her seat to help, then remembered where she was and what her business was at Ryhope Grange. It felt different, unusual and not altogether pleasant to be waited on after all the years she'd worked in service. She glanced at Bessie, who looked to be scowling at Em, but as soon as she caught Sadie's eye, her face expanded into one of its smiles and the scowl disappeared.

As Em was pouring the tea, Mrs Marshall

walked into the room. She did it quietly, without announcement; she just seemed to appear out of nowhere and her entrance took Sadie and Bessie by surprise. Less surprised was Em, who simply poured a third cup and placed it on a small table by the side of the sofa.

'That's all. You may go,' Mrs Marshall said. Her voice was little more than a whisper, as if she was having difficulty speaking through a sore throat.

Em stood for a second, and Sadie wondered if she would curtsey to her mistress, as she had seen maids do in Hartlepool. But she simply turned her back to Mrs Marshall, smiled at Bessie and rolled her eyes before taking her leave and walking from the room.

Sadie watched as Mrs Marshall made a fuss of picking up her teacup and bringing it to her lips. For a pit manager's wife, she looked ill-fed, thin and wan, as if she was in need of a day at the beach in the sun, kicking off her shoes and paddling in the sea. She looked unhappy, too. Her face was pale, almost translucent, and the skin on her bony hands and fingers was paper white. Her hair, though, was wondrous; Sadie had seen nothing like it before. Draping around her shoulders in soft curls, it wasn't red, not exactly, but neither was it brown. Sadie decided at last that it was the colour of oatmeal biscuits left in the oven for just a minute too long. The whole impression of Mrs Marshall was of extreme delicacy and lightness, almost as if the woman wasn't of this world, and certainly not of Ryhope. It wasn't the picture that Sadie had built up of Mrs Marshall in her mind. She had expected a robust character full of vigour and life, someone perhaps Bessie's age, and yet the woman in front of her looked only a little older than Sadie herself.

She cast her mind back to the day at Freda's lodging when Birdie had been taken. All she had seen of Mrs Marshall then, if indeed it had been her, was a fancy hat in the back seat of a car. She had no reason, no proof, to think this might be the same woman.

Bessie caught Sadie staring across the room. 'Thank you for seeing us, Mrs Marshall,' she said, breaking the silence.

The woman smiled, but Sadie noticed no warmth there. It was just her lips that moved slightly; the rest of her face gave little away.

'I apologise for the noise you must have heard when you arrived,' she said. 'There was a slight accident in the kitchen. I dropped . . . it was a pan that dropped to the floor.' She looked at Sadie, seeming to take in her appearance fully for the first time. 'What strange hair you have, girl,' she said abruptly.

Sadie lifted her right hand self-consciously to her head.

'Nits,' Bessie said quickly, eyeing Sadie. 'The girl had nits and the hair had to go. But that was some time ago now and she's long been clean of infestation.'

'Glad to hear it,' Mrs Marshall said. 'Otherwise I would have had to ask you to leave.'

'About this picnic, Mrs Marshall,' said Bessie, changing the subject again. 'I hear you'd like the Forester's Arms to cater it for you?'

'Saturday next,' the woman replied with a bored sigh. 'Two o'clock. On the beach if the weather is fair, otherwise in our garden room. There are twelve invited although I'm not sure how many will be free to come. It's for the wives of the managers of the local pits, some as far away as Hylton. It's my husband's idea, although I dare say he won't be attending. Too busy working; I rarely see him these days. Some of the women will bring bairns. We'll need fresh pies, savoury and sweet, and good bread.'

'We can do it all, Mrs Marshall,' Bessie said.

'I dare say you can, Mrs Brogan. The point is, can you do it well? I mean, your food might be acceptable to the miners who come into your licensed premises for their beer, but you must realise that this picnic is for people of a higher class than you're used to catering for.'

Bessie cleared her throat and was about to respond when Mrs Marshall cut in again.

'And there's to be a cake. You can do cakes, can't you?'

'We can bake any cake you desire, and to the highest standard too,' Bessie said, nodding towards Sadie. 'This one's got magic hands.'

'I need a birthday cake for my child,' Mrs Marshall said.

Sadie felt her heartbeat quicken when she saw the woman lift her eyes to the framed picture on the mantelpiece.

'She'll be fourteen months old. Or as good as.'

Bessie saw her opening and took it, determined to get as much information about the child as she could. 'As good as?' she probed.

146

Mrs Marshall shot her a look. 'I'm sure, Mrs Brogan, that it's no secret that Mr Marshall and I had some difficulty with conception. I understand gossip travels fast in Ryhope amongst people with little better to do than chat about things that are none of their business. Since we came to live here over a year ago, when my husband was offered his position with Ryhope Coal Company, I've come to learn that Ryhope is a place of few secrets. Making a home here was not my choice, I want to make that clear. I'm here at my husband's behest and nothing more. And so you will have heard on the gossip grapevine, or whatever you people call it, that we chose our own child. Of course, when one does this kind of thing, there is no way of knowing what the actual birth date is. My ill-health prevented a celebration from taking place earlier this summer in the child's birthday month of July. And so the picnic can serve by way of celebration for her too.'

Sadie gripped her hands together in her lap.

'Of course,' Bessie said. She lifted her large black handbag from the floor and took out a small notepad and pencil. She licked the end of the pencil and set to writing a list. 'So that's catering for twelve. Pies, bread. Saturday next. On the beach if it's fair, here if it's not. Birthday cake for a bairn.'

'We'll pay you the going rate,' Mrs Marshall said dismissively. 'You can sort that out with the maid.'

Bessie looked up from her notepad. 'Em?'

'I said you can sort that out with the maid!'

Sadie stifled a giggle that threatened to rise.

147

She knew she shouldn't laugh, oh, she shouldn't, not here.

'No,' said Bessie. 'I mean, I was asking if I should speak to your maid. She's called Emily, Em for short. I've known her for years. Is she the one I need to talk to about the payment or is there someone else I should make arrangements with?'

Mrs Marshall lifted her hand and then let it flop down to the sofa armrest. 'Is that her name? Yes, then sort it out with her. And remember, I want the highest-quality ingredients, bought at the Co-op store only. Nothing must come from the markets, you hear me?' She pushed down on the sofa with both hands to support her as she rose. 'Now, if you'll excuse me, I have things to do.'

Bessie stood too, and Sadie followed. Bessie stretched her hand towards Mrs Marshall, but it was left hanging in mid air as the woman reached to steady herself against the mantelpiece.

'Are you all right, dear?' Bessie asked.

'I'm fine,' she snapped. 'And I'd be grateful if you'd leave me in peace now. I'm a very busy woman, and as I've said, I've things to do. I'll see you a week on Saturday.'

'You'll be seeing Sadie, not me,' said Bessie. 'I can't leave the pub on a Saturday, it's our busiest day. Sadie will look after the picnic for you.'

Mrs Marshall sighed. 'So be it. But I want you to know that it was my husband's idea to use your public house to cater for the picnic. If I had my way, we'd be bringing in the caterer my sister uses for her affairs in Newcastle. At least if the food fails to impress, it won't be my fault.'

148

'I promise you, it won't fail to impress,' Sadie said, finding her voice at last. She felt confident in addressing Mrs Marshall directly now that she appeared to pose no real threat towards her. Her weak countenance had shocked Sadie when she had first laid eyes on her, and she almost felt sorry for the woman in her poor state of health. 'I'll do the very best I can.'

Mrs Marshall dismissed Sadie and Bessie with a wave of her hand and they let themselves out of the front door.

'Well!' Bessie exclaimed as they walked away up the village green. 'What did you make of her? Who on earth does she think she is?'

Sadie felt her eyes fill with tears. 'My baby's mother,' she whispered. 'That's who she thinks she is.'

'Oh lass, now come on,' Bessie said gently. 'If that *is* your bairn she's got in the Grange, I've told you, I'll help you. But you have to take things slowly, see?'

Sadie wiped her eyes and turned to look back at the house. 'Why, Bessie? Why do I have to take it slowly? Why can't I just go and demand to see her, to take a look at her shoulder? I'd know the minute I saw it. That's all I need to do. I just need to see it. And if the birthmark's not there, I'll stop my search.'

Bessie took her arm. 'Come on, love. I've already told you, you can't go demanding such things, it's not right.'

'Couldn't your friend Em find out?' Sadie asked. 'She'd see the bairn in her work, wouldn't she?'

'She's the maid, love, not the child's nurse, and a woman like Mrs Marshall is bound to have a nurse. Makes her feel more important than she has a right to, and having staff to boss around gives her something to do with her time while her husband's out with his . . . '

'His what?' Sadie asked.

Bessie bit her tongue. 'Nothing, love,' she replied. Pat had told her more than once about the gossip in the pub that Mr Marshall was friendly with a younger woman; friendlier than he should have been, considering he was married and all. But she didn't want to burden Sadie with the rumour, given what else the lass had on her mind.

'But you'll ask Em, won't you? Please, Bessie?'

'Course I will, love,' Bessie replied. 'Course I will. Now come on, we've got to get back to the Forester's and help Pat.'

★ ★ ★

Pat was already settled on his stool behind the bar when Bessie and Sadie arrived.

'Everything go all right at the Grange?' he asked.

'We're taking things one step at a time,' Bessie replied with a quick glance towards Sadie. 'Oh, and Em Crawford's still working there. I got a bit of a shock when I saw her.'

'Em Crawford? We haven't seen her in a long time. I thought she'd moved to live up in Silksworth?'

'No, she's working for the Marshalls still.'

150

'Was himself in?' Pat asked.

'Just her,' Bessie replied. 'And she was every inch the stuck-up little madam that I'd heard she would be. It's no wonder she's got no friends in the village.'

'They reckon that's why she spends so much time helping out at the church,' Pat said. 'The vicar's the only one polite enough to put up with her.'

'Aye, well, that's as may be, but she's paying us to cater for a picnic on the beach next Saturday, and we're going to put on a spread to make us the talk of the town, never mind the village.'

Pat smiled. 'We might make a canny bob or two.'

Sadie went behind the bar and reached up to a metal hook where her cotton apron hung. She lifted it down and placed it over her head to protect her clothes from beer spills, tying the straps in a knot at her back. Then she ran a hand across her head, a habit she was finding hard to break after years of having long hair to push back from her face. Now she was ready to work.

The first customer who stepped through the door was someone she wasn't happy to see. She took a step backwards as soon as she saw Bill Scurfield striding towards the bar.

'All right, Bill?' Pat said. 'What can we get you?'

'Pint of the usual,' he replied.

Under Pat's direction, Sadie pulled the pint of stout, took Bill's money and rang it into the large, heavy metal till. As she worked, she was aware of his eyes searching her face, trying to place who she was and where they had met. When she handed him his change, he pouted his lips into a grotesque kiss, then lifted his pint from the bar and headed towards a table in the corner of the room.

'Ignore him,' Pat whispered. 'Thinks he's God's gift, that one. Bessie's had trouble with him in the past, but he'll give you no grief, not in here.'

The pub door swung open again, and this time in walked a short woman with dark hair who Sadie had not seen before. She was wrapped in a blue shawl that couldn't disguise how whippet-thin she was. Her eyes darted around the pub as she walked towards Sadie and Pat.

'He's not been in, has he?' she asked Sadie.

'Who?'

'My bloody no-good husband, that's who.'

'No, Lil,' said Pat. 'He's not been in. We've only just opened.'

'I'll have a tonic water to settle my stomach. He's got me bad with my nerves.'

'You two been arguing again?' Pat said as Sadie searched for a bottle of tonic. It was something she'd not yet served in the pub and she was unsure where it might be. Finally she found it tucked right at the back of a shelf beneath the bar.

'I'm taking it over there to drink,' Lil said. 'Give myself a bit of peace and quiet away from him at home.'

But as she turned to take a seat in the far corner of the room, in walked the very person she was hoping to avoid. She pulled out a chair, plonked herself down in it and turned her back to her husband. The tall man, heavy-set, with thinning grey hair, looked over towards her as he approached the bar.

'I'll have a pint, Pat,' he said.

'Sadie will get it for you, Bob. My hip's acting up again.'

'See my Lil's made herself comfortable,' Bob said loudly. Lil remained silent, with her back still towards her husband.

'And to think I came in here to get away from her!'

Sadie pulled the pint, and after Bob had handed over the money, he took the beer and sat in the opposite corner to his wife, with his back turned towards her table.

'Daft beggars, the pair of them,' Pat whispered to Sadie. 'Always falling out with each other. They need their heads knocking together.'

He thought for a moment. 'Sadie? Was there another bottle of tonic under there?'

'I think so. Just one, mind. Shall I put them on the list for the next order to the brewery?'

'Might as well,' he replied, then he beckoned Sadie to his side. 'Listen, I've got an idea . . . '

Sadie followed Pat's instructions as he whispered to her behind the bar. She poured the bottle of tonic into a glass for Lil and took it over to her table.

'That's from Bob,' she told Lil quietly. 'He says he's sorry and he doesn't want it mentioned ever again.'

Lil sniffed. 'Is that right now?'

153

Sadie went back behind the bar, pulled another pint and took it to where Bob sat with his back towards his wife. 'That's from Lil,' she said, placing the pint of beer carefully in front of him. 'Says she's sorry and she'd be grateful if you didn't mention it again.'

'Lil sent this?' Bob said, eyeing the drink. 'If she's apologised, that's all well and good. And I'd be pleased not to go over old ground again and bring up our argument from this morning.'

'Least said, soonest mended,' Sadie said, remembering one of her mam's favourite sayings.

'Indeed.' Bob nodded sagely.

For the next hour, Lil and Bob smouldered over their drinks at separate tables. Finally, Bob finished his second pint and walked towards his wife. From their spot behind the bar, Sadie and Pat watched, intrigued to see if Pat's plan had worked its magic on the warring couple.

'Time for a spot of dinner, Lil?' Bob asked. 'What do you reckon?'

Still Lil didn't turn to face him. 'Got a nice bit of ham in the pantry,' she said to the wall in front of her.

Bob turned towards Sadie. 'Got any bread for sale today?'

'Not today,' Sadie replied. 'Bessie and I had business to see to this morning, so there's been no baking done.'

Bob laid his hand on Lil's shoulder. 'We could call at the Co-op and get a nice loaf to go with it,' he said.

'Happen we could,' Lil replied. She lifted her glass of tonic and drained it completely. Then she stood, took the empty glass back to the bar and walked from the pub without a word. Bob followed behind.

As soon as the door banged shut behind them, Pat let out the belly laugh that had been threatening to explode as he watched the scene unfold.

'Bet you never thought I dabbled in match-making, Sadie, did you?' he laughed. 'Oh, speaking of which, here comes love's young dream now.'

Sadie's heart lifted when she saw Eddie walk in through the pub door. Finally she'd be able to talk to him! She was bursting to tell him the news about the Marshalls and their baby, about the picnic she was baking for, the picnic at which she might even see Birdie again.

'Can I borrow Sadie for a minute, Pat?' he asked eagerly.

'Just for a minute, lad. She's working.'

Eddie beckoned for her to follow him outside, and she walked from the pub wondering what on earth was going on to make him so excited.

Out on the street, resting against the wall of the pub, was a big black bicycle. It was little more than two wheels and a seat held together with a metal bar.

'What do you reckon to this, then?' he asked, his face beaming.

'It's a bike,' Sadie replied, trying to under-stand what Eddie was doing with such a thing.

'It's not just any bike. It's *your* bike,' he said. 'If you want it, that is.' He glanced at her face, hoping to see at least a smile, but Sadie was puzzled, trying to take it all in.

'But what would I be doing with it?' she asked.

'Well, I know it needs tidying up — it's got a bit of rust on it, and I can make the seat more comfortable for you — but I thought you might like it for your deliveries.'

'Deliveries?'

'Your pies! Your bread!' Eddie cried. 'Aw, Sadie, just think what you could do with it. You could start baking for the shops up and down the colliery, for the other pubs. You could even bake for the Railway Inn. I've had a word with Mam and she said she'd give it a trial. If you want to, of course. That's a breakthrough, Sadie. She's softening, I can tell.' He patted the black metal handlebars of the bike. 'And you can deliver all your wares on your chariot here. I'll fit a basket to the front, of course.'

Sadie was lost for words, her mouth only getting as far as the word *but* over and over again.

'No buts, Sadie,' Eddie said. 'See what Bessie and Pat say about it. You'll be making money for them; they're bound to think it's a good idea.'

Sadie walked from one end of the bike to the other, eyeing it keenly, taking in the wheels and the chain of it, wondering how she'd ever get it to work.

'Eddie, I don't know what to say.'

'A simple thank you will suffice,' he beamed.

'You're too generous,' she said at last. 'I can't take this. What must it have cost you?'

'Never you mind,' he said. 'It's a gift from me to you.'

Sadie was touched by the gesture. She struggled to remember the last time anyone had

156

given her a gift of any kind, never mind something this generous. She couldn't believe she had her very own bike! And it was all down to Eddie, her sweet and gentle Eddie. There was something about the warmth of his gesture that reminded her of her dad. She could never have believed she'd meet another man as kind as him, but here he was. Eddie Teasdale was living proof that such men existed, and right here in Ryhope too.

Finally Sadie found her voice. 'You've given this a lot of thought, haven't you?'

Eddie winked. 'Oh yes.'

Sadie took hold of the handlebars and swung one leg across the deep frame of the bike, then pushed her backside onto the seat, keeping her feet firmly planted on the pavement. Her skirt rose a little, exposing her legs at the top of her boots. Eddie did his best not to stare.

'Are you sure it's safe?' she asked him.

'Brakes work fine, I checked them over. Got it off a mate of mine at the pit. His wife used to ride it but she's not used it for years, he said, so I took it off his hands. Go on, give it a spin.'

'Hold me, Eddie,' she said, and the two of them exchanged a look. 'My arm, hold my arm to keep me steady until I get on.'

Eddie did as she asked, and Sadie lifted her feet to the pedals. The bike wobbled until she found her balance. Then she pressed down with her right foot and the wheels began to turn. Slowly but surely, she was off. Eddie walked beside her, holding her arm, until the wheels turned faster than he could walk, and he began to run alongside the bike.

'You're flying, Sadie!' he cried. He let go of her arm and slowed to a walk, letting her cycle ahead, her skirt flapping around her legs. 'You're flying!' he called again. 'Sadie Linthorpe, there's no stopping you now!'

7

Picnic

September 1919

'It's a bit of a bone-shaker,' Sadie cried, turning and cycling back to Eddie.

Eddie scratched his chin. 'I might be able to pad the seat for you, if that helps?'

Sadie braked to a stop outside the Forester's Arms, putting her feet to the ground for balance. 'Do you think Bessie will really let me deliver pies around Ryhope?' she asked.

'Don't see why not,' Eddie replied. 'You'll be making a profit for her. Go and ask her; what's the worst that can happen? She can only say no, can't she? And if she says no, you can still keep the bike, and I'll get one myself and we can go cycling along the beach to Seaburn when I'm off work.'

Sadie lifted her leg across the frame, taking care that her heavy skirt didn't catch in the wheels. She propped the bike against the wall of the pub.

'Thank you, Eddie. I love it, it's wonderful.'

'It's my pleasure,' he replied.

She turned towards him. 'I've missed you, Eddie. How are things at the Railway? How's your mam and Tom? I haven't seen you in days.'

159

'I've been working mainly,' he sighed. 'But I haven't half missed you too. One of the gaffers at the pit is bringing in all sorts of new rules and regulations, and the lads aren't happy.'

'What sort of rules?' she asked.

'Ah, nothing really. Some of the lads have said they've heard rumours about a crack hewer coming in. Could be dangerous work for us all.'

'What's a crack hewer?' Sadie asked.

Eddie dismissed her question with a wave of his hand. 'Let's not talk about work; you don't want to hear me grumbling.'

Sadie smiled up at him. 'Well, I have some news to share,' she said, her eyes widening with excitement. She glanced behind her to make sure she couldn't be overheard by anyone walking past. 'But not here. I told Pat I'd only be gone a couple of minutes. Come on in and we'll have a quiet word at the bar.'

Eddie wheeled the bike to the back of the pub and Sadie met him at the gate. She lifted the sneck and let him into the yard, where he leaned the bike against the netty wall. Then he followed her into the pub through the back door. Pat was sitting on his high stool behind the bar, his only customer Bill Scurfield, who eyed Sadie like a hawk from his seat. Bessie walked in from the sitting room and greeted Eddie, asking how his mother was doing. Then she turned to Sadie.

'Have you told him your news?'

'I'm just about to,' Sadie replied, lifting her gaze to Eddie.

'Go into the sitting room,' Bessie said. 'You'll have a bit of privacy in there. Me and Pat can manage here; looks like it's going to be a slow day.'

In the sitting room, Eddie took a seat at one end of the three-seater sofa. Sadie was about to position herself in the armchair opposite, then thought better of it. She wanted to sit closer to Eddie when she shared her news, so she took the seat at the other end of the sofa, leaving a cushioned space between them.

'There's nothing wrong, is there, Sadie?' Eddie asked. 'What is it? Are you all right?'

Sadie leaned forward in her seat, her hands together in her lap, and locked eyes with Eddie.

'I think I've found her,' she said. 'I think I've found my bairn.'

'No!' Eddie cried. 'Where is she?'

'Bessie says I'm not to get my hopes up, but I can't help it, Eddie. It's her, or at least I think it is.'

'You don't sound so sure to me,' he said carefully. He didn't want to upset Sadie, and he knew he'd have to choose his words carefully. He saw her body tense as the words started tumbling from her lips, and sat in shock as she told him about her visit to the Grange with Bessie. He heard about the picnic on the beach and about how Sadie was going to bake pies and cakes for it. He heard the excitement in her voice, the longing, as she described how Mrs Marshall had told them that she had acquired a baby around the same time that Sadie's was taken.

Eddie's eyes widened. 'You went inside the Grange?' He let out a long, low whistle. 'You sat

161

with the pit gaffer's wife in her home?'

'There was a photograph on her mantelpiece of the bairn,' she said. 'But I couldn't get near it to see it properly. And even if I did see it, even if I held that picture in my hands and gazed at every inch of it, all I'd see is a bairn that looks like every other.'

'So there's no telling if the Marshalls' child really is yours,' Eddie said quietly. 'Bessie's right. You're not to get your hopes up. I'd hate to see you disappointed if things don't work out.'

Sadie sat quietly for a moment, then slumped back against the sofa. 'You think I'm mad, don't you? Chasing a child, any child, in the hope that it's mine?'

Eddie turned towards her and reached out to hold her hands. 'No, I don't think you're mad. I think you're the best thing that's ever happened to me. You're the best thing that's ever happened to Ryhope, come to think of it.'

Sadie smiled weakly.

'And whether you find your child or not, you'll always be special to me. I hope you realise that.'

Sadie lifted her gaze to meet his. 'Really?' she said.

'Really,' he replied.

There was a beat of a moment, just a second, when the two of them looked deep into each other's eyes. Then Sadie turned her body towards Eddie, and gently and slowly they leaned towards each other, still holding hands.

Their faces touched, their cheeks brushed and their lips finally met in a tender, loving kiss. Sadie's only experience so far had been that of

Mick forcing his lips on hers. Eddie's kiss was different, more gentle, and she melted into it, wanting more. But it ended too soon, for they were interrupted by Pat as he limped his way into the sitting room.

Eddie jumped up off the sofa as soon as he heard the door open. 'Sorry, Pat, I was just — ' he began, but Pat waved his hand.

'You're all right, lad. I was young once, you know. Me and Bessie used to do our courting in the cow shed on the farm in Dublin.'

He looked at Sadie, who was still sitting on the sofa, Eddie's kiss warm on her lips.

'Sorry, Sadie. Bessie's got a run of customers at the bar and she asks if you can come through.'

'Course I will,' Sadie said, getting up and hurrying from the sitting room. She turned to Eddie before she disappeared out of the door and said goodbye to him with a smile that didn't go unnoticed by Pat.

Left together in the sitting room, Pat eyed Eddie from his black boots all the way up to his unruly brown hair that would never lie flat no matter how many times it was brushed.

'You watch what you're doing with that lass,' he warned him. 'She's a good 'un, and me and Bessie have taken her to our hearts. I wouldn't like to see her getting hurt, you hear me?'

'I wouldn't . . . I'd never . . . ' Eddie stammered, taken aback by Pat's suggestion that he would do anything to hurt Sadie. 'You and Bessie aren't the only ones who've taken her to their hearts. I want the very best for her too.'

'Then she's going to need you, lad,' Pat said.

'She's got it into her mind that she's found her bairn.'

Eddie nodded. 'She's told me all about it.'

'You're going to have to look after her, and me and Bessie will do the same. Because I've a bad feeling about this picnic she's been asked to cater for. Chasing a bairn that might not be hers. And the bairn of a pit gaffer too. It's not good, Eddie. It's not good at all.'

'I know, Pat,' Eddie sighed. 'But Sadie's got it into her head, and she won't rest until she knows the truth, one way or the other.'

★ ★ ★

After Eddie left the pub, Sadie and Bessie were kept busy at the bar. Bessie went outside to use the netty, and came back in demanding to know whose bike had been left in the yard. When Sadie explained it was hers, a gift from Eddie, a smile spread wide on Bessie's face.

'I used to have one myself, back home in Ireland,' she beamed. 'The farm was too big to wander on foot and we had a bike we all used. My mam would cycle into the village and my dad cycled to the pub. Mind you, he fell off it more than once when he tried to cycle back after a few pints of stout. But what'll you be wanting a bike for in Ryhope, Sadie?'

Bessie listened intently as Sadie explained Eddie's idea about selling her pies to shops and pubs on the colliery and in the village too. She nodded every now and then as Sadie outlined the plan, both of them wondering if it really

164

would work and bring in more money to the pub.

'I like your thinking,' she said at last, letting Sadie's words sink in. 'I like it a lot. Let me talk it over with Pat.'

Later on, Sadie was busy clearing tables when she saw Pat and Bessie deep in conversation. It didn't take long for her to guess what they were talking about, as Pat kept glancing her way as he listened to his wife's words. She saw him nodding his head and smiling, and then finally heard him say the two words that she knew Bessie had been determined to get out of him to seal the deal: 'Yes, dear.'

★ ★ ★

It didn't take much persuasion from Bessie and Sadie to convince the shops and pubs in Ryhope to buy Sadie's pies. Word had already spread, and many of the small shops on the colliery were only too keen to take them fresh each morning. By dinner time they'd already sold out. There was only one pub that Sadie hadn't yet approached, and that was the Railway Inn. Although she'd heard from Eddie that his mam wanted to sell the pies at the bar, he'd not offered up any more information, and Sadie didn't feel it her place to approach Molly without his support. Until she knew for sure, she avoided the Railway Inn and sold her pies in the village to the Albion Inn only, where Hetty and Jack Burdon were only too happy to offer them for sale.

Out on her bike, with her short hair, Sadie

proved a curious sight. But she paid no mind to those who stared at her because riding her bike proved to be more fun than she'd thought it would be. She'd lay a checked cloth across the wicker basket that Eddie had attached to the front of the bike, keeping the dirty coal-laden air from her pies, and set off at speed down the colliery bank, lifting her feet from the pedals to freewheel down to Nelson Street. She loved the feel of the wind against her face, the sun on her head, the freedom she felt to take herself any-where around Ryhope that she wanted. Coming back up the colliery bank proved difficult, and at first she had to get off and walk, pushing the bike back to the Forester's Arms. Apart from the exertion needed to cycle up the bank, Sadie's other problem was her skirt. It just didn't allow the room and space for her to work her legs as hard as she needed. She mentioned it to Bessie at work.

'You'll be needing a bifurcated skirt,' Bessie stated.

Sadie swung round, unsure if she'd heard properly. 'A what?'

Bessie swished her arms about her legs in an attempt to indicate to Sadie what she meant. 'Bifurcated skirt. Have you never seen one, lass?'

Sadie shook her head.

'My girls Cara and Branna tell me all about them. They keep me up to date on all the young fashions these days, not that I'm one for trying them myself. Anyway, it's sort of a skirt for each leg and it fastens around the waist like a normal skirt would.'

166

'You mean like a pair of trousers?' Sadie cried. 'I can't wear trousers! They already give me funny looks in Ryhope because of my hair. I don't want to be giving them any more reason to whisper and gossip about me.'

'No one will know,' Bessie said softly. 'They won't be able to tell, not really. There's plenty of material in the skirt. It doesn't hang like trousers do; it still swishes about your legs but it'll give you the freedom for each leg to move separately when you're on your bike, see?'

Sadie was intrigued. 'But where will I get one?' she asked.

'I'll ask our Cara to run you one up. She's good with the sewing. I dare say she'll do it for you for free if I ask her nicely enough and you offer to bake her bread and cakes in return.'

'It's a deal,' Sadie said.

*   *   *

On the morning of the last Saturday in September, Eddie borrowed a handcart from the Railway Inn and helped Sadie take the picnic food from the Forester's. There was still a warmth to the day, even as the beginning of autumn could be seen in the trees around the green as their leaves began to change colour and fall.

'I'd better check with Em where the picnic's going to be,' Sadie said as the cart pulled to a stop outside Ryhope Grange. 'It looks set fair for today but I don't want to take all the food to the beach if Mrs Marshall's changed her mind and

167

it's to be here in the Grange.'

Eddie waited while Sadie walked to the front door of the big house. It was Em who answered, and he could see her nodding her head in response to Sadie's questions. He waited as Sadie headed back towards him.

'As I thought, it's at the beach,' she told him. 'I'm to go and set up the food there. Em's already laid out picnic rugs on the sands. There's crockery and cutlery and Mrs Marshall is waiting there now.'

'With the child?' Eddie asked.

Sadie took a deep breath. 'Em said she's there with the bairn, yes.'

Eddie gripped the cart handles and stared straight ahead. 'I can come with you if you'd like me to,' he said.

'Thank you, but I need to do this on my own,' she replied softly. 'Bessie offered. Even Pat with his bad hip said he'd come. But this is something I have to do alone. I just need to see the bairn.'

'Then I'll collect you later this afternoon when I come back for the cart, if you're sure you don't need me?'

Sadie looked deep into Eddie's brown eyes, then laid her hand on his arm. 'Thank you.'

They walked along the beach road, under the bridge that carried the railway line above and then down through the cliffs to the sea. At the very end there was a turning space just wide enough for Eddie to manoeuvre the cart. He helped Sadie unload the boxes of pies, sandwiches and cakes and walked with her across the stones at the top of the beach.

Ahead of her, Sadie saw four women. Three of them were sitting on a rug in the shelter of the cliff; Mrs Marshall stood a short distance away, her hands on her hips. Sadie had expected more women to be at the picnic party after Mrs Marshall's words about the pit managers' wives from around the area being invited. She knew immediately that she had baked too much food. In front of the women, two girls aged about five or six ran around laughing, chasing each other and falling on the sand. Sadie looked for Mrs Marshall's child, but she was nowhere to be seen. Had the woman decided not to bring her to the picnic after all? Perhaps Em had got it wrong and the little girl had been left at home at the Grange. And if that was the case, had Sadie and Bessie's planning of the picnic been for nothing?

'Who's this?' Mrs Marshall hissed towards Eddie.

'He's helping me carry the food,' Sadie explained.

Eddie carefully placed a box on the blue-striped picnic rug, then turned towards Mrs Marshall and doffed his cap.

'Eddie Teasdale,' he said. 'I work up at the pit, as a hewer.'

Mrs Marshall sniffed. 'Good day to you, Eddie.' She turned her back on him and immediately started issuing instructions to Sadie on how she wanted the picnic arranged. Eddie caught Sadie's eye and mouthed farewell.

As Sadie worked, she kept turning her head, desperate to know if the child was there, impatient to see her. But all she saw were the three women, chatting and laughing. None of them came over to speak to Mrs Marshall, content as they were gossiping together on the rug. In front of them the girls played in the sand, digging with their hands and running barefoot from their mothers towards the frilled white of the waves. But neither of those children could be Birdie, for they were too old. Elsewhere on the beach people were walking, making the most of the warmth of the day. A skinny white dog with black spots ran into the waves, bounding and leaping then running back to shore, barking madly. Seagulls squawked overhead. An old man, pushing an empty tattered pram walked slowly on the sands. Every now and then he stooped to shovel up lumps of sea coal and drop the black stones into the pram.

Under the watchful gaze of Mrs Marshall, Sadie unwrapped the pies from their cloths and lifted the sandwiches and cakes from the boxes. She allowed herself a satisfied smile. The picnic looked good when it was all laid out on the rug, and she knew that the work she'd put into the preparation had been a job well done. There were sandwiches of fresh boiled ham with stuffing in stottie bread that she and Bessie had baked fresh that morning. There was a pie of steak and kidney, another of ham and egg and a third of brisket of beef. There were small mounds of coconut tarts and, of course, the birthday cake, a sponge sandwich decorated with lemon curd and cream. Around the edge of the cake Sadie had piped tiny yellow birds in flight.

She stood next to Mrs Marshall, who was inspecting the food laid out in front of her.

'And it's all been baked with ingredients from the Co-op, as instructed?'

'Every last crumb,' Sadie confirmed. 'Course, it made it more expensive than it might otherwise have been.'

'The cost is irrelevant,' Mrs Marshall said curtly. 'Quality is what counts. Stay here with the food, girl, until I'm ready for you to serve.'

She turned and walked towards the three women. Sadie was close enough to hear snatches of their conversation, and she noticed that when their hostess joined them, their talk quietened and became serious. Mrs Marshall took up a place on the rug, sitting at the edge of the group, who shifted to accommodate her. The women sat with their backs to Sadie, so that all she could see of them were their hats and jackets. Their skirts were arranged carefully so as not to get covered with sand, their formal dress at odds with the rugged cliffs and the natural beauty of the beach. With the tide out, the sands were golden and clear all the way.

Sadie watched the two little girls running and laughing, seeing how carefree they were, how untroubled and happy with nothing to do other than have fun. She was bitterly disappointed not to see Mrs Marshall's child and wondered where she could be and who was looking after her. One of the women stood from the rug and walked to where the children were playing. In her hand she held a box camera, and she spent some time lining the girls up, asking them to smile while she composed her shot. Sadie watched, transfixed, lost in the moment, feeling the sun on her face while listening to the rhythmic pull of the sea.

Suddenly a cry went up. 'Girl!' It was Mrs Marshall. She snapped her fingers. Two of the women sitting with her turned in Sadie's direction. 'You may serve now,' she ordered.

Sadie saw the two women exchange a look, and one of them raised her eyebrows, while the other smiled sympathetically.

She kneeled on the rug and began cutting the pies into generous slices. She knew from experience that each plate she loaded with sandwiches and pie would have to be handed to Mrs Marshall, who would then present the food to her guests as if she had made it herself. With the first two plates ready, she took one in each hand and walked towards the women, taking care not to stand on stones that could cause her to lose her balance. But as she approached, there in the middle of the rug was a sight that made her stop dead. It was a child, lying asleep, wrapped in a delicate shawl. The women sitting on the rug had surrounded the infant, keeping it safe and warm, away from sand blown on the wind, and Sadie hadn't been able to see it from her position next to the food. She gasped, and it did not go unnoticed.

'More food, girl,' Mrs Marshall said sharply, taking the plates from her hands. 'And don't keep us waiting.'

Sadie couldn't move. She stood gazing at the child, desperate to reach out and stroke her face.

'Are you all right?' the woman with the box

camera asked kindly as she rejoined the group. 'You seem a little distressed.'

Sadie snapped out of her trance. 'I'm fine,' she said quickly, forcing a smile. 'Thank you.'

She returned to the picnic and went through the motions of filling two more plates before walking back to Mrs Marshall's side. The girls had come running now, seeing that food was being served, crawling onto the rug and squeezing in between the women. This time when Sadie handed the food to Mrs Marshall, she kept her eyes fixed on the child in the middle of the group. Its pink face surrounded by a mass of dark curly hair peeked from the shawl, its eyes tight shut. Her heart beat wildly and she breathed deeply to keep herself calm.

The women were all eating now, enjoying the food, and Sadie heard them complimenting Mrs Marshall. She calmed herself with the routine chores of sorting the plates and arranging the cake. She had no proof that the baby was Mrs Marshall's; it could belong to any of the women there. But even as she thought this, the child began to cry.

'Oh dear,' one of the women said. 'She's waking, Ruth.'

'She must know there's food being served,' another joked, and a tinkle of laughter rang out.

Sadie watched as Mrs Marshall lowered her plate of food to the rug and leaned forward to the bundle in front of her. She picked up the crying child, shushing her, rocking her. The infant quietened, but she was awake now and Mrs Marshall laid her down on the rug again, this time on her stomach. The child wriggled free of the shawl, revealing a white cotton dress with long sleeves. The women laughed as she began to move, pushing herself along the rug towards Mrs Marshall.

'Is she walking yet?' one of them asked.

'Almost,' Mrs Marshall replied dully. 'Dare say I'll have to find a new nurse.'

'Lost another one, Ruth?'

She sniffed. 'Ryhope girls are so unreliable.'

Mrs Marshall turned her attention back to her food and Sadie saw the look that passed between the other women. She busied herself with cutting the birthday cake into slices, making sure that each slice had three of the tiny piped yellow birds at its edge.

'May I take your photograph?' said a voice.

She looked up and saw the dark-haired woman with a pretty smile who had spoken to her kindly before.

'Your food is delicious,' the woman said. 'I hoped you might allow me to photograph you with the cake. I'm writing up about the picnic, you see, for the coal managers' newsletter, and it'd be good to have a photograph to accompany my words.'

Sadie stood. 'You want to photograph *me*?' she asked.

'Only if you don't mind.' The woman pointed to Sadie's short hair. 'You have a most striking look that will photograph well. And I'd like to put your name next to the picture. Of course, they might not publish my article, but I've had some work accepted in the past and there's a chance they'd like to take this piece too.'

Sadie took a step backwards. The last thing she wanted was for her picture and name to be in a publication that anyone could see. She was feeling safer by the day living in Ryhope, but there was still the slightest chance that she wasn't entirely free of Freda and Mick's reach.

'You want my name?' she asked. 'Will it be published with my name in it?'

'Look, if you're worried about becoming famous, don't be,' the woman said breezily. 'It's only the pit bosses who read it. I never kid myself that my foray into journalism goes any further than a newsletter that ends up on a pit boss's desk to read while he's having his dinner.'

'Well, if you're sure,' Sadie said. She stood straight, brought her feet together and her hands behind her back, pushed out her chest and smiled brightly. She stood still for a few moments while the woman positioned the large black box camera, holding it with both hands.

'All done!' she beamed after a while. 'So, may I take your name now?'

Sadie hesitated just a moment.

'Barnes,' she said at last, too afraid to give her real surname to this woman she didn't know. 'Sadie Barnes.'

The woman took a notepad and pencil from her pocket and wrote down the name. Then she shook Sadie's hand in thanks.

'Don't let Mrs Marshall get you down,' she whispered. 'Can't be easy working for someone like her. We all know what she's like.'

Sadie's mouth opened in shock. She'd never

been spoken to that way before by anyone she'd worked for.

'Thank you,' she replied, and the woman turned and headed back to her friends.

Sadie finished plating up the cake and then headed towards Mrs Marshall to take back the empty plates and used cutlery. As she bent low to the rug to gather everything up, the child crawled towards her. Sadie noticed the tiny nose, the smile that played around the baby's lips, ready to break into laughter.

'Hey there, wriggler! Come back.' The woman with the camera laughed and held out her arms. The child gurgled with pleasure but continued crawling towards Sadie, intent on reaching the plate in her hand. A pair of hands reached towards the child and lifted her from the rug, holding her firm and standing her on her tippy-toes.

'She's got good strong legs,' the woman said. 'She'll be walking any day now.'

'She pulls herself up to the furniture in the Grange,' Mrs Marshall said without a trace of emotion. 'I dare say she'll be taking steps on her own soon.'

'Then you must find a new nurse as quickly as you can.' Mrs Marshall sighed. 'It's such a bore. I barely have the energy to go through the rigmarole of hiring new staff, and Joe's no help.'

'Are you still under the doctor, dear?'

Mrs Marshall nodded. 'The pain comes and goes,' she said, turning her gaze towards the sea, dismissing any further talk.

'Let's walk the child to the water,' the woman

with the camera suggested. 'It'd make a wonder-ful picture for the newsletter. What do you say, Ruth?'

★ ★ ★

Having her picture taken with the child was the last thing Ruth Marshall wanted, but she agreed to it anyway, knowing that when her husband found out, he'd be pleased. She'd have proof then that the picnic had been a success of some kind, even if only three pit managers' wives had turned up when twelve had been invited. Cards and letters had arrived at the Grange from those who couldn't attend, all bearing expressions of regret at having to be somewhere else on that day, at some event that had been arranged in advance, weeks, even months ago. And yet whenever one of the other pit managers' wives had arranged a luncheon or a soirée or a dinner, there had always been a good attendance. Ruth had never known just three attendees at any one of the events over the years since she'd married Joe.

She felt the disdain of her peers like a slap across the face, but it only served to strengthen her resolve against them. What did she need them for anyway? She had her sister Esther in Newcastle when she needed to get away from Ryhope, from the dark air of the pit — and from Joe. On those visits she left the child behind with the nurse at the Grange, so desperate was she to get away from the duties of looking after a bairn that would never truly be her own.

Since Joe had taken up his role with Ryhope Coal Company, his time had increasingly been spent away from his home, his wife, and now his child too. He was always working, always with his colleagues, or so he told Ruth. When they had first married, they had tried for a child but had failed many times, and according to the doctor, the fault lay with her. Even after demanding a second opinion from her sister's doctor in Newcastle, she was told the same thing. But Joe insisted on having a family, whatever the cost. For him it was a business decision, pure and simple. He knew that to rise up the ranks in his chosen career of mining engineering, he needed not just a wife who would cater for the dinners he would throw at the Grange, but also a child. He was desperate to be seen as a good, solid, decent family man by the pit bosses above him, whose approval he craved.

Back in the early days of their married life, Ruth had wanted to please her husband. She was determined to be a good wife to Joe and a good mother to a child, even if in the end, and in desperation, they had to resort to using an orphan house. Joe had wanted a boy, a strong, healthy lad to follow in his footsteps as manager of the Ryhope pit. But after a desperate search, the only baby they could find was a girl, and from Hartlepool of all places, far away down the coast. Ruth was reluctant to take her at first, after hearing about the mark on her skin, but Joe assured her that he would inspect the child carefully to ensure she did not harbour disease of any kind.

Ruth's desire was that the manner of their acquisition of the child would be kept a secret. But she was to learn that secrets were rare in a village as small and tight-knit as Ryhope. The wet nurse Joe brought in for the newborn told the maid, who told the gardener, who told a friend of his at the Railway Inn. And in this way the secret spread until it became common knowledge and everyone knew that the pit boss and his wife had bought themselves a child.

Ruth was desperate to bond with the baby; she willed herself to do so, but she felt little for it, truth be told. She hired a nurse to clean and feed it, a maid to walk and entertain it, leaving her with time on her hands that she used to travel to Newcastle to stay with Esther as often as she could. Many times she stayed overnight with her sister; sometimes she stayed away for as long as a week, leaving the child and her husband behind. And it was during those times that Ruth was away that gossip about Joe Marshall, pit manager with the Ryhope Coal Company, began. It was said that he'd been seen in the company of a woman, a young, dark-haired woman with smoky eyes and painted bow lips.

★   ★   ★

'Come on, Ruth,' the woman with the camera urged. 'Let me take your photograph, please?'

Ruth Marshall sighed. 'All right then, if you must.'

She pushed her hands to the rug to give herself support, but there was no strength in her

179

arms. The flu virus that had damaged her nerve endings had wreaked havoc on her body, leaving her with a debilitating infection that was still taking its toll. The two women seated beside her helped her to her feet. Without a word of thanks, she took the child by the hand, keeping her upright, and walked down towards the waves.

'How rude!' the photographer whispered to the other women.

'Dreadful woman,' one of them agreed.

'I'm only here because my husband said it'd be good for business. I can think of a million things I'd rather be doing than spending my afternoon with her.'

'It's no wonder her child's nurse has left,' the woman holding the camera agreed. 'That's the third one in a year.'

'Fourth, I heard.'

'She can't even hold onto her staff, never mind her friends.'

'Or her husband.'

Behind them, clearing the plates from the rug, Sadie heard every word as the women gossiped about their host. She worked as quickly as she could, stacking the used plates and cutlery in one of the boxes. The birthday cake was laid out ready on clean plates with fresh napkins and polished forks.

In front of her, the woman with the camera had followed Mrs Marshall to the water's edge and was giving instructions on where and how she should pose for the photograph. They were too far away for Sadie to hear what was being said, but she understood what was going on when the photographer indicated for the child to splash her bare feet in the sea. The little girl was gesturing and pointing, gurgling with happiness as the photograph was taken, while Ruth stared into the camera lens as if she was fighting a battle with it that she was determined to win.

Just then, the other women and the two girls approached, and Ruth's child reached out her hand to them, causing her to lose her balance. She tumbled to the damp sand, unhurt but crying with the shock of the cold water, which soaked through her cotton dress. Ruth scooped her up immediately, scolding the child for falling although it was no fault of her own. Refusing any more photograph requests, she stormed back up the beach.

As they neared the rug, Sadie could see the child wriggling in Mrs Marshall's arms. It was clear that she wanted to head back to the older girls and the sea, but Mrs Marshall was equally intent on getting her out of the wet outfit and into another that was dry.

'Stay still, Alexandra!' she yelled at the squirming child.

Sadie stopped in her tracks. *Alexandra?*

The little girl began crying at the harshness of the command, causing Mrs Marshall's irritation to worsen. Sadie moved forward until she was standing at the edge of the rug.

'Here, girl.' Mrs Marshall thrust the child towards her. 'Put her in a dry dress and coat.' She nodded to a wicker basket set back towards the cliffs. 'You'll find them in there. And hurry. The child will catch its death if you don't look sharp!'

Instinctively, Sadie held out her arms. The weight of the child surprised her; she was heavier than she looked. She cradled her to her shoulder, her hands shaking with nerves and excitement, feeling the damp cotton of her dress under her fingers. The little girl's scent reached her nose, a smell that pulled on something deep within her so that she had to stop herself from planting a kiss on the warm skin of her bare arm. Her heart was beating nineteen to the dozen as she walked to the basket with the crying child in her arms.

'Shush now, little one,' she said softly as she lifted the lid on the basket. Inside were towels and linens and a cotton dress in eggshell blue with a matching jacket. She took the dress out and laid the child across her knee, hardly daring to look as she began to unbutton the wet garment. But she had to look, she had to know, she had to find out if this little girl, this beautiful little girl on her knee, was her own baby — her Birdie.

The child began to gurgle with joy as the wet dress was removed, thinking it a game. She was happy now, soothed and calmed by Sadie's words and her capable hands. Sadie glanced towards Mrs Marshall, who was sitting with her back turned. The pit managers' wives were still by the water's edge with their girls, the photographer taking a group shot with the waves behind them. No one would notice if she looked at the child's shoulder; no one would know. She had to do it, she knew that. She had to take this chance, for when would it happen again?

As she slipped the dry cotton dress over the

child's head, she turned her just enough so that she could see her back, her left shoulder. Her breath caught in her throat for she hardly dared to believe what she saw. Just a little birthmark, that was all it was, a small mark on the baby's left shoulder. Paler now than it once was, less scarlet, less raw than Sadie remembered. But it was there, the tiny mark like a ladybird with its wings spread, ready to fly.

8

Fresh Start

As Sadie ran her fingertips across the birthmark on the baby's shoulder, her breath caught in her throat and her heart filled with happiness, so much so that it hurt inside her chest. She wanted to stare at Birdie's face, drink in every inch of her. She wanted to study every feature, every line of her body, every finger, every toe.

'Birdie,' she whispered as she pulled the child towards her. Tears pooled and fell from her lashes, streaming down her face. 'My Birdie.'

The little girl snuggled against her, happy now, gurgling and smiling and lifting her tiny hands to Sadie's head, trying to touch her short hair.

'Girl!' Mrs Marshall cried, but her call went unheeded as Sadie's heart filled with love and fear and all kinds of emotions she'd never even known she could feel. There was something familiar about the pull of it, something that took her back to the days after Birdie's birth and her connection to the tiny girl in her arms.

And now, at last, they were reunited. All her hard work had come to fruition: hiding her savings for months under the floorboards, plucking up the courage to escape from Freda's house, searching for her child. Finally, here was Birdie, sitting on her knee, her own precious daughter.

'Girl!' The cry came again.

Sadie looked up and saw Mrs Marshall with a face full of thunder. Beyond her, the three pit managers' wives and the two girls were walking back from the shoreline.

'Serve the cake, girl!' Mrs Marshall called sharply.

Sadie stood with Birdie in her arms, the child reaching out her small doughy hands to her face as if to wipe away her tears. Then she walked slowly and calmly across the stones, holding onto her daughter tightly.

'Put her on the rug,' Mrs Marshall directed as she drew near. She did as she was told, then returned to fetch the plates of birthday cake. She was shaking, hardly daring to believe what had just happened. Quickly she wiped her eyes on a corner of her apron, then brought the first plates to Mrs Marshall, who handed them to her guests and received their compliments in return on the lightness of the sponge and the pretty yellow birds decorated around the edge.

Sadie kept her eyes on the child each time she neared Mrs Marshall and the group of women, for what else could she do? She couldn't cause a scene, not here in front of such important guests. She couldn't give in to her feelings, no matter how much she wanted to. Her heart was screaming: *Run, Sadie, run with the child in your arms. Run as far as you can,* but her head was telling her: *No.* If she ran, there was a risk that she might fall on the sand and rocks along the beach, and protecting Birdie was paramount now.

She was filled with the need to let Bessie and Eddie know what had happened. Bessie would know what to do. And Eddie, well, Eddie would keep her grounded, she knew that. He'd tell her not to do anything that might jeopardise her chances of seeing Birdie again. She swallowed the lump in her throat and squared her shoulders, sniffing back the tears as she carried on serving the cake, all the while trying to peek at the crawling child on the rug. The child that she now knew was her own.

The birthday cake that Sadie had baked with love and care that morning was gone within minutes. After everyone had eaten their fill, requests were made for slices to be wrapped up in napkins to be taken home for husbands and friends, and Sadie began to pack the rest of the plates and cutlery in the boxes. When everything was loaded onto the handcart, she sat on the sand with her skirt tucked under her knees, waiting for Eddie to return. She could have managed the cart herself, but she enjoyed the fact that he wanted to help and be part of her working day.

At last Mrs Marshall's guests stood to leave, dusting the sand from their skirts and pinning their hats as they said their farewells, leaving Mrs Marshall on the picnic rug with the child by her side. As they walked past Sadie, the woman with the camera gave a friendly wave goodbye, but the others acted as if she didn't exist. Sadie didn't mind; it was what she was used to, besides which, she now had more important things on her mind. She took a deep breath, then stood and walked towards Mrs Marshall.

'Your baby,' she said hesitantly. 'Her name is Alexandra, is that right? Is she well?'

Mrs Marshall turned sharply at her words. 'Of course she's well. Why wouldn't she be?'

'She's a beautiful child.' Sadie smiled, determined not to let the woman's tone upset her. Whatever happened now, whatever the future held for Sadie, for Birdie and for Ruth Marshall, the three of them were connected by an invisible bond. It was a bond that only Sadie knew of and she would do everything she could to ensure it was strengthened.

'Yes. She is,' Mrs Marshall replied without looking at Sadie or the little girl.

Sadie gave a gentle cough. 'Mrs Marshall?'

'Heavens! What now?'

'I wasn't meaning to pry, but when I served the food, I overheard you say that you might be in need of a nurse for the child. Am I right?'

Still the woman did not turn to look at her. She sighed deeply. 'What of it?'

Sadie pushed her shoulders back and clasped her hands in front of her apron. 'Would you consider me for the role?'

'You, girl?'

'Bessie . . . I mean, Mrs Brogan at the Forester's Arms will speak of my character. I've been working there since — '

Mrs Marshall turned her head and glared at her. 'You expect me to let you look after my child after you've been pulling pints and clearing slops?'

'Yes, I pull pints and I clear slops. And I never complain about any of it. Mrs Brogan will tell you that. And if I can cook and clean and fend for myself against some of Ryhope's hardest pitmen when they come in for a drink, then I know I can look after a small child.'

The expression on Mrs Marshall's face softened slightly. 'And you say Mrs Brogan will give a character reference if you were offered the position?'

Sadie's heart leapt. 'I am certain she will.'

'Then let me speak to my husband.' She looked at Sadie again, all the way from her boots to the apron covering her skirt, and up to her eager face and short hair. Then she turned her gaze back to the ocean and gave another long sigh. 'You can't be any worse than the other girls we've had working for us in the past.'

After a moment, Mrs Marshall gathered her shawl around her shoulders and steadied her hands on the rug, intent on pushing herself up from the sand. Sadie saw at once that the effort was proving too much for her, and she gently but firmly hooked her arm under one of the woman's elbows. She was not thanked for her assistance, however.

'The child,' Mrs Marshall barked, indicating the rug.

Sadie bent low and scooped Birdie up in her arms, delighting in the feel of her own flesh and blood against her skin.

'She needs wrapping up for the walk to the village,' Mrs Marshall directed.

Sadie did as she was told, draping the white shawl around the child before reluctantly handing her over. Mrs Marshall positioned Birdie in the perambulator and then ordered Sadie to collect up the rugs and take them back to the Grange.

'I could walk with you,' Sadie offered. 'I could carry the rugs on the handcart; it'll be easy enough to push if we walk slowly, and I can drop the rugs off at the Grange on my way back to the Forester's.'

'If we'll be walking slowly, then yes,' Mrs Marshall said with a defeated tone. 'Follow my lead, girl.'

Sadie gathered the rugs, folded them and laid them across the top of the wooden cart, which was loaded now with boxes of plates and uneaten food. She knew Bessie would be pleased to see so much food being returned to the Forester's Arms, where it would go on sale at the bar that night.

The handcart was heavier than Eddie had made it look, but soon she was walking slowly behind Mrs Marshall and the big black pram up along the track that led between the cliffs. Ahead of them, Eddie came into view, heading towards the beach to collect Sadie and the cart as he'd promised.

'This looks like your pitman coming down,' Mrs Marshall said. 'I'll leave you to him. And I'll send word to the Forester's once I've spoken to Mr Marshall about the position at the Grange.'

'Thank you,' Sadie replied, but it went unheard as Mrs Marshall upped her pace and walked on, passing Eddie, who raised his cap and said good afternoon. Mrs Marshall gave a weak smile in return. Once past her, Eddie beamed at Sadie walking towards him. When he reached her, he took the cart handles from her and began to push it along the track.

'What's happened?' he whispered. 'What are you doing walking back from the beach with her? Where have her guests gone?'

'Oh Eddie,' Sadie said softly. 'I've got so much to tell you, I don't know even where to begin.'

'Hey, hey. Come on,' Eddie said. He let go of the cart handles and hugged her to his chest. It hurt him to see her distressed like this and he wanted to do all he could to comfort her. She pulled away from his arms and looked up into his eyes. Eddie saw her tears falling. 'What is it, Sadie? What happened with the child? It wasn't her, was it? I told you not to get your hopes up. Oh Sadie. I'm sorry. We'll keep looking, I promise you. I'll help.'

Sadie shook her head. 'No, Eddie. It was her. The birthmark was there, right there on her shoulder, just as I remembered.'

Eddie's eyes widened. 'No! You saw it on the child?'

Sadie nodded. 'With my own eyes.'

'You're sure? You're absolutely sure?'

Sadie's silent tears turned into heaving sobs as the emotion of the day was finally released. 'It's her, Eddie. It's my Birdie.'

Eddie looked up ahead to where Mrs Marshall and the pram were disappearing into the dark of the tunnel with its railway lines above.

Sadie stroked the ladybird charm at her neck. 'There's more to tell you, too,' she said. 'Come on, let's get going.'

190

Eddie picked up the cart handles again and let Sadie set the pace for their walk back to the village. By the time they reached the village green, he knew all about the child called Alexandra, about how curt Mrs Marshall could be, and about the job at the Grange that Sadie had applied for.

At the house, Em opened the door and Sadie handed the picnic rugs over. As she did so, Em leaned towards her and whispered, 'She's just told me she's considering you as the child's nurse.'

Sadie smiled weakly in return. 'I hope so,' she said. 'I've not had much experience with children before, but I'll learn how to look after her.' She looked at Em shyly. 'Would you help me? I mean, if I did get the job?'

'Course I will, lass. She's asked if I know you or your family, but as far as I know, you're not from round here, are you?'

Sadie shook her head. 'Bessie will attest to my character,' she said.

'I'm sure she will,' Em agreed. She glanced behind her before carrying on. 'Ooh, but I'd give anything to be a fly on the wall when you tell old Bessie you're leaving her pub.'

Once Em had closed the door, Sadie headed back to Eddie, who was waiting at the garden gate.

'Come on,' she said. 'Let's get the cart back to the Forester's. It looks like I'm going to have to have a quiet word with Bessie, and I can't say I'm looking forward to it, not one little bit.'

★ ★ ★

Sadie had expected Bessie to be angry with her for wanting to leave her job at the Forester's, and braced herself for the worst. But Bessie wasn't angry; she was supportive of Sadie's decision, although desperately sad to let her go. She knew it was what Sadie yearned for, what she had come to Ryhope for, and if Sadie thought that Mrs Marshall's bairn was her own — and it seemed there was proof enough to suggest it — then Bessie Brogan was not the type of woman who would hold her back.

She had to let Sadie go, of course she did, and she gave her blessing, and that of Pat too. But after hours, in their sitting room at the back of the pub, Pat made known his concerns about losing Sadie and the business she had brought in, the extra money that they had been able to save since the pies had gone on sale. And so a deal was proposed to Sadie that she accepted without hesitation, not least because it meant that she wouldn't lose contact with Bessie and Pat, who she'd come to think of as family. It was a deal that would mean extra income for Sadie too, though it would be hard work and she knew it. She would bake the pies in Bessie's kitchen and deliver them around Ryhope first thing every morning before she started work at the Grange. With the bike that Eddie had given her, she'd be able to make short work of the distance between the Forester's on the colliery and the Grange in the village. And with the new skirt that Bessie's daughter Cara had made for her, it was easier to cycle up the colliery bank. Once she shared the plan with Eddie, he encouraged her to tell Mrs

Marshall about it before she took up her role at the Grange.

★ ★ ★

Mrs Marshall sent Em to the Forester's to speak to Bessie about Sadie's character reference. The maid wore her good hat, the brown velvet one she liked, for the walk up the colliery. A scarf was around her neck, tucked into the collar of her heavy coat against the coolness of the autumn wind. At the pub, she received a glowing report from Bessie about Sadie's work, her baking skills, her conversation at the bar, her character and her ability to get on with everyone she met. But Bessie kept quiet about what she knew about Sadie and Molly, about the betrayal that lay between the two women and still kept them apart.

Em took Bessie's verbal report back to the Grange, where she passed it on to Mrs Marshall almost word for word, embellishing where she could, for she knew that if Bessie and Sadie had got along well in the pub, then she and Sadie would get along together in the Grange. Em hadn't much taken to the previous nurses who had come and gone since Alexandra had been brought to the Grange. Most of them had been too young to know how to feed and clean a bairn properly, and she'd had to step in to help more than once, especially when Mrs Marshall's sharp tongue got the better of the girls. Then there were Mrs Marshall's aches and pains, which came and went depending on the day of the week, the weather and her mood. As for Mr Marshall, Em rarely saw him at home these days.

But there was something about Sadie that she liked the look of, and after speaking to Bessie, she felt sure in her heart that she was the right girl for the job. She seemed to have a good head on a strong and willing pair of shoulders, and was afraid of little. Well, her resolve would be put to the test sooner rather than later, Em knew, as Mrs Marshall had a way about her that didn't go down well with most folk. Her cutting remarks and conviction that, she was above all others was like water off a duck's back to Em, who just let the hurtful remarks slide. As long as she was paid to do her job, she kept her thoughts to herself and got on with her work. But still, having a lass like Sadie about the place was going to be a breath of fresh air, and she was looking forward to her coming to the Grange.

Em lived up at the colliery, with her husband and four boys, in one of the lime-washed cottages by the pit. Three of her lads were miners like their dad, and the fourth was at the village school. Sadie, however, would be living in at the Grange, to be there for the child when needed night or day. She and Em worked out a plan between them that would see Sadie being able to leave the house early in the morning for a couple of hours to cycle up to the Forester's to make her pies. Although she still had her folded pound notes hidden away under her mattress, she thought of it as Birdie's money, and wouldn't allow herself to spend it until, and unless, she was reunited with her daughter, and making the

194

pies meant that she could earn more than the pittance Mrs Marshall was paying.

The plan would involve Sadie waiting for Em to arrive at the Grange each morning while Birdie was still asleep. Em would then keep an eye on the child while Sadie was up at the Forester's, and would tend to her if she woke. It was an arrangement that they had considered carefully before Em put the proposal to Mrs Marshall over a cup of beef tea one afternoon. She did her best to present it in a favourable light, and by the time she had finished, she had managed to convince Mrs Marshall that the idea was her own.

'Think of the food we'll have fresh each morning,' she had said. 'If Sadie is baking for the pubs and shops, she can bake for us too. Alexandra will have fresh bread dipped in milk for her breakfast, and there'll be hearty pies for Mr Marshall when he comes home from work.'

Finally Mrs Marshall agreed — although not without a lot of sighing and fuss, which Em knew from experience was more for dramatic impact than anything else — and a date was set for Sadie to move to the Grange.

Sadie broke the news to Eddie as the two of them were out walking one evening. She squeezed his hand as she spoke of her excitement at taking on the role of Birdie's nurse.

'I'm going to work hard at the Grange,' she told him. 'And I won't do anything that could jeopardise spending time with Birdie. It's more than I could have dreamed of; I won't let anything spoil it, you know.'

'Don't forget that she's called Alexandra, Sadie. You've got to call her by the name the Marshalls gave her. My word, though, Mrs Marshall would have to name the child after one of the royals, wouldn't she?' He laughed. 'That's just typical of the woman, wanting to lord it over all and sundry.'

'She's an odd fish, that's for sure,' Sadie said. 'But I'm going to look after Bird — Alexandra as a nurse would, and I won't bring suspicion on myself.'

'You'll do just fine, I'm sure of it,' he said. 'And we're going to be living closer together when you move to the Grange. I'll be just around the corner if you need me — for anything at all.'

'I don't know what I'd do without you, Eddie. I'm not sure I would have had the strength for all this if it hadn't been for your help.'

'Don't do yourself down.' Eddie smiled and leaned in to kiss Sadie on the cheek. 'You're tougher than you think.'

★ ★ ★

In early October, as the trees on the village green shed their leaves to the grass below, Em set to cleaning the box room at the Grange, tucked away at the very top, on the third floor. It was to be Sadie's room and Em wanted to make it as welcoming as possible for the girl when she arrived. The small room contained a single bed under an eaves window. The only way to see out of it was to stand on the bed, but it let in a good amount of light. Em laid a freshly laundered

196

green eiderdown on the bed, and dusted the chest of drawers. On the bare floorboards she laid a worn and tattered clippy mat of red, black and blue stripes, which would give Sadie's bare feet some warmth when she stepped out of bed. When the room was prepared to her satisfaction, she headed down the three flights of stairs back to her work in the kitchen.

Later that morning, Sadie arrived at the Grange wearing Eddie's flat cap, carrying her blue linen bag of clothes and holding tight to her bike. Her heart was pounding with excitement at the thought that within minutes she would be with Birdie, looking after her, caring for her as best as she could. She pulled open the black iron gate, leaving her bike leaning against the railing that separated the Grange's garden from the pavement. Taking a deep breath, she squared her shoulders and pushed her feet forward in her boots. Then she walked briskly down the path and rapped hard at the front door, twice.

'Round the back,' Em told her when she opened the door. 'You can't come in through the front door any more, Sadie love.'

Sadie followed Em's directions, walking down past the village green and turning right as if she was heading to the Railway Inn. She stood still, taking in the scene of the pub in front of her, the place that had been her home when she'd first arrived in Ryhope, and where Eddie still lived. She saw movement at the side of the pub and realised it was a woman sweeping dirt into the road. Her heart lurched when she recognised Molly. Despite the worst kind of word that Molly had thrown at her that day in the kitchen at the Railway Inn, Sadie still hoped for a reconciliation. Molly was Eddie's mam, after all, and if there was any future for her and Eddie, then the two of them needed to make up. Sadie would forgive Molly for calling her a whore, of course she would, given time. She knew that Molly had used the word in anger at being deceived. She wanted to call out, to say hello, to chat and share a hug. But she still wasn't sure if that was what Molly wanted. Instead, she quietly rounded the corner with her bike, walking away from the pub, leaving Molly behind.

Around the corner, a dirt track ran along the back of the houses that stood proudly at the edge of the village green. Sadie followed it, making sure she walked along the centre, where cinder and ash had been sprinkled to soak up the mud. The cinder crunched underfoot and under the wheels of her bike. She kept glancing up at the back of the big houses, trying to work out which one was the Grange. Then Em bustled out of the back gate into the lane, beckoning Sadie towards her.

'Here, pet,' she said. 'You can leave your bike in the garden. This is the door you've got to use from now on. Only use the front if you've got the bairn out for a walk in her pram. She should never come through the back door and you should never go through the front without her. Got it?'

'Of course,' said Sadie. She felt an unexpected anger rise in her. After all her years working in service, she was used to being told her place and what she could and could not do. But this time she felt it personally. Yet what could she do? She knew she had to take it, for the joy of being with Birdie was too great to let something as trivial as a door spoil her excitement. If this was the way things had to be, then so be it, but it rankled with her still. She leaned her bike against the gardeners' wooden shed and headed towards the house.

'What on earth's that you're wearing?' Em asked, glancing at Sadie's legs.

'It's a bifurcated skirt,' Sadie smiled.

Em scratched her head and gave a hearty laugh. 'You young 'uns today. I don't know where I am with you, what with your short hair and your new-fangled clothes.' She pushed open the plain black wooden door that led into a scullery kept cool with white tiles on its walls. 'Here, come on in, Sadie,' she said. 'Welcome to your new home.'

The first thing Sadie noticed was the smell, the sweet, earthy scent of the rosemary that was dried in bunches hung from the beams. It was very different to the Forester's Arms, where the stench of beer was soaked into the very soul of the place. The scullery was a square room with wooden shelves around all four walls. On one shelf Sadie saw a plate of ham stored next to packets of flour and butter, and sugar lumps in a wide, low brown bowl. On another shelf were bottles of wine and spirits — whisky, brandy and gin.

'Kitchen's through here,' Em said, bustling forward. Sadie followed. 'Front parlour's through to the right, but you've been in there already.

199

Dining room's on the left.'

The dining room was as over-stuffed with furniture as Sadie remembered the parlour to have been on the day she and Bessie met Mrs Marshall. The walls were painted a dark shade of green to the picture rail, and white above that. From the rail hung framed prints showing views of the sea and a coastline that Sadie didn't recognise. They were arranged in groups of five and six, as if attempting to cover as much wall space as possible. The whole effect was dizzying, and she wondered how any dinner party held there could be relaxing or enjoyable. She felt seasick just looking at them all.

'Is Alexandra ready to meet me?' she asked. She was mad keen to set eyes on Birdie again; it had been all she had thought of and dreamed about since the moment her daughter had left her arms on the day of the picnic. But she knew she had to keep her cool; she couldn't jeopardise her position now she was so close. She had to keep up a pretence of formality in front of Em and the Marshalls.

'My word, you're keen!' Em smiled. 'Don't you want to see your room first? All the other young lasses who've worked here, that's all they've been bothered about: what their room was like, when their first afternoon off was and whether the gardeners were married.'

Sadie laughed. 'I don't think I'll be going after a gardener.'

'You've got a good fella in young Eddie, you know,' Em said, patting Sadie's arm.

'I know,' Sadie replied. She felt a warm glow

of pride whenever Eddie's name was mentioned. It wasn't the first time she'd heard people sing his praises. Bessie and Pat had done it too. In fact, now she thought about it, she hadn't heard a bad word said against him by anyone.

'Come on then, upstairs,' said Em, then she put a finger to her lips. 'And be quiet. Mrs Marshall's not feeling so good today; she's had one of her turns.'

'What's wrong with her?' Sadie whispered.

Em shrugged. 'The doctor gives her bottles of pills and medicines, but they don't seem to do a lot of good. She gets pains all down her back and her legs. That's why I put no store in a lot of what she says. I know she's got a nasty streak and a sharp tongue on her, but I reckon it comes from the pains, not from the badness of her heart. So don't let her get to you, you hear me? Anyway, let's go quietly, as she's taken to her bed.'

They climbed to the first landing, where Em pointed to the various doors and told Sadie what lay behind them.

'That's their bedroom, the master and missus,' she said, then gave her head a little shake. 'He's hardly ever home, though. And this door here, that's the nursery, they call it. It's a room for Alexandra, somewhere she can crawl about and play when she can't get out into the garden for fresh air. Next to it is the bairn's bedroom.'

'Can I see her?' whispered Sadie.

Em gave a quick glance towards Mrs Marshall's door. 'Come on then,' she said, pushing down on the handle of the child's room.

The door swung open and she stood to one side, allowing Sadie to enter first.

The same sweet scent of rosemary, this time mixed with lavender, filled the room, but Sadie didn't look to see where it was coming from this time. She was focused on the wooden crib in the middle of the room. She inched forward, her breath catching in her chest, every heartbeat pushing her on towards her child. She saw Birdie's wavy dark hair on a tiny white pillow, her body covered by a blanket. Peering into the crib, she fully expected to find the little girl asleep, but she was greeted with the widest smile from a beautiful round face.

'Hello, darling child,' she breathed. She held out her hand and Birdie took hold of her fingers in a tight fist.

Em gave a little cough from her position at the door. 'I should show you the rest of the house, Sadie. And then you can come back here to begin your work.'

'Of course,' Sadie nodded. She reminded herself again to remain as professional as she could in front of Em; she mustn't give her any reason to think there was more to her relationship with the child than that of just being her nurse. But oh, her heart was leaping with the joy of knowing that at long last she would be spending her days with her daughter.

She freed her hand from the baby's surprisingly strong grip and followed Em up to the second landing, where there were a further three rooms. Two of these were spare rooms, she was told, for guests, although she saw that one of them looked very much lived in, with a man's jacket hanging over the back of a chair, and the bed sheets crumpled. A shaving brush and soap stood on a dark wooden dressing table with three mirrors. Em saw the puzzled look that passed over her face.

'Mr Marshall uses the room,' she explained with a raise of her eyebrows. 'He and the missus don't share their own room much, and when he comes home in the early hours it's easier for him to stay up here so he doesn't disturb her.'

The third room was a bathroom, with indoor plumbing the likes of which Sadie had seen only in the biggest of the houses she'd worked at in Hartlepool.

'Isn't it grand?' Em said proudly. 'Takes a bit of cleaning, what with all the porcelain.'

'A bathtub too!' Sadie said. She reached out her hand and ran it along the cool bath top and around the taps, marvelling at it all.

'And your room's upstairs,' Em said, heading back out to the landing. 'It's small, but it's clean, and I've made it as nice as I can. If you need anything, just let me know.'

'Thanks, Em,' Sadie said as she followed the maid up the final flight. This time the stairs were narrow, with no patterned runner carpet that had been in place on the first two flights.

'Did you bring your things?' Em asked her. 'There's a chest of drawers here for your clothes.'

'I don't have anything other than what's in this bag,' Sadie said. 'And there's a spare skirt at the Forester's, one of Bessie's old ones, that I'll collect next time I'm there.'

'That's all you've got?' Em asked, surprised.

'And an apron, but that's at the Forester's too. It's for when I do the baking.' Sadie thought of her child, her little dark-haired beauty, who was lying in her crib just two floors below her. She touched the ladybird charm at her neck. 'I've got everything I need right here.'

'Well, if you're sure. I daresay you'll be able to afford to buy some new clothes as soon as you start earning. There's a good market by the docks; a woman called Florrie Smith runs a decent second-hand clothes stall there. With two jobs under your belt, here and working for Bessie, you'll be able to spend a few pennies on something nice. Maybe even get yourself another one of those bikefurrated skirts.'

'Bifurcated,' Sadie smiled.

Em shook her head. 'Women wearing skirts that look like trousers? Whatever is the world coming to?' And with that, she plodded back down the stairs, leaving Sadie alone in her room.

Sadie sat on the bed and gently bounced on it, once, twice, to get the feel of it. It wasn't bad. She'd slept on harder, lumpier beds and in much smaller rooms. Her new room wasn't as big or as homely as the room above the hardware shop next to the Forester's Arms, but it was certainly better than the storeroom in the yard at the Railway Inn where she'd slept when she'd first arrived. And she knew that she'd sleep in much worse to be this close to Birdie.

The thought of the Railway Inn, knowing it was just around the corner from the Grange, made her stomach turn with anxiety. She needed to speak to Molly, she knew that. She had to make her peace with her, especially if there was to be a future for her and Eddie.

★ ★ ★

As Sadie settled into her new life at the Grange, she saw little of Mrs Marshall, who remained in her sickbed. She was left to look after Alexandra, which she was delighted to do. Every morning when she woke, the first thing on her mind was her daughter, though she had to delay those first moments with her until she had done her baking at the pub.

While Sadie was at the Forester's, Em would look in on Alexandra to make sure she wasn't awake, or crying or needed tending to. At the pub, Bessie would feed Sadie breakfast while they waited for the pies to cook, and over a cup of tea, Sadie would talk about life at the Grange. Bessie could see how happy she was, reunited with her child. She saw the way Sadie had blossomed in the short time since she'd moved there. After the pies were taken from the oven, they were stored carefully in a basket at the front of her bike, and in another at the rear that Eddie had fixed on. Then off Sadie went, freewheeling down the bank to the shops and the pubs to drop off her wares.

Once she had finished her deliveries, it was time for her favourite part of the day, waking Birdie and feeding her, bathing her and dressing her. Em left her to her work with the child, trusting her fully. Even John the gardener soon began to greet her as a friend when they passed each other in the kitchen or the back garden at the Grange. With Mrs Marshall lying in her darkened room with the curtains drawn and visitors shunned, Sadie offered to help Em cook for her, delicate food that would not upset her digestion and would hopefully induce some sort of appetite. With the ingredients that Em bought from the Co-op, Sadie prepared nourishing clear soups, steamed whiting and even broiled chops, but all of the dishes went untouched, returned to the kitchen for them to eat themselves.

It was the time spent with her daughter — who she had no choice but to call Alexandra, never Birdie — that Sadie loved the most. She relished the time they were alone, playing in the nursery with wooden blocks the child would grab and then drop, gurgling with laughter. Mrs Marshall never once asked to see Alexandra as she lay in her sickbed, and Sadie took this as a sign of the depth of the pain and illness that had racked her employer's body. But neither did Alexandra appear to be missing her adoptive mother, and she took to Sadie immediately, with Em commenting that the child seemed different somehow since Sadie had moved into the Grange, happier and more content. She had even taken her first steps, encouraged by Sadie in the nursery, a milestone of which Mrs Marshall remained unaware.

While the child napped in the daytime, Sadie helped Em with the baking, cooking and cleaning. But still she never crossed paths with the elusive Mr Marshall, although she often heard sounds on the stairs below her room in the dark of the night. In the mornings, she was already up, dressed and cycling to the Forester's when Mr Marshall rose and prepared himself for work. And by the time she returned to the Grange after delivering the pies, the master had left for work. Not once did Em complain to Sadie about the extra responsibility she'd taken on in keeping watch over Alexandra. Fortunately, most days Alexandra slept long and well, waking only when Sadie returned at about eight o'clock.

Even though the pit was less than fifteen minutes' walk from the Grange, Joe Marshall drove himself to work each day. The black car that had for so long been shared between the three pit managers had now been offered to him by the regional manager for his personal use. He took it willingly and with much pride. It was a sign that his show of being a family man, outwardly at least, was standing him in good stead with those whose influence he sought at work. Investing in the Hartlepool child, he realised, was paying off, beginning to bring the benefits that he felt he deserved.

Because of the routine kept by Sadie and Mr Marshall, they never saw each other. He was aware that there was a girl in the house who had been employed by his wife as the child's nurse. He understood her to be competent, but he knew nothing more of her, not even her name. As far as he was concerned, the less he saw of her, the better, whoever she was.

★ ★ ★

As Sadie settled in at the Grange, a picture in the autumn edition of the coal managers' newsletter had caught the eye of David McAdam, a young journalist at *The Sunderland Echo*. David decided he would like to share the news about Mrs Marshall's picnic on the beach with the readers of his weekly column. He liked the unusual look of the girl in the picture — Sadie Barnes, according to the photographer's caption. From his desk at the *Echo*, he called the editor of the newsletter, who gave him permission to reprint the article and the photograph, as long as the photographer was credited. This was duly done, and the item appeared in the newspaper the following week.

A copy of *The Sunderland Echo* with this news item inside was discarded by a passenger travelling by train from Sunderland to Seaham Harbour. It was a quiet day, and the train's ticket collector, a hefty chap from Hartlepool nicknamed Potato Ned for the unfortunate lump on his right ear, had little to do. He picked up the paper and flicked idly through it. By the time the train arrived in Hartlepool, he'd torn out the news article about the girl he recognised from his visits to Freda's house.

It was the same girl he'd seen travelling to Ryhope months ago, he felt sure of it, the same girl he'd told Mick about. She might have shorn hair now, but he remembered her bonny face. And there, underneath the photograph, was a name printed in bold type: Sadie Barnes. He had always known her first name was Sadie, but he was sure her surname wasn't Barnes. He racked his brains, trying to dredge up the memory of the name that Mick had told him months ago. What what it? Linskell? Linsdale? He shook his head and then clicked his fingers when it came to him at last. Linthorpe! Why had she changed her name from Linthorpe to Barnes? He wondered about this only briefly before giving a shrug. Maybe she'd been wed. Well, whatever it was, he planned to take the photo to show Mick just as soon as he finished his shift.

9

Truth

Tom didn't recognise the tall, dark-haired young man who'd been blown into the pub on a gust of autumn wind. He wasn't one of the regulars at the Railway Inn.

'What can I get for you, sir?'

Mick nodded towards the closest hand pump. 'Is that any good?'

'Vaux? Course it is,' Tom replied. 'Beer doesn't come much better around here.'

'I'll have a pint, then.'

Tom pulled the pint slowly, eyeing the stranger in front of him. It was a rum do when his customers questioned the quality of the local beer.

'You passing through?' he asked as the beer settled under its foam top. He gently pulled down on the pump to top the glass up to the brim.

'Something like that,' Mick replied, handing over the coins in payment. 'I'm looking for some-one.'

Tom's interest was piqued. 'Oh aye? Anyone in particular?'

'A girl.'

Tom laughed. 'Aren't we all, mate?'

'This girl,' Mick said.

He rummaged in his coat pocket and pulled out the folded page of newsprint from *The Sunderland Echo*. He slid it across the bar towards Tom and pointed at the picture of Sadie on the beach.

'You seen her? It says in the paper she was catering a picnic for the wife of a pit boss, a Mr Marshall who lives at Ryhope Grange.'

Tom stared hard at the grainy black-and-white picture. If he wasn't mistaken, it was the lass that Eddie had been going around with. He hadn't seen her in weeks, but he would swear blind it was her, although heaven only knows what had happened to her hair.

'I've seen her. And I know where the Grange is,' he said, eyeing Mick suspiciously. 'What's it to you?'

'She owes me,' Mick said, shifting uncomfortably under Tom's steely gaze.

'Is that right now? So she's worth something to you then?' A flicker of a smile played around Tom's lips. He could do with some extra cash to pay off his card game debts, and if he played things right with this young lad, he might be able to make some easy money.

'Well, I reckon I could tell you where you'd find her right now if I was so inclined.'

'And are you inclined?'

'Depends what's in it for me. A crown might do the trick.' Tom knew he'd have to keep this quiet from Eddie; he wouldn't want his brother finding out that he'd led a stranger to his girlfriend.

'Five bob?' Mick cried.

'Shush!' Tom demanded. 'Keep your voice down! Now, do you want to find this girl or not?'

'I can give you two bob and that's your lot.'

Tom glanced behind him to make sure their conversation wasn't being overhead. 'Make it three and you're on.'

Mick reached into his coat pocket. He pulled out a handful of coins and handed over the three shillings. Tom leaned towards him, their heads almost touching across the bar.

'She's working at the Grange, just as you said, for the Marshalls. I think she's the cook or something; she makes pies anyway.'

'I didn't come in for a cookery lesson,' Mick sneered.

Tom felt a rage start to burn at the back of his neck as he struggled to keep his temper against the lad's sarcasm.

'You'll find the Grange just around the corner from here,' he continued, doing his best to keep his cool. 'Walk out of the door you came in just now, head to the village green and turn left. The Grange is the big house with black iron gates at the front. If she's not there, you'll likely find her up at the Forester's Arms; it's a pub up the colliery. Ask anyone in Ryhope, they'll tell you where it is.'

Mick lifted his pint and took a long swig. Then he picked up the page from *The Sunderland Echo*, folded it carefully and placed it back in his pocket.

'Pleasure doing business with you,' he said before he turned to walk out of the door.

Tom watched him leave, turning over the three shillings in his trouser pocket. They'd make a good investment, he thought; he could double his money in a poker game in the Select that night once his mam had gone to bed. The rage he'd felt when the lad was at the bar started to disappear, and he helped himself to a nip of whisky from a bottle behind the bar.

★　★　★

Up in the nursery of the Grange, Sadie was kneeling with her arms stretched out wide.

'Come on then, Alexandra!' she called. 'Come on, you can do it. Walk to Sadie. Come on, walk to Sadie.'

Alexandra wobbled on her chubby legs. She took an unsteady step, and then another, the novelty of propelling herself forward making her gurgle with laughter. Sadie smiled widely as she watched her daughter toddle towards her. Alexandra's legs were getting stronger every day, and at the same time she was becoming more capable with her hands. She was able to feed herself with a spoon now, with Sadie's patient help, although there was usually as much food left on the child's face as went into her mouth. As she tottered towards Sadie, her laughter filled the nursery. Sadie clapped her hands with glee and cheered when Alexandra finally made her way into her arms.

'Again?' she asked. 'Again, for Sadie?'

'Dee! Dee!' Alexandra gurgled in reply.

Sadie held the child with both hands until she

was steady on her feet, then walked to the other side of the nursery and called to her. But before Alexandra could set off again, the nursery door swung open and Mrs Marshall stepped into the room. She looked as pale and wan as Sadie had ever seen her, but her auburn hair had been brushed and tidied.

'Mrs Marshall.' Sadie stood to attention. 'Are you feeling better today?'

'I'm up, aren't I?' she replied. There was a rasp to her voice that took away any sting.

'I hope we didn't wake you,' Sadie said. 'Alexandra has been walking, taking steps all on her own. Would you like to see?'

Mrs Marshall's eyes flickered across the room to the child. 'Later, perhaps,' she said coldly. 'Is there food ready downstairs?'

Sadie nodded. 'Em has prepared lunch. She's left it warming in the coal oven and it's ready to be eaten whenever you would like.'

'Where *is* Em?' Mrs Marshall demanded. 'Do you mean to tell me she's not here?'

'She's at the Co-op, shopping,' Sadie said gently. 'If she'd known you were leaving your bed today, I'm sure she would have been here for you.'

'And my husband? He'll be out too, I expect?'

Mrs Marshall didn't wait for Sadie to reply before she turned and walked back out to the landing. Sadie picked up Alexandra and followed. She watched as the woman gripped the handrail with each step she took, heard her laboured breathing as she headed down the stairs. It was hard not to notice Mrs Marshall's bony shoulder blades through the thin silk of her gown. She had not eaten in days, had refused the plates of food that Em and Sadie had prepared. All she had taken was water and a plate of plain boiled rice.

'Mrs Marshall, please let me help you,' Sadie said when they finally reached the bottom stair.

'I'm fine, girl!' Mrs Marshall snapped. 'You can put the child down and then bring lunch to me in the dining room.'

'Would you be more comfortable in the parlour?'

'In the dining room! Are you deaf?'

Sadie sighed and headed towards the kitchen with Alexandra in her arms. She was just about to let the child down to the stone floor and serve up the lunch of beef stew that Em had prepared when there was a loud knocking at the front door. It was an insistent knock, impatient, not the polite tapping of Reverend Daye when he came calling. With Em still at the shops, Sadie had no choice but to answer.

She took Alexandra by the hand and led her towards the door, the little girl unsteady on her feet. As she passed the dining room, she saw Mrs Marshall holding on to the back of a chair, her breathing laboured. With her free hand, Sadie pulled open the heavy front door. There on the doorstep was the last person she had expected — or wanted — to see.

She tried to push the door closed, but she was no match for Mick and it swung open against her. She stood to one side, shielding Alexandra behind her, keeping her out of Mick's sight as much as she could. He stepped inside and kicked the door shut behind him.

'What do you want?' Sadie gasped.

An evil smile played around his lips. 'What do you think?'

'I'm not going back!' Sadie hissed.

'Don't kid yourself,' Mick snarled. 'I don't want you, never did. You know what you took from us. You know what I've come to get. Thought you'd escaped me, did you? I came looking for you once before and I went home empty-handed. Mam wasn't happy about that. Well I'm not going home with nothing this time, I'll tell you now.'

Sadie gripped tight hold of Alexandra's hand. 'How did you find me?' she asked.

Mick tapped the side of his nose. 'That's for me to know, isn't it? Think you can fool Mick McIntyre? Think again, Sadie Linthorpe.'

His fist shot out, and Sadie felt the pain deep in the side of her face. She stumbled backwards to the wall. Without Sadie's support, Alexandra lost her balance and dropped to the floor, wailing from the shock. The pain gathered and throbbed in Sadie's cheek, causing tears to stream from one eye. She put her fingers to her damp face, and when she pulled them away, she saw blood mixed with her tears.

Mick saw the horror in Sadie's eyes when she realised what had happened, but that didn't stop him lashing out, hitting her again and again. She tried to stop him, tried to grab his hands, but he kept punching her, grabbing hold of her apron so that she couldn't move as he slapped her hard across her face. She lashed out with her boots,

216

kicking him in the shins, but she was no match for Mick's brutal attack. Throughout it all, Alexandra continued to wail, but Sadie was powerless to do anything other than cover her face as best as she could to protect it from the blows raining down.

Finally Alexandra's cries caught Mick's attention, and he noticed the bairn behind Sadie. He pulled his foot back ready to kick at the child.

'No!' Sadie yelled. She jerked her body as hard as she could to get in front of Alexandra. The force of her movement ripped her apron where Mick still held tight to it and she was free of him. She stumbled to the floor, sitting beside Alexandra, both of them sitting on the cold linoleum. Sadie staggered to her knees and positioned herself so that Alexandra was behind her. The fear that had been running through her had given way to something else now, something deeper, something she had never experienced before. She jumped to her feet and took a step towards Mick, glaring at him, furious. 'Don't . . . you . . . dare!' she cried, pushing him hard in the chest with both hands with every word she spat at him. 'Don't you dare harm my child!'

'*Your* child?' Mick sneered. 'What's it to you?'

She could have told him. Right there, in that instant, she could have told him the truth. But a bond with Mick McIntyre was a bond she did not want.

'Stop it!'

It was Mrs Marshall, standing by the dining room door, her face aflame. She was gripping the

217

frame with both hands to keep herself upright.

'I said stop, or I'll call the police!'

Mick glanced at her quickly, and once he realised that the weak, thin woman posed little threat, his turned his gaze to Sadie's bloodied face. His breathing came from him thick and fast, as if he was ready to take up the beating again.

'Get out,' Mrs Marshall ordered in her rasping voice. 'Get out now.'

'Not without what I came for,' Mick grunted, still not taking his eyes off Sadie.

Mrs Marshall took a step towards the front door. 'I'm telling you, you'd better go now unless you want to spend the night in the Sunderland cells. You've picked the wrong house to bring your fighting to, whoever you are. Don't you know who I am? I can have the police here in minutes and have you locked up before you know it.'

Mick leered at Mrs Marshall, eyeing her carpet slippers, the silk housecoat tied tight at her tiny waist, and the sickly, pale skin of her face. But Sadie's words were beginning to sink in, and he felt a rush of nausea as the penny dropped. He knew then whose child this was. He glanced from Alexandra, still sitting on the floor, to Sadie and back again.

'Get out,' Mrs Marshall ordered again. 'And don't let me see you here again.'

'You won't,' Mick said quickly, shaking his head. He had seen the likeness — the eyes, the way the bairn's mouth turned — and he knew the truth of Sadie's words, of what she was protecting. He turned to Mrs Marshall.

'You lot make me sick,' he said. 'You, her — and her ugly bastard bairn.'

And with that, he pulled the front door towards him and disappeared into the garden, heading towards the iron gate. His mind whirled with thoughts of the child he'd just seen in there, the child with dark curly hair like his own. He knew the bairn was his, and he wanted nothing to do with it, nothing at all. He'd tell his mam he couldn't find Sadie, he'd lie through his teeth — his mam would believe him, she trusted everything he said. But one thing was for sure: he wasn't coming back to Ryhope, not now he knew that his child lived there. He'd felt nothing for it when he saw it. And now he needed to get as far away from it and from Sadie as he could.

His mate Ned had promised him another free ride back to Hartlepool. Mick kicked a rock that was lying on the road ahead of him; it flew against a brick wall and smashed into pieces. He put his head down, staring at the pavement. Then he began to run, his heart pounding, his feet flying as he made his way to the railway station.

★ ★ ★

Mick stormed from the Grange, crashing the iron gate behind him, just as Em returned from the Co-op with her basket on her arm. She looked on as the tall, gangly lad rushed away, trying to figure out if she knew who he was. She had intended to go around to the back of the

219

house and enter through the scullery door as she usually did. But there was something about the way the lad had run off that made her think again. He'd left the front door wide open too.

Em pulled open the iron gate and walked down the garden path. What she found inside the Grange startled her. Sadie, with blood on her face and her apron torn, was clutching a sobbing Alexandra, while Mrs Marshall was slumped to the floor in the doorway of the dining room.

'Holy Mary, Mother of God!' Em cried. 'What's gone on here?'

She ran to Mrs Marshall and knelt beside her. Her basket spilled to one side and two onions rolled across the floor.

'Come on, love,' she said to her employer. She put her hands under Mrs Marshall's arms. 'Sadie, put the bairn down and help me move her to the sofa,' she directed.

Sadie walked into the parlour and sat Alexandra on the clippy mat in front of the fireplace. Then she hurried back to the dining room to help Em, and between them they managed to get Mrs Marshall into a standing position.

'Come on, into the parlour,' Em said, taking a step towards the room.

'No,' Mrs Marshall said. She glared at Sadie. 'I want to know the truth, girl. Why did you call her *your* child? I heard you, just now, and I heard the boy's remark too.'

Startled, Em glanced at Sadie for an explanation, but she remained silent.

'I demand to know,' Mrs Marshall continued, but her words came from her with less power

220

than she would have liked. Her breathing was shallow and her body was weak.

'Let's get you comfortable on the sofa,' Em said, guiding her towards the parlour. 'You've had a terrible shock. Sadie, go and get a glass of water and some food from the kitchen and bring it here quickly.'

Sadie did as she was told. When she returned to the parlour, Mrs Marshall was sitting on the sofa with her back supported and her legs up on the cushions. Sadie handed the tray of food to Em, who set to feeding her mistress the beef stew from a spoon. Alexandra crawled towards the sofa and pulled herself up to standing.

'Not now, child,' Mrs Marshall whispered, then she glanced at Sadie. 'Take her away.'

'Yes, Mrs Marshall,' Sadie replied.

'And girl?'

Sadie turned.

'When the child has her nap, I want to speak to you about what just happened out there. I want to know who that boy was, and what was meant by those words between you. And you'll tell me the truth or the police will be called. You hear me?'

'Yes, Mrs Marshall.'

'And clean your face up before you come back down.'

Sadie took Alexandra in her arms and walked slowly upstairs. The shock of what had happened — seeing Mick, the attack, the words that Mrs Marshall had heard — made her stomach turn, and she felt sick inside. Her legs began to shake and she quickly placed Alexandra in her crib, much to the child's displeasure, and walked to the bathroom to wash the blood from her face and hands. Her cheek was cut and starting to swell.

She wanted Eddie. She wanted to hold him and talk to him right then more than she wanted anything. She hadn't seen him in an age; he'd given her time to settle into her new job and new home, knowing how important it was for her to develop a bond with her child. But what if he saw her with a cut face and swollen cheek? She'd have to tell him about Mick returning to Ryhope to find her, but first there was Mrs Marshall to deal with.

She took a piece of cotton from the bathroom cabinet and held it gently to her cheek until the bleeding stopped. Then she returned to Alexandra's bedroom, where the child was standing in her crib, gripping the top of it with her chubby little hands and stomping her feet against the blankets. Sadie watched as she alternated between crying tears of real anguish one minute and then laughing at her stomping game the next. She smiled and walked towards the crib.

'Dee, Dee,' Alexandra cried, holding her arms out, then losing her balance again and falling gently to the blanket, still laughing, the shock of the morning's events seemingly forgotten. Sadie reached into the crib and Alexandra grabbed tight hold of her fingers. She whispered softly to the child to calm and settle her, and then began to sing until Alexandra closed her eyes and drifted off to sleep.

Sadie tucked the blanket around her daughter

to keep her warm before heading to the kitchen, where she took a clean apron from the cupboard and put it on in place of the torn one. She took a deep breath, which caught in her chest with the pain of Mick's beating, then gathered herself up, squared her shoulders and walked towards the parlour. She was ready to answer Mrs Marshall's questions as honestly as she dared.

Em was leaving the parlour with the food tray, and Sadie saw the bowl of beef stew had hardly been touched.

'Close the door,' Mrs Marshall said from the sofa.

Em did as she was told, but she didn't go straight back to the kitchen. She waited outside the parlour, with one ear to the door, determined to find out what on earth was going on.

'Sit, girl,' Mrs Marshall barked at Sadie. 'I demand an explanation.'

Sadie remained silent, wondering where to start, and how much she should reveal. Eddie's words came to her about being honest, about not keeping secrets. She thought of the hurt she had caused Molly at the Railway Inn, losing her as a friend after she'd taken her in and given her a job and a home. But she hadn't lied to Molly, not really; she just hadn't told the whole truth. Then she thought of the advice Bessie had given her about biding her time and not getting involved for fear she'd be carted off to the funny farm if she went around demanding her child.

She took a long breath and tried to stop her legs from shaking, but when she looked at Mrs Marshall, she saw that her eyes had closed, as if she was sleeping. She sat quietly for a few moments, waiting for the woman to speak again. Mrs Marshall's breathing rasped in her chest and her eyes finally opened. She stared ahead of her, to a picture of a white boat on a foaming grey sea, a boat in turmoil, frozen in action and framed.

'Tell me the truth, girl,' she said at last. 'The child who lives in this house. Is it really yours?'

Sadie's silence told her everything she needed to know.

'And who was that boy?'

'Someone I knew . . .' Sadie began hesitantly. 'From Hartlepool.'

Mrs Marshall nodded slightly. She kept her gaze fixed firmly ahead, not looking at Sadie as she spoke. 'We were given assurances that the child's mother would never follow her. How did you find us?'

'I searched,' Sadie said, keeping her voice as even as she could. She was determined not to cry, not to show weakness in front of her employer.

'You were paid, girl,' Mrs Marshall said, turning to face her now.

Sadie felt the sting of the words: all the money involved in the sale of her baby had been taken by Freda. She bit her tongue.

'We bought that child. You have no right coming here demanding it, taking it!' Mrs Marshall slumped back against the cushions.

Outside the parlour door, Em's mouth opened in shock.

'I demand nothing, Mrs Marshall,' Sadie

began. 'All I want is — '

'Do you think I care what you want?' Mrs Marshall hissed.

Sadie looked down at her hands in her lap. She swallowed hard.

Outside, Em bustled away from the parlour door. She had heard enough.

'Mrs Marshall, I — ' Sadie continued.

'Get out.'

'What?'

'You heard me. Get out. I never want to set eyes on you again, you hear?'

'But — '

'Forget the child. Forget your job here. And remember, I can make life very difficult for you if you go up against me. I have influence in this village. I can make sure that no one in Ryhope will ever buy your pies and your bread and your pretty little bird cakes. And don't imagine you will ever see the child again. Now go.'

Sadie's eyes filled with tears as she turned and walked towards the parlour door. But Mrs Marshall wasn't finished with her yet.

'And there's one more thing. The child must never know who her real mother is, you hear me? Never! If the truth comes to light, I will destroy you, and don't think for one minute that I wouldn't. The Marshalls of Ryhope have power, girl. We run the pit that keeps the village going. So don't think I don't have it in me to stand up against those who oppose me. Now leave the house immediately, or I'll call the police.'

Sadie opened the door and stood in the hallway, unsure of which way to go next. She wanted to run upstairs to see Birdie, to kiss her and hold her and tell her she loved her. But she knew that if she did, Mrs Marshall could make things worse for her. Instead, she headed towards the kitchen, where Em was scraping the uneaten beef stew from the bowl. At the sight of Sadie, with her cut face and the tears streaming down her cheeks, she reached out her arms to the girl.

'Is it true?' she asked. 'Is that your bairn upstairs?'

Sadie nodded, wiping the back of her hand across her eyes.

'Oh Sadie love. Don't worry, things have a way of turning out all right,' Em soothed. 'Go on up to the Forester's and talk to Bessie. She'll know what to do.'

Sadie lifted her apron over her head and folded it neatly across the back of a chair in the scullery before heading out to the back yard. But then she stopped, remembering her pound notes, folded and tucked away under her mattress at the top of the house. Should she go back to collect them? She knew that only Em would go into her room; Mr and Mrs Marshall would never lower themselves to enter a staff member's room. She decided she could trust Em with the money if she found it — and she knew she could trust her with Birdie too. What she needed to do now was get away from the Grange, and if she needed to collect her belongings, she'd ask for Em's help when the time came.

She wheeled her bike away from the gardeners' shed but was in no mood to cycle with the pain from Mick's beating still raging in her. Instead, she flung Eddie's cap on her head and walked with her head down. What Bessie would think when she saw her, homeless again, with bruises and cuts on her cheek, was anyone's guess. But Sadie knew that Em was right: she had to go to Bessie for advice. For where else could she turn? Eddie would be at work and there was no one else she could speak to.

As she made her way out of the back yard and on to the cinder-covered dirt track, John the gardener came ambling towards her. Sadie sniffed back her tears, ready to speak to him and let him know that she wouldn't be working at the Grange any more. But just as they neared each other, a shout went up behind her, and she turned to see Em, frantic, waving and yelling.

'Get Dr Anderson!' she called. 'John! Fetch the doctor. Find him now!'

'What is it?' Sadie yelled, unable to disguise the fear that ran through her. 'It's not Alexandra, is it?'

Em shook her head. 'It's the mistress, but it's best if you leave, Sadie. She'll not want to see you. She's taken badly, tried to get herself up from the sofa and fell. John! Quick! Fetch the doctor! Get Mr Marshall from the pit!'

John turned and fled down the cinder track, heading to Dr Anderson's surgery up on Stockton Road. Sadie watched as he disappeared around the edge of the village green, then continued on her way, walking past the front of the Grange, past its black iron gates and railings, past the front gardens still vibrant from the evergreen shrubs that John had planted and tended for years. She glanced up at the front bedroom window where she knew her daughter was sleeping, and her breath caught in her throat. Then she pushed her bike on, holding fast to it with one hand on the saddle and the other on the handlebar.

As she walked, Sadie was so lost in herself, churned up in a whirl of emotions and feelings, that she didn't even realise how cold the day was until the rain began to fall. She pulled her shawl tightly around her, but it was little protection against the biting wind that was now blowing the rain sideways, lashing it against her. When she reached the Co-op, she huddled in the doorway and watched a group of miners walking down the colliery together in a tight group. They'd finished their shift, she could tell just by looking at them; every last bit of skin that was exposed to the weather was black from the coal. Their flat caps were pulled low against the rain, but Sadie recognised one of them immediately from the way he walked and held himself.

'Eddie!' she called across the road. She waved, and he waved back, then excused himself from his friends and ran across the road, joining her under the canopy of the doorway, out of the rain.

'What the . . . ? What's happened to your face?' he cried when he saw her. 'Have you fallen off your bike?'

Sadie's fingers flew to her swollen cheek. There was so much she wanted to tell him, but she didn't know where to begin. The raindrops streamed from his flat cap, catching the side of his face and streaking his coal-black face.

'Sadie? What it is it?' he asked her.

'I've had to leave the Grange, Eddie,' she said at last. 'I'm heading up to see Bessie now, but we need to talk. I need to tell you what's happened.'

Eddie nodded grimly. 'Give me half an hour,' he said. 'I'll run home and have my bath, then I'll come up to the Forester's and we can talk there.'

Sadie heaved a sigh of relief. She walked on through the rain the short distance up the colliery bank to the Forester's Arms. Once there, she popped her head around the door, managed to catch Pat's attention and asked if the gate in the yard could be opened. Then she wheeled her bike to the back of the pub.

It was Bessie who let her in, taking in the sight of her bruised and cut face, her cheek swelling black and blue. 'Come on through to the sitting room,' she said once the bike had been leaned against the netty wall. 'It looks like you might need to talk. Who's looking after the child?'

'Em,' replied Sadie as she sank into Bessie's chair by the fire. She took off her wet shawl and placed it by the fireside to dry. Over tea and a cheese scone still warm from the oven with butter melted on it, she told Bessie all that had happened. Bessie listened and asked questions, and once she had heard everything, she offered to take Sadie in.

'I didn't want to ask,' Sadie said. 'I didn't want to presume, or take you for granted, Bessie. But I'm grateful. I do need somewhere to stay.'

'I'd have been upset if you'd gone anywhere else,' Bessie said. 'Your room's as it was. I'll give you some fresh bedding and you can stay as long as you need. Have you spoken to Eddie yet?'

'He's coming here later,' Sadie replied. 'I'll tell him everything then.'

Bessie sighed and shook her head. 'That Mick lad's made a mess of your face, love. Have you put anything on it yet?'

Without waiting for an answer, Bessie disappeared, leaving Sadie sitting by the fire. When she reappeared, she carried a small white enamel bowl and some strips of white cotton. She cleaned the wound on Sadie's face, softly and gently working around the cut under her eye.

'You'll live,' she smiled. 'But you're going to have a beauty of a black eye for a few days.'

'I'll work behind the bar for you while I'm here,' Sadie said. 'I can't take your kindness for free.'

'You'll do no such thing,' Bessie replied. 'If you go behind the bar looking like that, you'll put the customers off their ale. You look like you've done ten rounds in the blood pit. But I can use you, lass, that's for sure. Once you feel up to it, how'd you fancy baking a few more pies and some bread for sale in the pub?'

Sadie leaned across to Bessie and gave her a kiss on her cheek. 'I'd love to,' she said.

'Stay in here and rest for today, then. We can put you to work tomorrow. And when your black eye fades and your cheek goes down, we'll think about letting you back behind the bar. And we'll have a think, Sadie, about the bairn. You've come so far and done so much. You can't just let her go now.'

Bessie walked from the room, heading back to work. Sitting alone by the fire, Sadie ran the ladybird charm through her fingers as her tears began to fall once again. By the time Eddie arrived, she'd pulled herself together a little. Her skirt was dry after sitting by the fire, and she felt safe and warm in Pat and Bessie's sitting room. Eddie sat on the sofa opposite her, and just as she'd done with Bessie earlier, Sadie told him all that had happened at the Grange. As her words spilled from her, she saw Eddie's face cloud over, then he stood and thumped the air in anger.

'I'll kill him!' he yelled. 'If I get my hands on him, I'll — '

'Eddie, sit down,' Sadie pleaded. 'He'll be miles away now and I'm fine, really I am. It's just a few cuts and bruises; they'll soon heal.'

Eddie sank into the seat next to Sadie and laid his hand gently on hers.

'Let it go, Eddie. Mick's history now, he's in my past,' Sadie said.

'Well if he turns up here again, he'll be sorry by the time I'm finished with him!' Eddie spat.

'He won't come back,' Sadie said, remembering the look of disgust on Mick's face as he took in the sight of his own child at the Grange. 'We've seen the last of him now.'

Eddie sighed deeply. 'What if . . . what if I had a word with Mr Marshall?' he offered. 'I could talk to him man to man, make him see sense and let you see the child again.'

'Speak to your gaffer? No, Eddie. I don't want you getting involved. You'd be putting your job at risk and I can't let you do that.'

'But I'd be speaking to him personally, at the Grange, as your . . . ' he smiled at Sadie, 'as your boyfriend, not at work as one of his miners.'

Sadie shook her head. 'I couldn't let you, Eddie. Really I couldn't.'

She thought of the man who had visited her in her bedroom at Freda's. The man who had walked away with Birdie in his arms.

'If anyone speaks to him, it has to be me,' she said. 'He doesn't even know I'm working at the Grange. It's going to be enough of a shock for him when he finds out who I am.'

'Then I'll come with you to tell him,' Eddie said.

'Perhaps,' Sadie said, and Eddie noticed a sadness in her voice. Sadie gently touched the side of her face. 'But not until all this settles down.'

'Then we've got a few days to think about what we'll say to him,' Eddie said. He stood from the sofa and paced the floor in front of the fireplace. 'We'll start off calmly but firmly. We'll tell him the truth, of course. Hell, we'll beg him if we have to!'

He turned when he heard a noise at the sitting room door. Bessie stood there holding the door with both hands, steadying herself.

'Sadie love. Some news has just come into the pub. Bad news, I'm afraid.'

Eddie took a step towards Sadie and laid a hand on her shoulder.

'What is it?' she asked.

'Oh love, there's no easy way to say this. John the gardener's just been in and he's asked me to tell you. Mrs Marshall, she — '

'They called the doctor when I left,' Sadie said hurriedly. 'What's happened, Bessie? What did John say?'

'He said she's gone, love. Mrs Marshall's passed away.'

10

Funeral

Winter 1919

Sadie jumped from her seat. 'I've got to go to her!'

'There's nothing can be done now, lass,' Bessie said softly. 'You'd best stay well away.'

'No!' Sadie cried, gathering her shawl about her. 'I don't mean Mrs Marshall. I've got to go to Birdie.'

Bessie and Eddie exchanged a look.

'I'll go with you,' Eddie said.

'Be careful, Sadie,' said Bessie. 'Let Em guide you through what's happening. They're not like us, those with money, and Mr Marshall is a stickler by all accounts. Grief can take a person a funny way; you have no idea what state he'll be in.'

Eddie put his cap on and buttoned up his coat. Then he took Sadie's arm and led her out of the sitting room and into the back yard of the pub. They walked past her bike, leaving it leaning against the netty wall as they headed out and away from the pub. The cold air of the autumn day felt raw against Sadie's swollen face, and she pulled her shawl tight. They walked in silence to the Grange, and once they reached its black iron gates, Eddie took Sadie's hands.

'Shall I come in with you?' he asked, but Sadie shook her head.

'It's best if I go in alone. I'll see what's happening, see if I can help Em. I need to make sure Birdie's looked after.' She glanced towards the bay windows of the house. 'They might not want me, I know that. There's a chance that Mr Marshall might already know that his wife dismissed me, if he spoke to her before she died. But I've got to see how things are in there. You understand that, don't you?'

Eddie leaned towards Sadie and kissed her lightly on the cheek. 'I've never met anyone like you, Sadie Linthorpe,' he smiled.

They walked past the big black car that was parked outside the Grange, to the back lane, where Eddie blew Sadie a kiss before she disappeared into the scullery. Em was there, boiling water on the coal fire with the big brown teapot ready by the fire. From the passageway leading off the scullery Sadie could hear men's voices. Em turned when she heard a noise at the door and wasn't surprised to see Sadie there.

'You've heard, then?' she said.

'Just now.' Sadie nodded. She took a step into the room. 'Em?'

Em was busy with the kettle, wrapping the handle of it with a cloth so that it didn't burn her hands. She kept her concentration on her work, preparing the tea for the doctor and Mr Marshall, who were waiting in the front parlour.

Sadie tried again. 'Em?'

Em filled the teapot with boiled water and

placed the lid on it. Then she set it down on a tray with cups, saucers and a jug of milk.

'Listen, Sadie,' she said. 'I haven't got time to chat, not right now. The doctor's still here and Mr Marshall is with him. Mrs Marshall's body has been taken but there's work to be done. The house will be in mourning, there's the funeral to think about, there's a million things I need to do.'

'And Alexandra?' Sadie asked. 'Does Mr Marshall know anything about who I really am?'

Em shook her head. 'I don't know, love. He spent a little time at his wife's bedside after John fetched him from the pit. We have no way of knowing whether she told him the truth about you before she passed on. If she didn't, then I'm willing to keep it a secret if you are, for heaven only knows I could do with an extra pair of hands around the place, especially in the coming days when the house will be busy with the wake.'

Sadie sank into a chair by the fire.

'If they did speak of it, she might have told him she'd dismissed me from my job.'

'No use worrying until we know what's been said,' Em replied. 'Now, don't just stand there looking gormless. I'm going to take this tea into the parlour and you can tend to Alexandra; she'll be waking soon from her nap. I'm just thankful she's too young to know what's gone on down here.'

She picked up the heavy tea tray and bustled away along the passage to the front of the house, leaving Sadie with much on her mind. She thought about what lay ahead, about finally coming face to face with Mr Marshall for the first time since that day at Freda's house. She'd remember him anywhere, that small, black, tidy moustache, his dark hair, the air of self-importance about him. But would he remember her? And if he did, what then? Would she be back out on the street, back at Bessie's begging for a bed for the night?

She took a deep breath and started to remove her shawl as she walked slowly up the stairs to Alexandra's bedroom. What would Mrs Marshall's death mean? she wondered. The child would never know of the death, not for many years to come, and only then if she was told. Would she remember the woman, have memories of her as she grew up? From all that Sadie had witnessed, there had been no maternal bond, indeed no bond at all, between the two of them. She had never once seen Mrs Marshall act towards Alexandra with kindness or love.

As Sadie played with Alexandra in her nursery, she heard a crashing noise from the room above. She picked the little girl up and walked with her in her arms to the landing. Something must have fallen, she thought, perhaps an ornament or a picture from the wall. But when she reached the second floor, the door to the spare room was open. This was the room where Sadie had seen a shaving brush and soap laid out on the dressing table, the room that Em had explained was used by Mr Marshall.

She edged towards the open door and pushed it with her free hand, then gasped with shock. Mr Marshall was sitting in front of the dressing table. She hadn't heard him walking up the stairs as she'd played in the nursery with Alexandra. He had his back to her, and his eyes met hers in the large central mirror. On either side, his face was reflected from the smaller mirrors too, three thin, pinched faces stared at Sadie. Three pairs of steely grey eyes, three tidy black moustaches. He was dressed in a black jacket, white shirt and black tie, his dark hair neatly parted and combed to one side.

Sadie stared at his reflections in the mirrors, unable to pull her gaze away. The room smelled not of the lavender and rosemary that scented the bedrooms and nursery of the house, but of something different and bitter. Mr Marshall's beady eyes took in Sadie's reflections in turn, the bruises from the beating from Mick and her shorn hair.

Alexandra cried out, breaking the silence that hung in the room, and wriggled in Sadie's arms, trying to free herself.

'Take the child away,' Mr Marshall said abruptly without turning around.

Sadie did as she was told. As she went to leave the room, she saw broken glass at Mr Marshall's feet, the remains of a bottle. She could clearly see the whisky label attached to a shard of glass as the spirit soaked into the mat.

She took Alexandra back to the nursery but left the door open, seating herself close by so that she could listen to what was going on in the rest of the house. From downstairs she heard the front door open and Em exchange words with a man who Sadie took to be the doctor. The front door closed again. She wondered if there might be sobbing from the floor above, the tears of a man who had just lost his wife. But all she heard was the sound of the dressing table stool being scraped across the floor, and Mr Marshall yelling: 'Damn it! Damn it to hell!'

★　★　★

Over the next few days, Sadie kept out of Mr Marshall's sight as much as she could. The bruises on her face faded, leaving no physical scars of the beating she had suffered. But the pains in her chest and back took longer to heal, serving as a reminder if one were needed of the evil that grew inside Mick.

Mr Marshall was spending time at home, taking the days of compassionate leave on which the two other pit managers insisted. Although he felt in need of no such leave, he knew he had to do what appeared the right, decent thing, especially where his fellow managers were concerned. Sadie looked after Alexandra and helped Em with the housework, including the tidying of Mrs Marshall's room, where, at her husband's request, the bed was stripped of its sheets and eiderdown. He also demanded that his wife's clothes be taken from the wardrobe and laid into wooden trunks. Personal items — a hairbrush, her perfume, jewellery and handbags — were kept separate, laid out on the naked double bed just as he'd asked.

Em assisted Mr Marshall in arranging the funeral. Reverend Daye of St Paul's called at the house to offer his condolences and to talk through the arrangements for the day. There was a small turnout expected, mainly Ryhope Coal Company officials and their wives. Ruth Marshall's spinster sister Esther was due to attend too, coming all the way from Newcastle by train.

On the evening before the funeral, Sadie was working with Em in the kitchen, cleaning glassware and polishing brass. Alexandra had already been put to bed and Mr Marshall was in the parlour, or so Em and Sadie thought. They were startled when he appeared unannounced at the kitchen door.

'I want to talk to the girl,' he said, nodding towards Sadie. He glanced at Em. 'Alone.'

Sadie and Em exchanged a look and Sadie laid down her glass cloth.

'Follow me,' he instructed, and headed towards the parlour.

Em was tempted to follow too, to listen in at the door, but then thought better of it. If she had learned one thing recently, it was that nothing good came from eavesdropping on a conversation not meant for her ears.

In the parlour, Mr Marshall settled into the large armchair beside the coal fire. Sadie stood in front of him, waiting for him to speak. He did not invite her to sit. He picked up a glass from a table at his side and took a sip from it. Keeping hold of the glass in both hands, he cleared his throat, then looked up at her, holding her gaze.

'How did you find us?' he asked.

The shock of his question made Sadie feel as if she had been punched in the chest. She wanted to reply with a question of her own — *How did you find out who I am?* — but thought better of it. His wife must have told him before she passed away, for who else had known? Em would not have betrayed her, and neither would Eddie or Bessie, she knew that.

She gave the same answer that she had given Mrs Marshall. 'I searched.'

Mr Marshall threw back his head and let out a bark of forced laughter. 'Oh! So you're a detective now, are you? And how, pray tell, does a penniless orphan in a lodging house become a detective?'

From his words, the way he spat out each one, and from the redness in his cheeks, Sadie could tell he was drunk. She'd seen the same look on Freda and Mick's faces back in Hartlepool and she knew she had to be on her guard.

'Thought you'd search us out, did you? Find your baby? Well, I paid for that child, and you know it. A deal was done with that woman you lived with. You can't just turn up here expecting a reunion.'

'No, sir,' Sadie said. 'Mrs Marshall employed me as the child's nurse. I have been working here for some time.'

'But Mrs Marshall is no longer here, of that I'm sure you are aware.'

Sadie didn't rise to the dark tone of his voice and the sarcasm of his words. She waited for him to say more, to tell her she was no longer employed as Alexandra's nurse, but he remained silent. It was a silence that Sadie dared to break.

'I'm a good nurse, sir. A good mother. I only

want the best for my child, you must see that, surely?'

Mr Marshall took another swig from his glass. 'And I want the best for the child too. Or should I say, the best price. That's why I'm sending it away.'

'No!' Sadie cried.

Mr Marshall held up his hand. 'It will go to my sister-in-law in Newcastle until she finds a buyer for it. There was a reason I bought your child, a reason that has everything to do with my position at the Ryhope Coal Company!' He banged his fist down on the armrest of the chair. 'Suffice to say, I have no need for it now, not with Mrs Marshall gone. I will not be saddled with a brat for no reason. So you see, your search has been in vain.'

'But — '

'And don't you dare refer to it as *your* child again! That child was bought in good faith; a financial transaction took place. It belongs to me in the same way . . . ' Mr Marshall scanned the parlour before his eyes rested on one of the framed pictures on the wall, 'in the same way as that painting!' He pointed to another picture. 'Or that one, or that. Alexandra is my property. Remember, girl, I bought her and I have the power to place her where I choose. You may stay in my employ as nurse until such time as she leaves for Newcastle. But the deal has been done. The child will be leaving in the new year. Now go.'

His words hardened Sadie, making her want to strike out, to pick up his whisky glass and throw

242

it at the wall. She felt her chest heave and tears spring behind her eyes. She turned to walk from the room, but before she reached the door, Mr Marshall called her back.

'And don't even think about taking her yourself, you hear me? I'm a man of position. All it would take is one call to my friends at Ryhope police station . . . '

Sadie turned her back on Mr Marshall and walked from the room, leaving his words hanging in the stuffy parlour air. She wasn't daft enough to get herself into trouble with the police. If it was her word against that of a pit boss, she knew who the authorities would believe. No, she had to think of another way that she and Birdie could stay together. There had to be one. She had come so far and gone through so much to get where she was now. She was not prepared to give up on her baby. She knew now, after being reunited with Birdie, that she would fight for her daughter every way she could — fair or foul.

★   ★   ★

The morning of Mrs Marshall's funeral dawned under a dark autumn sky. John the gardener had spent the previous day sweeping leaves from the path and raking them from the soil, making the garden look as presentable as possible for the bigwigs from the pit who were due for the wake. Em and Sadie were also pressed into service, baking fresh bread for beef sandwiches. These were to be laid out on the best china plates on the dining table, which had been lifted and pushed back against the dining room wall. Mr Marshall needed space for the mourners to wander freely, he'd told Em.

'Course, what he really means is he doesn't want them getting too comfortable,' Em confided to Sadie as they kneaded the dough for the bread. 'He wants them in and out as quick as you like. He'll give them a stiff drink, say a few words, and then that's it. You just watch, they won't stay long, he'll make sure of that.'

'Where does he go, Em?' Sadie asked. 'Before Mrs Marshall died, he was rarely home. He can't have been at work all those times, can he?'

Em cast a look towards the scullery door to ensure they weren't being overheard. She lowered her voice. 'Some say he's got a woman, a mistress. My husband Neville says he's heard gossip about him carrying on with a younger woman.'

'What's she like, this woman?' Sadie whispered.

Em shrugged. 'Young, pretty, bit on the common side, I've heard. But I can't say for sure as I've never seen her myself, and we shouldn't go repeating gossip outside the Grange, Sadie. Not if we want to keep our jobs.'

'He says he's giving Alexandra to his sister-in-law in Newcastle. He says she's going to sell her on to someone else.'

Em paused in her work, her hands deep in the bowl of dough. 'Is that right now?' she said at last.

'You didn't know?' Sadie asked.

'No,' Em replied. She started working the

244

dough again, harder this time. 'I've only met her once, when the Marshalls first moved in here.'

'Is she kind?' Sadie asked. 'Does she have children of her own?'

Em didn't reply, just kept on working the dough.

'She's Mrs Marshall's sister,' she said at last. 'There's something that must run in that family because no, she doesn't have children of her own either. And if you thought Mrs Marshall's bark was bad, then her sister's is even worse.'

Sadie's stomach churned. 'Would she take me on, Em? Do you think she'd employ me as Alexandra's nurse?'

'You'd do that?' Em asked, surprised. 'You'd leave Ryhope? But you don't even know how long the sister-in-law is going to keep the child. If she sells her on, as Mr Marshall says she will, would you really leave Eddie and move to Newcastle just to be with Alexandra for what could be a short time?'

'Maybe Eddie will come with me,' Sadie said softly. She hadn't yet thought things through. 'And if not, Newcastle's not too far away, is it?'

Em sighed. 'It's far enough to spoil a perfectly good couple who should be spending the rest of their lives together.'

Sadie knew, deep in her heart, that if it came to a choice between staying with Eddie and leaving to be with Birdie, she had to go with her child. No matter how much Eddie meant to her, Birdie was her flesh and blood. And if he wouldn't, or couldn't, leave Ryhope behind and follow her, then she'd have to go alone. Oh, but it would hurt to leave him. Just thinking about it made her heart feel as though it had been ripped from her chest. She felt closer to Eddie than she'd ever been to anyone before.

'I don't know what's to become of the Grange without the mistress,' Em said, interrupting her thoughts. 'It'll be just Mr Marshall to look after from now on. Mind you, I'm not complaining. Things will be a lot easier for me with him out at work all day, and no more pandering to Mrs Marshall's aches and pains and minding her sharp tongue.'

'Was she never friendly towards you, Em?' Sadie asked.

Em shook her head. 'Them lot never are. Think we're beneath them and only good enough to skivvy for them. Mr Marshall's not so bad, I've known worse, but he's an odd one deep down. Keeps himself to himself around the house; very private he is. I don't know what he's thinking, I really don't.'

Sadie remembered Mr Marshall's slurred, drunken words to her in the parlour earlier that week, and the smashed bottle of whisky under the dressing table. But she kept quiet. As Em had said, it was best not to repeat gossip about what went on in the house, not if she wanted to keep her job.

★   ★   ★

It was a small gathering at the Grange for the wake. The dining table was covered with a heavy black cloth on which the plates of sandwiches were laid out. Bottles were lined up on a side table with glasses into which Em measured whisky for the men and sherry for their wives. Sadie did as Mr Marshall had instructed and brought Alexandra into the parlour for inspection by his sister-in-law. She held tight to the child's hand as she took hesitant steps towards the mourners. There were several representatives from the Ryhope Coal Company, along with their wives, two of whom Sadie recognised from the picnic at the beach. They smiled at Alexandra and passed compliments to Mr Marshall on such a bonny bairn, and their condolences on her being left without her dear, doting mother.

Sadie recognised Esther the minute she saw her. Her face wore the same pained expression as Mrs Marshall's had, as if everything around her was unpleasant and deserving of disdain. Her hair, from what Sadie could see escaping from the black hat she wore tied with a black ribbon, was the same gentle auburn as Mrs Marshall's had been. But she was taller and sturdier than her sister, healthier, with a ruddiness to her cheeks.

'Is *this* the child?' Sadie heard her ask Mr Marshall as she pointed towards Alexandra.

Sadie looked at Mr Marshall, who indicated with his hand for her to come forward. She gently manoeuvred Alexandra in his direction, and then she and the child stood hand in hand under Esther's steely gaze.

'You know I can't take her until well after Christmas.'

'Yes, Esther, you've told me,' Mr Marshall

replied. 'In fact, you've said so many times.'

The woman stared at the child. Then she turned her head and spoke in a low voice.

'And you're certain there's no one who will buy her from you in Ryhope? You can't get a return on your investment here? There must be someone, surely?'

Mr Marshall looked at Sadie and caught her gaze for the briefest of moments.

'No one,' he said firmly. 'Now come. I need to refill my glass.'

He took his sister-in-law by the arm and led her into the dining room, leaving Sadie and Alexandra standing alone.

★ ★ ★

After the mourners had left, the Grange fell silent. Em and Sadie cleared away the plates and glasses, washed them and stored them away. Sadie bathed Alexandra, running her fingertips across the ladybird birthmark on the child's shoulder, delighting in the bond between them. Her daughter was happy and laughing, unaware of the events that had unfolded around Mrs Marshall's death and the uncertain life that lay ahead for them all.

Once Alexandra was asleep, Sadie and Em sat by the fire in the kitchen, talking for a while, before Sadie headed to her room. Sleep didn't come easy as her mind turned over thoughts of Alexandra, and the cruel hardness to the faces of Mr Marshall and Esther. She thought of Bessie and Pat at the Forester's Arms, and of Eddie too.

For the first time in her life, she felt settled and happy. She had friends, and a boyfriend she could finally admit she loved. Eddie had proclaimed his love for her that day he'd stood up to his mam in the kitchen of the Railway Inn. And now she knew she felt the same way. The thought of him made her feel happier than anything else, apart from being with Birdie. And yet she would have to give it all up to start again in Newcastle if that was what it took to be with her daughter.

Confused, jumbled thoughts fluttered across her mind as she fell into a fitful sleep. When she woke, it was still dark outside. Too dark to be morning, she knew, even though it was October now and the days were darkening towards winter. She lay still in her bed and listened. Was that a woman's voice she could hear? A tinkle of laughter reached her, a shushing noise, then more laughter, a man's voice now. And then a door slamming shut on the floor below.

Sadie eased herself from her bed and tiptoed to her bedroom door. She pulled it open and listened. Again she heard the voices; again there was laughter. She began to make her way downstairs, treading the floorboards as gently as she could so as not to make herself heard. Just before she reached the landing, the door to Mr Marshall's room flew open. Sadie stepped back quickly, pressing her body against the wall, making sure she couldn't be seen by whoever was in the room. A woman danced across the landing, her hips swinging from side to side, her arms waving in the air. She was humming a tune

Sadie didn't recognise.

'Don't be long, Dinah!' a voice called out in a childish sing-song. 'Joe's waiting!'

Sadie gasped with shock. It was Mr Marshall's voice, and it was coming from his room. She craned her neck and peered across the landing. She saw the woman disappear into the bathroom and then emerge a few moments later, heading back to Mr Marshall's room. The door was slammed shut behind her.

Sadie froze, unable to move from the shock of what she'd seen. Who was Dinah? She didn't look familiar, and Sadie was sure she'd have remembered that face if she'd been at Mrs Marshall's wake earlier. Was she the young, pretty woman that Em had mentioned? From the glimpse that Sadie had been given of her, there was a touch of something common about her as Em had described. Yes, she would definitely say that, having seen the woman's heavily made-up bow lips and smoky eyes. Sadie judged Mr Marshall harshly, with his wife not yet cold in her grave.

★ ★ ★

When Sadie woke again, she heard the sound of heavy rain belting against the small window in the sloping roof above her bed. She was due at the Forester's that morning to help Bessie bake pies, and she prayed the rain would ease before she set out on her bike. She lay still, listening to the rain, remembering the woman from the night before, turning her name over in her mind. She wondered if Dinah was still in the house, still in bed with Mr Marshall.

She got out of bed and washed at the bowl in her room, as Em had told her never to use the indoor bathroom while Mr Marshall was about the house. It was a rule she adhered to strictly, apart from when she was bathing Alexandra. She dressed quickly in the cold room, pulling on as many layers as she could and covering her head with her shawl, then crept down the stairs. The last thing she wanted to do was wake Mr Marshall and Dinah if they were still sleeping. But she needn't have worried, for the door to the bedroom was open when she passed, with no sound from within.

When she reached the ground floor, she looked out of the window but saw no sign of Mr Marshall's black car. She wondered what a woman like Dinah, a pretty woman who could have any man she wanted, saw in someone like Joe Marshall. He was short and thin, not unpleasant-looking but certainly not handsome. And there was something about him, something a little oily in the way he comported himself, as if he was bestowing his presence on those around him and they ought to feel grateful to have him in their company. Sadie thought him a strange man, but she had no choice other than to stay on his good side while she was living under his roof. All she knew was that she had to make the most of every day with Alexandra. For who knew what would happen when Mr Marshall's sister-in-law came to take the child? But that was for the future, still weeks away. For now, she had to continue to make ends meet, and that meant getting up to the Forester's as quickly as she could through the rain.

★ ★ ★

Bessie was more than happy to see her, and especially glad to see that Sadie's hair had started to grow and soften around her face. She wanted to hear all about Mrs Marshall's funeral, and Sadie shared the previous night's revelations. Bessie was not surprised to hear about Dinah; it merely confirmed the gossip that she'd heard. But she was saddened and upset to hear of Sadie's plans to move away if Mrs Marshall's sister accepted her as the child's nurse.

'Esther's coming back after Christmas,' Sadie explained. 'But Bessie, she wasn't a good woman, or a nice one. She didn't so much as look at Birdie when she came to the Grange.'

'Birdie? You call the child by the name you chose?'

'Never at the Grange,' Sadie explained. 'I wouldn't do that, Bessie. It'd confuse the child when she's still getting used to her own name.'

'Good on you, lass,' Bessie replied.

'But the sister-in-law, she's taking Birdie to sell,' Sadie continued. 'Mr Marshall says he has no need for her since Mrs Marshall passed on, and he says Esther will find a buyer. They're treating her worse than a dog, passing her from home to home like an unwanted mongrel. And it's all for appearances' sake only. Mr Marshall never wanted a child. Em said he only came and

252

took mine because Mrs Marshall couldn't have a bairn of her own and they needed to look as if they were a happy family, to help his career at the pit.'

'And I bet he thinks his career at the pit will be hampered now he's a widower with a small child?' Bessie bristled. 'It's not right, I tell you. I wish I could do more to help, Sadie. Me and Pat might have been able to offer you the money to buy her yourself, but we're barely able to scrape a living as it is.'

'No, Bessie! That's not what I'm asking, I would never ask it of you,' Sadie cried.

'I know, pet,' Bessie said. 'But if I could buy the bairn for you, you know I would.'

As the rain threw itself against the windows and bounced up from the flagstones in the yard, Bessie hugged Sadie tightly to her.

'Oh love,' she said softly. 'I can't bear to lose you to Newcastle. But I'd never stop you from following your bairn.'

'I have no choice,' Sadie replied. 'If that's what it comes to, then that's what I must do.'

Bessie let her go and put her hands on the girl's shoulders. 'In Ireland, you know, women helped each other, we always did. And I've found that same spirit in Ryhope.'

Sadie nodded in agreement.

'I'd like to do something,' Bessie said. 'It's something I've not done since I left Dublin, but it feels right to do it now, especially if I'm going to lose you. It's something I've often thought of doing for my girls, Branna and Cara. And I think of you as one of my own now, you know.'

'What is it?'

Bessie sank into a chair by the fire. The pies were cooking in the oven and the aroma of pastry baking with corned beef inside filled the small room. Sadie sat in the seat opposite.

'Christmas is coming, and in Ireland we used to have two of them.'

'Two Christmases?' Sadie smiled.

'One for the family, on Christmas Day, and one for the women afterwards. Little Christmas, we called it. We had the main one on Christmas Day itself. And then on the twelfth day of Christmas, the sixth of January, we had the Women's Christmas. And that's the best part of all, Sadie, it's just for us girls.'

'No men?'

Bessie shook her head. 'No men, no boys. No Pat Brogan, no Eddie, no Mr Marshall, none of them. This is just for us, Sadie. A day to call our own, to get together and eat, drink, share our secrets and open our hearts.'

Sadie's face dropped. 'But does it mean we need to bring gifts? I know I couldn't afford to pay.'

'No gifts,' Bessie said. 'No need to bring anything. You and I will do the baking — pies, cakes, the works. We'll hold it right here in the pub.'

'In the sitting room?'

'No, love. I mean in the front bar. I'll close the pub for the night and send Pat next door to the Colliery Inn. His bad hip will allow him to walk that far, at least.'

'You'll close the pub?' Sadie laughed. 'But there'll be ructions on! You'll have a crowd of angry punters at the door banging on it until you let them in!'

'Let the buggers bang on as long and loud as they want,' Bessie cried. 'This is going to be our day, our Little Christmas.' She started counting on her fingers. 'So, let's see. There'll be you and me and our Branna and Cara and their daughters. Branna's got two girls and Cara's got one. Then I'll invite Hetty from the Albion, Lil Mahone, Em . . . and I was thinking of asking Molly from the Railway Inn.'

'Oh.'

'Don't tell me you two haven't made up yet?'

'I haven't seen her,' Sadie said quietly. 'I don't even get to see Eddie much these days. He's working night shifts right now, and looking after Birdie at the Grange takes up all of my time when I'm not baking and delivering pies around Ryhope.'

Bessie stroked her chin. 'Well, Molly's my friend and I can't imagine organising a Little Christmas without inviting her. You've got time, love, a few weeks yet. See if the two of you can't make things up, eh?'

Sadie gazed into the fire. 'Could I bring Birdie?' she asked.

'I'd be disappointed if you didn't,' Bessie replied. 'But how are you going to get Mr Marshall to agree to you taking the child from the house? And what if the sister-in-law reappears before then?'

Sadie thought of Dinah, the woman with the painted face, the bow lips and smoky eyes. She thought of Mrs Marshall, who she had judged so

255

harshly when she'd been alive. But now she knew what a life she must have led with her philandering husband, and how coping with the lie of living with such a man could have hardened her to people.

'I think I might have a bit of leverage with Mr Marshall,' Sadie said slowly. She lifted her gaze to meet Bessie's. 'Knowing things about him, knowing what he gets up to at home and how at odds it all is with his professional life . . . '

'No,' Bessie said firmly. 'You can't be talking like that, Sadie. That's blackmail, and it's wrong.'

Sadie sat back in her chair. 'Not blackmail,' she said, shaking her head. 'Knowing his secrets means having a little bit of power over him, that's all.'

'Well, just you be careful,' Bessie warned.

She stood and took a heavy cloth from the kitchen table, wrapped it around her hands and pulled the tray with the meat pies from the oven, setting it on a cooling rack on the table.

'Now then, how about some breakfast while we're waiting for these to cool down?'

'Sounds perfect,' Sadie replied, grateful beyond words for Bessie's love and care.

★ ★ ★

In the following weeks, the wet and windy days of autumn gave way to frosty mornings and bitterly cold nights. In the big houses around the village green, Christmas trees were put on display in the bay windows, as much to impress passers-by as to be enjoyed within, and lights from candles sparkled. Sadie found the sight magical, taking her back to her childhood with her parents. There'd been no such festivities while she'd been living at Freda's.

Up at the Forester's Arms, Christmas decorations were hung. Paper chains of all colours were strung across the ceiling, and the glass cases on the walls with the stuffed dog and pigeons inside were festooned too. Shops on the colliery changed their window displays, offering all kinds of sweet items as Christmas treats. The windows of the Co-op were stuffed full of fruit cakes and pastries, sugared mice and marzipan fruits. There was an air of goodwill about Ryhope. Everywhere, that was, apart from at the Grange.

'He's never liked Christmas,' Em confided to Sadie. 'And now Mrs Marshall is no longer here, he'll see no need to pretend he's feeling jolly or festive.'

'Will there be a Christmas meal?' Sadie asked, but Em shook her head.

'He's not asked for anything this year. And he usually lets me know by now if he wants a turkey bought.'

'Will you be working here on Christmas Day, Em?'

'Not if there's nothing to do. I'll take the day off like everyone else. You'll be all right with the child, won't you?'

Sadie smiled. The thought of spending a whole day with Alexandra, just the two of them together, playing and singing and laughing, filled her heart with glee.

'Oh, I'll be fine,' she said. 'And Eddie said he'd call on Christmas morning.'

'Just as long as he calls at the scullery door, remember,' Em told her. 'He'll be welcome in the kitchen, but not in the rooms at the front. They're not ours to enjoy. I dare say you two could make yourselves cosy here with the fire going, the kettle on to boil, a piece of fruit cake and a slice of fresh pie.'

★   ★   ★

When Christmas morning broke, Sadie leapt out of bed. A whole day lay ahead, hers and Birdie's alone. Mr Marshall had told her that he planned to spend the day with friends, and Sadie wondered who these friends might be, for she had seen none ever visit the Grange. Of his return he had made no mention, and she suspected he might be staying out overnight with Dinah.

She dressed quickly then hurried to Birdie's room, where the child was already awake, laughing in her crib. Sadie peeked out of the window by the front door, but Mr Marshall's car was nowhere to be seen. She breathed a sigh of relief, knowing that she had the whole house to herself. With no Em around the place, the Grange seemed quiet and much bigger. She dressed her daughter and took her to the kitchen to feed her.

Eddie called at the scullery door at mid morning and Sadie greeted him with Alexandra in her arms.

'Merry Christmas, Sadie,' he said, leaning in

to kiss her lightly on the lips. Then he kissed the tip of his finger and pressed it gently to Birdie's nose, making her giggle. 'Merry Christmas, little one,' he said. He took off his coat and scarf and warmed himself by the fire.

'Sit down, Eddie,' said Sadie. 'I'll make us some tea.'

Eddie reached for the child. 'May I?'

Sadie passed her daughter over into his strong, capable hands.

'I've never held a bairn before,' he said.

Sadie smiled. 'You look a natural to me.' She busied herself with the kettle at the fireplace.

'What should I say to her?' Eddie asked.

'Say anything you like, it doesn't matter. All she needs to hear is your voice and how you sound. She likes a song, if you're up to singing.'

'A song, eh?' Eddie thought for a moment and then softly began to sing, a song about coal mining and the men who hewed the dusky diamonds from the earth. Alexandra wriggled in his arms, reaching out with her chubby little hands to his face and his mouth.

When the tea was ready, Sadie took the child from him and she and Eddie sat facing each other in their chairs by the fire. Birdie was between them, sitting on a clippy mat, playing with a wooden spoon.

'Cold out,' Eddie said.

'Not much warmer in here,' Sadie replied. 'Think I'll stay in the kitchen all day, have my dinner in here and play with her until it's time for bed.'

'The mister not in then?'

Sadie shook her head. 'And I don't know if he'll be back later, either.'

'What do you mean?'

'I think he's got a mistress.'

Eddie put his mug of tea down on the fireside. 'Mr Marshall?' he cried. 'Are you sure?'

Sadie nodded. 'She was here. The night of Mrs Marshall's funeral, he had her in his room upstairs. I saw her with my own eyes.'

Eddie sank back into his chair. 'Well I never! I'd heard gossip, of course. But he's one of the pit gaffers, he shouldn't be getting up to things like that.'

Sadie took a sip of her tea. 'There's something else I need to tell you, Eddie, and I don't think you're going to like it.'

Eddie listened as Sadie poured out the story about Mrs Marshall's sister planning on taking Birdie to Newcastle. And when she told him that she was thinking of following her child there as her nurse, even for what might be a very short time, his heart broke with her every word.

'I couldn't bear to lose you, Sadie, I just couldn't.'

'You could come with me,' she said quietly, hopefully.

'Leave Ryhope? Leave Mam and the pub and my job?'

'I don't know what else to do.'

A silence hung between them for a few minutes, the only sound the crackle of the flames as they licked around the coal in the fire.

'Well, I know what to do,' Eddie declared at last.

He stood and gave a little cough to clear his throat. Sadie watched, puzzled, as he sank to the kitchen floor on bent knee. He whipped his flat cap off his head and clutched it to his heart. With his free hand, he reached for her.

'Sadie,' he said, looking straight into her eyes. 'Whatever comes next, whatever happens to you, to your child, I won't let you go through it alone. We're going to face things together, you and me. That's if you'll have me, of course.'

Sadie felt her heart quicken. 'Are you asking me to marry you, Eddie Teasdale?' Tears sprang to her eyes, unbidden. Knowing that Eddie was offering himself to her, forever, overwhelmed her. She took hold of his hand, this man that she loved, that she wanted to spend her life with. She knew she wanted nothing more than to accept him.

Eddie nodded. 'What do you say, Sadie? I can't bear to lose you. Whatever happens, let me help you, let me look after you and Birdie.'

She gently squeezed his hand. 'Oh Eddie, my heart says yes. You must know it says yes. But my head says I can't.'

Eddie's face clouded over as she explained. 'I can't, Eddie. Not yet. There's something I need to do first.'

11

The Women's Little Christmas

1919–1920

'Mam? Have you got a minute?'

'What is it, Eddie? Can't you see I've got my hands full? I could do with your help behind the bar. God only knows where Tom's gone. He still hasn't come home from last night.'

'Mam? Please?'

Molly looked up from the pint of Vaux stout she was pulling at the bar. She froze when she saw Sadie there, standing with a bairn in her arms.

'What's *she* doing here?'

'We need to speak to you, Mam. Sadie's got something she wants to say.'

Molly slid the pint across the bar to her customer and took payment for it. Then she turned to pull on the thick cord that rang the heavy old bell at the bar. 'Time, gentlemen, please!' she yelled.

'You can't close yet, it's far too flaming early!' a voice called back.

'It's Christmas Day, Mam. Let the fellas stay and have a drink,' said Eddie. 'I'll come and help you behind the bar until closing time.'

'Tom should be here. Where the devil is he?

262

Anyway, I can close when I damn well please. It's my pub and I'll do what I want.'

A murmur of grumbling went up around the bar, but the customers knew that no matter how much they protested, they'd never sway Molly Teasdale once she'd made up her mind.

Over the course of the next fifteen minutes, the pub began to empty.

'I'll take my business over to the Albion Inn if I can't get served in here,' one of the customers hissed. But Molly was too exhausted to care.

With the last customer gone, she bolted the pub doors and walked through to the kitchen at the back, Pip at her heels. Eddie motioned for Sadie to follow, and they trooped after her. Molly sank into her chair by the fire.

'Shall I put the kettle on, Mam?' Eddie asked.

'Might as well. Dare say you might as well bring a bottle of brandy through from the bar too.'

'That's very generous of you, Mam.'

Molly looked towards Sadie. 'Oh, it's not to celebrate the day. It's to take the shock off whatever it is she's come to tell me. Now sit down and stop making the place look untidy.'

Sadie took the seat opposite Molly and positioned Birdie on her knee. She saw Molly take in the child's features, and a soft smile settle itself around her lips. Eddie returned with three glasses of brandy. He handed one to his mam and another to Sadie.

Molly raised her glass. 'Merry Christmas to you both, and to the little 'un.'

'Merry Christmas,' Sadie replied. She put the

glass down by the fireside without taking a sip. She wanted to keep a clear head. Eddie stood behind her chair with his hand resting on her shoulder.

'Come on then, out with it,' Molly said. She swirled the amber liquid around her glass.

Sadie took a deep breath. 'I've come to apologise, Molly.'

Molly took a sip of her drink but said nothing, simply waiting for Sadie to explain.

'You took me in when I had nowhere to live, no job and no friends. I should have told you, Molly, I should have. But you can see how I'm fixed. A young girl with a child, I . . . ' She dropped her gaze to the floor. 'I was terrified you'd throw me out if you knew the truth, knew the real reason I'd come to Ryhope.'

'You shouldn't have lied,' Molly said quietly. 'I can take pretty much anything from folk, but not lying, Sadie.'

Sadie sat forward. 'I'm sorry, Molly, please let me — '

'No,' Molly said firmly. She looked into Sadie's eyes and saw them brimming with tears. 'It's me who should be apologising. I called you something that day that I shouldn't have, and I've regretted it ever since. But I can see how close you and Eddie are now and I just hope you can forgive me. And please, promise me one thing: that you'll be honest with me from now on. That you'll never lie again. I just wish you'd been honest from the start.'

'I know,' Sadie said. 'There's not a day since I moved out of here that I haven't said that to myself. I've a lot to learn, Molly. About being a mother, about being — '

Eddie gave her shoulder a gentle squeeze. 'My wife.'

Molly turned her gaze towards her son. 'Your what?'

'I've asked her to marry me, Mam.'

'I haven't said yes,' Sadie added. 'I couldn't, Molly. Not until I'd spoken to you face to face to find out if you'd accept my apology. I love Eddie with all my heart. Since the minute I met him, I've always known. But if you can't forgive me, I'll move on and away, for I'd never want to come between you and your son. I don't want to be the cause of any more problems for either of you.'

'You'd take on another man's bairn?' Molly demanded of Eddie.

'I'd be taking on Sadie's bairn,' he said proudly.

Molly held her glass out. 'Put another drop in there, son, a big drop. I think I'm going to need it.'

Eddie did as he was told. Molly sat quietly at the fireside, lost in her thoughts. Birdie began to squirm in Sadie's arms, mewling as if ready to cry.

'Shush now,' said Sadie. 'Shush.'

Molly looked from Sadie to Eddie, and then at the little girl. She put her glass down.

'Give her here,' she said.

Sadie stood, walked towards Molly and handed her daughter to her. Once the child was settled, Molly looked up at her son.

'This is what you truly want?'

Eddie simply nodded in reply.

She turned her gaze to Sadie. 'And you'll look after him?'

'Every day,' replied Sadie. 'Every minute of every day.'

'No more lies? No more keeping things from us?'

Sadie shook her head. 'Never.'

Molly eyed her keenly. 'What have you done to your hair, lass? Why cut it all off? It was beautiful the way you had it.'

'It's a long story,' she said. 'But I will tell you, Molly, I promise. And I'll tell you about the Marshalls and what's going on there, too.'

Molly looked deep into Birdie's big brown eyes. She stroked the child's hair back from her face. 'And what's the name of your little one?' she asked.

Sadie paused. She had been about to offer the name that she'd been using at the Grange, the name that had been given to her bairn by another woman. But there was no need to use that name with Molly, not now the truth was being told.

'Birdie,' she said. 'I named her Birdie.'

'And at the Grange?' asked Molly. 'Does Mr Marshall call her that?'

'Her name there is Alexandra.'

Molly stroked the child's cheek with her finger and was rewarded with a wide smile. 'Well, she'll be called Birdie here.'

Eddie and Sadie exchanged a smile.

'And you have my blessing, the two of you.'

Molly raised her gaze and Sadie saw the tears in her eyes. 'Welcome to the family, Sadie love,' she said. 'Welcome back.'

★　★　★

The days between Christmas and New Year were bitterly cold, with sleet brought in on biting winds. Mr Marshall had returned to work, but his evenings were spent alone in the parlour at the Grange, drinking and poring over paperwork. Em told Sadie it was pit work he was doing there each evening, as she'd seen the crest of the Ryhope Coal Company on the piles of papers he read. Sadie noticed that he seemed preoccupied, with much on his mind.

The year turned without any celebration at the Grange, and still Mr Marshall locked himself away in the parlour each evening. It was Em who persuaded him to allow Sadie to take Alexandra to Bessie's Little Christmas on the evening of 6 January. He wasn't happy about it at first, but he soon relented when she pointed out, in no uncertain terms, that Sadie was due a night off. When faced with the option of either letting her take the child with her or looking after Alexandra at home himself, Mr Marshall gave in.

Em and Sadie knew nothing of the real reason for Mr Marshall's tense and anxious frame of mind. He had much to think about, troubled by events that his lady friend Dinah had brought to his door. He tried to immerse himself in paperwork to take his mind off matters, and he was glad of the quiet of an empty house on the night Sadie took the child to the Forester's to celebrate the Women's Christmas.

★   ★   ★

Pat Brogan was not a happy man. He had his coat, scarf and hat on and was ready to leave the pub.

'I can't believe you're closing tonight,' he sighed. 'I just can't believe it. Do you know how much money we'll be losing?'

'Aw, Pat,' Bessie replied. 'It's a bitterly cold Tuesday night in January. We're hardly going to be doing a roaring trade, now are we? Anyway, the women are coming, it's all arranged. I'm not going back on it now. We've never had a Little Christmas here in England, and nothing's going to spoil it, you hear? So, where are you off to?'

'Might be able to manage to walk next door to the Colliery Inn, I guess,' Pat sniffed.

'Well, don't come back before midnight,' Bessie warned him.

'Yes, dear,' said Pat.

Bessie hugged her husband to her.

'Have a good night,' he said. He kissed her on the cheek and then headed out of the door.

Left alone inside the pub, Bessie busied herself pulling the small wooden tables and chairs into a semicircle by the fire, arranging them so that the women could sit and chat. She took a handful of candles from behind the bar, lit them and placed them in old jam jars dotted around on the tables. The light from the candles glittered and shone, the whole effect cosy and welcoming. On the bar top was laid out a selection of pies, cakes and freshly baked stottie bread.

There was a loud bang at the front door and she heard a man cry, 'Bessie? You open? I'm dying of thirst here!'

'We're shut!' she yelled back.

'Shut? But you're never shut!'

'We are tonight!'

She would open the front door only when she was good and ready, and only when she heard the voices of her daughters and granddaughters and the friends who had been invited for the night.

Bessie stood with her hands on her hips, surveying the scene in front of her. Never had the pub looked so pretty, never had it twinkled so brightly, with the candlelight dancing in the shadows. The only other light came from the coal fire around which the chairs and tables were placed. As a girl growing up in Ireland, the Women's Little Christmas had been as important to Bessie's mam, aunts and grandma as Christmas Day itself. It was the day when the women relaxed after the rigours of looking after their families during the busy festive time; the day when they let their hair down with no men to judge them or spoil their fun. It was a time for talking, for telling stories and exchanging fragments of their lives, a gathering like no other. And now here she was, hosting her own Little Christmas in her own little pub. It might just be for a few hours, but by God, she'd spent a long time looking forward to it.

First to arrive were Branna and her two

daughters, teenager Ellen and seven-year-old Ada. Branna was the double of her mother, everyone said so, with a face that could have soured milk, but oh, when she smiled, she could light up a room. They were followed by Cara and her daughter, who was named after Bessie herself and known to all as young Bess. She was just four years old. Cara took after her dad in the way of looks, but both girls had their mother's no-nonsense way about them. Lil Mahone arrived next, flushed with excitement at being away from the house without Bob, a rare night out on her own. She couldn't recall the last time she'd done that, as she told Bessie over again.

The women set to placing the food from the bar on the small tables in front of the fire as they waited for the others to arrive. Sadie was next, with Molly and Hetty Burdon who ran the Albion Inn. Molly and Hetty had walked arm in arm from the village, Sadie alongside them carrying Birdie. Last to arrive was Em, who received a warm cheer as she entered the pub.

'We're all here, ladies,' Bessie cried. 'Let our Little Christmas begin!'

The women took their seats and the children — Ellen, Ada and young Bess — sat on the floor at their mothers' feet, warming themselves by their fire.

'So, this is an Irish thing, is that right, Bessie?' Hetty asked.

'It's called Nollaig na mBan,' Bessie replied, her Irish brogue coming through strong.

'I wouldn't like to try saying that after a couple of glasses of sherry,' Lil Mahone called out, and the group dissolved into laughter.

'Speaking of sherry,' Bessie said as she walked towards the bar. 'The drinks are on the house tonight. Whatever you want you can have.'

Ellen turned to Branna. 'Can I have a beer, Mam?'

Branna shook her head. 'Nice try, young 'un. You'll have a lemonade and be thankful I've brought you.'

Branna walked to the bar to help Bessie pour the drinks. 'The bread looks great, Mam,' she enthused. 'It's good to have it made with proper flour again. While it was being rationed I had to mix it with maize and it brought the bairns out in a rash. War-bread face, they were calling it.'

'Not any more,' smiled Bessie. 'Proper flour's back in the shops now, sugar too at the Co-op. Everything all right at home, love? How's Daniel?'

'Moaning about being left at home on his own. But apart from that, he's much the same. How's Dad?'

'Moaning about having to go all the way next door to the Colliery Inn for a pint instead of having one in his own pub.'

'How's his hip?'

'Not good, pet. But he won't see the doctor; you know what he's like, the stubborn old goat.'

Bessie and Branna exchanged a smile.

'Here, take this to the lasses,' Bessie said, handing her daughter a tray of glasses filled with wine, gin and sherry. A small glass of stout was also on the tray, as Bessie knew that was Lil's choice of tipple. When everyone had a drink,

Bessie proposed a toast.

'To friends,' she said, raising her glass. 'To us.'

Sadie sat with Birdie on her knee. After the initial excitement, the child had fallen asleep in her arms. The food that she and Bessie had baked earlier was served on plates with red patterned paper napkins.

'Can I take some of this pie home for Bob?' Lil asked, but she didn't wait for an answer and was already wrapping slices of beef and potato pie in a napkin and sliding them into her hand-bag. 'He likes a nice bit of pie.'

'How's things down at the Albion, Hetty?' Bessie asked.

Hetty nodded, chewing furiously on an egg sandwich. 'Good,' she said at last. 'Got the new Vaux beer in last week, it's going down a treat.'

'And how's your Jack coping?' Bessie asked.

Hetty took her time to answer, and when she did, she spoke quietly, averting her gaze. 'Philip's passing remains hard on us both.'

A silence hung over the group and Molly reached out to pat Hetty's arm. Hetty shook her head, and wisps of her auburn hair fell around her face.

'Never mind me. How's things with you, Molly?'

Molly glanced at Sadie. 'I'm fine,' she said. 'We're fine.' She looked at the faces of the women sitting around the fire. 'We've got a bit of news, Sadie and I.'

Sadie gave her the tiniest of nods, allowing her to tell the tale.

'We're going to be family. Our Eddie's proposed . . .'

' . . . and I've said yes,' added Sadie.

Bessie's hand flew to her heart. 'Oh, that's fantastic news!' she cried. She moved from her seat and leaned down to Sadie, planting a kiss on her cheek. 'I've never met a more well-suited couple. I'm over the moon about it, I really am.'

She turned to Molly. 'And you're getting a good one here for your daughter-in-law,' she said, pointing towards Sadie.

Molly laid her hand on Sadie's arm and the two women exchanged a smile.

'To Sadie and Eddie!' Bessie cried, raising her glass.

'Sadie and Eddie!' everyone replied as the toast was drunk.

'And I'm heartily glad you two have made up,' Bessie said sagely, glancing between Molly and Sadie. 'It's about time.'

'Many congratulations to you both.' Lil nodded towards Sadie, taking another sip of her drink.

'What about you, Lil?' Molly asked. 'What have you been up to when you're not stealing Bessie's pies?'

The joke was lost on Lil, who took umbrage at Molly's remark. 'I'll have you know I don't go stealing nothing,' she sniffed. 'If you must know, I've been out and about, doing what I can to make ends meet. Which is more than can be said for some in Ryhope.'

Around the fire, the women nodded to each other. There was a lot of eye contact and raised eyebrows, but no names mentioned, for fear that the bairns would overhear and pass on names at school.

'I was in town yesterday with Bob, like,' Lil said.

'What on earth were you doing down there?' Bessie asked. 'Where've you been getting money to spend in town?'

'Oh, I wasn't spending,' Lil said. She took a long gulp from her glass of stout. 'We were looking at rooms to let.'

'You thinking of moving, then, Lil?' Molly asked.

Lil shook her head. 'There's always rooms to let, and Mondays, I'd heard, are the best days to go and look. There's one landlord in the town gives you the keys so you can view the rooms yourself. So it's not that we're wanting to move, but it gets us inside and we can see if the previous tenants have left anything behind.'

Bessie sucked in air through her teeth and Molly tutted loudly.

'Eeh! Lil Mahone, you should be ashamed of yourself,' said Bessie.

Lil sat up straight in her chair. 'Don't see why. We're as skint as anyone else in Ryhope. If there's free stuff going, then who's to know if we take it?'

'Jesus knows,' Ada piped up from her place at Branna's feet. 'That's what they tell us in Sunday school.'

Branna stroked her daughter's hair. 'That's right, love,' she said, smiling towards Lil and rolling her eyes.

But Lil wasn't finished. 'And Jesus also knows that me and Bob are so skint that not so long ago we didn't even have a pot to pi — '

'Lil!' Cara said, nodding towards the children.

274

'Mind your language.'

'We didn't have a pot to call our own,' Lil went on, careful of her words now. 'When we were first wed, we were so poor that we couldn't go out together; one of us had to stay at home.'

'Why on earth was that?' Hetty asked.

'We only had one pair of boots between us,' Lil laughed. 'Oh, I can smile about it now, but I tell you, if Jesus ever saw what was going on back then, he did bugger all to help us out. I had to stuff the boots with balled-up pages of *The Sunderland Echo* because they were Bob's, too big for my tiny feet. I wore them when I went to the shops and the market, and he had them to go to work at the pit and when he went to the pub. So now that you've asked, I'll tell you again — no, I feel no shame in going looking in lodging rooms for anything that's been left behind. Why should I?'

Bessie walked towards Lil and took her empty glass from her.

'I'll get you another, love,' she said, and headed towards the bar.

Sadie shifted in her seat, positioning the sleeping Birdie so that she was more comfortable holding the child.

'Thanks for the cycling skirt you made for me, Cara,' she said.

'My pleasure,' Cara smiled. 'Mam said you've been helping with the baking and selling pies around Ryhope.'

Molly leaned towards Sadie. 'Will you be bringing them down for me to sell in the Railway Inn, love?'

'Course I will,' Sadie said.

'How old's your bairn?' Cara asked, nodding towards Birdie.

'Well, she's not . . . I mean, I'm her mam but I daren't believe that she's really mine,' Sadie confessed.

All eyes turned towards her. Even the children sitting on the floor looked up, waiting for an explanation. Sadie took a deep breath and started to tell her tale. She told them about her baby being taken from her arms by the man she now knew as Mr Marshall, about how her search for Birdie had led her to Ryhope, to the Railway Inn, to Molly and Eddie. At this point she faltered slightly, unsure how much she should reveal, but with Molly's gentle encouragement, she confided about their falling-out and her move to the Forester's Arms.

'Sadie love, you've been through a lot,' said Cara. 'Mam's told me and Branna a little of what went on, but we had no idea things had been so bad. If you need anything, just let us know and we'll do what we can to help, won't we, Branna?'

'Anything, Sadie, just say it,' Branna agreed. 'Mam's always spoken highly of you.'

Young Bess shifted from her position on the floor, turning and staring right at Sadie.

'So is that baby yours or not?' she asked, pointing at Birdie. 'And if it's not yours, do you have to give it back?'

Sadie and Bessie exchanged a look and Bessie rolled her eyes.

'Never mind all this grown-up talk,' she said

brightly. She smiled at Sadie and shook her head before turning to her granddaughters. 'What have you young girls got to say for yourselves while we're sitting here telling stories from our lives? What about you, Ellen?'

Ellen shrugged and looked at the floor.

'No boyfriend to tell us about?' Bessie teased.

'Urgh, Grandma!' Ellen cried, pulling a face of distaste.

'Ada?' Bessie asked. 'What about you, my love. What makes you happy?'

'I like going to Sunday school and I like my teacher at the village school too, Miss Bewick.'

'Young Bess?'

'I like . . . ' She glanced up at her mother. 'What do I like, Mam?'

Cara laughed. 'You like eating me out of house and home, that's what you like.'

'And what about you, Cara. How's things? Still doing the sewing?'

'Still sewing,' Cara replied. 'Stitching clothes all day at work and then sewing at night after young Bess has gone to bed. I can make more money that way than I make all week long in the factory. I get to create my own designs at home and sell them on the market.' She paused and glanced at Bessie. 'But I've got some news, Mam. And as we're all sitting here sharing secrets, it seems as good a time as any to tell you.'

Branna shot her sister a look. 'Are you sure you want to say this now?'

'I'm sure.'

Bessie's heart dropped. 'What is it?' she barked.

'Nothing bad, Mam,' Cara said, taking the sting from Bessie's worry. 'Young Bess here, she's going to have a little brother or sister.'

'You're pregnant again?' Bessie cried. 'Oh Cara! Love!'

Cara scraped her chair back, then stood and walked towards her mam, and the two women embraced.

'You knew?' Bessie asked Branna.

Branna nodded. 'I told her not to tell you, not to say anything yet; it's too early.'

'Now come on, how could I not tell her tonight of all nights?' Cara said. 'It's the first Little Christmas we've ever had in England. It feels right to share these things.'

'I think this news deserves another drink,' Bessie declared, and she headed back to the bar, calling the women to her to fill up their glasses and raise another toast.

'Who've we not heard from tonight, then?' Bessie said, glancing around until her eyes locked with Em's. 'Anything you want to share, Em?' she asked.

'I've four lads at home, and a husband to cook and clean for. There's no gossip to share, I'm just enjoying sitting here in the company of women.' Em smiled. 'Oh, don't get me wrong, I love my lads to pieces, all four of them, and I worry about them all the time. Neville's a good husband, we keep a tidy house and I'm grateful for my job at the Grange. But no, I've nothing to share. No news, no baby I've gone in search of like Sadie, no pregnancy to announce like Cara.'

'I should think not, at your age,' sniffed Lil.

'What about you, Bessie?' asked Sadie from her chair by the fire. 'You've brought us all here tonight to celebrate the . . . what was it you called it?'

'Nollaig na mBam,' Bessie repeated, the rhythm and poetry of her words as magical a sound as Sadie had ever heard. 'The Women's Little Christmas.'

'We're all here because of you, Bessie. What story would you like to share?'

Bessie made sure that everyone had their glass topped up before she took her seat by the fire again. 'Come here,' she said to her granddaughters, and they scuttled along the floor on their bottoms to sit at her feet. Young Bess crawled up to sit on her grandma's knee.

Bessie raised her glass of port, and the deep brown liquid caught the reflection of the flames from the fire.

'I want to thank you all for coming, first and foremost,' she said. 'It means a lot to me, to my family. When I was a girl in Ireland we always had these Little Christmas nights for the women. Like my girls here, I remember sitting at my grandma's feet on her kitchen floor in Dublin, listening to tales told as lives were untangled and secrets spilled out.' She looked hard at Lil Mahone. 'And they are secrets, Lil. Not for idle gossip, you hear? What you hear at Women's Christmas stays in this room with us.'

'As if I would!' Lil bristled.

'I remember sitting with my mam, listening as she told tales of growing up in Dublin — '

'Skippy Johnson,' barked Lil.

Bessie glared at her. 'What on earth . . .'

'Skippy Johnson. I should have married him, not Bob. There, I've said it.' She locked eyes with Bessie. 'You said this was a night for secrets. You said that what we say in here stays in here. Well, now I've told you. I should have married Skippy Johnson when he asked me. I've regretted it ever since.'

'Isn't he that fella with the gammy leg who lives on Dinsdale Street?' asked Molly.

'He works as a butcher, doesn't he?' Em asked. 'I'm sure I've seen his name painted on the side of a van that drives around the village.'

'That's him. I had to turn him down because my mam and dad weren't keen, said he came from rough stock and he wouldn't treat me fair. Then Bob asked my dad if he could have my hand in marriage, and before I knew it, I found myself engaged. And the rest, as they say, is history.'

'Did you love him?' asked Bessie. 'Did you love Skippy Johnson?'

Lil gazed into the flames of the coal fire. 'Yes,' she said softly. 'Yes, I did as it happens.'

'And do you love Bob?'

Lil took a few seconds before she gave her reply. 'I do now.'

The women fell silent, shocked at the revelation, unsure of what to say, but it was Lil who spoke next.

'What were you saying, Bessie? Just now, you were remembering days past, the Women's Little Christmas from when you were a girl?'

Bessie smiled. 'I was about to say I never

280

thought for one minute that I'd find myself this old. I never thought, sitting with my grandma in Dublin, that I'd ever reach the age when I'd be a grandmother myself. I never thought I'd even be here in England, but we had no choice other than to move when the famine struck. The rest of the Irish went to live down by the docks, but that was no place for me and Pat, not when I knew I was already pregnant with Branna. I never even thought I'd marry Pat Brogan, nasty little piece he was back then in Dublin, always stealing chickens from our farm.'

'Grandad stole chickens?' Ada asked, her eyes wide with astonishment.

Bessie looked around at her friends and her daughters. 'What I'm trying to say is that life moves too quickly. You turn your back on it and you lose five years, ten.' She nodded towards Sadie. 'People come into your life and change you for the better, but you've got to let them know how you feel. It's no good storing things up inside. When there's love to give, give it.'

'Oh Mam, now you're being melodramatic,' Branna laughed.

'Am I?' asked Bessie, looking around at the faces turned towards her. 'We women have to stick together. We've always known it, always felt it. We have to help each other, always.'

Hetty stared into the flames, thinking of her son, who had died fighting for his country. She thought of her husband, who had hardened since Philip's death. She and Jack were drifting apart instead of uniting in their grief.

'We love our families, as we should,' Bessie

continued. 'But tonight, we're here for each other. Let the spirit of Little Christmas remain in our hearts for the year ahead, for who knows what the future will bring.'

Sadie raised her glass. 'To Bessie,' she said. 'And the Women's Little Christmas.'

The women sipped their drinks, and then Branna began to sing, softly at first, gently, and Sadie saw Bessie's eyes glisten with tears. She sang in a language that Sadie didn't recognise but guessed must be Irish. Bessie joined her, her voice lower, carrying her daughter's as it soared around the pub. Then Cara joined in too, the three Brogan women singing the most beautiful, mournful tune that Sadie had ever heard. Young Bess hugged her grandma close until the song finally came to a close.

'It's been a long time since we sang that one,' Bessie said.

'Too long,' Branna replied.

Young Bess reached a hand to Bessie's face and wiped away a tear that had fallen to her cheek. 'Don't cry, Grandma,' she said. 'Don't be sad.'

'Oh, Grandma's being a silly old fool.' Bessie smiled at her granddaughter. 'That song always makes me cry.'

And then, from out of nowhere, Lil Mahone began to sing. It was a song Sadie knew, one she had heard men singing when she'd worked in the Railway Inn, a song of lost love and of what might have been. Lil gripped her glass of stout in both hands in front of her as the tune left her lips. The sweetness of her voice took them all by surprise: she was note-perfect, crystal clear, the words coming out of her with an honesty and a power that no one could have guessed. Sadie joined in, hesitantly at first, and then, when they reached the chorus, Em added her voice. Soon they were all singing, the music filling the pub.

When the last note died away, it was Hetty who took up a new song, this one about a mother who had lost her son to war. The older women there knew the song too, but they let Hetty sing alone, knowing how much of herself she was putting into it. When she finished, her head dropped and she wept. Molly embraced her and wiped away her tears.

'At work in the Albion, behind the bar, there's a person I have to be,' Hetty explained once she'd collected herself. 'I have to smile at the customers, ask them how they're doing, enquire after their wives and their bairns. I put on my smile with my pinny every morning. And every evening, I take them off. The pinny goes back on its hook behind the bar and the smile — well, the smile disappears until it's needed the next day. I grieve for Philip and I think about all the other lads, all the other good and honest young lads, who were killed out there. And I wonder what it was all for.' She looked around the room at her friends, searching their faces for the tiniest hint that they understood her pain. 'What's changed? I ask you. My Philip has gone, and what's changed? They say it was the war to end all wars. Well, I hope so. Because as God is my witness, I cannot bear to think that other families, other mothers, will go through the hell of what I'm going through now.'

Bessie raised her glass again. 'A toast to those no longer with us but who will always be in our hearts.'

★ ★ ★

It was almost midnight when Bessie unlocked the door to let Sadie, Em, Molly, Hetty and Lil out into the bitterly cold night outside. Bessie's daughters and granddaughters were staying overnight at the pub. Em and Lil walked off together towards the pit cottages, bidding the others farewell. Sadie, Molly and Hetty huddled together for the walk to the village. Sadie gathered Birdie inside her shawl and hugged her close to her chest to keep her as warm as she could.

When they reached the village, the lamps had been lit, casting a misty glow around the green. Hetty kissed the other two goodnight and headed down to the Albion, leaving Molly and Sadie at the black iron gates to the Grange. Mr Marshall's car was parked on the road outside. Sadie pushed the gate open.

'He lets you enter by the front door?' Molly asked, surprised.

'Only when I've got Birdie,' she whispered. 'Otherwise I have to go around the back.'

'It's been a good night,' Molly said.

'The best.'

'Look, love, if there's anything you need, anything at all, you know I'm just around the corner.'

'Thanks, Molly.'

The two women hugged before Molly set off in the direction of the Railway Inn. Sadie walked down the garden path towards the imposing front door. She pushed it open and stepped inside. An oil lamp was burning on a table in the hallway, and she was both surprised and grateful that Mr Marshall had left it there so that she hadn't had to step into blackness with the child in her arms. Perhaps there was a grain of decency about him after all.

She picked up the lamp and began to climb the stairs. On the first-floor landing, she saw that the door to the room that had been Mrs Marshall's was wide open. This meant that if Mr Marshall was home, as his parked car suggested, he must still be using his own room on the floor above.

She settled Birdie into her crib, laying an extra blanket across her to make sure that the child would be warm. Then she sat by the crib for a while, watching her daughter as she slept. Sadie was tired and needed to head upstairs to her room, but after the night with Bessie's family and the friends she'd made in Ryhope, there was a happiness she wanted to savour. She knew that as soon as she went up to bed, that feeling would be gone, and she wanted to capture it in her heart for as long as she could before sleep took her over. In the crib, Birdie turned and let out a little cry.

'Shush, my darling,' Sadie said softly. 'Sleep now, little one. You're safe here with me. You know I'll take care of you for as long as I can.'

She reached into the crib and stroked Birdie's

face, the child's soft skin like silk. And then, in a whisper, she began to sing the song she'd heard Lil singing that night, humming the tune when she struggled to remember the words. She broke off sharply when she heard a dull thud from the room above.

She picked up the oil lamp and stepped onto the landing, fully intending to head straight up to her room. But even before she reached the second floor, she heard more noises, voices now. She recognised Mr Marshall's immediately, loud and angry. And there was a woman's voice too. Was it Dinah again? She stood just below the landing, hardly daring to climb further in case Mr Marshall or the woman should leave the bedroom and head to the bathroom, as had happened before. She held the lamp up and saw that Mr Marshall's bedroom door was closed. Did she dare risk it?

She was just about to take a step when she heard the sound of a woman's sobs. Sadie bit her lip. She couldn't spend all night on the stairs, she had to get to her room. She took one step up, determined to run as quickly as she could. But she was stopped in her tracks a second time by the sound of Mr Marshall's voice again.

'How do I know it's even mine?' he cried.

The woman's sobs, which had begun softly, now turned into a wail. 'You know it's yours, Joe! You know it! I haven't been with any other man.'

'You've got to get rid of it, Dinah. Do you know what this will do to me? It'll crucify me if news gets out. Joe Marshall and his bastard! What do you think they're going to make of that at work, eh? I've got to look respectable! I've only just smoothed things over with them about getting shot of the first kid. Now that Ruth's dead, they said they could quite see why a widower wouldn't want the responsibility of a child. Don't you understand? Things were settling down nicely for me. Ruth's sister is going to take the child. But if news gets out about you being pregnant, I'll be a laughing stock around Ryhope.'

'You could always make an honest woman of me, Joe,' the woman pleaded.

There was silence for a few moments, and Sadie wondered if she should make the most of it and run like the clappers up the stairs. Then the sound of the woman sobbing reached her again, followed by Mr Marshall's voice. This time there was a softness to it, a gentleness that Sadie had never heard before.

'Come now, Dinah. We're in a mess and no mistake, but we'll sort things out.'

'How, Joe? How?'

The voices lowered and faded to whispers. Sadie took her chance and ran to the second landing, then up the next flight of stairs to her room at the top of the house. She set the oil lamp on the floor and undressed quickly, throwing on her nightshirt and jumping into bed, where she lay still with her thoughts, turning over the secret she had just overheard.

12

Crack Hewer

Spring 1920

'I need your help tonight, Sadie.'

'Of course, what's happening?'

Em held up a sheet of lined paper on which Sadie saw a list written in pencil. 'He's wanting a dinner cooked, for seven of them.'

Sadie's heart quickened. Was this the moment she had been dreading? 'Is it the sister-in-law coming?'

Em shook her head. 'No, lass.'

'Who's the dinner for, then?'

'Fellas from the Ryhope Coal Company, he told me. He says they'll be going into the parlour after dinner too, where he wants drinks and ginger cake served. It's been a while since we had such a dinner at the Grange. I'm quite looking forward to doing all the preparation, truth be told. But I'll need an extra pair of hands to get the food from the kitchen and served at the table.'

'I'd be more than happy to help, Em,' Sadie replied, but she wondered why the dinner was taking place, and if it had anything to do with the conversation she'd overheard between Dinah and Mr Marshall. But surely something like that was private and secret, not something that Mr Marshall would be keen to share with other senior men from the pit.

Em was running her finger down the list, making a pencil mark against items she would need to buy.

'Em?' asked Sadie. 'Have you heard anything more about Mr Marshall's sister-in-law?'

'Can't say I have, no,' Em replied. 'Is there any reason you ask?'

'He said we'd hear from her at the turn of the year. But that was some time ago now. Do you think she's changed her mind?'

'Don't get your hopes up, love,' Em warned her. 'You never know what's going on with this lot.' She turned her attention back to the shopping list, and Sadie returned to her chores.

⋆　⋆　⋆

The first gentleman from the Ryhope Coal Company presented himself at the Grange at five minutes to seven. The others arrived in ones and twos over the next fifteen minutes. Sadie answered the door to them as Em cooked in the kitchen. She took their heavy coats, along with hats, gloves and scarves, and hung them on pegs in a small alcove beside the scullery. Then she showed the men into the dining room and poured each one a tot of whisky.

Mr Marshall was in his element, cheerful and full of energy with a ready smile for his colleagues. But as soon as he needed to address Sadie, to call for another glass to be poured, or for the door to be answered to allow another gentleman to enter, his tone darkened and his face clouded over. He had no patience to waste on her; all his energy went into pleasing his guests. Sadie wondered if he knew she was aware of the secret about Dinah being pregnant with his child. But how could he have been? Sadie had been as quiet as a mouse on the night she'd heard the argument between the two of them.

The group of men stood talking for a while with their drinks in their hands. Cigars were smoked and voices were raised; hearty laughter streamed from the dining room along the hallway to the scullery where Em and Sadie worked. Sadie's thoughts went back to the night of the Little Christmas at the Forester's Arms. There, the women had been seated and calm as they sang, talked and laughed, sharing secrets and love. How different to this group of powerful men, full of their own importance. They looked uncomfortable in their stuffed shirts and ties, their waistcoats and jackets, surrounded by the patterned wallpaper and framed pictures looking down.

The clock in the hall chimed the half-hour and Mr Marshall beckoned everyone to take a seat at the table. He sat at the head and directly opposite him sat Sidney Wright, another of the three pit managers at the Ryhope Coal Company. Sidney was the eldest at the table, a man with greying hair swept back from his face and a thick grey moustache. Next to him sat Benjamin Pascoe, the third manager. He was younger than his colleagues and Mr Marshall did not trust him; the two men often disagreed over decisions at the pit. Benjamin had short, clipped fair hair and a bland face that Joe Marshall thought held as much interest as a newly scrubbed potato. The remaining four men at the table were the two assistant pit managers, Matthew Gowland and William Sorley, the chief engineer, John Ratcliffe, and his most trusted man from the engineering department, Brian Ridley. Trust, Ratcliffe had been told, was key to being invited to this dinner.

Once they were all seated, Mr Marshall picked up a small brass handbell from the side table and rang it three times.

'They're playing your tune,' Em smiled to Sadie. 'Go and take their starters in.'

Sadie picked up a tray containing a dish of Moscow mince, which Mr Marshall had requested. It was a favourite of his and one that Em cooked well, tiny pieces of ham mixed with pepper and onion, fried and served on hot buttered toast. An agreeable murmur went up around the room once Sadie had served the food. Mr Marshall dismissed her and she returned to the kitchen to help Em with the main course.

Once the starter plates had been cleared, Sadie brought in the plates of beef roll and two gravy boats, one for each end of the table. A large white dish of vegetables was placed in the centre, a curl of steam rising from it. Again Mr Marshall dismissed her, barking at her to close the door as she left.

'How will I know when they're ready to have

their plates removed?' she asked Em when she returned to the kitchen.

'You'll have to listen at the door,' Em replied. 'There's nothing else for it, not if they've closed themselves in.'

While the men ate, Sadie watched Em making the ginger cake that had been requested for dessert. She took a seat by the coal fire as Em combined white flour with dark spice, sugar and treacle, margarine and eggs. She worked without a recipe, her nimble fingers following their own pattern learned through the years. When the mixture was ready, she spooned it into a flat square metal tin and placed it in the coal oven. Soon, the soft aroma of ginger filled the kitchen. Sadie could have stuck out her tongue and tasted it on the air, the scent was that strong and delicious. She longed to have the cake in her mouth, to taste it warm there and make it last forever.

'If we're lucky, they might leave some.' Em winked. 'Men don't usually have such a sweet tooth, but he asked for a pudding just in case they wanted something for afters.'

'When do you think I should go to see if they're finished their beef roll?' Sadie asked.

'Don't see why you can't go now. Listen at the door first; you'll hear knives and forks scraping against the china if they're still eating. If it's quiet, you can give a little knock, pop your head round the door and ask Mr Marshall if he's ready to move into the parlour for the cake. If he says yes, tell him it'll be ready in ten minutes. That'll give them plenty of time to sort themselves out. Some of them might want to use the bathroom.'

Sadie stood from her chair and took the tray from the kitchen table. She walked towards the dining room, and as she did so, she heard raised voices. There was no mistaking the voice of Mr Marshall, for it was one she knew well, but she had never heard him so angry. His tone was more direct, more vicious than the night when she had heard him turn on Dinah. It was commanding now, indicating that he was not to be messed with or contradicted.

She took a deep breath and squared her shoulders, then leaned to her right and pressed her ear to the dining room door. There was no scraping of knives on plates, as Em had told her to listen for. All she could hear were the voices of the men inside, shouting and arguing, each of them trying to talk over the other.

'We've got no choice, man!' Mr Marshall yelled. 'You can't argue with the figures. It's all there in black and white. I've been going over the books for weeks now, you know that. And yet you still say we should hold back from changing things?'

Sadie heard another man speaking, a quieter, less angry one, who gave his reply calmly and evenly.

'There's ways and means of doing things, Joe. All I'm saying is I'm not sure that bringing in a crack hewer at Ryhope is the right thing to do.'

Sadie felt certain she'd heard of a crack hewer before. Hadn't Eddie mentioned it once? And when she'd asked him what it was, he'd suddenly changed the subject and it had never been spoken of again.

'Benjamin, if you'll forgive me.' Mr Marshall spoke again, more calmly this time but with just as much force and strength. 'I've been in this business a hell of a lot longer than you have and I've seen it work at other pits. There's no reason on God's earth why it can't work at Ryhope. I say we give it a try.'

'Gentlemen, please!' another voice cut in, an older man this time. 'We could go round in circles arguing for and against bringing in a crack hewer to Ryhope. It's been much in discussion over the last few months already. What we came here for tonight, may I remind you, was to vote on the matter and get the thing over and done with.'

Sadie heard a low grumble from inside the dining room.

'You're right, Sidney,' said Mr Marshall. 'I say we vote now before tempers become any more frayed. All those in favour of bringing in a crack hewer to Ryhope pit, raise your right hand.'

There was silence from the room as the men cast their vote. After a few seconds, Sadie heard Mr Marshall speak again.

'And those against?'

There was another silence.

'Three for and three against, Joe. This is what you've always wanted, isn't it! To divide the management!' Benjamin Pascoe exploded.

'Of course it's bloody not,' Mr Marshall spat.

'Then it's your vote that decides,' Benjamin said.

'You know my feelings. My vote goes to bring in the crack hewer.'

'Four votes to three in favour,' Sidney Wright said. 'Motion carried.'

'You'll regret this,' Sadie heard the younger man say. 'Just you mark my words.'

There was a scraping of chairs against the wooden floor and she jumped back from the dining room door as it flew open and Benjamin Pascoe stormed out. Instead of heading for the parlour, where drinks were to be served, he went straight to the front door. Sadie laid her tray on the table in the hallway and went to fetch his coat, and he left without so much as a thank you or a goodbye to any of the men he'd been dining with moments ago. Slowly, the other men left the dining room too, filing towards the parlour.

'Clear the room, girl,' Mr Marshall directed Sadie when he caught sight of her waiting. Sadie gave him eye contact but nothing more, then disappeared inside the dining room to collect the empty plates.

'You took your time,' Em said, glancing up when Sadie walked into the kitchen.

'Had to get a coat for one of the gentlemen,' she replied quickly. She knew that with her husband and sons all working at the mine, it was likely that Em might know what a crack hewer was, and it was on the tip of her tongue to ask. But she kept quiet, wanting to speak to Eddie first before she told anyone else what she'd heard.

The rest of the evening passed without any more raised voices or arguments, at least none that Sadie heard when she entered the parlour with plates of Em's ginger cake and cups of tea. The cake was met with approval, disproving Em's words about men not having a sweet tooth, but the tea was left untouched as Mr Marshall insisted that whisky be served instead.

When the gentlemen finally left the Grange, stepping out into the cold night air, Sadie gave a sigh of relief. But for Mr Marshall, the night was not yet done.

★ ★ ★

As soon as Em had finished work and left to head home, Mr Marshall set out in his car. He was gone not ten minutes before he returned with a passenger beside him in the front seat. When he entered the house, Sadie was preparing an oil lamp to be left in the hallway. She jumped when she heard the door open behind her, but it was hard to say who got the bigger surprise as she locked eyes with a woman she recognised immediately as Dinah. Mr Marshall followed Dinah into the hall.

'Give the girl your coat,' he barked.

Dinah giggled self-consciously and removed her chocolate-brown jacket. She held it with both hands, unsure of what to do with it, until Sadie reached out and offered to take it. Dinah smiled gratefully in return, and Sadie looked at the other woman's face properly for the first time. She was young, that much was clear, barely older than Sadie herself, her pale skin almost translucent. Her dark hair curled around her face, and her fringe fell to her big brown eyes. Without the heavy make-up that Sadie had seen her wearing on her earlier visit, when she'd spotted her dancing across the landing, she could make out a natural beauty there, and it was easy to see how Mr Marshall had fallen for her.

Mr Marshall gave a gentle cough. 'I shall be entertaining in the parlour,' he told Sadie. 'You are dismissed for the evening.' He took Dinah by the arm and led her away, and as he did so, Dinah turned and smiled at Sadie again.

Sadie placed Dinah's jacket on a peg in the alcove. It was a thin garment, she noticed, not made for keeping out the cold, but for fashion, for showing off. A sweet smell of cologne came from it as she ran her hand along its soft collar. She sighed, and headed up the stairs to check on Alexandra before she fell into her own bed, exhausted.

* * *

Downstairs in the parlour, Mr Marshall poured a single glass of whisky and sank into a chair in front of the dying fire. Opposite him on the settee, Dinah lay stretched out with her legs up on the cushions. Her black high-heeled shoes lay discarded on the floor.

'No drink for me, Joe?' she cooed.

'Not in your condition,' he replied sharply. 'Did you see the doctor, like I told you?'

'If you mean did he confirm what I already knew, then yes, I saw the doctor. It's your child,

297

Joe. I'm pregnant with your child.'

Mr Marshall took a long slug from the whisky glass. 'And what about your family? If you're insisting on keeping it, can't they look after it for you?'

Dinah took her time before replying. 'You're my family now,' she said softly. 'I've only got you. There's no one else I can call my own.' She turned her face towards him and ran her tongue around her lips. 'I was hoping I could move in here, with you.'

Mr Marshall closed his eyes as if to distance himself from her words, but in truth, it was something that he had already forced himself to give thought to. 'We'd have to do it properly,' he said at last. 'Make it look respectable. I need to make it appear as if I'm doing the right thing, at least.'

Dinah gasped. 'Respectable? Oh Joe! Are you saying that you want to marry me?'

Mr Marshall sighed heavily. 'I'm not saying that I want to. I'm saying that I will, for appearance's sake and nothing more.'

Dinah allowed a smile to play around her mouth as she snuggled into the soft cushions of the sofa. She stared up at the heavily patterned wallpaper, and at the framed pictures hanging on the walls. It was the first time she had been into the parlour, into any of the rooms apart from Mr Marshall's bedroom and the bathroom. Yes, she was sure she could be very happy here.

'I'll get the paperwork drawn up,' Mr Marshall said, gazing into the fire. 'But there'll be work for you to do, Dinah. You'll be expected to become the lady of the Grange. We'll need to take you to Sunderland and buy you new clothes, the right kind of clothes.'

'New clothes?' She smiled, stretching her shapely legs along the cushions and wiggling her toes in her stockings. But then her face clouded over. 'What sort of work will I have to do? Can't your girl do it all? You pay her, surely? And what of your daughter, Alexandra? I can't be taking on another woman's child, Joe. You know that, don't you?'

'Have I ever asked you to take her on?' he said sharply.

'No, but — '

'The child will be leaving just as soon as Esther, my sister-in-law, advises when she can take her. I'm expecting a letter from her on the matter any day.'

Dinah bristled at his tone. 'I just wanted to make it clear that if you were harbouring any thoughts of keeping the child — '

'I'm not,' he barked. 'She was a business transaction, pure and simple, brought into this house for reasons that don't need to bother you. All I want is a return on my investment, something Esther has offered to secure on my behalf.'

The thought of Esther made Mr Marshall's stomach tighten. He took no joy at all in the thought of breaking the news to his late wife's sister that he was to marry again, and so soon after Ruth's death too. He knew that Esther would no doubt be free with her sharp tongue when he told her. And as for what his fellow managers at the Ryhope Coal Company would have to say on the matter, well, he'd deal with that when the time came. They were family men, through and through, and it would kill his career if he didn't do the right thing and marry Dinah. He just hoped her pregnancy wouldn't show until well after their wedding, an occasion that he needed to arrange as quickly as possible, before the whole of Ryhope found out the news.

★　★　★

The following morning, Sadie was tending to Birdie in her bedroom. She treasured these moments when, in the early-morning quiet of the Grange, the only sounds were of her child laughing and forming sounds into words. Some mornings when she entered Birdie's room, the little girl was already standing in her crib, her chubby arms reaching out, waiting for Sadie to pick her up and cuddle her. Every single minute, every single second that she spent with her daughter was becoming more precious. She never took them for granted, aware that within weeks, or even days, her life could turn over yet again, this time with Esther's arrival. When that happened, Sadie would need her wits about her, ready to offer herself as the child's nurse and show how capable she was. For she was not prepared to let her daughter go.

At the sound of a footstep at the bedroom door, Sadie swung around to find Dinah there.

'Oh! Miss!' She called out in shock. 'I didn't know you were there.' Dinah looked lost, Sadie thought, lost and alone, vulnerable and small. Without her make-up and heels, she looked just like a child herself.

'I've been watching you,' Dinah said. 'You and the child there. She trusts you, doesn't she? She's always smiling, and when you were talking to her just now, she was laughing so much. Do you know a lot about working with children?'

Sadie shook her head. 'No. Just this one. I'm her nurse.'

Dinah slowly walked towards her. 'I'm Dinah,' she said shyly. 'You're Sadie, aren't you?'

Sadie nodded. 'If you're wanting breakfast, it's Em who does the cooking,' she said hurriedly. 'She'll be downstairs.'

'I don't think I could manage breakfast,' Dinah said.

Sadie knew the feeling; she remembered only too well the morning nausea when she was pregnant and living at Freda's house. But she remained silent, aware that Dinah didn't realise she knew about the baby, or even indeed about what she was doing at the Grange.

Dinah glanced behind her towards the open bedroom door. 'I think I need some help,' she whispered.

'With what?' Sadie replied.

'Understanding Mr Marshall, for a start.' Dinah smiled. 'I'm to move in here, he's said.'

'To the Grange?'

'And there's to be a wedding too,' she added.

Sadie's eyes widened with shock. This was turning out to be quite the morning, and she'd been out of bed for less than an hour!

301

'What about . . . ' she began to say, but stopped herself short. She wanted to know how the marriage would affect her and Birdie. She had so many questions that needed answering, but it was impossible to know where to start. And it wouldn't be right to ask Dinah, of all people, when they'd only just met, especially as Dinah was taking on the mantle of lady of the Grange. But it was Dinah herself who broke down any barrier between them.

'You'll help me, won't you, Sadie? Please? You look like you know what you're doing with the child. I'm going to need all the help I can get when mine comes along.' She laid her hands to her stomach.

'Is it your first?' Sadie asked.

'Yes, I'm hoping for a girl, just like yours,' Dinah replied, glancing towards Birdie in her crib.

Sadie kept her voice as even as she could. Had Mr Marshall told Dinah the truth? 'Mine?'

'Well, the child you look after for him, I mean. He says it was bought for his wife as she couldn't have none of her own, and that it's going to live with Hester, some relative of his in Newcastle, is that right?'

'It's Esther, his sister-in-law, and yes, that's what I've been led to understand.'

'The child will miss you when she goes, I can tell that just by watching you together and seeing the way her face lights up when you look at her.'

'Not as much as I'll miss her,' Sadie said quietly, so quietly that Dinah didn't catch the words on her breath.

'Are you a Ryhope lass, Sadie?' Dinah asked.

'Hartlepool. What about you?'

'Lived in Ryhope all my life. But my mam chucked me out when she found out I was pregnant and carrying a bairn, even if it is the pit manager's. I've been sleeping in my friend Nell's house, on the floor. She lives in North Tunstall Street, do you know it? That's when I've not been staying overnight here.'

'You said you needed some help, miss, with understanding Mr Marshall?' Sadie saw tears in Dinah's eyes.

'Please, Sadie,' she begged. 'I've never been anywhere as fancy as this place before. I've never had a cook to make my breakfast, I've never had cotton sheets the likes of those on the bed here. He wants me to become the lady of the Grange, but I don't know where to start. I don't know who to ask. I can't go back to my mam and I can hardly ask Nell; she won't know about such things. I can only ask you, if you'll help me. Will you?'

There was a tremor to Dinah's voice, a hesitancy that made Sadie warm to her. She remembered Bessie's words from the night of the Little Christmas, about women being there for each other, helping and supporting one another.

'I'll help you, miss,' she said.

Dinah's breath caught in her chest as the tears threatened to fall. She turned and headed towards the bedroom door.

'The cook's name is Em, you say? Think I'll go down and introduce myself and see if I can get a pot of tea.'

That evening, Sadie bathed her daughter and put her to bed, singing a lullaby that her own mam used to sing to her when she was small. Her night ahead was free, as Em was working late at the Grange and had agreed to keep an eye on Alexandra.

'Get yourself out for an hour or two,' she'd told Sadie. 'You need to spend time with Eddie; he'll be forgetting what you look like if you don't go round and see him soon!'

Sadie made her way to the Railway Inn, looking forward to seeing Eddie and Molly again. Molly looked up when she walked in. She was working alone behind the bar, apart from her little dog Pip, who was running around at her feet, in desperate need of some attention and a scratch behind his ears. Sadie noticed Tom seated alone at one of the tables with the remains of a pint of ale in front of him. And there was Eddie, standing at the end of the bar reading a book. The two brothers could not have placed themselves further apart if they had tried; they were clearly still not getting along. It saddened Sadie to see them like this, but she also knew that there was little use in trying to understand how other people's families worked. She spotted that the door to the Select was tight shut and wondered how much it had been used since she'd cleaned it after Molly's plans to reopen it.

It was a quiet night in the bar. Apart from Eddie and Tom, there were just two customers sitting quietly, one of them reading that day's *Sunderland Echo*. The other customer, a man sitting on his own, glared at Sadie as she entered. A shiver ran down her spine when she recognised Bill Scurfield. She wondered how he'd managed to worm his way back into the pub. Hadn't Molly barred him after the trouble he'd caused last time? Bill kept his gaze fixed on Sadie as she greeted Molly. Eddie's eyes lit up, and he came over and kissed her.

'Eddie, can we sit somewhere to talk?' Sadie asked.

'Course we can,' he replied. 'Everything's all right, isn't it?'

Sadie nodded and pointed to a table in the corner where she was certain they wouldn't be overheard. Molly pulled a pint of ale into a dimpled glass with a handle for her son, and a glass of shandy for Sadie. Eddie took the drinks to the table, and Sadie sat down, drawing her chair as close as she could towards Eddie's and leaning in towards him.

'You wouldn't believe what's gone on at the Grange,' she whispered. She went on to tell Eddie all about Dinah moving in, about her asking for help with her baby and about the plans for the wedding too. Eddie took it all in his stride.

'As I told you,' he said, 'they're a funny bunch, those pit managers. Different to us, Sadie.'

'And that's not all,' she said, glancing round to make sure that no one was listening. She told Eddie about the dinner for the pit managers and about the arguments she had heard from the dining room.

'Mr Marshall shouted them all down,' she explained. 'Oh, you should have heard him, Eddie. And then they voted, all seven of them.'

'Voted? What for?'

'Do you remember you told me that someone at the pit wanted to bring in a crack hewer?'

'They voted on that?' he whispered.

'Four to three in favour. They're bringing it into Ryhope pit.'

Eddie let out a heavy sigh and slowly shook his head. 'No! I can't believe it. I won't believe it.'

'What is it, Eddie? What's a crack hewer?'

'A crack hewer isn't a thing,' Eddie said at last. 'It's a man. The pit managers bring them in on private contracts. They're big fellas, crack hewers, bigger and stronger than any of us who've worked in the pit all our lives. I can't believe he's doing this, Sadie. Are you sure you heard right?'

Sadie nodded, taking Eddie's hands as he continued. 'These crack hewers, they're that strong and they work that fast that they're able to hew many more tubs of coal from a seam than the average lad. Oh, it's not good news at all, love. See, what happens is, once the crack hewer's set the pace, it makes the rest of us look like we're not trying. But the pit bosses argue that if he can do it, then so can the rest of us, and they adjust our targets based on the crack hewer's performance.'

'And if you don't come up to the same standard as the man they bring in?'

'We have no choice. If we want to keep our jobs, we have to match the crack hewer's standard. And the worst thing of all? Once the

306

targets have been fixed against his performance, off he goes to another pit, where the managers there get him to do the same thing all over again. It leaves us lot working longer and harder for not a penny more.'

'But that's not fair,' Sadie whispered, appalled.

'Forget fair,' Eddie said. 'This is serious business we're talking about. There's one rule for us lads underground and another for those who work above that we all have to doff our caps to. Your Mr Marshall's been keen to make a name for himself at the pit, and if he goes ahead and does this, his balance sheet will have a shine on it, but by God, the miners won't be happy. Just you mark my words.'

He took a long drink from his pint and then stood, scraping his chair along the floor.

'I'm just nipping out the back,' he told Sadie. 'I won't be a minute.'

Alone at the table, Sadie took a sip of her shandy. She felt uneasy after what Eddie had told her about the goings-on at the pit, and she worried for his safety too. Pip appeared at her feet and sat obediently, waiting for some attention, but Sadie was lost in her thoughts. She never noticed two muddy boots appear on the floor beside the dog, and she got a nasty surprise to find Bill Scurfield standing next to her. As he sank into the seat where Eddie had been sitting just moments before, Pip let out a low growl.

'What's a lovely lass like you doing with a dead-beat like Eddie Teasdale?' Bill sneered. Sadie could smell the ale on his breath and she turned her face from the stench. Bill reached out a gnarled hand and scraped a finger down her cheek.

'Come on, lass. What do you say? Give old Bill a try, would you? I can show you a good time, better than Eddie.'

'Get off me,' she hissed. 'I thought you were barred from this pub?'

'Molly let me have a second chance,' he whispered.

Sadie tried to stand, to move away, but Bill Scurfield caught her by the arm and pushed her back down. Holding tight to both arms, he forced himself forward, trying to kiss her full on the lips. Sadie whipped her head away just in time. Pip started barking and Bill kicked out at the dog, but he jumped away.

'Get off,' Sadie said again, more loudly this time. 'Get off me!'

A fist shot out and caught Bill Scurfield on the side of his face, knocking him off his stool. Sadie looked up, astonished to see Tom there, towering over Bill, who was lying on the floor holding his face. Tom reached out a hand to Sadie, but just as he did so, the back door of the pub swung open and Eddie walked in. What he saw didn't please him one bit.

'Get your hands off her!' he yelled at Tom. 'What the hell do you think you're doing?'

'No, Eddie, it's not what it looks like,' Sadie cried.

Eddie grabbed the front of his brother's shirt with such force that Tom's feet lifted from the floor.

'I was helping her, for God's sake!' Tom cried.

308

Eddie glanced at Bill Scurfield, who was on his knees now, trying to stand, holding tight to a tabletop.

'It was that piece of rubbish who was trying it on with her,' Tom yelled, pointing towards Bill.

'It's true, Eddie,' Sadie cried. 'Leave Tom alone. He was helping me, that's all.'

Eddie looked from Sadie to Tom and back again, then released his grip on his brother.

'What's going on, boys?'

Molly had come to see what all the shouting was about. She took one look at Bill Scurfield on his knees.

'Get up,' she told him. 'Get up and get out and don't you ever come back. I should never have given you a second chance; you're not worth it. Don't let me see you in here again. You hear me?'

Eddie hooked an arm under Bill Scurfield's and pulled him to a standing position. Then Tom hooked Bill's other arm and the two brothers half walked, half dragged the man to the door and threw him onto the pavement outside.

'You're drinking elsewhere from now on. Got it?' Eddie told him.

Bill turned, trying to focus on the two brothers. 'Ah, go to hell, the lot of you,' he slurred.

Eddie put his hand on the door, intent on going back inside and making sure that Sadie was all right. But he was stopped by Tom, who blocked his way.

'You thought I was trying it on with her, didn't you?'

'Wouldn't be the first time,' Eddie replied. 'I know what you're like. She told me you asked her out when she first came to Ryhope.'

'I did — and she turned me down. How was I to know you two would become as thick as thieves? You've found your soulmate there. Think yourself lucky, Eddie. She's a nice lass. You've done well.'

Eddie stared hard at his brother. 'What do you want, Tom? You've hardly said two words to me since you came back from the war, and you've spent most of that time lost in drink. You've barely lifted a finger to help Mam — she's had to drag you out of bed most mornings to lend a hand down here. And now all of a sudden you're Sadie's knight in shining armour and you're treating me like I'm your best pal. What's got into you?'

Tom gazed past his brother to the railway station up ahead.

'It's changed me, Ed,' he said at last.

Eddie looked at his brother, really looked at him, and saw for the first time the lines etched into Tom's face, the dullness in his eyes.

'The war?' he asked, as if he needed confirmation.

Tom tapped his index finger against the side of his head. 'It's all in here, going round and round. It never leaves me, never eases. Men died, Ed. Men died at my feet, at my side, men I thought of as friends. And now I'm back home, I'm alive. They tell me I should be thankful for that, but inside I'm dead. I don't feel right any more. I saw things, witnessed the most terrible things I know I'll never forget.'

Eddie put his arm around his brother's

310

shoulders. 'Come on, mate, let's get you inside.'

Molly did a double-take when she saw her boys walking into the pub, Eddie with his arm around Tom, supporting him.

'He needs help, Mam,' he whispered to Molly.

Sadie was down on her hands and knees under the table where she'd been sitting. In all the commotion, she'd lost her ladybird necklace again. She knew she'd had it around her neck when she'd left the Grange, and so it must be on the pub floor somewhere. But she paused her search, startled to see Eddie and Tom walking into the pub, arms around each other. Tom slumped into the nearest chair by the door and Eddie sat next to him. Molly poured a glass of brandy for him and took the seat opposite. Sadie got to her feet and took the fourth seat at the table. Slowly, hesitantly, Tom told his story, the bits he felt able to talk about, the bits he knew wouldn't upset his mam too much.

'Shell shock, they call it,' he explained. 'We were told to pull ourselves together. *Man up*, they said. Some of the lads did, or at least they seemed able to; some weren't so strong. I didn't think I'd ever be one of those who couldn't get over what I'd seen.' He raised his brandy glass. 'I thought this would help, all the drinking, all the ale. But it hasn't. It's just made things worse. I don't sleep. I'm constantly thinking, wondering, remembering.'

'We'll get him help, Mam, won't we?' Eddie urged.

'I don't deserve it,' Tom replied. He bit his lip and turned towards his brother. 'I've shown you nothing but spite since I came back, Eddie. I've bottled it all up inside for so long that when I have been able to talk to anyone, it's come out wrong. I've been rotten to the lot of you and I don't deserve your help.'

Molly laid her hand on her son's arm. 'Now come on, Tom. There's no use thinking like that.'

'But it's true, Mam,' he continued. 'These feelings I get . . . they're like rages inside me. I just want to strike out all the time, hurt people, and I've been doing it to you all. I can see how happy Eddie and Sadie are. But he's been here at home all the time I've been away and — '

'I've been working, Tom,' Eddie reminded him. 'Some of us had to stay or what state would the country have been in? And mining was a reserved occupation, you know that.'

Tom banged the table with his fist. 'But you haven't suffered, man! You haven't been to war! You haven't been through what I have.'

Eddie shifted uncomfortably in his seat and Sadie reached for his hand to comfort him against the sting of his brother's words.

'We'll look after you,' he said at last. 'Me, Mam and Sadie, we're going to do what's right and get you the help you need.'

Tom sighed deeply. 'See? I went off again, that's what it does to me, I strike out at people, and I never used to be like that, did I, Mam?'

Molly put her hand on her son's knee and looked him straight in the eye. 'We'll go and see Dr Anderson together. He might know where we can turn.'

Tom sighed deeply. 'Thanks, Mam,' he said

312

softly, and then his tears began to fall.

Pip walked towards where they sat at the table. His tail was wagging so hard that his back legs were in danger of lifting from the floor. As he approached, Sadie saw something hanging from the corner of his mouth. She gasped when she realised that it was the string with her ladybird charm attached. She took it from him and put it into her coat pocket. Pip sat, waiting for a rub behind the ears, which Sadie duly gave him. Then his little head darted from Sadie to Molly and then to Tom, who was wiping his hand across his face to dry his eyes. Pip padded over to him and launched himself up from the floor to Tom's lap, where he circled once, twice, his little paws kneading Tom's legs, before collapsing in a contented heap.

'Well I never!' exclaimed Molly. 'He's never done that before.'

As Tom stroked the dog's head, Sadie noticed, for the first time since she'd met him, the beginnings of a smile on his face.

13

Wedding

'Miss, you shouldn't be in here,' Sadie said, casting a glance at Dinah standing by the kitchen door.

'Could you call me Dinah, not miss?' she asked, not moving.

Sadie gave a quick nod. 'Dinah it is. But never when Mr Marshall is home. He'll have me shot for not addressing you properly.'

Dinah strode into the kitchen, her arms swinging by her sides. 'Can't I just sit with you and watch what you're doing?' she pleaded. 'I'm so bored, Sadie. I don't know what to do with myself. The Grange is too big, with all those rooms, and I can't seem to settle in any of them. Joe's gone off to work and what am I supposed to do when he's not here?'

She made herself comfortable in a chair by the fireplace. Despite the warmth of the spring day outside, the fire was roaring in the hearth, ready to heat up water when needed. The black iron fireplace that wrapped around the hearth protected Sadie and Em's skirts and legs as they worked.

'Let me help, please, Sadie,' Dinah said. 'There must be something I can do.'

Em had her back to the two girls. She was

working at the kitchen table, preparing a tin for the fruit cake she was baking, the cake that Mr Marshall had asked her specially to make. She wasn't altogether pleased to find herself having to work for a mistress as young and inexperienced as Dinah. But she kept her thoughts to herself. She had worked for some odd people over the years, but by goodness, she thought, Joe Marshall took the biscuit.

'Sadie, go and tend to Alexandra upstairs,' she said at last. She turned towards Dinah. 'And you, miss,' she said. 'Do you really want to make yourself useful?'

Dinah stood carefully from her seat, supporting the weight of her growing stomach, pressing one hand against her back. 'Yes, I do.'

Em held out a wooden spoon. 'Here, take this.'

Dinah took the spoon from Em's hand.

'See that?' Em asked, nodding towards the big earthenware bowl on the kitchen table, into which she had measured sugar and margarine.

Dinah peered into the bowl as if afraid that something would jump out and bite her.

'Give it a good mix,' Em ordered. 'You want the butter to go creamy. And when it's done, we'll stir in the dried fruit. There's some cut prunes in the pantry, and a bowl of raisins I've soaked overnight in brandy. I'll show you how to add vanilla essence, but for now just mix it, Dinah, as hard as you can.'

'But what is it?' Dinah asked, still peering into the bowl.

Em stood with her hands on her hips. 'He hasn't told you?'

Dinah shook her head, confused.

'It's your wedding cake, lass,' Em explained.

Dinah lifted her gaze. 'But we haven't even arranged the date yet,' she said softly.

Em's chest heaved and she let out a long sigh. Despite her reservations about working for this slip of a lass, her heart went out to her. She didn't envy her one bit having to spend the rest of her life with someone like Joe Marshall. Oh, the Grange might be a fancy enough place to live, but at what cost, having to share it with an uppity fella like him?

'He told me this morning before he left for work that the wedding's on Saturday, love,' she said gently. 'He's got a special licence and it's taking place at the register office on John Street in Sunderland.'

Dinah reached a hand to the kitchen table to steady herself. 'He never said a word to me, Em. Not one word.'

'Well,' said Em. 'That's for you and him to sort out, love. If you're to be married, you need to talk to him, get him to tell you what's going on. Secrets will never do, not between a husband and wife. You need to tell him straight, you hear me? Have it out with him as soon as you can; it'll save you from more heartache in the future.'

Dinah dropped her hands to her sides and the wooden spoon hung ready to fall to the floor.

'Now come on,' Em urged. 'No use moping. There's nothing you can do about it now, with him out at work. But if you take my advice, you'll get him on his own tonight after dinner and talk to him. Pour him a whisky, get him relaxed and then put your foot down with him. Be firm but fair. He can't go organising something as important as your wedding without telling you about it. Don't stand for it, Dinah.'

'Yes, I'll do that,' Dinah said. 'I will.'

Em lifted Dinah's hand and pushed the wooden spoon into the slab of butter in the mixing bowl. 'Now go on, give it a good beating, get it nice and creamy and light. I bet you never thought you'd end up making your own wedding cake today, did you?'

Dinah started attacking the butter with the spoon, working it around the bowl. 'There's a lot I've got to learn about him, Em. And about life at the Grange.'

'You'll learn, pet. Just take it one day at a time.'

As Dinah worked the butter and sugar together, she glanced out of the kitchen window into the back yard at the Grange. She saw the brick outhouse where the netty was, and Sadie's bike leaning up against the wall. There were flowers there too, their leaves covering a wooden fence, the flowers like delicate pink stars spilling over into the back lane. She could see the rooftops and chimney pots of the Railway Inn just around the corner from the Grange, and beyond that, the blue of the sea.

She'd never given much thought to her wedding before. She'd just assumed it would happen one day; that she'd marry a Ryhope lad, a miner or a farmer, someone her mam would approve of. She had always pictured the lad that she'd marry to be tall, strong, a grafter. And she'd never thought she'd be living in anything more grand than one of the lime-washed cottages by the pit. But now? Here she was in one of the biggest houses in Ryhope and about to be married to one of the gaffers at the pit. She'd want for nothing, she had a child on the way and she had Sadie and Em, her own staff. But the thought of it made her embarrassed. She couldn't tell other people what to do; it wasn't in her nature, nor how her mam had brought her up.

None of this new life was making her happy. Joe was a cruel man, she was finding. Oh, he wasn't abusive or violent, at least not towards her, but he was cold and distant — and fancy him arranging their wedding without even telling her about it! Well, she'd take Em's advice and tell him he had to share things with her. It was only right, now that she was to become his wife. If only she could go to her mam, she'd know what to say to make things right. Dinah felt a knot in her stomach when she thought of her mam and of the night when she broke the news she was pregnant with Mr Marshall's child.

'What's a man like him, a bit of top brass, doing with a girl like you?' Mam had demanded to know. 'Is he paying you? Is that what it is?'

Her own mother, accusing her of spreading her legs for money. They had argued, mother and daughter, shouting at each other long into the night before Dinah was forced out to the street. Her mam had told her never to darken her door again after bringing such shame to her home.

Dinah had first met Joe Marshall in the Albion Inn on one of the nights when she'd been called in to help Hetty Burdon behind the bar. She'd served him with beer and in return he'd tipped her generously, asking her to join him for a drink as soon as she was free. She didn't join him, not then, not in public, where everyone would have seen them and gossiped about the pit manager and the barmaid. But she kept her eye on him, watching him as she worked. There was something about the tidiness of him that she liked. She admired his smart suit and his hat. It wasn't a cloth cap like the miners wore. His was solid, shiny and clean.

Joe Marshall was different to any of the lads she'd met before, older, more worldly, and he offered her power and influence. She could have had any lad in Ryhope she wanted, she knew that; with her looks, people said, she could have had the pick of them all. But she wanted none of them, only Joe. She saw him often when he came into the Albion for a drink, and they secretly flirted. Dinah blushed every time he let his fingers brush her hand as he handed over coins to pay for his ale. She knew he was married, had even heard about their child, but she didn't let his domestic arrangements trouble her. She was young and wanted fun, and what was wrong with that? All she cared about was the way he made her feel when she saw him in the pub, how his discreet smiles and winks when no one else was looking made her body yearn for his.

Their opportunity came suddenly. During a quiet night at the bar, Dinah headed to the yard at the back of the pub and Mr Marshall followed. There, under the autumn moon above, they gave in to their lust after weeks of flirting and smiling. No one saw them there, no one realised that they'd even left the pub together. Mr Marshall headed back inside first, leaving Dinah to straighten her skirt and tidy her hair. But when she entered the pub just moments after him, he was nowhere to be found.

It didn't take long to track him down. Being the pit manager in a place as small as Ryhope meant that she knew where he lived and worked. She took her chance and made her move. And now here she was, at the Grange, where Mr Marshall's wife had lived just weeks before, sleeping in a warm double bed under soft sheets and wearing the finest cotton nightgown. But still she missed her mam and she missed her friend Nell, and she choked back the tears as she gripped tight to the handle of the wooden spoon and continued beating the butter and sugar to bake a cake for her wedding to a man she didn't truly know.

★ ★ ★

Sadie found herself warming to Dinah. She liked having someone of the same age to talk to. She liked the girl's spirit and admired the way she made herself at home in the Grange in a way that Sadie had never felt able to do as a member of staff. Dinah showed no interest in tending to Alexandra, for which Sadie was grateful. She liked having her daughter to herself, singing tunes remembered from her own childhood. The little girl was now at the age where she would try to join in with the tune, forming words as best as she could, delighting both herself and Sadie. Dinah spoke kindly to her when she saw her, but since Mr Marshall had told her that his sister-in-law would be coming at some point to take the child away, she saw her as little more than a piece of luggage waiting to be picked up and removed from the house.

Sadie had questioned Mr Marshall on the subject of Esther's arrival date many times since Christmas, and his answer was the same every time — when he had something to tell her, he would. The truth was, Esther's letters expressed no immediate desire to come and get the child at all. Gossip had travelled on the wind from Ryhope pit boss Benjamin Pascoe to his wife Sarah. Sarah told her sister Jeanette, who knew a pit manager's wife in Newcastle called Mrs McNally, who had a friend who knew Esther. The news had taken its time, but word finally reached Esther about her brother-in-law taking on a pregnant young woman and moving her into the Grange. She told him firmly in her letters that she would collect the child when she was good and ready and not a moment before.

With each passing week, and no word of Esther's arrival, Sadie relaxed a little, enjoying her time with her child, treasuring every second. But she needed to find out what was going to happen; her future depended on knowing how much time she had with Birdie. She had asked Dinah to enquire of Mr Marshall on her behalf, but the matter was of little interest to Dinah, for she cared nothing for another woman's child, as she had already made plain to Joe. Still, Sadie persisted, and one evening Dinah put the question carefully to Joe, on a rare evening when they were alone in the parlour together. He dismissed her with a wave of his hand and told her to be quiet. Dinah knew that a man who truly loved her wouldn't treat her that way. But she bit her tongue, this time. Far better to be quiet until after she was wed and had the ring on her finger that entitled her to the luxury of life at the Grange. She walked from the room and left him to his drinking.

On the night before Dinah and Joe's wedding, there was no concession given to tradition or what was deemed correct. Mr Marshall's bride-to-be spent the night under the same roof and in the same bed as her groom. There was no air of celebration about the Grange; it was a night like all the rest.

The morning of the wedding dawned bright with an eggshell-blue sky and few clouds. The sunlight on the flowers in the front garden of the Grange turned the tulips into jewels of purple and red floating on a frothy cloud of forget-me-not blue. Sadie and Em were pressed into service; Bessie had understood when Sadie had asked her for the morning away from her pie-baking duties. Em had been ordered to cook a full breakfast for Mr Marshall and Dinah, which they took together in the dining room with the door closed. Afterwards, Dinah asked Sadie to help her get dressed, and with Mr Marshall waiting downstairs in the parlour, Sadie took Alexandra in her arms and walked up to the bedroom that Dinah and Mr Marshall now shared.

'Come on in,' Dinah said, striding into the room with Sadie following. 'Sit the child on the bed; she'll be fine there, won't she?'

Alexandra began to crawl about on the eiderdown, with Sadie keeping an eye on her in case she veered too close to the edge. At the same time, she watched as Dinah pulled out a garment from the dark wooden wardrobe.

'He bought it for me,' she said, holding up a floaty peach-coloured dress for Sadie to see. 'Went into Binns yesterday and picked it specially.'

'He chose your wedding dress?' Sadie asked, shocked. 'Wouldn't you have liked to have chosen it yourself?'

Dinah shrugged. 'It's nice enough. And it fits me, although it's a little tight across my tummy, of course.'

She slipped the dress over her head. Sadie zipped it for her at the back and Dinah smoothed it over her stomach. The material of the dress felt smooth and cool to Sadie's touch, and she wondered if it was silk. She glanced at Dinah's bare feet.

'What about stockings and shoes?'

'My black high heels will have to do; they're the best shoes I have.'

Sadie glanced at the worn shoes lying on the floor and thought for a moment. 'There's polish downstairs in the kitchen. Let me go and shine them for you.' She swooped Alexandra into her arms and picked up the shoes with her free hand.

As she walked down to the kitchen, she chatted to the little girl.

'Shoes,' she said. 'Can Alexandra say shoes?'

The child tried with the unfamiliar word, but all that left her lips was the 'shh' sound, which made Sadie laugh. When Alexandra caught sight of Sadie laughing, she joined in too.

Once the shoes were shined, Sadie and Alexandra made their way back up the stairs. Sadie gasped when she saw Dinah. She'd applied rouge to her cheeks and her bow lips were now as juicy red as raspberries. Her hair was pinned back and her eyes had been darkened with shadow the colour of midnight.

'You look beautiful, miss,' she said, taking in the sight.

Dinah smiled and sat on the edge of the bed. She took the shoes from Sadie and slipped them onto her feet. Then she stood and wiggled her toes down into them.

'They're old and a little tight, but they'll have to do. Thank you, Sadie.'

'Come on then, let's get you downstairs.'

Dinah led the way to where Mr Marshall was waiting by the front door, checking his watch. He glanced up and Sadie saw his gaze lower, falling to the swell of Dinah's stomach as it pressed against the dress that he'd bought.

'You'll have to do,' he told her. 'Now come on, we've got to be at the register office for half past ten.'

Em walked into the hallway, wiping her hands on her apron.

'Lunch will be ready for noon, Mr Marshall,'

she said. 'And we'll have the dining room decorated for your return as you requested.'

'The best china and glasses, remember?'

'Yes, sir, for four of you, as we discussed.'

Mr Marshall nodded at Em. Sadie hung back with Alexandra in her arms and watched as he walked out to his car. Dinah started to follow, but then turned towards Sadie.

'Thank you,' she said.

Sadie simply nodded in reply, and then she and Em watched from the front door as Dinah disappeared into the passenger seat of Mr Marshall's black car.

'That poor girl,' Em whispered as the car drove away.

'Lunch for four of them?' Sadie asked. 'Who's coming?'

'One of the other pit bosses, the older one, Mr Wright. He and his wife have been called in to act as witnesses at the wedding, and then they're coming back here by way of the only celebration that poor girl's going to have on what should be the happiest day of her life.'

'No party, then? No big announcement?'

'Think he wants to keep it as quiet as he can,' Em sniffed. 'Anyway, I can't stand here chatting, I've got to get lunch on the go. He wants fried whiting for starters, then veal cutlets with brown gravy, and there's the fruit cake for afters, the one that Dinah helped make.'

'Is there anything I can do, Em?'

Em shook her head. 'Just let me crack on with things, love, and keep out of the kitchen with the little one today. I'm in no mood for chatting. I've a terrible feeling in my bones that I can't seem to shake off.'

★ ★ ★

Sadie spent the rest of the morning with Alexandra in the nursery, reading to her from a storybook that Em had brought into the house for her. There were no other books that Sadie could find, nor even any toys or dolls. She wondered whether Ruth and Joe Marshall had ever loved the child they had bought from her in Hartlepool. Alexandra was taken by the colours of the pictures in the book, and when something caught her attention, Sadie went over it again and again, forming the words for the little girl to copy.

'Horse,' she would say, pointing to a picture of the farmyard animals. 'And there's a cow, and a chicken.'

'Icken! Icken!' Alexandra repeated, looking to Sadie for confirmation that the right sounds were leaving her lips. She stabbed a plump finger at the sky above the farm, where a flock of birds were flying.

'They're birds,' Sadie explained. 'Birds, Bird . . .'

She stopped, catching herself just in time before she could say any more. It had been there, right on the tip of her tongue, the word *Birdie*, the name she had given her child. She had never uttered it in the Grange before, but it had almost come out without her thinking. And although there was no one to hear them, with Em working in the kitchen below and Mr Marshall and

Dinah not yet back from the register office, Sadie knew that she must never let her guard down again. For who knew what trouble it might land her in if the child thought of herself as Sadie's own special Birdie? She needed to stay in Mr Marshall's good books, for whatever he said about her to Esther when she came to take the child could mean the difference between Esther taking her to Newcastle and . . . the alternative was something Sadie couldn't allow herself to think about. She was determined never to be parted from her baby again, even if it meant leaving Ryhope behind.

★ ★ ★

After feeding Alexandra and settling her down for her nap, Sadie went downstairs to the kitchen. She found Em busy preparing the wedding meal.

'Will you help me serve, Sadie, when they arrive?' Em asked.

'Course I will,' Sadie said.

Em nodded towards the dresser, where the plates and cutlery were. 'You could set the table if you don't mind. Two sets of knives and forks, please, one for starters, one for mains. And no pudding spoons needed; I'm preparing small plates for the fruit cake, which I'll slice up later.'

Sadie set to laying the table in the dining room, putting down the best cloth first and then arranging the place mats. She didn't like the mats, with their pictures of boats on storm-tossed seas. There was nothing restful about them, she thought, and the pictures made her feel uneasy, the waves in turmoil and the boats in danger. She laid the larger knives and forks at the edge of each mat and then the smaller pieces of cutlery, to be used for the fried whiting starter, further out. When it was done, she admired her handiwork. It looked smart, she thought, and she knew that she'd done a good job.

In the hallway, the grandfather clock struck the hour. A movement outside caught Sadie's eye and she pulled back the lace curtain and peeked out. There was Mr Marshall's car, and there was Dinah, stepping out to the road.

'They're back!' Sadie yelled as she walked through to the kitchen. 'Em, they're back!'

'Go and take Mr and Mrs Wright's coats, love,' Em directed. 'I'll get this fish plated up and then you can take it into the dining room when they're all settled in.'

Sadie waited in the hallway and, as instructed by Em, took the coats from the pit boss and his wife. She recognised Mr Wright from the night of the dinner at the Grange, but if he remembered her, he gave nothing away. There was no hello, not even a hint of a smile. His wife bustled into the hallway after him; she was as tall as her husband and smiled broadly at Sadie as she handed over her shawl.

'Thank you, my dear,' she said. 'Is there somewhere I can freshen up before we eat?'

Sadie directed her to the bathroom on the landing and watched as the woman walked up the stairs. Her ample backside wobbled underneath her flowered dress as she moved. She was friendly, Sadie thought, polite too, and she was glad of it, for it didn't happen often that those in service were spoken to so kindly.

'We'll take drinks in the dining room,' Mr Marshall barked. 'The food can be served as soon as Mrs Wright joins us.'

'Yes, sir,' Sadie replied. She tried to catch Dinah's eye, to give her a smile of congratulation, but Dinah kept her eyes on Mr Marshall, as if needing to be told what to do.

Sadie hung the coats on the pegs and went to collect the plates of whiting. By now, everyone was seated and she served Mrs Wright and Dinah first. She glanced at Dinah, hoping again to show her support with something as simple as a smile. But when Dinah eventually looked up, there was an expression of horror in her eyes.

Sadie wanted to ask what was wrong, but she knew she couldn't say a word, not in front of everyone there, so she simply raised her eyebrows. Dinah quickly and subtly put her hands to the two sets of knives and forks in front of her. And suddenly Sadie understood. She hurried to the kitchen to bring the whiting for Mr Wright and Mr Marshall, and as she laid the master's plate in front of him, she flicked her eyes to Dinah to make sure she was watching, then gently reached out with her little finger and nudged his smaller fork.

It was a movement of no consequence to anyone else at the table, but it meant the world to Dinah. Now she knew which knife and fork to use. She watched as the others around the table picked up their cutlery and started to cut into the fish. The smell of it turned her stomach, but she knew she had to make an effort.

'Thank you both for this morning.' Mr Marshall addressed Mr Wright and his wife. 'It means a great deal to me that you agreed to be witnesses today.'

'Yes, thank you,' Dinah added quickly. 'Thank you, Mrs Wright.'

Mrs Wright laid her knife and fork down and finished chewing a mouthful of whiting before she allowed herself to speak.

'My dear child,' she said with a smile. 'Please, you must call me Margaret.'

'Margaret.' Dinah nodded.

'But never Peggy,' Mrs Wright continued, laughing. 'Nor Meg and certainly not Maggie. Why some people change the name they were born with I will never understand. My dear mother, may she rest in peace, named me Margaret the minute she clapped her eyes on me. And so Margaret I'll always be. I simply detest it when people call me anything but my true and proper name.'

'Yes, I see,' Dinah replied, although she didn't really understand.

Mr Wright gave a gentle cough. 'It's all going well at the pit with the new addition, isn't it?' he said, turning to his colleague.

Margaret glared at her husband. 'Must we really talk of work on a day like today?'

Mr Marshall chose to ignore her and replied directly across the table to Mr Wright.

'Very well,' he said. 'Better than expected. Production is up, as I thought.'

'Any more trouble from those agitators who

330

were complaining about safety on the seam?'

'None that you and I need be concerned about, Sidney.'

Eventually Mrs Wright managed to steer the talk from the pit to the weather: the warmth of the spring day and the forecast for the week. She was sensitive to the young girl's anxiety, and had been aware of her being quiet and reserved at the register office. She'd always thought of Joe Marshall as a bit of an unusual man, and he'd proved her right today. Marrying Dinah, who was just a slip of a lass, and so soon after Ruth's death too . . . well, she wasn't one to gossip, but she knew that word of this was going to make its way around Ryhope very soon. It was difficult enough to keep a secret in such a tight-knit community, where everyone seemed to know everyone else's business. But when the secret involved one of the pit bosses, his suspiciously quick marriage to a barmaid and the obvious way Dinah's belly strained against her silk wedding gown, it was easy to see that the villagers and the pit folk were going to have a field day.

She reached a hand to Dinah's arm and gave a warm smile. 'I could call on you each week if you'd like me to, Dinah. I usually go to visit friends in Seaham on Fridays and it'd be easy for me to drop in here as it's on the road back to Silksworth. Perhaps we might be friends?'

'I'd like that,' Dinah replied. 'I'd like that very much indeed.'

★ ★ ★

Once the main meal was served, Sadie helped Em in the kitchen, drying the pots and pans that Em was washing. They worked companionably together in silence, neither of them mentioning Dinah and Joe's wedding for fear that the other would think they were gossiping. But in truth, both of them were desperate to know what had gone on that morning in town.

With the washing-up done, Em wiped her hands on her apron and set to slicing up the fruit cake with her sharpest knife. The knife slipped easily through the cake; it had been a good bake and one she was proud of. The tang of brandy escaped with each slice she cut. But just as she was arranging them on the delicate blue china plates decorated with tiny pink roses, the scream of a siren cut into the very heart of the Grange. Again it sounded, and again. Three times, three blasts, as long and as loud and as evil a sound as Em had ever heard.

'My God! No! No!' she cried.

'What is it, Em? What's that dreadful noise?'

Em dropped the knife on the stone floor, where it clattered and slid. She ran out of the kitchen into the hall, heading for the front door but she was not the first to reach it. Mr Marshall and Mr Wright had already leapt into action. The sound of the siren from the pit was something that everyone in Ryhope lived in fear of, and three blasts meant only one thing.

The men flew from the Grange and into Mr Marshall's car, and before Em had even reached the end of the garden path, the motor had started up and was pulling from the kerb. She

332

ran after it as fast as she could, puffing and panting with every step. She had to know if her menfolk were safe. Three blasts from the pit meant the worst: a death underground. It wasn't the first time in her lifetime that she had heard the dreaded sound. But it was the first time that she'd had three of her sons and her husband all working at the colliery.

As she ran, doors were flung open and other women rushed out to join her, all heading in the same direction, all wanting to know what had happened, needing to know who had died.

'Please, God,' Em whispered under her breath as she ran past St Paul's church. Reverend Daye was running too, his bible in his hand, joining the women and children as they headed to the pit.

★ ★ ★

Back at the Grange, Sadie stood in the hallway, at a loss as to what was happening. What did those blasts mean?

'It's the pit,' Mrs Wright explained. 'When there's one blast, there's been an accident. Three blasts mean a death. We've got to get up there and do what we can to help.'

She and Dinah headed to the door, Dinah still wearing her wedding gown and best shoes.

'Dinah, it'd be best if you stay here,' Mrs Wright instructed. 'You don't want to get caught up in whatever's going on up there, not in your condition.'

Sadie ran up the stairs and took her daughter

from her bed. Alexandra was awake and crying; the noise of the blast had woken her from her sleep. Sadie held her to her chest, kissing her gently on her brow, then walked downstairs carefully and slowly with the child in her arms, trying to focus, to keep calm, to keep breathing in the midst of the panic around her. There was only one word on her mind. *Eddie.*

* * *

Sadie walked as quickly as she could, but by the time she arrived at the pit, there was a throng crowding the entrance, shouting and crying and demanding answers. She stood at the edge with Alexandra in her arms, watching and waiting for news. Her heart pounded and she pulled her daughter close. *Not Eddie, please, not Eddie,* she begged over and over again. Ahead of her, the crowd quietened, became solemn and then slowly began to part, allowing a stream of miners to leave the pit, their heads bowed, their faces streaked black.

No one spoke, no one dared ask the question, not yet. And then slowly a murmur started up. Sadie stood on tiptoes, watching the men file from the pit in groups of two and three. She scanned the crowd for the man she longed to see, but still there was no sign. Finally word was passed back from those coming out of the pit, and she heard the whispers about what had happened.

'Should never have brought him in,' one miner told another. 'Bloody crack hewer. The management needs a good shake-up. It should never have been allowed.'

'The younger lads don't understand, though, Billy. They try and match his pace.'

'Never stood a chance, did he?'

'Poor lad. What a waste of a life, and for what, eh? Answer me that!'

'For what? To make the bosses richer, that's what!'

Sadie watched and listened, and a chill ran through her. Hadn't Eddie told her how dangerous it was to bring a crack hewer in?

And then she saw him, Eddie, walking towards her. His head was down, but she knew it was him. Her heart lifted and a yell came from her that she didn't know she was capable of. She called his name, once, twice, and he spotted her in the crowd. She waved her free hand, hugging Alexandra to her chest. 'It's Eddie,' she whispered to the child. 'He's alive, my darling, he's alive.'

When he reached Sadie, he fell against her, holding onto her arm, and she had to set Alexandra on the ground, holding tight to the child's hand, so that she could wrap her free arm around him, hugging her to him as best as she could. When he lifted his head, Sadie saw that his face was as black as death and streaked with tears.

'It's Jacky Crawford,' he told her.

She closed her eyes, willing the name away, hoping it had been a mistake, that he'd been given the wrong name. 'Em's son?' she whispered.

'He was trying too hard, Sadie, pitching

himself against the crack hewer. And he was doing well, all the lads were cheering him on. We're just as much to blame.'

'No, Eddie!'

'He was tipping the coal tubs and he was that full of himself, he didn't see it coming: one of the tubs caught him and crushed him. Oh Sadie, I saw it all and there was nothing I could do, it all happened in a flash. One minute he was as happy as Larry, showing off how many tubs he could fill, joking that he could be a crack hewer himself, and the next . . . '

He shook himself free of Sadie's hand and leaned back against a shop window for support. Scared by the noise of the crowd, Alexandra began crying again.

'Come on, Eddie,' Sadie said, linking her arm through his. 'Let's get you home to your mam. She'll be worried sick.'

Eddie let himself be led away, and the three of them walked towards the Railway Inn. They'd only got as far as St Paul's church when Molly came hurrying towards them with Pip at her heels. She'd also heard the three blasts and had prepared herself for the worst. The minute she saw her son, she held out her arms to him. They stood together, arms wrapped around each other, on the pavement outside the church, as other mothers, sisters, aunts and wives streamed past on their way to the pit. When Molly at last released her grip, Sadie embraced her warmly, sharing her relief that it wasn't their boy who had been taken.

'Molly? Could you take Birdie to the Railway

Inn with you?' Sadie asked. 'There's something I need to do.'

'Course I can, love. But where are you off to?' Molly took Birdie from Sadie's arms and the child nuzzled into her neck.

'Back up to the pit. I've got to go and find Em.'

'It's Em's lad Jacky. He's the one who's gone, Mam,' Eddie explained.

'Jacky Crawford? But he's just a lad, a young lad. Oh, his poor mother. You be sure to give her my love, Sadie, please? Tell her I'll call up as soon as I can to see her, and she's to send word down to the Railway Inn if she needs anything, anything at all.'

'I will. I won't be long,' Sadie promised.

'Take as long as you need,' Molly replied. 'I'll look after Birdie for you, you know I love having her.'

Sadie clasped Eddie's hands, then kissed Birdie on the cheek before turning and racing back up the colliery, her skirt flying behind her in the wind. She would call at the Forester's Arms first. Bessie would know what to do, and the two of them would give Em all the love she deserved, and all the care she needed too.

14

Moment of Truth

Summer 1920

'The brass band was good, very moving,' Sadie said.

Eddie nodded. 'No self-respecting pit village would be without a colliery band, and Ryhope's got one of the best. Jacky would have loved it, the whole band turning out to play at his funeral like that.'

'Em didn't look well, though, did she?'

'No surprise,' Eddie replied. 'And you say she's not returning to the Grange?'

'She says her mind's made up. She can't be working for one of the pit bosses, not after what happened to Jacky.'

'You haven't told anyone you knew about the crack hewer being brought in, have you?'

Sadie shook her head. 'I haven't said a word. You know I don't gossip about Mr Marshall's business to anyone outside the Grange.'

Eddie looked ahead of him, to the blue of the ocean sparkling under the summer sky. 'I've been hearing things about him myself. And it might just be gossip, Sadie, that's why I haven't said anything to you before. But I've been told that he's involved in something crooked with the

338

books. Financial irregularities, they're calling it.'

'Who told you?'

'One of the engineers at the pit, a fella called Brian Ridley; his mam is good friends with mine. She told Mam on the quiet last week in the pub. Mam's only told me; she won't breathe a word to another soul. It mustn't go any further, Sadie. But it gives us an insight into the kind of man Joe Marshall really is.'

Sadie pushed her fingers into the warm sand as she let Eddie's words sink in. There was something she needed to tell him: a letter had arrived at the Grange that morning. But she pushed the thought of it to the back of her mind as they sat enjoying the sunny day on the beach.

'Will you be taking on Em's duties at the Grange?' Eddie asked.

Sadie shrugged. 'Nothing's been said. I've barely seen Mr Marshall since the day Jacky died. He's working day and night at the pit, or at least that's what he tells Dinah. She and I have the house to ourselves; she sits in the kitchen with me, chatting. I like her, Eddie. She asks my advice, and I share what I can. I've been doing some baking for her, and it seems to keep her happy. Bessie said I can take a break from making the pies to sell until things are settled at the Grange and a new cook comes in.'

Eddie turned his attention to Birdie, who was toddling around happily in front of where he and Sadie sat on a checked picnic blanket. 'And what's to become of us, Sadie?' he said, gazing at the child.

'It depends on Esther.' Sadie touched her

ladybird charm. 'If I can go to live with her in Newcastle, even if it's just for a short time, before she . . . ' she faltered and looked out to sea, 'before she sells Birdie on, maybe there's a chance I can go with her as her nurse. If I can, my future lies there.'

'*Our* future,' Eddie reminded her.

Sadie felt a lump rise in her throat. If anyone had seen them sitting there on the sands, they would have thought them a perfect family — Sadie, Eddie and a little girl who could be their own. But Sadie had to try her best not to let her thoughts run that way, such was the uncertainty of what was going to happen once Esther arrived. She didn't dare hope that she and Eddie could stay in Ryhope, or that Birdie would always be a part of her life. Her own parents had died when she was so young and her heart yearned for a family. But she mustn't dream about life with both Eddie and Birdie, not yet. For now, sitting on the beach under the warm summer sky, she had the family she had always wanted. But how long was it going to last?

'Come on, Alexandra!' Eddie called, and he jumped to his feet, running towards the child. She squealed with delight as he scooped her up from the sand and ran with her in his arms to the sea.

Sadie stayed where she was, watching them playing in the shallows, Birdie tiptoeing into the water and then running from the waves as they kissed the shore. She watched as Eddie kneeled on the sand in front of Birdie and held out his arms for the child to cling on to as she kicked and splashed the water with her bare feet. She saw him lean his head close to Birdie's as if he was whispering in her ear, and she wondered what he was telling her. She saw Birdie's face light up with glee as she repeated the words Eddie encouraged her to say. She was learning more words every day, and Sadie could not have been more proud of her. Her heart was bursting with love for the man who would become her husband, and for the child she had been blessed to spend time raising as her own. But she knew, deep in her heart, that their life together and what lay ahead of them remained in the hands of Mr Marshall and his evil sister-in-law.

When they had finished playing in the shallows, Eddie picked Birdie up and carried her across a patch of pebbles so that she didn't hurt her feet. He sat her down on the picnic blanket beside Sadie and then sat down himself on the other side of her.

'Eddie, I need to tell you something,' Sadie said.

He looked at her with concern.

'A letter came to the Grange this morning. It's Esther's handwriting. It's sitting in the hallway right now, waiting for Mr Marshall to open and read it. It might be news of her visit at last.'

'We'll know for sure one way or the other soon enough,' Eddie replied. 'But you know, Jacky's death has started me thinking. Life's too short to wait, Sadie. That could have been me caught up in the accident at the pit; it could have been any of us. One day you're there and the next you're six feet under and the Ryhope brass band is giving you a send-off.'

'What are you saying?' Sadie asked, confused.

'What I'm saying is, we should set a date for the wedding. Let's not leave it until it's too late. And if we do have to make the move to Newcastle, we'll be doing it as husband and wife.'

Sadie's face lit up. 'We could go and see Reverend Daye this afternoon, see what he's got to say.'

'There's no time like the present. Let's do it now.'

★   ★   ★

'Sadie? Could I have a word?'

It was Dinah, standing in the doorway to the parlour. Sadie's heart sank when she saw the pale blue envelope in her hand. Was this it, then? Finally, news of Esther's arrival?

'Could I put Alexandra to bed first?' she asked. She hugged the sleeping child to her chest, both of them tired and happy after their day spent at the beach with Eddie.

'Of course,' Dinah replied. 'And then please come into the parlour. It's all right, Joe's not here. He's asked me to speak to you.' She held the blue envelope aloft. 'There's news.'

★   ★   ★

When Sadie entered the parlour, Dinah was seated to one side of the fireplace. The fire was unlit, the room already too stuffy and warm.

Dinah filled the chair completely, her growing belly straining against the thin cotton of her dress. She looked tired, Sadie thought, tired and overwhelmed, and she remembered how she had once felt when she was pregnant with Birdie at Freda's house.

'Please, have a seat,' Dinah said.

Sadie took the chair opposite and placed her hands in her lap. There was a new directness to Dinah, she noticed; the girl had clearly heeded Em's early advice about making her own mark at the Grange. She straightened her back and prepared herself for whatever Esther's letter contained.

'I won't beat around the bush. She's coming this weekend,' Dinah said. She searched the other girl's face, fearing that the words she had been asked to pass on would hurt Sadie deeply. She'd seen the bond between Sadie and the child, she'd seen how happy they were in each other's company, how content and settled. 'She's to stay Friday night and travel back first thing on Saturday morning.'

'Taking Alexandra with her?' Sadie asked.

'I think you knew that was always her plan.' Dinah picked up the letter from a small table beside her and held it towards Sadie. 'Would you like to read it?'

Sadie shook her head.

'Joe has asked if you could make up the guest room and cook the meals while she's here. He'll pay you extra, he said, until such time as I appoint a new housekeeper.'

Sadie swallowed hard. The very last thing she

wanted to do was look after the woman who was coming to the Grange to take her child away. But she knew she needed to keep herself in check, to bide her time until she could have a private word with Esther about joining her when she left.

'If you don't mind, Dinah, I think I'll go to bed,' she said at last. 'It's been a long day.'

She stood and walked from the parlour, taking the stairs slowly. Once in her room, she lay down on the eiderdown, mulling over the news. Nothing was more important now than staying with Birdie. She was not prepared to let her go. The only option she had now was to appeal to Esther's conscience, if she had one. Could Dinah speak for her? she wondered. No, she decided, this was something she needed to do on her own. She'd have to prepare herself, think of the words she would use, the tone she would need to convince Esther to take her on as Alexandra's nurse. She could see no other way around it. Mr Marshall had warned her against running away with the child. Sadie knew it was his investment he was afraid to lose, with little thought for Alexandra's welfare. But who would believe her word against that of a respectable pit boss? Yet the more she thought about Mr Marshall, the more an idea began to form in her mind. And when she woke the next morning, still in her clothes from the day before, still lying on the eiderdown, Sadie knew exactly what she needed to do.

★　★　★

On Friday evening, Mr Marshall's car pulled up outside the Grange with Esther in the passenger seat. Sadie waited anxiously in the hallway. She had made up the guest room and baked chicken pies to be served with new potatoes. It was hard to know who was the more nervous about the woman's arrival. Dinah had never met any of her husband's family before, and knew little of what to expect.

Mr Marshall stepped into the house, Esther following him with a look on her face that suggested she would rather be anywhere else in the world. She was wearing a black cape and hat, which Sadie thought made her appear as if she was still in mourning garb, which perhaps was her intention. Once Sadie had taken her outdoor things, and Mr Marshall had brought her travelling bag from the car, Dinah walked from the parlour with her hand outstretched, as Sadie had advised her earlier.

'Nice to meet you, Esther,' she said.

Esther took Dinah's dainty hand and held it for a second, no longer. 'Is my room ready?' she said. There was no smile, no warmth in her tone.

'Let me take you up,' Dinah suggested.

'No need,' Esther said. 'I know where it is.' She turned to Sadie. 'And you? You'll have the child ready for seven thirty in the morning. I will be leaving on the first train. As for breakfast, I'll take an egg, lightly poached, at seven. And I want none of the stottie bread that you people like so much. It plays havoc with my digestion.'

'Will you be down for dinner this evening?' Mr Marshall asked her.

Esther glared at Dinah, deliberately letting her gaze settle on Dinah's stomach, bulging with Joe Marshall's child, the child her sister could never bear.

'No,' she said firmly. 'I have work to do in my room, letters to write and papers to prepare.'

'I'll bring you a tray of tea, miss,' Sadie offered. 'With a slice of chicken pie warm from the oven.'

'As you wish,' replied Esther. She turned to her brother-in-law. 'My bag, please.' Mr Marshall picked up her overnight bag from the floor and followed her up the stairs.

'My word, she's a one!' Dinah whispered once Esther was out of earshot. She followed as Sadie headed back to the kitchen. 'Sadie? Can I ask you something?'

Sadie turned. 'Of course, what is it?'

'When the child goes tomorrow, how would you like to stay on here as the nurse to my child?'

Sadie felt the words like a punch to her chest. She had never been sure whether Dinah knew the truth about Alexandra being her own child. But if Dinah had known, if Joe had told her, Sadie knew she would've never been so insensitive, offering Sadie such a role staying on at the Grange looking after Joe's real child. She reached out to one of the kitchen chairs and gripped it to steady herself as Dinah continued.

'I mean, I've seen the way you are with Alexandra: you're capable, you're loving, you're calm. We'd have to get a new cook and house-keeper, of course, now that Em's not coming back, but what do you say, Sadie? Would you

346

stay? I'd have to run it past Joe, but I'm sure he'll say yes. I'm getting better at putting my foot down with him, you know, just like Em told me to. And he's out at work all the time anyway, isn't he? Would you stay on, Sadie? You've helped me so much, I don't know what I'd do without you if you weren't here any more.'

Sadie couldn't reply, she was so choked with emotion, and in the silence, Dinah looked at her and saw the tears in her eyes.

'I can't stay, Dinah. I have plans of my own once the child goes.'

'You do? What plans? Sadie, are you all right?'

Sadie lifted the edge of her apron to wipe her tears away. 'I'm fine,' she said. 'Sorry, Dinah. Please, I need to get on and prepare the tray.'

She turned away, busying herself with the teapot by the fire, and Dinah slipped out of the room.

⋆　⋆　⋆

Esther didn't reappear that evening; she stayed in her room with the oil lamp burning. Sadie could see the light from under the door when she walked up the stairs to check on Alexandra. She settled herself into the chair at Alexandra's bedside and watched the sleeping child, going over in her mind what she needed to do.

Downstairs in the parlour, Dinah and Mr Marshall sat talking. Sadie heard the odd word floating up the stairs. She made out Dinah's voice, forceful, pleading, demanding to know where her new husband was spending his time

347

after he finished work at the pit. In return came Joe Marshall's voice, calming and hushing his bride, telling her he was a busy man, that she needed to get used to it if she was to fit in at the Grange. And then there were footsteps, heavy, slow footsteps coming up the stairs, a door slamming and the sound of Dinah's sobs.

Sadie leaned across Alexandra's bed and kissed her daughter on the forehead. She took a deep breath, then straightened up and smoothed down the front of her apron. At the bedroom door, she turned, took a final look at the sleeping child and whispered. 'Goodnight, my angel. Sleep tight.'

She closed the door softly behind her and went downstairs to the parlour. The parlour door was closed, and she raised her hand to knock, but then thought better of it and stopped. She removed her apron, folded it and laid it on a chair in the hallway. She was going to deal with Mr Marshall on her own terms; not as an employee at the Grange, but as Sadie Linthorpe, a mother. Without giving herself a chance to change her mind, she pushed open the door and strode inside.

Mr Marshall was sprawled in an armchair, a glass of whisky in his hand. 'What the hell do you think you're doing?' he asked her. 'You can't come barging in here uninvited!'

Sadie felt her earlier resolve crumbling, her legs starting to shake. The words that she'd gone over in her mind just minutes before wouldn't leave her lips. Her mouth felt dry and her hands were clammy. She forced herself to swallow and breathe deeply, readying herself for a fight she knew she had to win.

'I need to speak to you, Mr Marshall.'

'Bloody women! That's all you ever do! You never shut up, do you, the lot of you!'

He threw the remains of the drink down his throat and filled the glass again from the bottle at his side. From the look of him, and the way he slurred his words, Sadie guessed he'd been drinking since Esther's arrival.

'My home has become a nest of bloody women!' he cried again, addressing the room. 'And all you ever do is talk! You don't work! You don't know the responsibility of running a business, a pit!' He tapped the side of his head forcefully with his forefinger. 'You have no idea what goes on in here, do you? Inside a man's mind?' He took a gulp of whisky and eyed Sadie from her boots all the way up. 'You'll return to Hartlepool after Esther leaves with the child tomorrow.'

'No, sir,' Sadie said. She gripped her hands together in front of her. 'I'm staying in Ryhope.' She took another deep breath. 'And so is my child.'

Mr Marshall's eyes narrowed. 'What did you say?'

'I said my child is staying in Ryhope, with me. I'm her mother and I won't let anyone take her again.'

Mr Marshall snorted with laughter. 'You don't have any say in the matter, girl.'

'Oh, I think I do,' Sadie said softly. 'You see, I know a lot about you, Joe Marshall.'

She took a step towards him and saw his body stiffen. He raised his glass to his lips and took another gulp.

'I know about your women, about how you courted Dinah while Ruth was in her sickbed, carrying on with her when you should have been at home tending to your dying wife. And I know you're cheating on Dinah too.'

This last was nothing but a guess on Sadie's part, deduced from what she'd seen of his treatment of Dinah and from the argument she'd heard between them. But from the way Mr Marshall's mouth twisted, it was clear that her words had found their target.

'And what of it?' he asked, smirking. 'A man's not a man unless he's got a few trinkets he can play with.' His tone was breezy, carefree; he was trying too hard. Sadie knew she had him squirming and she took another step forward.

'And that's how they view things at the pit, is it? That it's all right for respectable bosses to be adulterers behind closed doors? Perhaps I could tell that to the wives of the other managers I've met while I've worked here. I'm sure Mrs Wright might be interested to know what goes on in your private life . . . ' Sadie paused, 'sir.'

Mr Marshall sucked air through his teeth.

'Or should I tell Dinah?' she continued.

'What is this? What do you want? Do you want money? Is that what you're after?'

'You know what I'm after,' Sadie said, keeping her breathing steady and her tone calm. 'And there's more, Joe Marshall. There's more gossip going on about you around the back streets of

Ryhope than you could possibly know.'

'Rubbish!' he spat.

'Financial irregularities at the pit, I heard,' Sadie said. 'Now I wonder if the area manager of the Ryhope Coal Company would be interested to hear about that? Or maybe I should write a letter to *The Sunderland Echo*?'

Joe Marshall dropped his gaze to the floor, his breathing fast and shallow. Sadie stood her ground. It was just a piece of gossip that Eddie had passed on. It could be wrong, she could have misjudged it, but she also knew Eddie would never have told her if he'd thought there was no truth in it.

'You'll never prove anything,' Mr Marshall said at last, glaring at her. He stood, but the whisky made him unsteady on his feet and he fell back into his chair.

Sadie wasn't finished with him yet. She took another step forward so that she was standing right in front of him. He reached for the bottle again, but she grabbed it from the table before he could refill his glass.

'What do you want?' he hissed at her.

'Just one thing. My child.'

Mr Marshall shook his head. 'Impossible. The child is leaving in the morning.'

'The child will stay, Mr Marshall. You hear me? She will stay, with me. But not here at the Grange. I'm moving out tonight and taking her with me. And if you stop me, if you even try, I'll tell Dinah all I know about your other women, and I'll tell the Ryhope Coal Company about your creative financial work too.'

'They wouldn't believe you,' he spat.

'If they don't, then the people of Ryhope will. Your reputation is in my hands. There's more I could tell them too, about the death of Jacky Crawford at the pit. About how your vote was the deciding one in bringing in the crack hewer. You killed Jacky, Mr Marshall. You cast your vote and you killed a Ryhope lad.'

'Get out!' he screamed. 'Get out of my bloody house!'

'Oh, I'll go,' Sadie said quietly. 'In fact I'm going now. I'm all packed and I'm taking my child. You took her from me once and that will never happen again. Never!' She thrust the whisky bottle at him and he slumped, defeated, in the armchair, hugging it to his chest.

Sadie turned to head from the room, but before she reached the door, Mr Marshall called out: 'You take that child and I'll kill you. I swear I'll kill you with my own two hands. Esther is taking the child. A deal has been agreed and money's been paid.'

'More than tuppence this time, I trust?'

'Tuppence? What are you on about, girl?'

Sadie ignored his question and reached out her hand to the door. But before she could open it, it swung open. Outside in the hallway stood Dinah, her eyes red and her face streaked with tears. She stepped into the parlour and turned her fury on her husband.

'I've heard every word, Joe. Every single word.'

Sadie shot her a look, but Dinah was fully focused on her drunken husband.

'I know all about you now, and if you think I

352

didn't hear your threats to kill Sadie, think again. I heard every word with my own ears. I'm moving out of your bedroom to the room above, the room where I'll live as Mrs Marshall, lady of the Grange, and you'll do right by me and my bairn. My God, I'll make sure that you do. I'm not giving up the soft sheets and the warm rooms and the comfort I've been denied so far in my life. And if you don't want a scandal, you'll agree to my terms. I'm going to move my mam into the guest room. I'll beg her if I have to, but I need her here with me. And there'll be a job for my friend Nell, too.

'Every Friday, I will open the Grange to Mrs Margaret Wright and to any of the other pit managers' wives who want to come here to visit and talk. And we *will* talk, Joe Marshall, we will talk of our husbands and of the things they do. And if you want me to keep quiet about what I've heard tonight, you'll do right by Sadie here, let her take her child and send that witch of a sister-in-law of yours back to Newcastle empty-handed!'

Sadie watched as Mr Marshall tried to form words, tried to say something to get himself out of the mess he'd created. Dinah laid her hand on her arm.

'Go,' she smiled. 'Take your child and go.'

'Did you know she was mine?'

'I began to suspect she might be,' Dinah replied. 'But I swear I didn't know when I asked you to stay on here to look after my child. I'd never be so unthinking towards you. But I've seen the way you are with her and the love that flows between you. I've watched you, Sadie. You and Alexandra are meant to be together.'

'I call her Birdie,' Sadie said.

'Then go to Birdie and take her now. I'll make sure he sends on any wages that you're due. Promise me that you'll keep in touch, that you'll let me know where you are and how we can reach you?'

'I promise.'

Sadie fled, taking the stairs two at a time. She ran all the way to her room and grabbed her bag of clothes. Then she went down to the child's bedroom and picked up her daughter, holding her in her arms.

'Come on, Birdie,' she whispered to the sleeping child. 'It's time for us both to go home.'

15

Birdie

'Another drink, love?' Molly called from behind the bar. Eddie shook his head and glanced towards Tom, who was helping their mam, working a cloth around a pint glass, his eyes downcast. But at least he was up and out of bed, and sober, which was something of an improvement.

Eddie watched as his mam pulled pints for her customers, chatting to them, asking how they were doing, remembering the names of their wives, daughters, dogs and even pigeons, and enquiring about the health of them all. For a lot of the customers, the welfare of their pigeons took priority over family members. It always made him smile. He saw his mam lay her hand on Tom's arm as they passed each other behind the bar and mouth softly to him: 'You all right, son?' And he saw Tom give a gentle nod in reply.

He was just about to finish his pint and head up to bed when the pub door burst open with such force that many of the customers turned to see what was going on.

'Sadie!' he cried as soon as he saw her. Her face was flushed and streaked with tears. In one arm she carried the crying child; in the other were two cotton sacks, which she flung to the pub floor.

355

'I've done it,' she sobbed.

Molly dashed from behind the bar and held her arms out. Sadie gratefully handed Birdie to her and then sank into the nearest chair. Molly shushed the little girl, calming her. Birdie was awake now and crying after the walk in the night air from the Grange.

'What is it, Sadie? What's happened?' Eddie asked, concerned.

'I've done it, Eddie. I've left the Grange. It's over. And the bairn, she's all mine now. She's ours.'

Tom appeared by Sadie's side. Without a word he planted a glass of brandy on the table in front of her.

Molly looked from her son to Sadie. 'It sounds like you two have got a lot to talk about. I'll take the bairn and settle her in my bed upstairs.' She turned to the drinkers gawping and whispering about Sadie's arrival. 'And you lot? Mind your own bloody business!'

★ ★ ★

Over the next hour, Sadie told Eddie about everything that had happened at the Grange. When she reached the part about confronting Mr Marshall over the financial irregularities at the pit, Eddie took a sharp breath.

'You didn't tell him where you'd heard that, did you?'

'Course not,' Sadie replied. 'But it's true, Eddie, you were right about it all. I saw it on his face; he didn't even try to deny it. I told him

356

what I knew about the crack hewer, too. I had to, Eddie. I had to throw everything I had at him.'

Eddie took her hand, then pulled his chair closer to hers and wrapped his arm around her shoulders. 'I'm proud of you, Sadie. I've always known you were special.' He put his hand to his chest. 'I've always felt it, you know. In here. I know I don't say much, not about my feelings and that, but I don't half love you, Sadie Linthorpe.'

Sadie leaned towards him and kissed him hard on the lips. 'I'm pleased to hear it,' she said. 'Because I think we should take up Reverend Daye's offer of the free Saturday in July he told us about. I want to marry you as soon as I can, Eddie. I want to be Mrs Sadie Teasdale. I want the three of us to be a family.'

Eddie thought his heart would burst with pride and he swallowed a lump in his throat. 'I spoke to Mam,' he said. 'Asked her if we could move into my room after we were wed.'

'And what did she say?'

'What do you think she said?' Eddie teased. 'She's over the moon. She even said she's going to get Bessie's daughter Cara to run up some new curtains on her sewing machine. It's not a big room, Sadie, but it'll do until we can afford a place of our own.'

'I've got a little money saved,' Sadie said, thinking of the pound notes tucked into her boot. It was money she had kept all of this time for Birdie, and now with Eddie's love and care, her daughter would want for nothing.

She glanced around the pub. It looked no

different from the first time she'd seen it, when she'd taken shelter from the rain on the day she'd arrived in Ryhope, alone and desperate to find her child. And not only had she found her, but she'd found Eddie too, Molly and Tom and even little Pip. She'd found her family at last, in Ryhope of all places. And in the Railway Inn she'd found her home. Who knew what her future might bring her, or where it might lead? All she knew at that moment, sitting by Eddie's side with her child safe in bed above, was that she'd never felt more happy or secure.

A movement at the end of the bar caught her eye, and she glanced over to see Molly walking towards them.

'Bairn fell fast asleep the minute her head touched the pillow,' she smiled. 'There's space for both of you to sleep in with me until you and Eddie are spliced. I can't send you back to live in the storeroom, it wouldn't be right, not now you're almost family.'

'Thanks, Molly,' Sadie smiled.

'You two all right?' Molly asked, glancing at Eddie.

'We're fine, Mam,' he replied. 'I'll let Sadie tell you everything that's happened. I've got to get myself up to bed; I need to be up early for my shift.' He stood, kissing Sadie on the cheek, and then he kissed his mam too.

'Night, love,' Molly said.

'Molly?' said Sadie.

'Yes, pet?'

'Can I tell you everything in the morning; would you mind waiting till then? I'm done in, and I really want to be with Birdie right now.'

'Course you can, love.'

'And there's something else I hope I can talk to you about,' Sadie added.

'Whatever it is, I'll help you.'

'It's about the wedding. We want to take the Saturday in July that's free at St Paul's.'

Molly clasped her hands to her heart. 'Oh love, that's fantastic!'

Sadie glanced towards the bar and leaned closer to Molly. 'Do you think Tom will come if we invite him?' she whispered.

'I hope so,' smiled Molly. 'Because Eddie's already asked him to be his best man.'

'And he's agreed?'

Molly nodded. She reached across the table to hold Sadie's hands in hers, and Sadie saw her eyes fill with tears.

'I knew you were a good 'un the minute I saw you,' she said. 'And I apologise again for doubting you, lass, and for calling you what I did.'

'Let's never mention it again,' Sadie said.

'It's a deal,' Molly agreed. 'Now, about this wedding, who will you ask to give you away?'

Sadie replied without missing a beat. 'Pat Brogan.'

'Of course,' Molly replied. 'Now go on, get yourself up to bed with your little one. We'll talk more in the morning.'

Sadie walked through the doorway at the end of the bar to where the stairs led to the rooms above. It was the first time she had ever been up there, and when she reached the landing, she wondered which way to turn. How would she know which room was Molly's? It didn't take her long to find out, for there was one room that had its door open to the landing. She peeked her head around it, and there was no mistaking it was a woman's bedroom, with its floral eiderdown, and bottles of lotions and perfume on a dressing table. She pushed the door further open and there was her daughter, lying in the middle of the big double bed.

She walked into the room and pulled the door closed behind her. An oil lamp threw flickers of light into the room from the top of a dressing table. Sadie lay down on the bed next to her daughter. It was the first time they had shared a bed since the day Birdie had been taken from her arms. She looked at her little girl, really looked at her in a way she had never done before, savouring the fact that they never need be parted again. Birdie's eyes were closed tight as she lay fast asleep on Molly's soft pillow.

Thoughts raced in Sadie's mind in the quiet of the room with just the gentle breath of Birdie at her side. She thought about Dinah at the Grange and the power she'd displayed standing up to Joe Marshall. She thought about what Esther would say when she discovered what had happened. And then her thoughts turned to what was to come: her wedding to Eddie and all it would involve. She needed to speak to Reverend Daye to confirm the date. And she'd speak to Bessie to ask if Cara could make her wedding dress.

She pictured a floor-length white gown, the simplicity of its lines set off by a small bunch of lilac and the sweet peas that grew wild along the beach road, tangled on the old wooden fence. She would pick the longest stalks she could find, bunching the flowers together until she had enough for her own bouquet and a smaller one for Birdie, her bridesmaid. At her neck would be her ladybird charm, glinting silver against her pale skin. And she'd ask Molly to do her hair for her; now that it was no longer shorn, Molly would make it look pretty.

She thought of Bessie and Pat Brogan. If the pain in Pat's hip allowed, she'd ask him to walk her down the aisle, her arm linked through his. She pictured the congregation waiting inside the church to see her and Eddie get wed. She'd invite Dinah and Em, Lil Mahone and Bessie's daughters with their families. And there'd be a cake — oh, the cake that Sadie could make with Bessie and Molly's help, decorated with tiny birds made of lemon fondant.

Suddenly her heart sank. She'd have to return to the Grange at some point, as she'd left her bike in the back yard. Maybe Eddie could collect it for her, or she could go on a day when Mr Marshall's car was absent from the street and she'd be able to sneak into the scullery to chat to Dinah, her mam and Nell. She thought of her life ahead, living at the Railway Inn, getting the Select up and running properly, making it her own. She pictured herself sharing Eddie's room, his past, his future, his family, and the thought of it warmed her, made her smile and sent her to sleep at last.

The next morning, Sadie was roused by Birdie's cry. It was the first time the child had woken outside of the Grange and she was confused by her surroundings. Sadie sat up in the bed, pulling her daughter towards her, calming her, telling her that everything was all right, for she felt sure in her heart that it was.

Birdie reached her hands to the ladybird charm at Sadie's neck, laughing now, her tears drying, forgotten.

'Dee!' she cried. 'Dee.'

Sadie shook her head. 'Mama,' she told the child with a smile.

16

Hartlepool

Three days before Eddie and Sadie's wedding, there was a surprise caller for Sadie at the Railway Inn. She was in the yard with Birdie and Eddie, the three of them running around, making Birdie scream with delight as she chased them, calling out to them with the new words Sadie had taught her to say.

'Mama! Dada!'

Each time Eddie allowed himself to be caught, he'd sweep the little girl up in his arms to the Ryhope sky above and tell her: 'I love you, little one, our sweet Bird.'

'Visitor for you, Sadie,' Molly called from the back door of the pub.

Sadie stiffened. She wasn't expecting anyone and feared it might be Mr Marshall. No matter how many times Eddie reassured her that it would never happen, that she was home and clear now, that Birdie would never be taken from her again, there was still a tiny piece of her heart that couldn't yet believe his words.

'I'll come with you,' Eddie said when he saw how worried Sadie looked. He scooped Birdie into his arms and followed her into the pub.

'Dinah!' Sadie cried when she saw her standing by the pub door. And then she noticed the black perambulator at Dinah's side, and Molly peering into it, smiling at the baby asleep under the softest cotton blankets that money could buy. Tom was working behind the bar, and he and Dinah exchanged a shy look and a smile. Sadie walked towards her and held out her hand, but Dinah pulled her close and hugged her to within an inch of her life.

'It's a girl!' she said, smiling. 'I'm calling her Joan Emily after my mam.'

Sadie looked at the baby's tiny pink face, its eyes screwed up as it slept.

'She's beautiful,' she said.

Dinah nodded in agreement.

'You look well,' Sadie told her, and it was true, there was a sparkle about Dinah, and Sadie took in the pretty summer jacket and matching hat that she wore.

'Listen, Sadie, I was wondering . . . well, I was hoping you might give me some help.'

'With your baby? No, I won't go back to the Grange if that's what you mean.'

'No, not the Grange. I need some help in finding a housekeeper and I wondered if you knew anyone I could ask. Em still refuses to return. I've even offered her a pay rise, but she says she's never coming back to work for Mr Marshall. My mam's moved in to help me nurse the baby and my friend Nell's coming in every morning to clean the place and get the fires burning. But I need help with the cooking and the baking and the dinners I have to throw for the pit bosses. I haven't a clue where to start.'

Sadie thought for a moment. She didn't know

of anyone in Ryhope who would want such a job, but then an idea struck her.

'What are you doing for the rest of the day, Dinah?'

'Walking the baby. Joe's at work and I don't expect him back until the early hours.' Dinah held Sadie's gaze, both of them fully aware of where Joe went when he wasn't at work. But she kept her head high, for there was more to the Grange than being married to an oddball like Joe Marshall. The more time her husband spent outside her new home, the more Dinah could make her own mark on the place, enjoying the fruits of Joe's labour, relishing the perks of being married to a pit boss without any of his demands.

Sadie glanced at the clock behind the bar. 'Eddie, would you mind if I disappeared with Dinah for the rest of the day? I want to take Birdie too. We'll be home early evening.'

'But where are we going?' Dinah asked.

'Hartlepool,' Sadie replied. 'The morning train leaves from Ryhope East just before eleven. We'll go and find you your housekeeper; I know just the place to look.'

'Sadie, are you sure?' Eddie asked, concerned. 'What if you see Mick or Freda?'

'They can't hurt me now. I need to do this, Eddie. I need to go to Hartlepool one last time, then I can turn my back on it finally before I enjoy my future here.'

'The lass has got a point,' Molly sighed. 'Let her do what she needs to do, son.'

Eddie thought for a moment. His mam was

right; he needed to let Sadie spread her wings. But he'd seen the mess she'd been in after Mick had beaten her when he'd found her at the Grange. There was no way he'd allow that to happen again. 'I'm coming with you,' he said.

'There's no need,' Sadie said. 'Really, Eddie.'

'Please let me come, Sadie. If you go on your own, I'll not rest all day until I see you walk back through the pub door. Let me come; you can show me Hartlepool, share a bit of your past with me before our wedding.'

Sadie hesitated a moment and turned to Dinah. 'Is it all right if Eddie comes and we make a day of it?'

Dinah smiled. 'The more the merrier. We might need some help getting the baby's pram up onto the train, if Eddie's keen to help?'

Sadie ran up the stairs to the bedroom she shared with Molly and grabbed her shawl, hat and bag. Then she picked up a shawl and hat for Birdie too, that Molly had knitted for her in red and white stripes. She kissed Molly before she headed out of the pub holding tight to Birdie's hand. At her side walked Dinah, pushing the pram with her newborn inside. Eddie hung back a few steps, letting the women walk together.

Dinah leaned towards Sadie. 'I've never been on a train before,' she confided. 'In fact, I've never been outside of Ryhope.'

'Don't worry, I have,' Sadie smiled. 'I know what to do. I'll ask the ticket clerk for our tickets. It'll be first-class for you and the baby. Eddie and I will travel in third with Birdie.'

'You'll do no such thing! Joe Marshall has

given me a purse full of money this morning. I reckon there's enough for first-class return tickets for us all.'

★   ★   ★

When the train finally reached Hartlepool West, Sadie led the way to the market square. It seemed smaller than she remembered, more densely packed with shops and buildings, the streets crowded with more people than she could recall from her time living there. She felt a tightness in her chest as she scanned the features of those walking the pavements, in case there was a familiar face she might want to see, or one she might want to avoid.

Time had moved on, and Sadie knew that better than anyone, for how different her life had become since the day she'd escaped from Freda's lodging house. And now, here she was, back in the market square, amongst the hawkers and the pedlars and the stalls set up with fruit and vegetables, trinkets and ornaments, pots and pans and cups and saucers. And then she saw it. The stall with the tiny silver charms where she had been given her ladybird. She walked past the stallholder, but there was no recognition in the old lady's eyes when she saw Sadie's smile. She just gave a little nod and returned her attention to where a customer was looking over her wares.

Sadie walked to the edge of the market, where she used to line up each morning waiting for work. There were five girls standing there. She pointed them out to Dinah, told her what

367

questions to ask and how much to offer based on the experience the girl might have. Then she hung back with Eddie, holding Birdie's hand.

Dinah spoke to the first girl in the line and Sadie saw her shake her head in a definite *no*, as did the second and third. It wasn't going to be easy to find a girl who'd want to move from Hartlepool to Ryhope. Dinah would need to find someone with nothing and no one to hold her back, perhaps someone wanting to flee, waiting for an opportunity like the one she was proposing. Sadie knew in her heart that it was a chance she would have taken had it been offered to her. It would have been her way out, an easier, less costly escape than the one she had made.

Finally, a deal was done and Dinah walked towards Sadie with a young girl in tow, a girl who reminded Sadie of herself, how she had been at that age.

'She's called Florence.' Dinah beamed. 'Says she's a good worker and she's got clean hands and no nits. I checked her hands, Sadie, just like you told me to do.'

'Hello, Florence,' Sadie smiled. 'Have you ever been to Ryhope before?'

The girl shook her head.

'Well I think you're going to be happy working for Mrs Marshall at the Grange. There's a good team of women there.'

They walked back to Hartlepool West railway station, Sadie and Eddie ambling with Birdie between them. Dinah and Florence walked ahead deep in conversation, Florence pushing the pram. As the little group neared the station,

Dinah handed the girl some money, enough to buy a first-class ticket for herself so that she could sit with the rest of them.

Florence approached the ticket office on her own.

'Where to, miss?' the clerk asked.

'Ryhope, please,' she said,

'Single or return?'

'Single, please.' She had no intention of ever coming back.

Other titles published by Ulverscroft:

BELLE OF THE BACK STREETS

Glenda Young

'Any rag and bone!' Everyone recognises the cry of Meg Sutcliffe as she plies her trade along the back streets of Ryhope. She learnt the ropes from her dad when he returned from the War. But when tragedy struck, Meg had no choice but to continue alone. Now the meagre money she earns is the only thing that stands between her family's safety and a predatory rent collector . . . Many say it's no job for a woman — especially a beauty like Meg. When she catches the eye of charming Clarky it looks like she might have found a chance of happiness. But could Adam, Meg's loyal childhood friend, be the one who really deserves her heart?

THE SHOP GIRL'S SOLDIER

Karen Dickson

Southampton, 1905: Ellie-May and Jack have been inseparable since birth. They are best friends, having grown up together on the same street. But when Jack and his mother fall on hard times they are thrown into the workhouse, and he and Ellie-May are forced into a goodbye. Four years later, now aged sixteen, Jack returns to Southampton and is reunited with Ellie-May. Quickly they both realise that their feelings for each other go beyond friendship, and with Jack home for good the pair are finally free to be together. But when WWII approaches, Jack's duty to his country is hard to ignore and when he enlists to fight, they are once again torn apart. Will Ellie-May and Jack find their way back to each other before it's too late?

THE GIRL FROM GALLOWAY

Anne Doughty

1845: Since following her heart and moving from her comfortable home in Scotland to the harsh mountainside of Ardtur, County Donegal, Hannah McGinley hasn't had the easiest life. But surrounded by her two children and her loving husband Patrick, she has found happiness. When her daughter returns home with news that her school may close as one of the teachers is moving away, Hannah feels compelled to take the vacant post. With the schoolmaster Daniel having lost his sight, Hannah knows that he won't be able to manage the children alone. But the money from teaching is poor, and as the potato crops begin to fail all around them, times are getting tougher still. Will Hannah be able to help her family and save the school?

THE CORNISH LADY

Nicola Pryce

Educated, beautiful, and the daughter of a prosperous merchant, Angelica Lilly has been invited to spend the summer in high society. Her father's wealth is opening doors and attracting marriage proposals, but Angelica still feels like an imposter among the aristocrats of Cornwall. When her brother returns home, ill and under the influence of a dangerous man, Angelica's loyalties are tested to the limit. Her one hope lies with coachman Henry Trevelyan, a softly spoken educated man with kind eyes. But when Henry seemingly betrays Angelica, she has no one to turn to. Who is Henry, and what does he want? And can Angelica save her brother from a terrible plot that threatens to ruin her entire family?